The Legacy Stone
Book Three: Part One

Jasper's Magick Corset:
Convergin'
on the
Ridiculous

The adventures of Verity Sauveur
and her most Righteous Blade of Wrath,
the Fell Sword Morphageus,
hereafter known as Jasper

Terry Kroenung

RARE MOON PRESS
Longmont, Colorado

Jasper's Magick Corset:

Convergin' on the Ridiculous

(revised edition)

Printed in the United States of America

Cover image by Solarbearstudio

ISBN: 978-1-7378947-8-0

www.terrykroenungink.com

The experts speak about
Jasper's Magick Corset!

"This book is both a crime and a punishment."
—*Dostoyevsky*

"May the snows of Kilimanjaro cover it."
—*Ernest Hemingway*

"I may tilt at windmills, but this book tilted over and sank."
—*Don Quixote*

"My deal with the devil did not include
having to read this trash."
—*Faust*

"This plot is dead, it is no more, it has ceased to be, it's gone to meet its maker, bereft of life, it rests in peace, it's kicked the bucket, it's shuffled off this mortal coil. This is an ex-plot!"
—*Monty Python*

"I wish this book were Less Miserable."
—*Victor Hugo*

"A novel of no importance."
—*Oscar Wilde*

Also by Terry Kroenung
www.terrykroenungink.com

<u>Novels</u>
Brimstone and Lily: A Blade of Dubious Glory
Brimstone and Lily: Beware the Sword of Mirth
Jasper's Foul Tongue: The Avenging Arm of Sarcasm
Jasper's Foul Tongue: How Sharper Than a Serpent's Tush
Jasper's Magick Corset: Partying is Such Sweet Sorrow
Paragon of the Eccentric
Rapiers & Rogues
The Gaze of Zeus

<u>Drama</u>
The Three Musketeers
Coolness and Courage
Blood and Beauty
Gentle Rain

<u>Nonfiction</u>
HeartSnark

<u>Anthologies</u> (contributor)
Customs, Castles, and Kings, v. 2
Broken Links, Mended Lives
False Faces
Found

<u>Awards</u>
Colorado Gold Literary Award
Paragon of the Eccentric (winner)
Brimstone and Lily (finalist)

Independent Publishers Book Award
Brimstone and Lily (Bronze Medal)

Next Generation Indie Book Award
Reader's Choice Award
HeartSnark (finalist)

Colorado Short Story Contest
"The Day the Earth Couldn't Stand Still"
(winner)

To Molly
After reading this
you may never put on a saucy corset again

Attention all students, teachers, and other crazed literature geeks!

There are several dozen references to famous books in *Jasper's Magick Corset*. Twain's *The Adventures of Huckleberry Finn* is most represented, along with some Charles Dickens, but so are *To Kill A Mockingbird, Romeo and Juliet* (and a lot more of Willie's work), *Monty Python*, and *The Hitchhiker's Guide to the Galaxy*, among others.

See how many you can spot! Sponsor *JFT* Lit Parties! Amaze your friends! Kick butt on *Jeopardy*! Be smarter than a 5th grader!

Contents

A howdy-do from y'all's intrepid narrator

Five books so far? Jumpin' Jehosaphat! My little fingers'd be worn down to nubs if I hadn't made Jasper copy it all down fer me. Purt near upchucked all over Ma's new carpet after I ate a whole Dutch apple pie to pay fer him turnin' into a magick fountain pen with never-endin' ink that wrote all by itself.

*Ma says there may be some poor innocent readers who pick up this book first, all unknowin'. I oughta make double-sure y'all understand that this here ain't the one to start with. That'd be the misbegotten **A Blade of Dubious Glory**. Then slog yer way through the other three till you arrive back here.*

This one looked uglier than a monkey's armpit when I first scribbled it (sort o' like this here introduction). Believe it or not, I get purty good grades in readin' and writin' but I feared Miz Finch'd expire of apoplexy when she first eyed the rough copy. We cleaned up the narration parts some but tried to leave most o' the dialogue stuff alone, so y'all get the flavor o' the thing. Jasper says it's sort o' a ipecac flavor.

Took a month o' Sundays t' put lipstick on this here pig, let me tell ya. If I'd known what a trouble it was to write a book I never would o' tackled it. Shoulda got on my raft and took a nap.

As far as the talkin' bits go, I guess I oughta apologize in advance for Jasper. You'll see what I mean.

JASPER'S MAGICK CORSET:
Convergin' on the Ridiculous

A snooty voice woofed at me in a Parisian accent.
"You can dress up le pig, as they say,
but it will still make le oink."
The floppy basset hound lying on the rug
rolled his eyes as he spoke.

1 / Fie on Corsets!
Saturday, July 14, 1804

"Scorn...oomph!"

Four to go.

"Defiance...urrk!"

Three now.

"Slight regard...yow!"

Only two. I can do this.

"Contempt...aack!"

Last one. Don't let 'em see you sweat.

Jasper, the voice of my magick sword that only I could hear, snickered. "What on earth are you mumblin' about?"

"Shakespeare," I grunted between clenched teeth. "*Henry V.* We studied it in school some."

Ma yanked on the laces that were threatening to crunch my ribs into dust, her knee in my back. Jasper kept on yapping in his snide boyish tones. "And this is helpin' you...how?"

"I'm dreamin' up all manner o' tortures-vile," I hissed.

"Poison toads fer breakfast. Itchin' powder in his underwear. Dearth-demons munchin' on his wretched innards. Prussic acid pourin' down from the heavens as he begs fer mercy from every woman in the States United and Europa."

"All this misery is for...?"

"Fer the misbegotten bastard what invented the corset!" I yelped as Ma hauled in on those lines as if she was trying to land some great fish.

"Language, dear," Ma purred, knowing that I'd heard a whole lot worse since coming aboard the *Penelope's Kiss*. What she didn't know was how much worse, mostly from Jasper. Our salty privateer crew could really burn your ears when they got goin'. Jasper loved to imitate them. Boys will be boys, even if they're disembodied spirits.

"Ain't you done yet?" I whined, trying to peer over my shoulder to check Ma's progress. All I could see out of a corner of my eye was a veil of my short red hair. Blowing at it did no good.

"Just getting ready to tie it off. Take a deep breath and hold it, please."

"Will I be able to let it out or is this the last breath I ever get to take?"

She smiled, the crinkles at her eyes looking like starbursts. "Oh, don't be so dramatic, honey. It's a corset, not an iron maiden."

Jasper, resting on her sewing table in the form of an old tin cup, melted and reformed until he became a miniature torture rack. A rag doll was lashed into it, an expression of agonized horror on its little face.

"Aiee!" it wailed in my head. "Do your worst, Torquemada! You'll never make me a slave to your dark fashion sense!"

I felt it a pity that Ma couldn't hear him. She was the costume designer at Ford's Theatre and had no truck with what passed for *La Mode* among some of our lady patrons. Enormous cage crinolines that made women resemble walking lace mushrooms. Over-trimmed hats that look like wedding confections. Magenta silk fabrics that gave you a pounding headache to look at. Ma would just shake her head and mumble to herself. Most of the time she wore a simple blue or gray cotton work dress and a snood for her dark brown hair. No fiendish devices to slim or reshape her. All natural, that was her motto.

But I had to travel incognito through Gaulle and into the Scepter'd Isle, so dressing like a native would be required. Walking about in Napoleon's time of 1804, to say nothing of Queen Elizabeth's 16th century, dressed in my preferred overalls, straw hat, and bare feet would attract the kind of attention we couldn't afford. Our do-or-die mission to rescue my friend Tommy from a Merchantry dungeon in London was going to be hard enough without getting arrested as a lunatic or a witch.

I talk to spirits and can sling all sorts o' magick about....might be sort o' hard to mount a defense.

So Ma had decided to train me for the kind of disguises I'd have to use. Stays and corsets, along with Empire waists, farthingales, and shoes designed by the Spanish Inquisition were all part of it. I'd have preferred a vizard glamour spell that would let me wear what I liked but fool onlookers into believing that I wore the local rags. My mind got changed by Jasper's gleeful explanation of how much I'd have to pay him for such a long-term use of magick. A whole bunch of whiskey, cigars, skinny-dipping, and even shoplifting would just about cover it, he'd said. After considering the disadvantages of sneaking through hostile territory staggering and upchucking I'd decided to take my chances with the corset.

A snooty voice whoofed at me in a Parisian accent. "You can dress up le pig, they say, but it will still make le oink." The floppy basset hound lying on the rug rolled his eyes as he spoke. A formerly-human aristocrat from the losing side of the 1789 Revolution, Jean-Luc D'Arcy Evremonde, le Duc du Ponteau, had a difficult time letting go of his imperious attitude towards us 'peasants.'

"Look who's talkin'," I shot back with as much force as my constricted lungs allowed. "The Merchantry dressed you up as a pooch, permanent-like."

"But I am still every inch a peer of the realm, even in this ridiculous shape. It proves my point." He lifted his long nose and posed as if David was painting his portrait.

Jasper turned himself into a six-inch long Roman ballista, bolt aimed at the Duke's rump. "Just say the word and I'll make my own point."

"Naw," I said with a shake of my head. "That'd just give him a bigger excuse fer his 'poor little me' act. He's tough enough to tolerate as it is."

"What is your ill-mannered toy saying about me now?" the Duke wanted to know, one eyebrow raised. "Mon Dieu! It never ceases to amaze me that you two are supposed to be civilization's only hope."

With a thought I returned Jasper to his natural self, the ancient sword Morphageus. Holding it up as high as I could while stuck in the corset, I showed him the black recurved blade covered in fiery runes. "Hey, it weren't no bright idea of mine, , Drooly. I just fell down a hole one night and here we are."

The same night three weeks before that a grotesque dearth-demon named Venoma had tranced poor Tommy and disappeared with a green flash into the Washington Monument. I'd been heading to London to spring him ever since.

So far I'd been attacked by giant ravens, zombies, the Assassins Guild, Hellenic Furies, the Hellfiend Legion, a cast-iron submarine, my own insane sorceress aunt, a shipload of disguised demons, Dionysus himself, and those creepy corrupt mages who look like little blonde boys, the Bullies.

Oh, yeah...and poop-monsters. Loads of poop monsters.

Welcome to my world, y'all.

I looked in the Dread Pirate Roberta's full-length mahogany mirror and winced. We were the master's cabin she shared with Commander Aloysius Pitcairn, the two-acre bed piled high with lacy petticoats and dainty unmentionables. Only we were sure as heck mentioning them now, since that was all I had on. Dumb as girlie stuff looked like on me at the best of times, it was a dadburned sight worse when there was no frilly frock to cover up the ridiculous foundation. Trust me, nothing's more ridiculous than a husky no-bosomed tomboy in a cotton shift and corset.

Jasper snickered and changed himself into a rag doll, hanging its red-yarned head in shame. "My mighty mistress looks like an ugly ship's figurehead. Woe is me!"

There wasn't much I could say to contradict him. I hadn't been in a dress in at least four years, when I'd been dragged kicking and screaming to Mr. Ford's niece's wedding. That hadn't gone well. Artie Radley had made some smart-aleck remark about my not looking very lady-like and I'd had to wrassle him down on the church lawn and Dutch-rub him into an apology.

"Yep," I sighed, throwing up my dirty hands, "this sure is a bust."

The doll produced tiny binoculars from thin air and looked me up and down. "Bust? Where? I see no such animal."

With a twitch of her nose Ma casually magicked a gag onto the doll's mouth. Though it had no real effect on him, Jasper played along and made muffled noises in my head. "I think you look pretty," she told me. "And once we get this dress on you, you'll turn all the boys' heads in Gaulle."

"Ma, you are such an awful liar." I hugged her. "But thanks anyway."

Jasper tore off the gag and gasped for air, the doll thrashing in feigned suffocation. "Your new-found beauty takes my breath away."

I wished him into the shape of a fireplace bellows. "Better?"

It expanded to its full volume, hopped onto the floor, and exhaled, buffeting the hound's long ears as if in a gale. The Duke raised that patrician eyebrow again, none of the rest of his floppy frame stirring. "Sacre bleu!" he grumped. "Can you not put a leash on this thing?"

Oh, don't I wish I could, Yer Grace.

Ma turned me around and dropped a pale blue muslin dress over my noggin. As it settled down around my shoulders and then the rest of me, I just knew it'd itch something awful. Already I was hankering for my denim overalls, cotton plaid shirt, and straw hat. And I had a wretched feeling that she was going to insist that I wear shoes, too. Yuck.

It hung all the way to the tops of my feet, a sky-colored cocoon. Like every other lady's dress of Bonaparte's time, the waist was a tight satin band around the bottom of my breastbone, tied into a bow in the back. At least the sleeves were short and puffy, it being mid-July. But the rest of it made me feel like a fancy sausage, unable to move with any kind of freedom.

"Jeepers!" I wailed. "How am I supposed to fight demons in this get-up?"

"You aren't," Ma mumbled, her mouth full of pins. She adjusted something at the back of my neck. "The plan is for you to sneak across Gaulle and into the Scepter'd Isle, not call attention to yourself by brawling without need."

Jasper transformed into a jack-in-the-box with bobbing clown's head. "Plan? You have a plan? Since when?"

"We always have a plan, boyo, " I thought to him. "It just generally falls apart five minutes after we start, is all."

"Yeah, and the back-up scheme is always the same: Jasper exhausts himself saving Verity's freckled hide."

"Moan, moan, moan. You love every minute of it."

"Except for the part where I get covered in poop-monster sludge or demon-goop. Do you have any idea what that stuff tastes like?"

"No, but I got me a pretty healthy imagination, so don't bend over backwards to enlighten me, thank you very much."

To complete the humiliation Ma plopped a poke bonnet onto my head. It blocked most of my side vision like blinders on a horse. Plus, it was trimmed with little pink silk flower blossoms. I sagged, wishing for a hole to crawl into and hide.

Oh, well, at least it's a straw hat. That's somethin'.

The hound snorted through his dangly lips. "The Merchantry minions shall wet themselves in terror at your approach."

As soon as he said that Jasper became an umbrella with little bare feet at the end of the handle. He ran all over the rug, ending up atop the Duke's prominent rear end. "Don't worry! I've got this under control!"

Ignoring them, I glared into the mirror again, mourning the demise of the tough girl tasked with saving the world from the forces of darkness. Then I gave Ma another sour stare. "You ain't my real mother, are you? You're a secret agent sent by the

Proprietor to grind your heels in my self-respect."

She tapped me on my pug nose and smiled. "You've found me out, clever girl. When I make you carry a handbag my mission will be complete."

"A handbag!" I howled.

Naturally the umbrella melted and reformed as a draw-stringed purse, complete with tassels at the corners. "What well-bred lady would dare leave the house without her reticule?" tittered Jasper. "It just isn't done!"

"He's awfully frisky today," Ma observed, rummaging through the pile of clothes on the bed. "What's he saying? Anything important?"

"When has he ever? He's just like all the other boys." I picked up the bag and hung it on my wrist with a sad sigh. "Dopey."

A booming woman's voice filled the cabin. Its owner's broad-shouldered frame did the same for the doorway. "Aw! I declare, ain't you just the purtiest little squid!"

Before I could react the Dread Pirate Roberta had squeezed the stuffing out of me. After the corset-donning nightmare I hadn't thought it possible for my innards to be smooshed together any tighter, but she proved me wrong. By the time she let me go I was seeing stars.

"That's what I've been telling her," said Ma, "but she won't believe me."

The *Kiss'* lady slapped me on the rump. She peered down at me through her wire-rimmed spectacles. "And here all this time I've been thinkin' we've had a boy on board."

Roberta gave the hound a rough pat and plopped down on her bed amidst the heap of garments. Curly chestnut hair hung out of her feather-bedecked tricorn hat. She had a pleasant face with a generous mouth that smiled often and well. Her full bosom swelled out of the top of a green velvet bodice. Brown silk pantaloons and knee-high bucket boots dangled beneath a gold brocade overskirt. In place of a lady's usual jewelry she sported at least half a dozen knives. A small ivory-hilted flintlock pistol peeped out of her wide leather belt.

"Y'all are just hilarious," I grumped to both of them.

"Well, you do have to fit in, missy," Roberta pointed out. "This is what all the girls are wearin' hereabouts."

"Yeah? And do all the girls hereabouts have to suddenly defend themselves against violent outrages from monsters and assassins?"

"No," said the Duke, standing and shaking, drool flying everywhere, "they have to defend themselves from the Corsican upstart's absurd ideas about governing the masses."

I held up my hands. "Ain't gonna start a political discussion with a transmogrified and bitter aristocrat, Yer Grace. Too much else to do today."

The dog muttered under his breath and slunk out of the room, no doubt on the hunt for food. I swear, he ate so much he must've had hollow feet. When he'd gone I turned back to Ma and Roberta. "Fittin' in is one thing. Fightin' is another. We all know that sneakin' ain't my specialty. So far every disguise I've used has lasted about as long as butter on a tin roof in August."

Ma wiped the seat from her face with a rag she kept tucked in her apron. Gaulle was powerful hot in July. "That's not so, sweetie. You fooled General Lee into thinking you were a Merchantry agent."

"But that was a glamour spell, not a real dress-up disguise."

"You pretended to be Mary Williams when you met Captain Tyrell. That was three whole days."

"And he knew who I was from the minute he laid eyes on me. Told me so."

"What about in Iberion, when you made those raiders and Rom believe you were an Arabe orphan?"

"A whole day and a half, maybe? Then I started swingin' Morphageus about and that was that."

Roberta waved that off with a sword-callused hand. "None o' this is to the point. You don't have to pass muster fer long, nor up close. The aim is to not be recognized by every Merchantry spy as the girl who wears the Stone. It's the overalls and bare feet you can't display, not to mention that head that's as bright as a new penny. Pryin' eyes aren't lookin' fer a cute Gaullic girl in a nice frock."

"But if I get jumped —"

"Then all bets are off. Though you aren't required to lop off heads with that wonder-sword as your first response. Use that big old brain of yours before drawin' the iron."

I clumped around the cabin, trying to get used to having my legs and feet all bound up by fabric. "Fair enough. But if somethin' as simple as runnin' is needed, this mess o' muslin is gonna slow me down to a caterpillar's crawl. Can't we just take passage with the owls again and fly by night instead of all of this play-actin'?"

A man's voice came in atop mine. "Ah, if it were only that simple." Commander Pitcairn, a vision of elegant manliness in a black-and gold brocade waistcoat and cream-colored leather breeches, sauntered into his cabin with a wink to his lady. "But the owls have already contracted to venture to Irlann. Apparently that isle is overrun with mice."

"And they need owls as big as Virginia barns fer that?"

"These mice are be-spelled and are the size of draft horses. Plus, they are venomous."

"So no quick and easy wings then." I took off the bonnet and scratched my head. "What about sailin' the *Kiss* up the coast?"

Pitcairn strolled over to the vast expanse of windowpanes which served as the cabin's rear wall. He waved out at a smudge on the sea's horizon. "Alas, no. It seems that three of Bonaparte's men-of-war have chosen this very bit of coast as their very own. Whether they are merely guarding against a Britannic fleet action or are actually disguised Merchantry hunters is impossible to say. My guess is the latter. Luckily we are well-hidden in this cove thanks to my crew's skill at camouflage and your mother's talent for vomit spells. No one can venture within a mile of this spot without heaving his poor guts out. But it is too dangerous to attempt a sly escape right now."

I stuck out my lip in an exaggerated pout. "So no easy way out for Verity...again."

Instead of wiping her tears away, she witched them off her cheeks. They floated off as soap bubbles which popped in the air, leaving faint little rainbows behind.

2 / Answers...and More Questions

It had been two full days since I'd returned from Lusitania, that horrid land next to Iberion where I'd nearly been devoured by a horde of undead acolytes of Dionysus. With time so short I'd naturally wanted to get right back on the road north to London. Tommy needed rescuing. A Merchantry prison held terrors way beyond your typical jail, that I was sure of. Ma said that the few who'd ever returned from a lengthy stay there tended to drool and shiver the rest of their lives.

But I'd taken quite a beating on that trip, even though it had only been a three-day affair. Sure, Ma had spelled me some to take the edge off, but all that fighting and running had plumb worn me out. Even smoking my corncob pipe that first day till I was green in the gills hadn't gained me enough strength from Jasper to contemplate a 700-mile trip through hostile territory. So I'd been stuck in my bunk, fidgeting to beat the band and wishing that the Stone could make me some sort of super-kid and let me get going.

"But it has already done so," said Sha'ira, standing beside me at the starboard rail of the *Kiss*. Back in my preferred duds, I'd been grumping about this to anybody within earshot and she'd steered me off to jaw at me.

I scrunched up my forehead at that. "How d'ya mean?"

"Consider what trials tested you there." Her long black hair danced across her handsome tattooed Arabe face. The coastal breeze was freshening. "Little sleep or food, constantly on the run in a strange land, battling the troops of that devil Carrasco, pursued by the god's cannibal women, engaging three giants..."

"Giants? Oh...them flamin' poop monsters."

"Indeed. And finally dueling with Dionysus himself." The former assassin shook her head. "Any other girl would be dead or in a hospital ward. You, however, are merely bruised and weary. I suggest that the Stone has served you well."

Jasper, of course, had his two cents to offer. "Not to mention yours truly." The cup turned into an ancient Greek tragedy mask, crying real tears. "No. Seriously. You haven't mentioned me."

I made a tired sound through my lips like a cranky donkey. "Why bother when I can depend on you to do such a bang-up job of it every chance you get?"

In reply the mask became a wind-up toy monkey beating a tiny drum.

Ignoring his 'look at me' antics, I turned back to Sha'ira. "Since we're talkin' about the Stone...where'd it come from? Who made it? Why does it have the power it does?"

She shrugged, staring out at the blockading ships. "That is a mystery to me."

The monkey waved a little paw over its head. "Ooh! Ooh! I know! I know! Ask me, teacher!"

I dropped my ragged straw hat over him and pressed the Dreamwriter. "Really? You ain't got no inlkin' at all? So many years as a Shade and then your time with Romulus and...nothin'?"

"One hears things, of course. But solid facts? No."

"Shucks, I'll settle fer wild rumors and crazy guesses at this point. All I've heard is that Pa hung it on my just-born neck as he was dragged back into the Obverse. Jasper says that it was on his master's finger as a ring the day he was put into the sword. And judgin' by hints he's dropped, like two moons instead of one, I'm guessin' that Jasper comes from the Obverse, too."

"That is likely. Hiding Morphageus and the Stone on this world would make it more difficult for enemies to find them. Since you are born from parents of both worlds it is only proper that the talismans would also claim dual citizenship, so to speak."

"But how'd Pa get the Stone? Where'd it go after Jasper got transmogrified and sent here? Sounds like it stayed on the other side, since Pa brought it with him before he met Ma."

"You seek more knowledge than I can provide. I suggest you ask the Marshals, or your mother." She took up a brass telescope and gave the horizon a closer look.

Ma's voice came in right on cue from ten feet behind us. "Ask me what?"

I turned to face her, scooping up my hat and plopping it onto my noggin. Jasper turned into a kite and floated above me, a steely little cable anchoring him to the crown. "I'm just hankerin' to know about this." Digging a hand into my shirt, I pulled out the Legacy Stone, secure on its unbreakable maillon chain. "Fer starters, where'd Pa come by it?"

Her face twitched, like it always did when she'd rather be taking a bath in itching powder than doing something she hated. "He...never said, exactly. Family heirloom is all he ever called it."

Jasper turned into a brass bell and clanged something fierce. "Warning! Warning! Big fib alert!"

Yeah, I sort o' got that feelin;, too. Wonder what she's hidin'?

"And what do you know about his family?"

Ma shrugged and sat on a keg. "Sages. Keepers of wisdom and magick in the greatest city of the Obverse. To us they would be closer to librarians than anything else. Only their books are actual living beings, not just paper and ink."

"Whoa!" yelled Jasper in my head. "Books you have to feed? Watch your fingers!"

"Books live and breathe? Fer real?"

"Yes," said Sha'ira, still frowning out at the sea. "They feed off of the dreams of their readers. Many things are different in the Obverse. They use magick there like we employ trains and telegraphs. Toddlers can create glamour spells. Schoolchildren can raise the dead. It isn't hidden as it is on this world."

Raise the dead? Maybe that explains all of the zombies I've been runnin' into.

I pressed ma on Pa's history. "So his people – our people, I guess – know all about the secrets of that world? What, do they have long conversations with the books?"

Ma interrupted me as I laughed at my little joke. "That's exactly right. Only sages can speak to the books. Much of the wisdom on the page is hidden. Books don't give up their wonders lightly there. What is inked on the page is only a small part of what a volume contains."

"Jeepers! Then Pa was a big wheel? The sages must be awful important if they're the only ones who can fully read a book." Then it hit me. "That's really why he came here, huh? Because of one of them books."

She smiled and rubbed my cheek as Sha'ira scooted off to the stern. "You are so smart. That's it. Books are like people. They don't bare their souls to just anyone. Paul was a savant with books. That was what made him such a strong mage. He had close relationships with several arcane books which told him things no one else had ever been privy to."

"And naturally there were some nasty folks who wanted in on that. I can see where this is goin'."

"Of course you can. He brought a book over, a dangerous book which couldn't be found, else it might be employed by the demons for their revolt. Paul hid it in this world someplace. But that's all I know about it. He never told me the particulars. Said the less I knew, the safer I'd be. The closest he ever came was when they were about to drag him off to the Obverse again, that night you were born. As he hung the Stone around your neck he kissed me and whispered something. He —" She bit her lip and turned away.

"What?"

Ma turned away. I could hear the quiet sobs in her breathing. She shook her head.

I circled around to face her. "No, no, no, no, no! Don't do this! You gotta tell me."

Instead of wiping her tears away, she witched them off of her cheeks. They floated off as soap bubbles, which popped in the air, leaving faint little rainbows behind. "I know. But as soon as I do, you'll be so much more in danger than you already are. I would rather — "

"Aw, come on, Ma! I'm about to stroll into Merchantry headquarters and demand a prisoner release. You really think it gets any more dangerous than that?" I took her trembling hand in both of mine. "It'll be okay."

"I hope so." She took a deep breath and let it out. "He said 'it's a key.' Whatever that means."

"A key?" I touched my chest where the Stone lay. "What, this?"

"I suppose so."

"That's all he said? That's the big revelation?"

"Well, that's all he said...aloud."

Jasper snorted. "Don't you just love it when she gets all cryptic on you?"

"Well, what else? Did he write you something in one of them notes he still sends?"

"No. He can't trust that they won't be intercepted. This was...different."

"How?"

"As the demons were hauling him back into the portal, Paul managed to sneeze."

"Woo-oo!" hollered Jasper. "There's a wackin' great epiphany for you!"

I gave her a puzzled squint. "And...?"

"Remember how demons' noses run when they tell a lie, even in human form?"

"Uh-huh."

"Well, master sages can speak to others' minds in a limited way, when in great stress. But they must sneeze to send the message."

"You're kiddin', right? Messin' with little Verity so she won't bug you no more?"

Ma hugged me hard. "Sweetie, I'm fresh out of jokes."

"I'm not!" sang Jasper. "Two demons walk into a bar — "

I willed him into silence and held Ma's face in my hands. "So tell me."

She sighed and stared out at the water. "He said that he'd hidden the book's location inside of you."

Oh, this just keeps gettin' better, don't it?.

"Huh? What the heck does that mean?"

"I wish I knew."

"Well, is it a spell? Mesmerism? Did he tattoo it on my noggin? What?"

Ma held up her palms and shrugged.

"Maybe it's written on your stomach lining," offered Jasper. "With all of the upchucking you do, you might've erased it already."

"Thanks. Can't you think of somethin' more constructive right now?" To Ma I said, "So I have the key around my neck but I'm the lock-box? Ain't that just peachy."

Ma wrapped her arms around herself as if cold. "I'm sorry. That's why I never told you before. It's not helpful information."

"What other unhelpful stuff have you been keepin' from me?"

She winced as if I'd stabbed her. "Don't say it like that. You don't know. You don't have a child...an only child...who's also a..."

"Freak? Abomination? Obverse half-breed?"

Her eyes filled up again. "You know that's not what I meant." She cuddled me up as if she'd wear me for a coat. "You're all that I have of him, you know. I knew him for barely a year and he's been lost to me...to us...for twelve. Suffering who knows what terrors over there."

Never thought of that. She's a grieving wife, not just plain old Ma.

"We'll get through this," I told her as boots started clomping all over the deck. "I'm gonna yank Tommy outta that stinkin' dungeon and then we're gonna get Pa back from the Obverse. So help me."

Jasper, of course, just had to chime in. "I'm jumpin' up and down anticipatin' your detailed plan for managin' all of that."

"You and me both, bucko. One thing at a time."

A high little voice shrieked from right behind me. "Surrender the booty or I'll keelhaul you!"

My super-sensitive ears nearly exploded. If I hadn't known who it was I might've been mad.

"Bold words, buccaneer," I said, letting go of Ma and holding my hands up high. Turning, I looked into the most adorable little freckled pirate face ever.

"I can back 'em up with bold deeds, swabbie!" growled five year-old Freya. She was as red-haired as me and waved a short wooden cutlass about. Roberta had dressed her as the cutest sea dog imaginable, in a red late 17th century coat and lace jabot.

"Do yer worst!" I turned Jasper into an identical toy sword and got down on my knees. "You'll have to spill me blood to claim me treasure!"

Freya squinted around her false eyepatch. "I accept yer challenge, ye scalawag!" She slapped her black tricorn hat to seat it on her head, then leaned in nose-to-nose with me, scowling. It took all of my self-control not to laugh. "If ye has any prayers, I suggest ye say 'em now."

"I'm a-sayin' one fer you, ye scurvy dog."

"Then take what's comin' to ya!"

A tiny finger poked me on my snoot. "Tag! You're it!" she giggled, turning and dashing off amidships to the nearest hatch. I snorted and pursued her, hanging Jasper on my belt in his cup form as I went.

We dodged around masts, lines, and cargo, the dinky pirate remaining a step ahead (I might've held back a bit to help her out). This was all so cute and fun that I had a hard time remembering that Freya was on the ship to be trained as a Shade, a professional killer for the Assassins' Guild. Pitcairn took their money with the understanding that at age thirteen she'd be handed over to the all-women Guild for their brutal final schooling in the ways of professional murder. But since that was a voluntary act, Roberta and the commander had assured me that when that time came, Freya would have been carefully taught to decline the offer. That was a dangerous game, if the Shades found out, but Pitcairn lived on the edge of annihilation anyhow, so one more threat didn't much matter.

I noticed a lot of the crew dashing about as we played. Since Pitcairn had hidden the *Kiss* up an inlet and dressed it in leafy nets to avoid detection, the men hadn't had much to do except clean and paint. But now they were carrying cutlasses and pistols, stern expressions on their unshaven faces. A team manned the windlass, ready to weigh anchor. Others took to the rigging to work the sails and serve as sharpshooters. Pintle guns swiveled, looking for targets landward.

Something was up. And that usually meant that poor little Verity would get chased by icky and drooling monstrosities.

With one hand I scooped up the still-laughing Freya and with the other collared Fergus McPherson, our dumpy one-eared bosun. "Hey, what's goin' on? I figure this ain't just a drill, huh?"

"No, 'fraid not, missy. Your Dreamwriter spied those ships makin' a move. They're headed our way, gun ports all open."

"We sure they mean mischief?"

"Can't be sure o' nothin', but the cap'n's taking no chances. We're sittin' ducks up this inlet if they launch iron our way."

"So we're pullin' out?"

"That we are. You might want to get the little terror there to someplace safe below."

Fergus scampered off to give orders. Freya squirmed in my grasp and complained that I was ruining her game. After passing her off to the next crewman I met, I headed aft to the helm to talk to Pitcairn. He'd already shucked his coat and hat, ready for action. A gray silk scarf covered his head. While he pulled on tight black riding gloves and stuck a battered belaying pin in his sword belt he explained his course of action.

"We must assume the worst. They may be merely patrolling the coast or running exercises, but that is more of a risk than I'm prepared to take." Cupping his hands, he shouted at Fergus. "Mr. McPherson! Strike the camouflage nets, if you please!"

"Three against one is bad odds," I pointed out, as if he didn't already know that. "And the wind's against you."

He grinned and winked at me. "Got them right where we want them, eh?"

"Took the words right out of my mouth, handsome," purred Roberta, appearing at his side. She gave him a big old smooch, not caring who saw it. She rubbed my head. "Don't it get yer blood racin', shrimp, to see this fine figure of a man in his natural element?"

I shrugged, still not understanding grown-ups' ways. "If you say so."

"I do say so." She slapped him on his rump. "Honeybunch, when we've sent these arrogant fools to their reward, let's parley in our cabin for the afternoon."

Since they looked too busy to give me any more information, I headed forward to find somebody more forthcoming. Romulus popped out of a cargo hatch, sun glistening on his dark shaved head. Captain Tyrell, CSA, followed him close. His horse, the golden marvel Alcibiades, glided up the ramp soon after.

"We don't like to get trapped below if there's to be a ruckus," the handsome Confederate explained. "The Valkyries prefer their steeds to fight in the open."

He'd borrowed Alcibiades from the Valkyries. The horse not only took fallen warriors to Valhalla in the blink of an eye, but could battle on his own. I'd seen him and his fellows do so. They were real handy with their hooves, not to mention their other hidden weapons. Finding yourself on the wrong side of Al when his blood was up was a bad place to be.

Tyrell was a Redeemer, belonging to a shadowy group founded by disillusioned officers of Napoleon to rebel against both Bonaparte and the Merchantry. They hoped to reform the latter and use its magickal power for good in the world. I thought that was a fool's errand, but nobody seemed to care about my opinion. The captain was actually a member of the original Coterie Redempteur, still appearing to be in his 20's thanks to some kind of spell.

"We'll clear out once Pitcairn gets under way," he said, checking Al's cinch. "So will you. Your mother wants you on land and ready to move north."

I made a sour face. "Just once I'd like to get consulted about stuff."

Romulus chuckled, which sounded like a locomotive straining uphill. He was close to six and a half feet tall and weighed three hundred pounds, none of it fat. Until recently a slave in Washington, and a war dog for Emperor Hadrian before that, Ma had hired him to help us around the house. It turned out that he'd been planted by the Marshals of the Equity to guard me from Merchantry attacks before I'd even known that there was such a thing.

"We had ourselfs a meetin'," he said. "Decided that you was likely to do whatever you pleased, consulted or not."

I squinted up at him, his sleek dome eclipsing the morning sun. "Fair enough. But a girl does like to be asked."

Tyrell hauled himself up into the saddle, gloved hand holding Al's reins. Like fast-growing flowers, white feathery wings bloomed out of the horse's shoulders. "Alright, then. Miss Verity, would you like some shore leave? Or would you prefer to stay here and shoot it out with those three warships...and the other two about to join them?"

*"Look out!" I yelled, turning Jasper into a big iron
frying pan about twelve feet across. It covered
all of us as ordnance rained down.*

3 / Scorch

Before I could answer Ma hauled me below to my cramped berth
where she'd already packed most of my stuff into the rucksack
she'd spelled the week before. As it was bigger on the inside than
the outside and contained a small warehouse of gear, it had
come in right handy on my trip to Iberion and Lusitania. I could
crawl in and sleep, that's how special it was. Ma had filled it with
maps, food, water, clothes, even magick potions. But it only
weighed maybe three pounds.

"You have to hurry," she said as I scooped up the items that
lay on the narrow shelf above my bunk. If I forgot the corncob
pipe Jasper might cry himself into apoplexy. "Commander
Pitcairn has the mer-folk ready to tow the ship so he can sail out
to sea against the wind."

"I'm goin', I'm goin'," I told her. Stuffing the double handful
of goodies into the sack, I dropped one of them on my bare foot.
With two toes I snagged its chain and picked it up.

"What's that?" asked Ernie from his perch atop my hat.

"Good question. Let's see."

Ma took in a quick breath. "Oh! I'd forgotten about that."

A strange black jewel dangled from an interlocked web of three gold chains. Not quite jet and not quite glass, streaks of pulsating blue vibrated deep in its core. Hefting the gem in my palm, I could feel something I'd never noticed before.

It had a pulse.

"Ick!" I dropped it on the bunk and gave it a snarl.

"Getting' awful squeamish in your old age, ain't you?" mocked Jasper.

Ernie echoed him, though he couldn't have heard what he said. "What a girl! It's only an ornament."

"Yeah?" I retorted. "Easy fer you to say, you didn't feel the 'wrongness' of it."

Roberta came in, spectacles on the end of her nose. "We're about to shove off. You might want to – say, what's that lovely little bauble?"

Her eye for treasure led her to reach for it. I moved like a rattlesnake to grab her wrist before she could touch the evil toy. "No, don't! It's the life-stone of that Fury we brought down when the ladies from Hades jumped us."

She backed away as if it carried smallpox. "Hard about! You're welcome to it, shrimp. Don't match the rest of my ensemble anyhow."

A bunch of ancient Hellene Furies had swarmed the *Kiss* out on the open ocean the week before, drawn by the call of a Dreamworm planted in one of our poor unsuspecting officers. Whether sent by the Merchantry's Proprietor or one of the groups opposing him in their civil war, I had no idea. Didn't matter much. When somebody's aiming to snatch your head off you just pay him the same compliment and sort out the wherefores later.

"Nor mine, neither, but the foul thing might come in handy down the road. I'll box it up and stow it deep."

We did just that. Ma wrapped it in oilskin and jammed it into an old wooden compass box that Roberta wired shut. Then I crawled into the sack and hid it in a carpetbag. No sense in making it too easy to lose...or too easy to escape. Who knew what it could do? I'd already learned to expect the worst where magick was concerned.

To my annoyance Ma made sure that the fiendish corset and dress didn't get left behind. Roberta cackled at that. Easy for her to laugh, she only wore the awful things for her special romps with Pitcairn. I gathered that they didn't stay on very long. Also going in were 16th century rags for a respectable London girl. On the Scepter'd Isle Queen Elizabeth and Shakespeare still lived, so if we made it that far I'd have to change clothes to blend in with the citizenry.

"I gave you a corset that will do for both places," Ma explained as we headed back to the main deck. "That way you won't have to change it after crossing the Channel."

"Gee, thanks. Sounds more like you didn't want to give me an excuse to chuck it into the water on the way."

We reached the gangplank and rushed down to shore. Once we hit dry land she pulled up short. I frowned and turned to eye her. "Ain't you goin' with us?"

"No, not yet. Commander Pitcairn asked that I remain aboard in case my magick might be needed. Taking on five sloops and frigates is no easy thing. Romulus, Sha'ira, and Ernie will travel with you for now. Once we shed these other ships we'll meet up with you. Stay near the coast road. Keep out of sight as much as you can. We'll send one of Matilda's gulls with a message where to meet us. If we're forced away from land she'll tell you what to do."

I hugged her hard. "We spend more time apart than we do together," I mumbled into her hair.

"Don't I know it, sweetie." She smooched me on the cheek. "Be careful. Listen to Romulus. He's been traveling this same route since the Romans ruled Gaulle. He'll keep you on the right road."

"Okay."

"And be careful with your magick. The more you use, the easier you'll be to spot. Your enemies know you're not good at cloaking yourself yet. Once we meet up again, I'll find a strong Chauntline and chant you a veil for it that even the Proprietor can't see through."

"Sounds good to me. I'm getting' tired of runnin' into bad guys every five minutes."

"**You're** tired?" moaned Jasper. "What about poor exhausted Morphageus over here, defendin' you night and day against all and sundry the past three weeks?"

I snickered and slung the rucksack onto my back. "Oh, you're right. What was I thinkin', bein' so selfish and not considerin' your tender delicate feelings?"

"There you go. That's the tone I want to hear from you. All properly compliant and solicitous."

Romulus stomped down the gangplank like a great fairy tale giant, tucking his Bowie knife into his belt. I knew he'd prefer to be in his natural form as the great Neapolitan Mastiff that had protected the Roman Emperor Hadrian, but Ma said it'd take a long time and a powerful Chauntline to permanently break the punishment curse thrust onto him by the Merchantry. In his human form he was no slouch, having saved my bacon more times than I could count.

Beside him Sha'ira wore her green-and-gold silk Arabe robes and soft boots. Her wicked scimitar, curved dagger, and boot knives announced that she was nobody to trifle with. Slung across her back was the deadly recurved bow and quiver which had accounted for so many enemies in my service. Though when she'd forsworn the Shades she'd taken an oath never to kill another human being again, that promise didn't go for demons, monsters, and the like. It also didn't include non-mortal wounding of any nasty people trying to dispatch us.

"Are we all ready to go?" she asked, adjusting the chain of the crescent-shaped stone around her throat. Milky white and with a mother-of-pearl sheen, it held some sort of spell. Whenever she did Chauntline magick, amateur though she was, it glowed like the moon. So did her eyes.

"Looks like it," rumbled Romulus, already scanning the

woods for threats with his eyes and nose. He hadn't survived for nearly two thousand years by being careless.

Ma hugged me again. "Watch after her. The nearer we get to our goal, the more desperate the enemy will get."

"Don't you fret none, Miz Ellen. We gonna get her to London in one piece and bring Master Tommy back."

Jasper just had to add his two cents. "Everybody keeps sayin' that, but I don't hear anybody explainin' precisely how that's gonna come about."

I agreed with him there. Aloud I said, "Not that I doubt you, but how are we gonna cover 700 miles in a few days, especially if the *Kiss* is tied up in a runnin' sea fight?"

Sha'ira smiled grim and hard. "There are ways, though all carry risk. In a day or two we shall know which route is open to us. Have patience."

Backing up the gangplank, Ma blew me a kiss and nearly went over on her backside as the Duc du Evremonde galumphed between her legs. The hound stopped there, enormous snooter poking out from beneath her skirt. Thick strings of slimy drool hung from his floppy lips like oozy stalactites.

"You pitiful peasants cannot think of traveling in my delightful Gaulle without me to guide you. Who shall steer you to the best patisseries if I remain behind?"

Ernie hopped off of my hat brim onto my shoulder, then leaped into the tall grass. "My charger has arrived!" He bounded up onto the dog's saggy neck, brandishing his knitting needle spear. "Now I travel in style!"

"Bonjour, mighty rodent. Shall we take the vanguard? Our foes shall part before us like la Mer Rouge did for Moses."

The pompous pooch waddled to shore, having to hop the last couple of feet. Crewmen were already pulling up the gangway. I could see that the approaching ships were much closer now, crowding on plenty of sail. Their gun ports were all open. Pitcairn really needed to get his ship moving. Mermen at the bow were preparing to turn the frigate's nose around and tow the *Kiss* out of the inlet before the oncoming craft could bottle her up. Ma stood at the rail, spelling a bit of magickal wind to aid them.

Once that had begun she turned to me and called out, "Verity! Stay safe! Watch for the gulls. And no Chauntlines!"

I frowned. "Huh? You taught me how to use 'em just yesterday."

"Your first baby steps. And the lines on the ship are weak approximations of the real thing. You aren't ready."

Our *Penelope's Kiss* had been taken from the Merchantry fleet by Pitcairn and Roberta. It had been the Proprietor's personal command vessel, though he hadn't been on it at the time. As an experiment its hull, keel, decks, rails, and bulkheads had been drilled and filled with samples of witched soil from strong Chauntlines on every continent. The result was that you could do some magick on her even while on the open ocean. Normally deep flowing water disrupted witchy energy and made it powerful dangerous to use. Like as not it'd rebound on the user. But on the *Kiss* you could sling some spells, though they weren't as strong or as predictable as on Mother Earth.

I reminded Ma that just a few days before I'd used a Chauntline to transport myself instantly across a mile of Lusitania by traveling between the barrier between the Obverse and our world. That didn't impress her much.

"You tagged along on Regan's spell. It's impressive that you survived that, but it isn't the same as calling it up yourself."

Her mad sister had tried to do us in by spelling a few thousand zombies. Regan was working for one of the nasty splinter groups allied against the Merchantry. At least, that's what she said. A bitter sorceress and born liar, you couldn't trust her to say that the sky was blue. When we'd taken her down she'd telegraphed herself away on a Chauntline. Just as she'd done it I'd grabbed her wrist and gone along for the ride. It'd come near to tearing me into little pieces. Only the Legacy Stone, the controlling chant *Nhana pana yolnyu,* and my inborn talent as a child of an Obverse sage had preserved me.

"Fair enough," I confessed, "but if my back's against a wall I might have to risk it."

A sad shadow passed over her face. "I know. But let's hope it doesn't come to that."

Jasper piped up. "If? If? What're the odds you can avoid it? That'd require a big change in our luck."

She blew me a kiss as the ship turned away and glided down the inlet much faster than a normal ship could've managed. The sea lay maybe half a mile away. With the wind from the north, Pitcairn would have to tack south along the coast to put distance between him and his five pursuers until he could manage to turn and fight. I just hoped that he'd get the chance. It looked like his foes might get into gun range before the *Kiss* could get underway.

Squinting, I used my Stone-boosted eyes to see who was after us. They all flew Britannic flags, but that didn't mean much. Merchantry hunters had chest-loads of colors and displayed whichever one would aid their chase. Pitcairn did the same thing when preying on rich vessels or blockade running. To make my point, he ran up a Swedish flag, which must've been the wrong choice, because before the pennant even made it all the way up the lead ship, a frigate similar in construction to the *Kiss*, let loose with a couple of forward-mounted deck guns even though it hadn't yet turned to free up its main batteries.

"Their captain must not like herring and lutfisk," chortled Jasper.

"What the heck is lutfisk?" I asked, keeping a sharp eye out for wayward cannonballs.

"Fish soaked in lye. Swedes love it. You oughta try it sometime."

"Yuck! Who in their right mind would ever think of eatin' that?"

"My guess would be drunken Vikings, on a dare."

The iron balls fell a good two hundred yards short. Pitcairn had reached the mouth of the inlet by then. Clear of trees now, he raised acres of sail and turned to port, heading for deeper water and maneuver room. Five hounds gave chase to the fox, which caught the sun beautifully with its pale grey and gold paint scheme. We hunkered down to watch the engagement, in no hurry to start our trek through unfamiliar woods. Romulus kept watch landward so we wouldn't be surprised by an enemy, though Ma's vomit spell still defended in that direction.

A sea battle is a wonderful sight when you aren't in the midst of it. I'd been on the receiving end of a chase and boarding and hadn't appreciated the slow-motion ballet then. It had been all chaos and terror, with cutlasses clanging and pistols barking in my too-sensitive ears. Granted, our attackers had been Darwins, demons from the Obverse who looked like blends of different savage beasts. That had made it hard to spy any artistry at hand.

This time, though, I was likely out of danger, though Ma and my friends weren't. That made it easier to watch the action as if it were a pageant. Attractive mounds of white canvas slid across the water like low-lying cloud banks. When the guns fired they spit puffy gusts of silent snow. Then the thunderous rumbles would reach us a few moments later. The flotilla of Britannic ships, if that was what they were, gracefully aligned itself like a troupe of deadly dancers. They came on in a staggered line which enabled them to see and fire on the *Kiss,* even with bow guns only, while not getting in one another's way. But they were mostly interested in catching their quarry and compelling it to surrender.

"Good luck with that," I muttered. "She's fast as a whippet. You'd need steam engines to have a chance."

As if to make a liar out of me, the enemy began to gain.

Minute by minute the gap between them and the *Penelope's Kiss* diminished. Since I knew how fast our ship was, there could be only one explanation. Pitcairn was slowing to give battle.

"What's he playin' at?" I asked aloud. "It's five-to-one."

Ernie spoke up from his seat atop the Duke. "Don't you fret. He knows what he's about, duckie."

"I darned well will fret. My poor Ma's on that boat!"

"Which makes everybody aboard that much safer, don't you think?"

True, I'd seen her turn a dozen demons to ash with Chauntline spells, but that didn't mean I thought a big sea fight was a mere church social. To my mind outrunning the enemy until they gave up seemed a sounder plan. Hadn't Ma just today told me to avoid fighting and use more stealth?

Sha'ira's warm tones caressed my ear. "Breathe, little one. You are as tense as a new bowstring."

I couldn't argue with her there. Concentrating on steady, even breaths, I started to relax myself with the calming chant she'd first taught me so I could control my seasickness. Since then I'd taken to using it any time my stress grew too much for even the Stone to handle. After a minute or so I felt as if I was soaking in a warm bath.

Jasper seemed to agree. In my head he sighed and yawned. The tin cup turned into a rag doll and curled up on my knee. Soon it napped there, snoring. Shaking my head, I concentrated on what was about to happen a mile out to sea.

Pitcairn was feigning a broken rudder. The *Kiss* wobbled and gave every sign that she could no longer be steered. Two enemy ships bought the deception and moved around to cut off the southern and western routes. To their mind the five ships now had Pitcairn dead to rights. As they closed in my magicked ears could almost make out what one of the commanders was saying via speaking trumpet. Calling for surrender, no doubt.

It must have been a trick of the water, for I had no trouble hearing our captain's laughing reply. "Surrender? When I have you right where I want you?"

As if the ships were individual people, there was a shocked pause. Mouths must have gaped at his arrogance. Aloysius Pitcairn appeared to have waiting for just that moment of stunned indecision, for in that pregnant instant he fired on all five ships at once.

And disabled every one of them.

Three of them lay more or less to his port side, blocking the way to the open Atlantic. Each of them took multiple hits to rudder or magazine before they could attempt their own broadsides. The center ship's powder exploded, rocking us all back even from our distant shore position. Smoke and oaken splinters shot into the air. Seconds later it rained men as the shattered bodies of unfortunate sailors fell back to the water's surface. To fore and aft the other two enemies took one cannonball apiece, one obliterating the tiller and helmsman, the other demolishing the mainmast so that it tipped heavily into the foremast, tangling sails and lines.

"Woo-eee!" yelled Jasper, now very much awake. "And it ain't even the Fourth of July!"

"That ain't even possible, is what you mean," I told him, shaking my head. "Nobody's that good a shot, not even Mr. Rochester. Some kind o' magick's helpin' out."

"You think so?"

"I know so. 'Cause I distinctly saw six o' them cannonballs turn in mid-air to smack their targets."

To prove my point, the two ships on Pitcairn's port side let go with their own volleys. At that range they couldn't miss, yet not a single shot landed. Every iron ball either dove into the water as if thrust there by an invisible giant's hand, or flew high over the *Kiss*.

And headed straight for us.

"Look out!" I yelled, turning Jasper into a big steel frying pan about twelve feet across. It covered all of us as ordnance rained down. Tree branches cracked as the iron split them. Mud flew in all directions when the solid shot thudded into the earth. One smacked right into our protective cover, ringing like a bell and making our teeth vibrate. When I was dead certain that all of the shots had landed, I shrank Morphageus back to cup form and took a look around.

All around us the terrain looked like the moon did when you peered at it through a telescope at the Smithsonian. Craters smoked, as if meteors had plunged into the Gaullic shore. Tree limbs hung like the limbs of dead monsters. Back out at sea, exchanges of fire continued, though only the *Kiss* could move. Again it miraculously avoided any damage.

Out of one of the shell holes crawled a tiny ember, staggering and unsteady. I crawled over to it, mindful of other errant shots which might come our way. When I got within three feet of it I could see that it was a little fellow about four inches tall, with hair made of flames and a body like a hot coal. He waved at me, hiccupped, and fell onto his backside.

"Wow!" he said, speech slurred. "That was some ride!" He pointed at himself with a dinky thumb. "Name's Scorch. And I am so drunk right now!"

*"Looks to me like you've imbibed just a wee bit too much
gunpowder. Didn't I warn you about that?"*

4 / Mysterious Horseman

"And you insist drinkin' is no fun," Jasper said.

"Drinkin', my eye," I told him, scooting closer to the itty-bitty figure. "Whiskey had nothin' to do with this and you know it."

The new arrival kept trying to stand but every time he made the effort he plopped right back down again. Now that I was nearly nose-to-nose with him I noticed he had two pairs of wings. But he didn't seem inclined to use them. Instead he folded them flat and slumped over on his back. Though he clearly was on fire, it didn't seem to hurt him any and it didn't burn the leaf he lay on.

"Is the earth spinning or is it just me?" he asked in a thick Irlann accent. "I'll tell you what, that Pitcairn has the best stuff! Yee-ow!"

I waggled my fingers at him. "Hey, there. You're one of them fire sprites that lives on the gun deck, ain't you?"

"That I am, m'lady!" He burped and a ring of orange flame poofed out of his mouth. "I beg your pardon. Manners."

"So you rode in on a cannonball then?"

"True enough. On a Merchantry twenty-four pounder, to be specific. Before that I left the *Kiss* on the bar shot that took down that mast. Must be why I'm so dizzy."

I gave him a wave. "Pleased to meetcha. I'm Verity."

"I know. You're the funny little human who's supposed to bring down the Proprietor and all of his ilk. Can't say as I have much faith in that but you're welcome to try. Nice hair, though. I like red. Can you tell?" He pointed at his fiery frame.

Ernie slid off of the Duke's back and ambled over to Scorch. They were about the same height, though the mouse was a darned sight plumper in the body. The sprite was needle-thin. "Looks to me like you've imbibed a wee bit too much gunpowder. Didn't I warn you about that?"

"Nagged me about it, you mean." Scorch leaned in close to me and whispered. "Terrible scold, he is. Won't let me have any fun."

"It isn't the fun I object to. It's cleanin' up your mess afterward." Ernie looked up at me. "You wouldn't think anybody so small could upchuck so much. Amazin', it is."

"I'm an Elemental spirit. It comes with the territory."

All around us other embers began drifting up out of shell holes. Many of them giggled as if they'd been touring taverns. They formed a blazing cloud in the air about ten feet above the ground. One of them called down to Scorch.

"Come on, we're gonna do it again! Pitcairn's counting on us."

Scorch shook his head. "You go on. I'll catch up. Need to clear my head a bit first. That last one was a real doozy."

"Okay, but don't stay too long. Looks like more ships are coming and the *Kiss* is heading farther out to sea."

"Aw, don't fret about old Scorchie. I'll be there for the big finish, like always." As he said that he tried to stand, spun in a figure-eight sort of way, and fell over again.

That prompted titters from the swirling mass of sprites. "Poor guy can't hold his heat. Come on, fellers! Last one there is a cold cinder!"

That crack about the cold cinder seemed pretty accurate. Scorch was cooling down now that he'd finished riding cannonballs. The flame on his head subsided to a mop of bristly blonde hair. His body glow faded until I could see that he wore a ruffled shirt, gray vest, and brown knee breeches, like they'd worn in Revolutionary War times. Instead of buckled shoes, though, his legs and feet were bare.

Ernie picked him up, throwing one of Scorch's arms around his mousy shoulder so that he wouldn't keel over again. "Here we go, mate. Let's walk it off. Just like usual."

"Don't wanna walk it off," complained the sprite. "Wanna get back with the swarm and help Pitcairn."

"You're in no condition to be flyin' just yet. Let's get some nectar into you and sober you up first."

"Nectar! Whee!"

I frowned at the sight of a roly-poly mouse trying to dry out a drunken a fairy or pixy or whatever Scorch was. Adding to the strangeness was the thought that this was a regular occurrence with them.

"Like usual?" I asked. "He does this a lot?"

"No, actually, and that's the problem," Ernie explained, hauling Scorch around like a rag doll. "He's a young sprite and hasn't yet built up a tolerance for flame. Tends to overindulge, he does."

"I can see that. And nectar will help?"

"Fire sprites actually live on flower juices. That's their real food. But they live for the thrill of the heat. Campfires, lightning, cook stoves, you name it. It's like moonshine to them. And riding a cannonball's the ultimate in excitement. That's why they're on the *Kiss*."

"Yeah, well, I knew that Mr. Rochester had 'em on the gun deck to help with the aimin'. But I had no idea that they could do such a bang-up job guidin' the shells. And it never occurred to me that they'd jump into the enemy's guns and throw off his fire."

"Oh, you betcha. That's why they're so valuable. Pitcairn spent years recruitin' 'em to the *Kiss*. How do you think he's survived so long against vast Merchantry fleets and the comin' of steam ships?"

"Makes sense. Sure seems to help economize on ammunition."

"That it does. Now help me find some flowers. He needs some real food in him."

With the help of Sha'ira's eyes and the Duke's nose, not to mention Romulus' doggy sense of smell (though stuck in human form, he still had some leftover canine skills), we soon came across a patch of honeysuckle. Ernie and the hound stayed to help Scorch gorge himself on the yellow blossoms. The rest of us huddled up to decide what to do next.

"We have perhaps six hours of daylight left," Sha'ira said, gazing out at the ocean. The *Penelope's Kiss* was no longer in view. Her five unlucky foes remained where they had been, decks swarming with crewmen repairing the damage the sprite-aided broadside had wreaked. Lifeboats hunted for survivors of the tremendous magazine explosion. Far off to our right the sails of two more vessels could be seen, hurrying to their aid and no doubt to pursue our friends. It appeared that our reunion might get put-off a while yet.

I looked at Romulus, big as a bear but as meek as a bunny, unless he was defending me from danger. Try as I might I still couldn't get used to the idea that he was really an ancient dog. All of my experience of him was as a handyman around our house the last few months. Even seeing him briefly transformed back into his true mastiff shape when fighting the *Croatan*'s demons hadn't changed that much.

"Ma says you're real familiar with this part o' Gaulle."

"True enough," he rumbled, eyes scanning the woods. "Trees are different, but the old Roman roads always stay the same. Folks just keep on usin' 'em. Just pave over 'em different, is all."

"So where are we now? And how do we travel without attractin' load of Merchantry attention? Or Bonaparte's patrols, fer that matter."

"North o' Bayonne, I figures. Lapurdum, it was called back in my day. Fortified army post. My master took me along with the Third Legion. It's a long, long way to London from here, Miz Verity. Hundreds o' miles."

"Which is why we should make haste," said Sha'ira, turning away from her survey of the water. "I count seven enemy ships. That is a large force for so sleepy an area. I fear we cannot count on an easy journey. One or more of our many foes has surely detected us."

I nodded and slung my rucksack onto my back. "Let's get movin' then. These woods are thick enough that I can wait to put on my corset and dress. I ain't in no hurry, let me tell you."

"There's a coast road," Romulus said, leading the way. "Easy to travel on and handy for the gulls to find us with messages. But it'll be the most likely place for Merchantry spies and ambushes, too."

Sha'ira chuckled. "And we hardly look like the typical residents of this time."

I snapped my fingers at Ernie to get his attention. He waved a paw and got Scorch up onto the hound's back. "I may have a way around that. But it'll require quite a lot of play-actin' on y'all's part."

"Shoot," laughed Romulus, "I been playin' at bein' human for months now."

"And I have been disguised ever since forswearing my Order," Sha'ira pointed out.

After collecting the Duke and Ernie, who told us that Scorch had gorged himself on nectar and passed out cold, I explained our cover story. It took a bit of adjusting as I went, and Jasper bouncing around in my head saying stuff like "Are you really gonna try to sell that?" didn't help much, but in a few minutes we had it sorted. It likely wouldn't keep me out of that hateful dress and bonnet, but it'd go some toward explaining a gigantic colored fellow and a tattooed Arabe woman.

"I love this plan!" crowed Jasper in my head. "Truly glad to be a part of it."

"Uh-huh," I retorted, "and my name is John Wilkes Booth."

Since Scorch was in no condition to return to the *Kiss*, which was out of sight and probably untold miles away, I tucked the woozy sprite away in my rucksack. The first chance we got I'd send him flying back to his swarm. Until then he'd just have to enjoy the pleasure of our company. I wasn't too happy about the prospect of having Jasper's antics in my noggin and Scorch's shenanigans out in the open, but that was a lot better than my usual run of 'monsters, monsters, everywhere' sort of luck.

Romulus led the way, since he knew the land and the route. The summer woods were lush and thick, which made the going slow, but the ground was flat this close to the coast and we weren't in a big hurry anyhow. I preferred to take it easy, feel out the situation, and conserve strength in case we had to run or fight. Running would be no fun, because if we had to run away from the sea we'd run into some awful steep hills, since the Pyrenees Mountains were at hand. And I'd had my fill of fighting in the past few weeks, enough for a lifetime. If I could just go back to stage combat at Ford's Theatre with Tommy, that'd be swell.

Tommy...what if you never see him again, kiddo? What if this is all a huge waste of time?

That thought had been stuck in my craw ever since Venoma had tranced him and taken him to London as a hostage. Maybe that was why I thought so little about him most days that it shocked me. A mental defense, possibly. I asked Jasper once if he was making that happen. He denied it, but pinning him down to a straight answer took more effort than wrestling a greased pig at the county fair. For whatever reason, it struck me as odd and disturbing. Heck, I'd only had one friend in the whole wide world, besides Ma, before this whole magickal mess rained down on me. You'd think that I'd see him in my mind night and day.

But no. Mostly I only had an image of him when the bad dreams came. Ever since my time in Iberion and Lusitania I'd been getting nightmares of Tommy being abused by his Merchantry jailers. Disturbing stuff, like you'd expect from that crowd. Whether they sent them from the Proprietor in London to upset me and hurry me along to my doom, or from somebody else, one thing I knew for certain. The dreams were sent. They were intentional, not just the ordinary muck that people conjured in their sleep. Too clear, too specific, too repetitive. Somebody had a Dreamwriter at his command.

Ravens in Elizabethan ruffs pecking at poor Tommy as he lay chained in the dark. Demons blowing fire at him. Venoma pointing at a huge hourglass as the sand ran out. And weirdest of all, a line of Bullies dancing the can-can with Napoleon.

That last bit bothered me the most. That dance hadn't been invented in Bonaparte's time. It didn't fit with the rest. What if that was the point? Maybe I was interpreting the dream all wrong. Rather than a Merchantry taunt, might it be a warning? Or a prediction?

Bonaparte and Bullies...was the dream saying that they were in cahoots? Or was it telling me that the Merchantry mages were pulling Napoleon's strings?

That last would be easy to believe, after my experiences in the States United. When I'd spoken to General Lee in Richmond he sure behaved as if the Merchantry was up to its foul eyeballs in our Civil War. The Proprietor just loved to manipulate conflicts. That's where his black power came from, by maneuvering people into suffering and misery. So why wouldn't he be involved in Napoleon's conquest of Europa? Even if it was a false conquest, since nobody outside of Gaulle was even living in the same time as Bonaparte's nation. In our tortured bizarre world there were no great armies duking it out at Austerlitz or Waterloo. A grand Merchantry spell merely made everybody think so. How the dark sorcerers in London arranged for the mass casualties that sold the lie didn't bear thinking about.

"Somethin' don't sit right," I thought.

Jasper snorted, "Three weeks of this and you're only figurin' that out now?"

"I don't mean in general. I know the whole world's a mess. Maybe more than one world, too. No, mean this Gaulle business in particular. I think somebody wants us to intervene with Napoleon somehow."

"In our copious leisure time while rescuing Tommy from the clutches of the Merchantry and restoring the entire planet to its rightful destiny while also preventing an inter-dimensional war with the Obverse."

"Funny, when you put it like that it don't seem like so much fun."

As I thought that I ran smack into a stone wall.

Well, it felt like a wall. Turned out to just be Romulus' back as he stopped moving and held up a huge hand. We all crouched down in the undergrowth and got real quiet. He pointed out front to indicate that there was trouble ahead.

Swell, ten whole minutes after we start and already there's mischief.

Beside me Sha'ira nocked an arrow onto her bowstring. To my rear the basset hound hunkered down in a bush until his black and tan body mostly vanished. Ernie scampered up a tree to get a better view. I held my breath and laid a hand on the tin cup, ready to transform it into a weapon or a shield if somebody got frisky. Until then I focused all of my Stone-senses on the situation up front.

One of Napoleon's cavalrymen blocked our way.

He sure wasn't dressed for concealment in the forest, that was for sure. His leather-lined trousers were a rich blue with all sorts of gold embroidery atop the thighs. The tight jacket, so high-necked it threatened to throttle him, was of the same stuff, the bosom crisscrossed by acres of shiny cording between three rows of brass buttons. Over his left shoulder hung a bright red jacket, trimmed in dark brown fur. More of that swanky yellow embroidery covered its sleeves and back. To my amazement, he had an enormously tall black fur hat on, despite the sweltering temperature. Beneath it hung silly braids which dangled alongside his face.

Jasper made a warm purring sound. "Aw, ain't he just the purtiest thing you ever did see?"

"Looks like a clown, if you ask me."

"I remind you that those clowns conquered most of Europa in their day."

"Yeah, well, in this heat the July sun's likely to conquer him any minute now."

He was faced three-quarters away from us on his gorgeous chestnut horse. The color of polished mahogany, it went a long way toward making up for his dopey clothes. I couldn't get a good look at the fellow's features, other than seeing that he sported a dark moustache and was fairly young. But something struck me as familiar about the pair of them. When I used my witched nose I instantly figured out what it was.

I laughed and pushed past Romulus, who reached out to stop me but missed. With a wave and a grin I called out, "Hi, y'all!"

"It's about time," said Tyrell with a wink. "Al and I have been waiting here forever."

To Tyrell I said, "Victoria, huh? She have a last name?"
He lowered his voice as if he feared the hound's scorn.
"Sponge."
My eyes widened. It took all of my self-control to keep a
straight face and to ignore Jasper's hoots in my mind.
"Victoria Sponge? You gotta be kiddin' me."

5 / An Old Quarrel

Sha'ira raised an eyebrow as she released the tension on her bow. Sliding it back into her quiver, she said, "Truly?"

Tyrell gave her a sly grin. "Yes, ma'am." His Virginia accent was pure and strong. "Took a deal of work but I managed to get my old glad rags ready in time for this soiree."

"Including a new horse, I see."

He gave his mount's neck a rub. The pale blonde mane was now black. "No, indeed. This here is Alcibiades. He just gave himself a fresh coat of paint is all."

"Norn horses can do that?" I asked, going nose-to-muzzle with Al. As usual, he snuffled around for treats but they were all stowed deep in my rucksack out of easy reach. That earned me a put-upon look.

"They were bred in Asgard to adapt to any situation. Color, breed, weight. All malleable. To say nothing of their talent for languages."

I'd heard that in Iberion Al had spoken Attic Greek when required, though I had a hard time buying it. He'd never spoken a single word in my hearing, not even in good old Britannic. But I supposed that if his magickal wings weren't beyond belief then nothing else should be, either. "Why shift his looks at all? He was a darned pretty horsey before. Quite the looker." Al's ears perked up at that. I swear he winked at me.

"Precisely the issue. I don't want him standing out to the casual observer. If he sticks in the mind then we aren't as unobtrusive as we'd like."

"Good point." I wondered how Tyrell gallivanting about in a circus ringmaster's outfit qualified as 'unobtrusive.'

From my feet came a disgusted snort such as only a patrician basset hound could make. The Duc du Ponteau's droopy features looked ready to cough up breakfast as he regarded the Confederate's fancy new duds. "If only your repellant ensemble were also less visible, then perhaps I would be less inclined to gag at the sight."

Tyrell returned his acid comment with a sneer of his own. "Say you so, Evremonde? Perhaps I should apply a gag to your snout so that I won't have to listen to your insufferable aristo belly-aching. Happy Bastille Day, by the way. Will you join me in a chorus or two of 'La Marseillaise'?"

"Such a gauche tune. And silencing me will not make your hypocritical cause any more proper."

"Hypocritical? The citizens rose up and threw your kind out."

"Yes, I say. That runt of a Corsican just crowned himself

Emperor two months ago, did he not? Such a man of the people."

"Compared to you parasites, yes. And the Coterie Redempteur is trying to return him to the true path."

"Ah, yes. You precious Redeemers. So sure that you can stuff the genie back into the bottle. A fool's errand, that."

From there they switched to jabbering in Gaullic and I lost track of what they were saying. I only knew that it was a mite less polite. Words like *cochon* and *ecume* and *vulgair* got bandied about thick and fast. Eventually I worried that they'd draw some unwelcome attention to us. So I turned my cup into a rolled–up newspaper and whacked the hound on his nose. Jasper snickered at that. When Tyrell laughed I pointed my corrective tool at him and threatened the same treatment.

"Look at you two! Actin' like fool schoolboys arguin' over a game o' ball. If I didn't know how serious your quarrel was I'd be inclined to lock you in an outhouse and let you settle it. But we ain't got the luxury, I tell you. Time's short as it is. We got a whole world in chains and you wanna carp about politics."

The Duke growled. "Politics! This is no mere power squabble, petit mademoiselle. My whole family was guillotined. I only escaped by swallowing all pride and fleeing in the guise of an old woman. Murderers they are. Promising *Liberte, Egalite, Fraternite* with one hand while sharpening the knives with the other." He spat at the grass near Al's foot, causing the horse to look hurt.

Tyrell waved the complaint away. "I had no hand in the

Terror. I was not much more than a boy then." But I could tell that he felt the sting of the accusation nonetheless. "I am a soldier, defending his country, nothing more."

When the Duke wound himself up to sling more heat, I jumped in between them again and tried to deflect the conversation. "I can see that. What uniform are you wearin'? Cavalry, that's plain to see." With a head jerk I begged Romulus to take the mutt aside and pacify him, dog-to-dog. Sha'ira slid off to watch for trouble.

Sitting up tall and proud, Tyrell twirled his moustache. "4th Hussars. Finest scouts and skirmishers ever to sit in a saddle."

"Hussars? Miz Finch taught us in school that they was, um, a handful."

He shrugged, letting slip a sheepish little smile. "Guilty. It takes a certain type of man to volunteer to scout ahead of the army, engaging the foe's bravest. We tend to only be happy in the charge, in a duel of honor, in our cups, or in a woman's arms. Our discipline can be a bit...slippery."

"Yeah? The way I heard it, your own Marshal Murat said that any hussar who wasn't dead by age thirty was a blackguard."

"An exaggeration, surely. Though he has lived far beyond that. I myself am only twenty-eight."

"Shoot. You're almost ninety. You told me so."

"I am well-preserved, am I not? In truth, I ceased to age when I swore myself to the Redeemers. Though they favor brains and science over magick, they do employ a few sorcerers' tricks."

Romulus was struggling to calm the Duke. They huddled

beneath a maple tree several yards away. I still had to keep Tyrell busy for a bit. Admiring his kit seemed like a good way to do it. Besides, I was curious about it. "Swell hat. Looks awful sweaty, though."

He nodded. "It is, I confess. Seal fur. But it absorbs saber blows well. And it is not, strictly-speaking, a hat. We call it a busby."

"What's that funny bag hangin' off it?"

An empty red sack with big gold tassels grew out of the crown of the crown of the busby and lay along the right side. Tyrell tapped it with a finger and chuckled. "Apart from its stunning stylishness? We tie it to the shoulder and it helps deflect sword cuts. Not very well, but every little bit helps."

"And them adorable girlie braids?"

"The same. We call them cadenettes. And what you call 'girlie' drives the ladies mad with passion."

"Yeah? Well, I don't need to know about that."

Jasper, of course, did. "Hey, not so fast, um, girlie! Let him talk. Your Uncle Jasper has needs."

With an eye-roll I pressed on. "What's that cute embroidered purse for? A place to stow the comb for yer braids or what?"

"It's a sabretache. The uniform is short on pockets. Too tight. We often deliver dispatches from commanders. This is where we keep them."

The hound seemed to be a bit less cranky now. Romulus had done his work well. Time to wrap up my diversion. "You know, it's the middle of July. That extra jacket seems way too much, don't you think?"

"What can I say? I am a slave to fashion, as the ladies say. It's a pelisse. The more layers, the less damage the enemy's swords do. In weather like this, we wear it as a cape, over the left shoulder, until engaging the foe."

I really wanted to get my hands on his gorgeous brass-hilted saber, but we'd already lingered too long. And the Duke was plodding in our direction. One last question. "How on earth did you manage to carry all this stuff with you? When we met in Virginia you had yer Confederate uniform and McClellan saddle. No sign of any of this. I know you didn't stuff it in those two saddlebags."

"Au contraire. That is precisely what I did."

"Huh? Impossible."

"Says the girl with a freight car of supplies in her rucksack. You aren't the only one with a magick pack, you know."

"Oh. Shoulda figured."

Ernie dropped onto my shoulder from a low-hanging tree branch. He tickled my ear with one furry paw. "If you're done with your history lesson, can we get goin'? Matilda's gulls ain't likely to spot us in these trees. We need to make some progress and find a place to lay up for the night."

"And I really need to taste the sweet savory goodness of your corncob pipe before bedtime," added Jasper.

Sighing, I gave the hound a stare. "Got yer hackles up still? Or can you swallow a little more of your Gaullic pride so we can get on the road?"

"It will be hard, little one, but I shall endeavor to be the bigger *chien*."

"Good fer you." I leaned in close so that Tyrell couldn't hear and whispered to the enormous long ears. "I'll let you in on a little secret. Napoleon loses in 1815. Exiled to a dinky speck o' rock in the Sea o' Atlas. The Bourbons return to the throne."

His brow wrinkled as his brown eyes widened. "Mon Dieu! Does he know this?"

"Nope. Let's just keep it between us fer now."

To Tyrell I said, "Truce? Okay?"

The Hussar nodded and took up Al's reins. I saw that he had a pair of flintlock pistols on his saddle, as well as a carbine musket. No sign of the nine-shot LeMat he usually packed. "Very well. All of our energies should be focused on young Thomas."

"Agreed." As I'd done with the Duke, I lowered my voice and told him something in confidence. "Don't let on that I said this, but Napoleon gets his comeuppance eleven years from now."

"I'm aware of that. Saw it from afar, in exile in the States United. But does the dog know?"

"How could he? He was a prisoner in a kitchen in medieval Iberion until I busted him out. I let on that his Bourbons are back on the throne."

"Let us not mention it then. It thrills me to imagine the day when I casually mention the election of Napoleon III."

That made me wonder just where Bonaparte's nephew, who took power two years before the Affluxion which transmogrified the whole word, was now. And all of the Gaullic nation of that time, come to think of it. Maybe no place. Though I kept asking what had happened to the millions of people who'd vanished on the spring equinox of 1850, my birth date, nobody could tell me. They'd been replaced by an imitation of the Gaulle of 1804, sure, but were the original folks all dead? In limbo? Stuck in the Obverse?

All that pondering got my head to hurting. Jasper humming the most gruesome verses of 'La Marseillaise' didn't help. We got back on the trail, Romulus in the lead again and Sha'ira covering our rear, bow ready to defend us. Tyrell walked his horse because the trees were so thick. They'd been snagging his splendid busby and over-decorated pelisse. In his scarlet and blue get-up he didn't exactly blend into the forest like the rest of us. You could probably spot all of that gold braid from Paris. I had the hound go with Romulus and apply his sniffer to the trail. Though the Duke was a literal royal pain in my backside sometimes, he could smell the faintest of odors. Even my witched nose wasn't that good.

Tyrell dropped back beside me as we picked our way through the forest. "How did you know it was me?"

"Huh?"

"When you came up on me from behind. You recognized me at once, despite the uniform and Al's changed appearance. How did you manage that?"

"Oh...well, you might've swapped out yer clothes but that rosy soap you use sure stays with you."

He blushed a bit, which I thought was adorable. "Ah, that. A present from a dear lady friend. Waste not, want not."

"Anybody I know?" I teased.

"Maybe it's your ma," Jasper chortled.

I changed him into a chamber pot and glared at him. "You know, I'm feelin' the call of nature somethin' fierce."

"Ouch! Somebody I know needs to grow a sense of humor."

"And somebody I know need to get his adjusted. No more Ma jokes, you hear?"

"All right! Touchy, touchy!"

Tyrell was looking at me with a twisted little smile. Beside him Al blew a horsey sigh through his lips.

"Just how I feel."

"Trouble with your gallant cup?" the Hussar asked.

"Naw. No more'n usual. And you won't shed me that easy. Now spill it. Who gave you that soap?"

"A fetching lass from the Scepter'd Isle, actually."

"Really? When were you ever there?"

"Never. Victoria was in Gaulle, on a concert tour. Playing the fortepiano. Lovely hands, of course."

"Naturally."

Jasper couldn't resist. "One does wonder about the circumstances which caused her to give him rose-scented soap. Were they sharing?" He imitated Tyrell's voice. "Say there, Miss Vicki, might I impose upon you to scrub my manly back?"

"Oh, ick," I growled at him. "Boys are impossible."

"Laugh now. Someday you'll change your tune and swear that

we are so very...necessary."

"Yeah, well that day ain't today. So stifle yourself."

To Tyrell I said, "Victoria, huh? She have a last name."

"Of course." He lowered his voice as if he feared the hound's scorn. "Sponge."

My eyes widened. It took all of my self-control to keep a straight face and to ignore Jasper's hoots in my mind. "Victoria Sponge? You gotta be kiddin' me."

"I swear on my honor as a Redeemer. That was her name. At least, that was what she told me. I confess that I didn't see her name on a parish register."

Jasper broke through, try as I might to keep him quiet. "Oh, boy! Sponge! I'll bet she absorbed his every romantic word."

"Ha-ha, Mr. Jokester."

"Sponge and soap...an unbeatable combination."

"Oh, you should go on the stage with this act. You'll knock 'em dead. I'll arrange it with Mr. Ford."

"She's Britannic? She must be from...Bath!"

I told him to go soak his head, quietly, and returned to Tyrell. "Well, she didn't pick her name. I sure as heck can't give anybody else grief when I'm named Sauveur. Not a soul can pronounce it."

Tyrell smiled. "They can here in Gaulle, though you wouldn't recognize it when you heard it."

He had a point. Ma's ancestors had been Huguenots who'd emigrated to the States United long before. Now we pronounced it 'sew-fair', which was kind of appropriate with Ma being a seamstress and all. But the locals in Gaulle would probably cry themselves to sleep at the thought of such sacrilege.

"Well, I ain't aimin' to give it out. That'd sure as shootin' draw down every demon, Shade, Bully, and poop monster fer a thousand miles."

My need for a new name reminded me that I had to include the Hussar in our cover story. That actually made things easier, since he was one of Napoleon's officers. I started to give him a quick explanation of our plan when he stiffened and put his finger to his lips. Following his narrowed dark eyes I saw that he was looking at the Duke. The basset hound had frozen in mid-stride and let out a tiny woof.

"Shh!" whispered Tyrell. "His over-bred nose is onto something."

He slid a pistol off of Al's saddle and crouched below the horse's belly. I did the same, tired knee joints crackling. Romulus had already flung himself flat beneath a shrub, bowie knife in hand. Behind us, Sha'ira's deadly eyes never wavered in making certain that we didn't get ambushed while concentrating on the Duke. My ears and nose didn't notice anything out of the ordinary, but a stiffening breeze from the sea was rustling the trees now and the noise made it hard to pick up sounds at any distance.

We all stayed put for a long time, until my legs started to shake from the strain. To relieve them I stood and crept along Al's flank until I got up to Romulus. Lying down next to his bulk, rucksack beside to me, I felt secure enough to risk anything. He raised one finger the size of a railroad spike and pointed it dead ahead of his nose. I followed it until I spotted our problem.

A cavalry patrol. Not Hussars, just a dozen ordinary enlisted horsemen. Still pretty fancy, though, compared to what I was used to in our Civil War. Tight blue jackets with yellow fronts and really odd helmets with square flat tops. Matching trousers with buttons running all down the outside. All of them carried wicked ten-foot lances.

They were stopped on a wide trail, tending to their horses and equipment. Likely they'd moved into the woods to get out of the stifling sun. Brows were getting wiped and water guzzled. A couple smoked pipes. None of them looked toward us or even seemed to be keeping much of a watch. Our lucky day. A mass rush at us wasn't in the cards.

It was still a good long way to open country and the coast road. Our best bet was to stay put and wait for them to leave the trees and continue their duties. After tangling with the Old Guard in Virginia when the Merchantry had made a big play for me, I was in no kind of hurry to start another ruckus with Bonaparte's boys. They took their fighting seriously.

But as usual things didn't go my way. Just as I gestured to everybody to relax and lay low for a while, I got reminded of just why Jasper said that he loved being with me: because my life was never dull and predictable.

Scorch woke up from his drunken nap.

The sprite crawled out of my rucksack, woozy and confused. Since I'd forgotten all about him being in there, I didn't react too quick when he staggered past my hand. Before I could nab him he'd staggered across Romulus' shoulders to rub his eyes and wonder just where the heck he was. From the tense look on his tiny face I guessed that he had a whopper of a hangover. Unfortunately for us, he spotted the one thing that might make him feel better.

Fire.

His dragonfly-like wings vibrated so fast they nearly turned invisible. Though I turned my cup into a bug net and tried to scoop him out of the air, he proved to be a lot more agile than his condition suggested. I missed twice as he took to the air. An instant later Scorch shot through the trees and went straight for his headache cure.

And dove into a lancer's pipe bowl.

"One day I'm the Righteous Cleaver of Doom and now I'm a bosom-buttress. How can I face the other magick swords?"

6 / Sparks

Sparks splashed up into the poor fellow's face as he stood beside his horse. He let go of the reins and commenced to swat at the orange fireflies. One of the embers landed near his mount's eye. The startled steed shied and bolted through the rest. In an instant the patrol lost all of its discipline. Men yelled and made frantic grabs at reins, manes, anything that might control their bucking, snorting, fleeing animals. Lances flew every which way like straws in a windstorm. Sent sprawling by panicked hooves, heads, and rumps, several soldiers smacked into tree trunks. All discipline evaporated.

In the chaos none of the troops noticed that one of the sparks from the pipe appeared a lot bigger than the others. It also somehow flew against the wind, changing directions in sudden jerky ways. I winced as Scorch zipped past enraged noses without being slapped out of the humid air. If the men could've heard what my magick-aided ears did, they would've made an effort to do just that.

"Yow-ee!" cried the sprite, turning loops, his hair and body ablaze. "Just the ticket for nectar-noggin! I feel good!"

I tried to get his attention and get him back to us before he caused any more ruckus, but he was way too excited. He darted all about, almost teasing the horses and lancers by circling their heads. And of course Jasper just had to pick that moment to get his own silly self into the act. My net shaped itself into a wind-up toy monkey that applauded Scorch as if he'd just won an election.

Through all of this Alcibiades stood stock-still, unflustered by all of the crazy goings-on. After everything I'd seen him deal with, from cannon bursts to Pluto's Bane volleys to angry chimeras tussling with zombies, this probably didn't even attract his attention. Beneath him Tyrell did the same, not moving at all except to holster his pistol. Romulus tucked his knife away, too, and motioned for Sha'ira to put away her bow. We were going to try to sneak away in the confusion and go around the pitiful patrol.

A good plan, but it didn't happen. One of the horses spun about, its broad back end knocking a lancer ten feet in the air until he slid face-first through the turf. The soldier, a boy of no more than eighteen, shook the dirt from his face and looked up.

Straight at Romulus. They could've spit on each other they were so close.

Okay, Verity, time to see if your cover story will hold water or just leak like a rowboat full of buckshot.

With a yelp the kid shoved himself backward and started yammering in Gaullic, pointing at the copse where we all hid. At first that only added to the fracas, which helped me out a good deal because just then I realized a couple of inconvenient things. First, I hadn't yet changed into my pretty dress and was still in my 1862 overalls and straw hat. Second, I couldn't understand a syllable of what anybody in Gaulle said.

Romulus hopped to his feet and pulled back behind Tyrell, who got into his saddle with as smooth a motion as I'd ever seen. It struck me that he'd been a cavalryman for about seventy years. Sha'ira and the Duke also joined Romulus, making a tight cluster which I could use. No sign of Ernie or Scorch. While the lancers finished gathering their mounts and weapons, a couple already reacting to the young man's discovery, I snagged monkey-Jasper, returned him to cup form, and scooted behind my friends.

"Stall 'em," I said. "Gotta make myself presentable. Two minutes."

With that Tyrell urged Alcibiades forward a bit, turned the horse sideways some, and made himself our spokesman. The rest created as wide a wall as they could to hide me. I yanked open the top of the rucksack and wriggled down into it. Inside it was the size of a tool shed. Shelves and chests held all manner of supplies. It looked like a small general store. Ma had stocked it with everything she'd expected that I might need if I got separated from her and had to go out on my own. Food, water, maps, and the like. There was even a supply of magick potions and instructions for Chauntline spells I hadn't yet learned.

But right now all I needed was that dress and bonnet. I

shucked my denim overalls and hat. In just my skivvies, I picked up the horrid corset. No time. Plus, it took somebody else's help to get into the wretched abomination. What a shame. *Sorry, Jasper. This'll be a humiliation fer us both. Can't be helped.*

With a wish I held the tin cup against my ribs, seeing an image of what I wanted to happen. Jasper's shrill howls of outrage bounced all around my skull as the cup flattened and flowed about me. I took a deep breath and held it as it became an ideal set of stays for a proper girl in 1804 Gaulle.

"Oh, the ignominy!" he wailed as if bound to a wheel of fire. "The disgrace! I'm mortified, I am!"

"Oh, shush," I told him, pulling the dress on over my head. "I'm the one that's gotta wear you."

"One day I'm the Righteous Cleaver of Doom and now I'm a bosom-buttress. How can I face the other magick swords?"

"It's not like you guys have meetings, you know." With the dopey bonnet on my head I rummaged through a bag of goodies. I had a favor to buy.

"You'll pay for this, Sauveur! My revenge shall be swift and terrible. Vengeance is mine, sayeth the sword. I shall loose the fateful lightning! I shall – ooh, yummy!"

I'd popped a wad of licorice into my maw, overdoing it some. He loved the stuff. Without a doubt it'd make him happy enough to forget the corset business and then some, even though it made me look like I was chewing tobacco.

"Don't be a baby," I said, tugging on slipper-like shoes. "It's just until we shed these guys and I can have Sha'ira do up the real corset all proper-like."

"Keep that ambrosia comin' and you can use me for diapers."

"Eeww!"

"Anything else Verity needs done? Dragons slain? Demons slaughtered?"

"I hope not, since I can't very well wear you on my chest and use you as a weapon at the same time."

"Not with this bosom. But give it time."

"Oh, oink. We gotta go. Here's what I need you to do."

It turned out to be a lot longer than two minutes by the time I'd dressed, arranged things with Jasper, and freed myself from the rucksack. When I poked my head out to see what was up, which would have really upset anybody who saw it, my friends hadn't moved. What that meant was that my nose ended up smooshed against the hound's butt. The Duc du Ponteau turned his head to give me a long disappointed look. Hey, he didn't like it any less than I did.

"Well, this is goin' from bad to worse," complained Jasper.

"Hush," I thought to him. "I gotta listen to this."

While I squirmed out of the bag I cocked an ear to try to make out what was happening. That I didn't arrive in the middle of a pitched battle struck me as a great first sign. What also made me happy was being able to understand what the Gaullic lancers were saying. Jasper's translation spell had come through. That licorice had some powerful influence with him.

A wide fellow who I took to be the sergeant in command of the patrol was talking to Tyrell. From the fairly relaxed manner of the conversation I gathered that things were going as I'd hoped. Considering that I hadn't really briefed the Hussar before things went sour, I couldn't have asked for much more.

"Gave us a fright, sir, and no mistake. Why the private's horse shied I have no idea, but old Lancelot would flinch at a sunrise if he took it into his head."

As usual, the spell let me hear every foreign word in Britannic, but with the accent of the speaker. That let me know what language I was listening to. Behind the sergeant his men were grouped back together, some still adjusting tack and calming their mounts. A quick scan of the area still didn't reveal where Ernie and Scorch had gone.

Tyrell gave Al a pat on his neck, raising a small dust cloud. "Old Tiresias used to do the same thing. Just spring into the air as if he could fly. Sometimes I thought he had wings."

Everybody laughed at that, which gave me my chance to slither all the way out of the sack. As the noise started to die down I backed up a little and then trod around to the right of 'Tiresias', rubbing his nose and pretending to breathe hard as if I'd rushed up to join them all. I gave the sergeant a curtsey and fiddled with my reticule.

"My apologies," I said, tucking a wayward strand of my newly-blonde and curly hair back up into my bonnet. Jasper had given me a new look to go with my mastery of Gaullic. The freckles which usually covered my features like a rusty constellation were gone, too. "I drank too much water this afternoon and I fear it quite ran through me."

Jasper hooted at me. "That's your idea of how a well-born lady talks to strangers?"

Beside me I could see Tyrell's eyes widen as he saw the new me. But he mastered himself at once. I hoped that Romulus and Sha'ira would do the same. The hound had sure taken it all in stride.

"Quite all right, miss. Mother Nature will not be denied, eh?"

"Very true, captain." I looked up at the sergeant, astride his nervous black horse. The man had an impressive nose like so many Gaulles. "Pleased to meet so gallant a soldier. My name is Lucy Gaspard."

The big lancer nodded and touched the golden brim of his odd helmet. "Sergeant Jean Gabelle, 7th Lancers. The honor is mine."

"You are too charming, sir. I trust that we were not the cause of your distress?"

"Oh, no. To my shame we were unaware of your presence until one of my men apparently blew through his pipe instead of drawing on it."

Gabelle glared at a gangly trooper who looked as if he wanted to ride his horse into the sea and vanish forever. "I swear something dropped into it. Then it — "

His voice cut off with a choke as if his commander used magick, though I saw that he only needed a dirty look. "That is good to hear. I would be mortified if we had somehow brought you trouble."

"That remains to be seen, miss. I am responsible for the

security of this district and when I encounter strange citizens wandering in the woods so near to an important port I naturally need to be assured of their good intentions."

"Of course. Your instincts do you credit. Then the good captain has not yet informed you of our situation?"

"That he has not. Captain Manette has insisted that you must explain how you came to be hiding here."

I took note of Tyrell's new name, as well as that of his horse, and hoped I could keep all of the fibs straight. "He did well. A *beau sabreur* he is, and he follows his orders well."

"Orders? From...you?" Gabelle tried not to smile as he pondered a superior officer taking commands from a kid. A girl, at that. A few of his men were less successful at controlling their snickers.

"No, of course not. From my uncle, General Marat."

Tyrell – Captain Manette, rather – cleared his throat. "Marshal Marat, that is to say."

Surprise showed on the sergeant's face. "You don't say?"

"Indeed. Two months ago, when the Senate made our Consul Emperor."

"They say that Fortune truly favors the bold."

Manette laughed. "Fortune also favors those who are wedded to the Emperor's sister."

That clouded Gabelle's features a little. He seemed out of his depth with that sort of political talk. I felt the same way, but for a different reason.

Jasper knew what the trouble was, since he was in my head.

"I bet you wished you'd paid more attention when your teacher taught your class this part of Europan history, huh?"

I sort of shrugged at him with my mind. "I got the basic details straight, and then some, but who memorizes promotion dates? We gotta watch our step here."

"All success to the new Marshal, however he came by it," said Gabelle. "May I live to be half the soldier he is."

Manette nodded. "Agreed. He is what we all aspire to be."

I wondered how tongue-in-cheek Tyrell was being, since we both knew that Murat would end his days in front of a firing squad a month before Waterloo. This tiptoeing-through-history business was like having a time machine with no instruction manual and it made my brains all gooey.

"Pleasantries aside, captain. Just why are you here?"

Ah. Time to spin the lies. Jasper, please hold up your end of our bargain.

I jumped in, since it was my brilliant cover story. Too bad it already needed adjustments. "Because of me, I'm afraid. I was at school in Bordeaux. When my term ended I took ship down the coast as a holiday, planning to come back up the Garonne and then travel home by diligence. Our family is all in Labastide-Fortuniere. Somewhat east of Bordeaux, in Lot."

"You sailed alone?"

"Of course not. My chaperone Therese accompanied me." I sniffed, mouth quivering. "Poor dear. I fear I may never see her again."

"Misfortune, then? On the sea?"

"Of the worst kind. You saw the distressing action today? All of those Britannic ships pouncing on that trader?"

"Smuggler, more like. No, we didn't get to see the fracas. Heard it, though. You weren't caught up in that?"

"Heavens, no. But some of those same ships pursued us. We had to flee all night, only escaping when they abandoned the chase in favor of a richer prize. One of our second-rates. They went over the horizon after it yesterday. I don't know what the outcome was. One hopes our fellows triumphed."

"So how did you end up in Bayonne?"

"The nearest port. Clearly the seas were too hazardous at present, so we decided to take the coast road. But before I could arrange a coach things became...interesting."

Gabelle clearly didn't think my story was all that interesting. He sighed and made a face which told me that I'd better hurry up. I checked back in with Jasper, who was feeding me tidbits about Gaullic geography, Marshal Murat, and anything else required. Making up an elaborate story while also having him babbling in my mind was hard work.

"We encountered the redoubtable Captain Manette here. He had been sent by my uncle to Bayonne on a different matter and was commanded to search for me."

Tyrell stepped in as the Hussar to help me out. "Optical telegraph message from the Marshal. Marvelous system. That Monsieur Chappe is a genius."

"Truly. Captain, can you be brief? We have other duties."

"My apologies. Lucy has now arrived at the meat of her tale.

I promise you that you will be intrigued."

I stepped aside to indicate Romulus and Sha'ira. "On the wharf Therese and I blundered into a tussle. Some men were trying to force these two poor souls into a wagon. It was quite apparent that they did not want to go. each wore shackles. Without thinking of danger or propriety Therese smacked one of them with her parasol and implored them to desist." I blubbered again. "She was always thinking of others before herself." Pretending to master my emotions, I went on. "They claimed to own these two. Exotics from the East, as you can see. The giant is called Oshaka, strong man and wrestler from the dark Continent, and the Arabe lady is Halam. She is famed as an archer, performing all over the Levant. No target is too challenging.

"Captives, they were. Slaves. Therese quite forgot herself. The so-called owners struck her down with bludgeons. I tried to aid her, but the violence of those men was too much. They flung my senseless friend into the wagon and were in the process of serving me the same way when the dashing Captain Manette, having scoured the docks for me, arrived to dispense justice. His saber and fists made short work of them and they fled in their wagon, taking Therese with them. We gave chase but lost them in the crush of vehicles in town." I gave in to my best fake tears at that point. "Oh, Therese! You were so good to me!"

You can always count on the waterworks to sell something to men. Sergeant Gabelle shrank in his saddle. He even offered me his handkerchief. "And you have still not found these men? Nor your chaperone?"

"Alas, no. That is why we are scouring these woods, in hopes that the scoundrels might be hiding here. You have seen no suspicious wagon?"

"Not yet. But we shall keep our eyes open as we patrol. What do you plan for these two exotics, as you call them?"

Tyrell jumped back in again. "We could hardly leave them to wander a stranger country, friendless, knowing little of our language. So I hit upon a plan for our mutual benefit. As you know, the Emperor's coronation will take place in Rouen later this year. He will doubtless desire to mark the occasion with festivities on a grand scale. I have been tasked, as an aide to the Marshal, to seek suitable performers. As the Emperor has spent time in the East, he may enjoy seeing examples of the best of that region. It is my hope that he will find a place for Oshaka and Halam or, if it is their will, return them to their homelands."

"We hid here because we foolishly hoped to chastise the offenders ourselves," I said. "Once you had passed, we planned to resume our search. But seeing your obvious capability, we leave them to you. If they are here, you shall apprehend them."

I gave Gabelle a detailed, and completely fictional, description of three dirty ruffians and a red wagon. After finishing with instructions that he should send the mythical Therese along to Labastide-Fortuniere, should he rescue her, we made ready to head north on the forest trail.

"So, sighed Jasper, "that was your idea of a simple cover story?"

He shuddered and shook his head.
"You've not seen the Channel nor been on it."
"Rough, huh?"
"You'll need all of your magick just to keep your meals down."

7 / A Busy Year

Sergeant Gabelle's lancers hadn't been gone half a minute when Scorch showed up. It turned out that Ernie had dumped him into a water-filled hoof print and sat on him until he cooled enough to be controlled. Now the dumpy mouse appeared with the unhappy sprite in tow. Scorch wore a pout.

"You ain't got no discipline at all, have you?" I asked him as I tried to figure out a lady-like way to haul my rucksack.

The little fellow laughed. "Well, no! Don't you know anything about Elementals?"

I gave him the same laugh right back. "Well, no! Miz Finch must o' forgot to cover that in school last year."

"Along with talkin' magick swords, combat pelicans, and zombie armies," added Jasper. "And by the way, you need to feed your sword again if you want to keep on talkin' the local lingo."

Scorch threw up his hands and flew up to my nose level, hovering there until my eyes almost crossed. Now I could see that he was not much more than a kid, with dark hair and a long nose. "We have the qualities of our element. Earth sprites are solid, beefy bores who take a long time to do anything. Air sprites have echo chambers for brains. Water sprites are cool and relaxed. They flow with whatever, and whoever, comes their way, if you get my meaning. Their cousins, ice sprites, are cold, calculating, and love schemes. And we — " Scorch burst into flames like a new-struck match. He flew in crazy patterns, leaving his name written in the air for a moment. "We're the fun-loving type. Our boilers are always at high pressure. Any time we see fire we just have to play with it."

"Ain't that just swell? Well, the next time you just have to play with some fire, do it a mile away from any armed troops, will you? Cause if you jeopardize us like that again, I'm likely to stick you in a jar like a lightnin' bug."

Scorch landed on the Duke's back and looked at Ernie, who already rode there, needle-spear held high. "Is she always this bossy?"

Ernie chuckled. "You have no idea."

I snagged some licorice and a peppermint stick from the pack, then gave up on wearing it and tossed it to Romulus. He opened up the straps as far as they'd go and put it on his ox-sized back. Up at the front of our group Tyrell fussed with his ridiculous fur busby. How anybody in Napoleon's time managed to accomplish anything dressed like that was a total mystery to me, but there was no denying that all of that gold braid and snug clothing caught a girl's eye, impractical or not. From what I'd heard about the disgusting behavior of Hussars, it had an even worse effect on the older ladies.

Sha'ira resumed her place at the end of the line to ensure that we didn't get snuck up on. Our hound tucked in next to Romulus, probably as a professional courtesy. I hustled up to join Tyrell, discovering that running in that awful dress was even more trouble than I'd feared it might be. And wearing Jasper for a corset was no Sunday picnic, either. Apart from the constricting of my breathing and the pinching, I had to put up with his whining about the mortification of it all. It made me long for the good old days in Iberion in my overalls and bare feet, fighting zombie hordes, flaming poop monsters, and Hellenic gods.

Okay, maybe I didn't long for it all that much. But still...

The heat was a good deal less on the trail, with the canopy of green overhead and mostly clear walking. Not as much work to walk. That ocean breeze felt nice, too. Relaxing a bit, but not too much because even an innocent-looking snake could be a Merchantry spy – as I'd discovered in Virginia – I tucked in beside Tyrell to pick his brain about our situation. Paying Jasper for a history lesson looked likely to upset my tummy at the prices he charged.

"It's July of 1804, right?" I asked.

The Hussar nodded, reins slack in his hand. Al mostly handled himself. "It is. Quite the amazing year, as I recall."

"Since you've already lived through it and the Affluxion spell nearly always makes things happen as they did in real history, maybe you'd better fill me in on what's goin' on in Gaulle, so I don't trip myself up."

He spent the better part of the afternoon lecturing me about Napoleon, the Gaulle of his youth, the wars, the plots, the culture. Some of it I already knew from school and reading, but it was good to have it from the horse's mouth, so to speak. Tyrell, who'd never told me his real name, had been born at the best (or worst, depending on your outlook) time to experience the entire French Revolution and the age of Bonaparte. He'd been born in 1776, amazingly. As a boy of about my age he'd witnessed the fall of the Bastille and the birth of that bloody uprising. To hear him tell it, an entire nation had lost its mind in blood lust against the aristocrats who'd kept them down for centuries and then against one another as the various factions tried to keep the Paris mob content by proving that they were more patriotic than the other guys. Chopping off heads seemed to be the favored way to do that. You could be the top of the heap on Monday, worshipped by all as the savior of Gaulle, and on Tuesday be denounced as 'counter-revolutionary' by your former best friend.

"I saw it many times," he said, shaking his head as he recalled painful memories. "Utter madness. Much the same as with the Civil War in the States United right now. Trying to end slavery overnight. Or the Protestant Reformation. Great sudden changes in a people's way of living or thinking can rarely be managed without apocalyptic chaos."

"How'd you manage you preserve your own head so that you could be here wearing that fine itchy hat?"

"By joining the army and keeping my mouth shut. It put

bread in my mouth. With all of the food shortages that was no small thing. And when the other nations of Europa invaded us to restore the aristocracy, well...one always defends one's fatherland, even in a situation such as that."

That reminded me that he was now in the Confederate Army, fighting against my side to preserve slavery. Did Tyrell do it for the same reason, because Lincoln's troops had invaded the South, or was there some complicated Redeemer plot at play in my country? I'd never asked. "I guess so. That's the argument Jeff Davis makes in Richmond, anyhow."

Before we got off on an argument about our nasty war of 1862, I steered him back to our Gaullic predicament. He seemed happy that I did. "But I need to know specific stuff about 1804. What're folks talkin' about? What's got 'em riled up?"

"Bonaparte's being made Emperor, of course. He was already First Consul for life, so the ground had been prepared. The Senate did that on May 18. By your calendar, I mean. The date here was 28th Ventose."

"Yeah, I recall tryin' to learn the Republican calendar in school. All them Brumaires and Thermidors. Made my brain woozy."

"You are not alone in that. The Revolution tried to sweep away all vestiges of the old order and create something utterly new, with complete equality of all citizens."

"Kind o' hard to have all of that equality when the guy in charge calls himself an Emperor."

"Agreed. That was why I joined the Coterie Redempteur two

days later."

"You mean this is the year you did that? "

"It is. I have not been back here since Waterloo. I hope I shall not encounter myself. That could be...awkward."

Imagining that scene made me giggle. "What else do I need to know about this year, besides the whole Emperor business?"

"Ironically, the civil code went into effect three days later."

That I did remember from school. "The Code Napoleon?"

"So-called, yes. Bonaparte felt that it was his greatest accomplishment. He may well have been correct. May nations adopted it or made it the framework for their own laws." Freedom of religion, equality of birth, a rule of laws rather than of one man's decree. No secret laws, no ex post facto laws. All fine in theory."

"But...?"

"But the day that it went into effect, Bonaparte had the Duc de Enghien kidnapped by dragoons and murdered. False evidence, drumhead trial, invasion of a sovereign nation in the dead of night. Turned all Europa against him, it did. At least, those who had been on the fence. A great strategic political error."

"A lot of big doin's this year, huh? New laws, new Emperor, a bunch o' new Marshals..."

"Not to mention the invasion."

"Invasion of what?"

"The Scepter'd Isle."

"I don't remember that from my history class."

"That's because it didn't happen. Naval reverses made it clear that Bonaparte could not cross the channel unimpeded."

"Hmph...news to me."

"Oh, you've studied about it, even if only indirectly. Every sou raised by the sale of Louisiana went toward the planned invasion." Tyrell stared out over Al's ears as if watching it all over again. "He spent the better part of two years preparing for it. Assembled an immense army at Boulogne, just across the Channel from Dover. Two hundred thousand men. I was one of them for a time. Camps, forts, constant training exercises in very unseaworthy little boats." He shuddered and shook his head. "You've not seen the Channel nor been on it."

"Rough, huh?"

"You'll need all of your magick to keep your meals down."

Jasper finally woke up from his nap or whatever it was he'd been doing. "No, no, no, no, no! Not again. Those first few days on the *Kiss* nearly did in your Uncle Jasper. Find another way."

"You do know it's an island, right?" I asked him out loud. "There ain't no other way."

Tyrell frowned at me. "I gather that Morphageus is unhappy with his options?"

"He feels everything that I feel, so yeah, he don't much look forward to upchucking all the way across."

"There are other methods. Safer ones. Mal-de-mer is, after all, the least of our concerns. The Channel is a Merchantry nightmare. With London as their headquarters they guard that patch of water with many ships...and other things."

"Yeah, I can just imagine what them things might be. Already had the pleasure of dancin' with their Furies. Not to mention a boatload of demons."

"But we are not without resources ourselves."

"Such as?"

"I'd rather not commit myself until I'm certain I can make use of them."

"Well, somebody better commit to somethin', and darned quick. We're seven hundred miles away from London and Tommy's time's runnin' out. I don't see no way to do it short of hijackin' an ostium and I hear that's impossible." The Merchantry's minions made use of a network of spots which used dark magickal energy to instantly transport them all around the world. Located at places of suffering or corruption, nobody but them could travel that way.

"Yes and no."

I squinted at him. "What's that supposed to mean?"

"It means that when the Stone Warden, a child of the Obverse who carries Morphageus, sets her mind to doing a thing it usually comes to pass."

"Is that so? This Stone Warden thinks her magick is at about a first-grade level yet. I'm guessin' that telegraphin' yerself takes more like an advanced degree from Sorcerer's University."

"Yet you did it in Iberion, did you not?"

"Yeah, but I just hitched a ride on somebody else's spell. That ain't the same as chantin' the trip myself. Ma says my head could explode."

"That sounds worse than seasickness," Jasper moaned. "Can we not do that?"

I paid him no never-mind as something hit me. "Say...hitchin' a ride may actually work."

"Yes? How?"

"In Washington's Monument Venoma took Tommy with her. He was out cold and in her arms. So obviously so long as one person, or thing, has the power to use the ostium, he can take others along who don't. Right?"

"So it would seem."

"Then all we have to do is capture us a Merchantry agent and convince them to take us where we want to go."

"Or more likely drop us all straight into their dungeon. How do we control the destination? That would be taking a great risk."

"I ain't got that far with the plan yet. But it might work."

"A better idea would be to discover just how they use the ostia and employ that for ourselves."

"Somethin' nobody's ever found out despite decades of tryin'. Believe me, I asked Romulus, Sha'ira, and anybody else who might know. The Shades are given the power to do it whenever they do a Merchantry job, but even Sha'ira don't know just how and she traveled to Virginia that way. Must be a spell. not an object like a Marshal's coin. She says nobody gave her anything like that."

"We Redeemers have been searching for the secret to no avail, also. It would be worth a great deal if we could."

"I need to dig into the magick lessons Ma wrote down and put into my pack. Maybe there's somethin' in there that could help. Mind control, maybe, that could make somebody take us where we want with no treachery."

"Doubtful. That's dark magick."

"Yeah? I kind o' figured so. Still, there may be somethin' we can use. In a pinch I'll try to send myself along the Obverse barrier, like in Iberion. If we end up with no other choice."

"Let us exhaust all other avenues first. You are too important to risk."

"Everybody keeps sayin' that. I ain't so sure."

"There is a prophecy, remember."

"Yeah, and a pretty dopey one, too."

"Lack of poetic skill doesn't make it any less true."

Scorch buzzed past my ear, turning over on his back and sticking a disturbingly-long tongue out. "Bored?" I asked, returning his rude greeting. "There's a big ball o' fire up in the sky. Why don't you go give it a ride?"

"Ah, if only I could. Old Scorch'd be the Great God of the fire sprites if he could manage that one."

"If you need somethin' to occupy you, maybe you could get up above these trees and see what's ahead."

The tiny man flipped me a lazy salute. "Why not? It beats listening to that mutt complain about your boyfriend here. Besides, he smells like dirty laundry."

With that he rose into the canopy of green and vanished. Romulus appeared beside me. For somebody the size of a warehouse he sure could move quiet-like when he wanted to. "Dey's a clearin' around da bend. Old charcoal-makin' camp. If nobody's dere we can use it for da night."

Sha'ira also came up to us, announcing that no one was tracking us. I took her word for it. If somebody trained by the Assassins' Guild says the coast is clear, you ought to believe them. Their lives depend on that sort of knowledge. We all hustled up to the clearing. I for one was in need of a rest. My girlie shoes were pinching.

It was more than some little old camp. The open space was a hundred yards across. I wondered why they weren't using it for charcoal any more. There was no shortage of trees, that was for sure. Several earthen mounds and a stone kiln surrounded a rude cabin. It even had a serviceable well. "Looks like a perfectly peaceful place," I said with a smile.

And then the trees tried to kill us.

*"Can't we just annihilate 'em all and get back on the road?
I'm tired o' bein' your unmentionables."*

8 / Treachery

Leafy limbs dipped down to grab at us. Bark peeled from trunks and attacked. The very roots rose up from the ground. Having seen that sort of thing in Virginia, though then the trees had been on our side, I didn't waste time being amazed. Instead I hitched up my skirt and high-tailed it for the cabin. All about me my friends fought the trees. Romulus' bowie knife seemed to hiss as it cut through the air. Arrows from the bow of Sha'ira struck home. A flash of red raced past. Tyrell dismounted, saber in hand. Even the hound battled our ambushers, his doggy teeth sinking into anything that tried to snatch him. Behind me Ernie's shrill little voice taunted his foes.

Crouching down, using the stone well as cover, I took a second to see what we were up against. Sure enough, Tyrell fought on foot against two assailants. Alcibiades was nowhere to be seen. Huh? He skedaddled? Romulus had laid low three enemies and struggled as six more tried to bear him to the ground with their weight. Already the Duke had fled. I couldn't blame him. A basset hound is only of so much use in combat.

Sha'ira moved through the trees, wounding several and avoiding all manner of assaults as if she had eight pairs of eyes. And on top of all of that, four trees headed my way, moving to surround me.

Only they weren't really trees, just cleverly camouflaged men.

Some wore elaborate net suits with leaves woven into them. Others were clad in canvas cleverly painted to look like bark. Still more had costumes with twisted wicker to resemble large roots. None carried a weapon any more lethal than a short club or a rope. All had grim, determined expressions on their faces. And they spoke not a single word.

Who are these guys?

"Took the words right out of my mouth," Jasper said.

"What mouth?"

"Exactly. I'm just a poor lowly corset, muffled by muslin."

The Stone was still warm, so no demons or black magick were present. *That's somethin', I suppose. But what do they want? And how'd they know we'd be here? This all took plannin' and preparin'.*

I had to stop pondering the wherefores and concentrate on preserving my hide. Something told me that that'd be tough to manage in a dress. That same something also suggested that keeping Morphageus hidden was smarter than whacking a lot of heads off. Murder didn't seem to be the tree-men's intent. Until I knew what this was about I needed to play at being poor little Lucy.

A grubby hand wrapped around my mouth from behind. I bit

it. Hard. He grunted in pain but didn't let go all of the way. His other hand wrapped around my middle. With Stone-strength I stomped on his foot and gave him a head butt. That did the trick. With a groan he tumbled six feet away, swearing. Somebody else snatched my arm. All that did was earn him a swift kick in his boy-bits. In my head Jasper laughed like he always did when there was fighting to be done. His defense magick, boosted by the Legacy Stone, warned me of threats I couldn't see and sped up my mind so that I could react to attacks quicker than a normal person. Two more of the silent fellows went down. One lassoed my wrist with his rope, so I yanked him face-first into the edge of the well stones. The other I spun into his comrade, tangling them both into an outraged sweating heap.

"Woo!" yelled Jasper in my head, "you're really convincin' 'em you're an innocent little girl, huh?"

He had a point. We'd been fighting bloodthirsty monsters for too long. My blood was up and I was really overdoing things. No normal kid could manage to embarrass professionals like these. I needed to behave more like a scared girl in a dress. After all, I had a good disguise if I played things right.

So I retreated until I thumped up against the wall of the cabin, its coarse logs scratching my back. The bonnet had fallen off during the scuffle and my new blonde hair spilled down to my shoulders. Hoping to play off my earlier success as the luck of a terrified child, I put on my best pretended-blubbering and clutched the reticule to my tummy, trembling all the while.

"Please, monsieurs," I begged, acting the cornered bunny to

the hilt, "do not slay me. Take what little money I have, but spare me and my poor friends."

I opened up the little purse as if to take some coins from it. Those assailants still standing paused, trading glances with one another. No one spoke. They seemed unsure what to do. One moment they'd had their prey dead to rights, the next she'd thrashed half of them. Now she was whining with a woeful countenance. Clearly they suspected a trick. Maybe they feared I'd throw the cabin at them or something.

"Can't we just annihilate 'em all and get back on the road?" Jasper asked. "I'm tired of bein' your unmentionables."

"No, this ain't a bunch of murderin' demons. This is more like...we're bein' hijacked and detoured, somehow."

While the leafy, rooty fellows closed around me, being careful to not get too close, I peeped around to see where my friends had gone. Scorch, Alcibiades, and the hound had vanished. Romulus lay beneath a sturdy rope net, held fast by five burly men. Unnoticed, Ernie crawled next to the giant Marshal's face, saying something to him. If anybody heard him it would just sound like mousy squeaks. There was no sign of Sha'ira, but I knew she'd gone to ground. If things got hot arrows would drop everybody around us with nasty yet non-fatal wounds. I hoped she'd show good judgement and hold off on that unless it was the only way out. We needed answers, not more blood.

I couldn't see Tyrell, either. Where could he be? In that Hussar outfit he couldn't very well be hiding in the greenery.

Nobody showed any interest in robbing me. That didn't

surprise me none. This was way too elaborate an ambush for mere thievery. My attackers wanted me for something, and it wasn't to take my head. Otherwise they would have kept on fighting. Only now they were hesitating, as if unsure that they had the right target.

"She has yellow locks!" a short, stocky bark-man called out, apparently to someone behind the clump I faced. I couldn't see who. A leader, I guessed.

"And clear skin!" hollered another.

"She speaks perfect Gaullic," a third added. "Not Britannic."

Hearing that gave me hope, so I kept up my charade. "Oh, my friends, you have mistaken me for another. Some brigand, perhaps, or a traitor to the Empire?"

Jasper hooted at that. "Yeah, they sent fifteen trained warriors to bring in that tiny outlaw chieftain Stumpy McBride, terror of the Gaullic hinterland."

My witched ears picked up somebody moving inside the cabin, stepping with care so as not to make much noise. A shuttered window above my head made me vulnerable to a sneaky attack, so I scooted to my left a bit.

"I see no tin cup," said the first man who'd spoken as he stared hard at me until I almost thought he could peer through my dress to the Jasper-corset.

"And why is that?" Jasper wanted to know. "I'm suffocatin' in here."

A husky woman's voice mocked them all. I couldn't see who it was, the others blocked my view, but she sounded tough. "You donkeys! She travels with a Marshal and a Shade. Who else would it be? Lord Nelson?"

The cabin shutter banged open and a long arm slapped the wall where I'd just been standing. Though I was tempted to give it a punch, I stayed in character. "Oh, gentlemen, please refrain! I want my mama!"

"I'll wager she does," said the unseen woman with a harsh laugh. "If her mother were here we might all be piles of ash."

Swell. Another bunch who know more about me than I do about them.

"You speak strangely, madame."

"No more than you. A quick study you are, to know Gaullic so well in a day. But then, you can do a great many impossible things, can't you, Miss Sauveur?"

"I fear you have the advantage of me. You know who I am but I cannot say to have ever made your acquaintance."

"Then proper introductions are in order." The men surrounding me parted like a stage curtain opening for a new act. Just behind them stood a tall brown-haired woman in tight buff male trousers and a short gray tailcoat with two rows of gold buttons. Her feet, in knee-high boots, were wide apart. A wicked smallsword hung at her hip. Handsome but not lovely, with more jaw and brow to be a beauty, she had more command presence than half a dozen colonels.

"Gloriana D'Aulnais, at your service."

She touched the brim of her black felt hat, tall-crowned and curly-brimmed with one hand. In her other was a cocked flintlock pistol, aimed at a man on his knees before her.

Tyrell.

Doing my best to ignore his predicament, I gave her the tiniest of curtsies. "Lucy Gaspard, ma'am."

She threw her head back and laughed as if I were the funniest girl in Europa. I noticed that though her whole body shook, the gun barrel never wavered. "Dear me, but you are a resolute child. Ramrod for a backbone and no mistake. But I'm afraid you waste your labor. My intelligence is excellent. You are Verity Sauveur, carrier of the Sagestone, bearer of Morphageus, so-called last hope of mankind, blah-blah-blah..."

Sagestone? Since when is it called that?

"Oh, yeah," Jasper muttered, "that's what its name is in the Obverse. Didn't I ever mention it?"

"No! Jeepers, what else you hidin' from me?"

"Who's hidin'? You never asked."

After reminding myself to strictly ration his licorice, I raised my chin at Gloriana. "Are you spinning fairy tales? Or is this some elaborate joke of my uncle's?"

Clouds passed over her already-stern face. "I fear my sense of humor has evaporated in this wretched heat. Playing the devil with my cravat." She pressed the pistol's muzzle against Tyrell's bare head. The busby was lying beside him. He looked more disgusted than scared. I wondered if Alcibiades was about to swoop in and rescue him. Fun as that might be, it'd wreck my hopes of finding out was going on here. "Come here, Miss Sauveur. Now. Or your friend's brains will bespatter his fine dolman."

She sure looked capable of pulling the trigger. And Tyrell seemed to be of the same mind. No arrows from Sha'ira arrived. Ernie had left Romulus. I didn't see him anymore. It was just me, Tyrell, and a bunch of cranky strangers. But they had knowledge I needed, so it seemed best to play along.

I took one step away from the cabin wall. "Kindly remove the pistol from Captain Tyrell's head first."

D'Aulnais snorted. "That isn't how the game is played, little one. I hold trump. The trick is mine. Come here. And surrender your tin cup."

You know, arrogant adults are so easy to fool when you're twelve that it's like fishin' in a horse trough.

I moved toward her, all of her tree-boys backing up as I did so. From my reticule I took the cup, rusty around the edges and with a couple of dents. "You know that you can't use it? It'd kill you."

"Yes, I am well aware of its power, and its curse. But I shall not relax until it is out of your hands, at least."

Shrugging, I tossed it to her as if it were worthless. She neatly caught it and handed it to Tyrell. The Hussar hooked a finger in its handle, smiled, and saluted me with it. All of the men around us cheered as if they'd just won some sort of horse race. Those holding down Romulus jumped up and released him. The man in the cabin came out of the door doing the same. Gloriana uncocked the pistol and handed it to the man she'd just threatened with it. Pretended to threaten, that is.

All I could do was stare at Tyrell as if he had two heads.

The redeemer had set this whole ambush up to get Morphageus. Maybe he'd planned it ever since the day we'd met.

He'd betrayed me.

That's the sort of thing that tends to affect the mother-daughter relationship. I mean, besides watching your mom throw magickal death at attacking monsters.

9 / Redeemed is a Dirty Word

Naturally my first response was plain-speaking, as Ma called it. "You dirty son of a — !"

"Hitch up your skirts and come here," Tyrell commanded with a chuckle. His men laughed, too. They began stripping off their camouflage suits. Underneath they wore similar outfits to Gloriana's except that they had no coats.

"Careful what you wish for," I hissed. "If I get within arm's reach of you there'll be a powerful deal of pain a-comin' yer way."

Smooth as a dancer he aimed the pistol at Romulus. "I am well-aware of your capabilities and do not intend to underestimate you like my men did. Now I say again, come here. Peaceably. And surrender the Stone."

I crossed my arms, silently running a chant through my mind in case anybody tried to rush me. "No. Ain't gonna happen."

Tyrell cocked the pistol. "I shall not ask again."

One corner of my mouth went up as I spotted grass rustling in the woods. Nobody else noticed since they were all watching us. "Big mistake, Cap'n."

With a crack the big gun leaped out of his hand, the lock ruined by an arrow. Sha'ira seemed to have understood that I needed information more than escape, but that didn't mean she'd put up with a threat to her long-time friend.

"Told ya," I sneered, backing up. Energy balled up into my palm. I kept it invisible for the moment, waiting to see what the forest-fools would do. They seemed more worried about the unseen sharpshooter than me. Gloriana cocked her head and the majority of them headed out after Sha'ira, using tree trunks for cover.

"So you did," the Hussar said with a shrug.

"I say we just shoot her and take the damned rock from her annoying little neck," grumped Gloriana.

That made Tyrell almost choke with mirth. "Go ahead. I wish you luck with that plan."

With no hesitation she yanked a small pistol from inside her coat and blazed away at me. But I'd been ready for that. My hand came up with a flat translucent shield of magic, the first magick Ma had taught me. The round bullet bounced from it like a rubber ball, putting a neat hole in the tail of her coat. She glared at her partner. Tyrell had leaped aside as soon as he'd made the suggestion, knowing that I looked too calm for his liking.

For my part I was just glad that the ricochet hadn't killed Gloriana. I needed answers and she looked like the one to supply them.

But there was no need to let her know that. "You try it again and I'll transmogrify you into a worm," I lied. *Though that'd be a neat trick. Too bad it's forbidden black magick or I'd ask Ma fer a lesson.*

She kept her composure, I'll give her that. Tucking the gun away, she took out a white silk handkerchief and dabbed the tiniest bit of nervous sweat away from her lip. "Well, can't have that, can we? These most excellent trousers do require proper legs to show to their best advantage."

I let the spell sink back into my soul-store. Magick was like drawing on a bank account, unless you stood on a Chauntline. It depleted awful quick. And I didn't know if real fighting lay ahead. One thing I did know for sure, and which proved to me that we were in a lot less danger than I'd first feared, was that Gloriana's shot had missed me by a country mile.

She'd aimed wide on purpose.

Takin' my measure, huh? Same as me with you, lady. Looks like we got ourselves a frisky little game goin' here.

Tyrell looked behind him to check on the progress of his men who were searching for Sha'ira. He had to know that they'd never find her. A Shade gets trained in evasion and concealment before she's ever allowed near a weapon. "If we are done with all of this roosterish posturing, perhaps we can proceed to the matter at hand?"

"You mean me tossin' ya across this clearin' like an old apple core?" I suggested. "That's what you deserve fer stabbin' me in the back."

His eyebrows shot up in genuine surprise. He even looked a little bit hurt. "Is that what you think this is? Treachery?"

"Well, if it looks like a duck and quack like a — "

"Oh, do close your bill, little one," sighed Gloriana. "It's much too hot to tolerate your American precocity." To Tyrell she said, "Let her keep the wretched Stone until we get to the Director."

He nodded. "My thought, as well. Much easier than forcing the issue here, against a mage-chick with a temper."

I glared at them both as if I could fry them with my eyes. That mage-chick comment hadn't improved my mood. "Just so we're all clear, I ain't visitin' this Director until I know what's goin' on and how come it don't qualify as betrayal."

Tyrell held up a hand as his men returned from their snipe hunt. The burly one I'd seen earlier reported, "No sign. Not even a broken blade of grass. I swear she's a ghost."

"Near as," the Hussar said. "They do call them Shades for a reason. Never mind. If she'd wanted to notch her tally stick there'd be a pile of bodies here by now. Let her follow us, if she's of a mind to. We won't make it difficult for her."

"What about your horse?"

"Lurking nearby, I suppose, until he chooses a side. Alcibiades is his own master. Eventually he'll discover that we are all on the same side and back he'll come."

"And the ridiculous dog?"

"We shan't be seeing that cur again. He's shown his true colors, as I always expected he would. I do not mourn the loss."

I stamped my foot. They all looked at me with the expressions of long-suffering parents. "A bunch of y'all are gonna mourn the loss of yer manly pride if I don't get some explanations and darned soon. Why the ambush? Where are we goin'? Who's this Director person?"

Gloriana waved at the knot of injured fellows from the tussle at the well and cabin. Their hurts were being tended to by the eldest of her group. "As to the ambush, that was an attempt to keep the damage minimal. We'd hoped to overwhelm you all without firearms or blades."

"That's peachy of you. Concerned fer our welfare, huh?"

"Of course. We are not your enemies, Miss Sauveur."

"Coulda fooled me."

"We'd hoped to. But you recovered your wits with alacrity."

I motioned Romulus over to me so that he could join in. Since I didn't even know who had grabbed us, two noggins had to be better than one. He had a lot more experience than me at this sort of thing. After some hesitation they let him pass. As he got up close to me, his back to everybody else, he winked and grinned.

Huh? Did I miss somethin'? Are we about to be rescued by a swarm of cavalry, maybe? That'd actually be really annoyin' right now.

Tyrell indicated that his men should head north, in the same direction we'd been going. Some hustled that way, spreading out to clear the path and ensure that nobody lurked in the woods on either side of it. Others hung back to perform the same tasks in our rear. Then he shooed me along as he spoke.

"My task has always been to keep you safe. And permitting you to take the Sagestone, Morphageus, and your very special hybrid self into the Proprietor's office would amount to a dereliction of duty."

I spat, disgusted. It almost soiled his fine boots. "You know, I've had just about all I can stand of so-called grown-ups bossin' me around. It was y'all who caused this great big mess in the first place."

"Granted, it was not children who reshaped the world into this travesty. Nor did they have a hand in the making of the Merchantry. But still, you must admit that you have only been Stone Warden for three weeks. Allowances must be made for your own unavoidable ignorance of how things stand."

Gloriana sipped from a small green glass flask covered in a silver filigree cage. "Debating with a baby. How the mighty have fallen."

I twitched, nearly letting myself pop her one with a puff of magickal force so she'd fall on her irritating backside. Or maybe just burst her fine drinkware. But Ma raised me to show restraint when dealing with idiots, so I bit my lip and concentrated on Tyrell.

"And in that three weeks I've traveled from Washington City to Richmond, tangled with a Grotesque and Bullies, been caught in a major battle, survived a Shade assassination and Rebel zombies, fought a whole shipload of Darwins, captured an angry chimera, tossed a Hellenic god into Hades — "

"Yes, yes, no one is disputing that you are a quick study in both the magickal and combative arenas, to say nothing of your native cleverness. After all, your parents are no mere farmers. And your mother made sure to teach you the human skills you might need in this business. But it is of the political arena that I speak. You simply do not know the lay of the land, so to speak."

"I know that the Merchantry has its nasty plan to rule the world usin' black magick. That it made a sick deal with the Obverse demons to gain the power they needed to pull it off. And that even then they messed it all up. And now they have a complicated civil war. Them Obverse baddies seem to have played both sides against the middle. On top of that the Merchantry has factions in its own ranks tryin' to undo the deal or just run it themselves. I'm guessin' that the Proprietor's management skills are a little sharp-edged, huh?"

"That would be a very accurate way of stating it, yes."

I patted Romulus' great log of an arm. "Then there's the Marshals of the Equity, who want the Merchantry to go the way of all dictatorships. That's been their job fer thousands of years, all the way back to the time of the Pharaohs."

"If not longer."

"And, of course, there's you Redeemers." I aimed my nose at all of the men around us. "That's what they all are, right? Coterie Redempteur, like you? Still believin' you can turn the Merchantry into a goody-two-shoes operation, twist its power to help instead of hurt."

"You think us deluded."

"From what I've seen of the Merchantry, you bet I do. Do you even have a plan to make that happen? You say I'm nuts fer tryin' to rescue Tommy from their headquarters, but how do you propose to accomplish somethin' a hundred times harder?"

"Of course we have a plan. That is precisely why we are taking you to the Director. And most of your questions shall be answered there."

"You don't say? Am I liable to be happy with them answers?"

"Unlikely. Knowledge does not necessarily bring joy."

"Yeah. I tried tellin' my teacher Miz Finch that. She made me stand in the corner."

Tyrell stared off into the distance. He looked like a boy who'd done a bad thing and didn't know how to tell his parents about it. I'd seen that in him before, that sad guilty expression. Something must've happened in his past to leave that shadow there. It could explain why he'd gone to the States United instead of spending his magickally-extended days in his native Gaulle.

"So, what's it like?" I asked him.

He shook the pain from his face. "Hmm?"

"Never gettin' any older. Always seein' the same face in the mirror."

"Odd, at first. Now I'm resigned to it." He sighed and fiddled with his sabretache. "It is what it is. A choice I made."

"Kids all are in a hurry to get older, it seems. To grow up and be able to make their own decisions."

"You'll find the opposite to be true when you're an adult, and desperately wish to be twelve once more. To have your mother taking care of everything again."

I thought of how swell things had gone since my twelfth birthday in March, especially the past few weeks. On the run from monstrous murderers and kidnappers. Befriending talking trees and combat pelicans. Meeting mermen. Finding out that Pa was alive but was a sorcerer from another world, that Ma could chant magick spells and turn demons to ash, that I was the 'chosen one' who was expected to bring down a centuries-old dictatorship.

"Actually, I think I may be the exception to that rule. Wantin' to come back to all of this don't seem too likely."

"Is that so? Tell me, how many friends besides Tommy did you have before falling through that basement floor at the theatre?"

"Um, none, really." I had plenty of enemies, though. Something about me, maybe the Stone's invisible energy, disturbed people, especially kids. They mostly kept their distance from the 'weird girl.'

"And has that changed?"

He had me there. Now I had oodles of folks who talked to me, played pranks on me, and risked their lives against creatures who were trying to kill me. But was that worth all of the running, bleeding, and terror?

Yeah, probably so.

Tyrell saw the answer on my face and smiled. "And what about Ellen, your mother? Are things better between you now?

Or worse?"

We did get along better now, or maybe it was so different that it just seemed so. Before she'd been sad a lot, still missing Pa despite him having been taken back to the Obverse twelve years ago, when I'd been born. But mostly she was just dull old Ma, working at Ford's Theatre as the costume mistress and making me do my chores. Trying to, anyhow. I was a handful, I knew that. The stubborn tomboy who hated frills and dresses and got into fights all of the time. Filling my days with imagined stories and fake swordplay with orphaned Tommy. Hanging out at the theatre fooling with the makeup kits. Learning pretended accents from the actors. Now I knew that she'd been nudging me toward all of that, knowing that I'd likely need those skills if and when I became Stone Warden.

And when that day came, a full ten years before anybody expected it to, I'd had to grow up almost overnight. Now those stories I'd acted out with Tommy were horribly real. You could end up dead, or worse. A lot worse. Ma had had to run off without me when the Merchantry had come after us both. Her little girl had saved her from being cooked and eaten by demons. Later she'd finally told me the truth about Pa, that he wasn't even human. That he was a powerful magick-flinger and a wanted man in two realities.

That's the sort of thing that tends to affect the mother-daughter relationship. I mean, besides watching your mom throw magical death at attacking monsters.

Death. There was a problem.

"We manage okay." I wrung the handle of my reticule. "You're a soldier born-and-bred, ain't you?"

The Hussar stood up a bit taller as I said that. He sure looked pretty, if a bit lost without his horse. *Where is Al, anyway? Did he up and abandon us when he saw Tyrell's turncoat actions?*

"Since the age of fifteen. Always had a knack with horses, so the cavalry was a natural choice. As far as this goes" – he indicated his glorious uniform – "what red-blooded lad could resist such finery. Heaven knows the mademoiselles couldn't."

"Yeah, well, spare the icky details about yer conquests."

"It's just as well. The tale would take days to relate. I was a Hussar's Hussar, if you take my meaning."

Men. Can't live with 'em. Can't shoot 'em. Mostly.

Which reminded me of why I'd brought the whole thing up. "That ain't what I want to know about. It's the...other stuff."

He seemed to read my mind. "Ah." His fingers automatically touched his saber hilt. "The killing, you mean."

"Yeah. How do you manage it?"

"Bothers you, does it? All of the violence that's come your way since finding this?" He waved the tin cup.

"Sure does. Makes me sick to my stomach. But only afterwards. When there's a fight I seem to shut down my conscience and just set to it."

"I'm the same. Thoughts of the awfulness of it evaporate. So long as the cause is just and I am compelled by circumstances to battle or die. To preserve my own life or that of others. We're made that way, I think. An inheritance from our savage past, if

Mr. Darwin's theories are correct."

"But a lot of folks ain't that way at all. Hordes of 'em seem to like it way too much. They seek it out, get a thrill. And as near as I can tell most of 'em work fer the Honourable Merchantry."

"Too true. Our foes recruit such twisted souls. Even then the supply falls short for their needs. So they manufacture men who do not shirk from inflicting pain."

"How?"

"It seldom requires magick. Blackmail, extortion, rearing an abandoned child with cruelty. Humans have done this forever."

"I do recall that poor feller in Virginia who'd been transmogrified into a bug to spy on us and then tried to massacre us all. He had ugly scars of torture all over him."

"That he did. They had broken him. And it would not surprise me if the Merchantry had made doubly certain of his loyalty by imprisoning his wife or child."

"Am I so different? I'm cuttin' a bloody path with Morphageus to get to them because they have Tommy in their dungeons."

Tyrell stopped dead and grabbed my arm so hard it might've hurt if I'd been a normal girl. His fierce eyes bored holes into mine. "No! You listen to me, Verity Sauveur. You are **not** like them. Don't you ever think that. They'd like nothing better than for you to believe such a thing and do their dirty work for them. Black thoughts lead to black deeds and then we **would** be in a pickle. The Proprietor relies on self-doubt and despair more than he does spells."

He glanced around. His men had stopped to stare. Gloriana looked both bored and amused. After a moment she strode past us, waving the group to get moving again. The sun was sinking pretty low by now, making the forest gloomy, and we needed to press on.

My Hussar friend raised the tin cup again. "Why do you think we want control of this? To use it? You know we cannot. No, we need to keep it out of your hands so that it can't fall into the Proprietor's. You're still a little girl. A malleable mind, vulnerable to his manipulation. I suspect that you disagree and I don't blame you. But consider your aunt Regan, the one who has become so twisted by his influence that she sent ten thousand undead women against you. Despite what your mother thinks, Regan wasn't born selfish and mad. He made her that way, subtly and indirectly."

"And you're afeared that the same thing might happen to me?"

"For my part, no, I think it unlikely. You are made of sterner stuff. I've seen that firsthand. But the Director of our order is and I am commanded to secure Morphageus and you until it is decided what to do. More training, I expect. Formal guidance."

"Swell. And you just let Tommy die while my schoolin' commences?"

Gloriana returned, a thin cigar in her gloved fingers. "Of course. This is a war. There will be unavoidable casualties."

Boy, I wanted to smack her one. "Easy fer you to say, Miss Prissy."

Her face hardened even more than usual. "You think so? I sat in the Place de la Revolution day after day in that dreadful summer of '94, a teenaged girl dragged there by her crazed mother. While they chopped off heads by the cartload she knitted. Knitted! Laughing and cheering all the while. Even when my father, her husband of twenty years, mounted those sorrowful steps to the Guillotine. The lot of them did, like it was a harvest festival. Hooting, clapping, stamping their feet. Mocking the doomed. Thus the Parisian mob. All humanity lost, blown away by their precious need for vengeance.

"My father was one of those unavoidable casualties, you see. A necessary sacrifice. For I could have saved him, got him out and across the border. Even then I was an underground fighter, a fledgling spy but still capable for all of that. We had a network, contacts. Blakeney, that faux-foppish Britannic fellow with all of the disguises, offered me a chance. I only had to nod my head and father might have lived. But if I had done so our entire organization would have been discovered.

They were onto us, you see. Snapping at our heels. I knew I was being watched. Mother suspected, maddened by the fever of revolution and burning to extinguish every aristocrat in the land, even the one she had married. If I had selfishly freed him, Percy and his men, as well as my own comrades, would have been exposed. Lost. And that would have meant the deaths of countless innocents whose only crime had been being born to the wrong parents. Our band had to be preserved at all costs, for who else could rescue the condemned? The rest of Gaulle thirsted for blood. Savagery and murder reigned in place of Louis Capet. The Age of Reason had truly ended.

"So yes, Mademoiselle Sauveur, when I speak of the cost of war, I am an unwilling expert. And if you think that I shall allow your juvenile infatuation for this unfortunate boy to jeopardize our chance at overthrowing the Merchantry scum, dubious as I am that you are the true Stone Warden of prophecy, then you are not as clever as my brother here believes you to be."

She stomped off, flicking ash from her cigar and muttering to herself. Watching her go, I could feel the tension between Tyrell and Gloriana, an unseen cable that connected them like two freighters pulling in opposite directions.

Now I knew the source of his mournful looks and miserable silences.

"Brother, huh?" I finally said as we followed along the trail after her.

"True enough," he admitted, holding his saber so that it wouldn't rattle. "She is a few years younger."

I considered his situation. This was pretty delicate. "But not really, right? Since this is all a Merchantry recreation from their Affluxion spell, she's just an imitation of your actual sister."

He sighed. "Don't let her hear you say that. I haven't mentioned it."

"Likely she'd just call you crazy anyhow."

"Yes, indeed."

"And we still don't know where all of the real people of that time went when the spell took hold?"

"No. I was in Philadelphia then. Gloriana was married to a judge in 1850, seventy years old and expecting another grandchild. I hadn't seen her since Bonaparte fell. How could I?" He pointed to his young face. "How would I have explained this?"

"Yeah, claimin' that you'd been to Florida and discovered the Fountain of Youth probably wouldn't have — "

Tyrell hooted like an owl. Gloriana and several others whipped their heads back toward him. He made a few complicated hand signals. In a flash everybody left the trail, diving behind trees or under shrubs. The Hussar's sword and pistol were out as he waited for trouble.

And from nowhere came the lancers, at full gallop and out for blood.

The smell of the creatures almost did that anyhow.
A combination of rotting meat and a summertime privy,
the stench amounted to a punch in the belly. Believe me,
a witched nose sure wasn't a blessing right then.

10 / Foul-Smelling Trouble

They rumbled down the trail three abreast, those long spears aimed at us like pencils from hell. A rattle of musket fire, which resembled the tearing of an enormous canvas sheet, announced that they'd brought infantry with them. Yelps came from our right as a couple of lead balls struck home. The other direction seemed clear of attackers for now.

The Stone froze, clinging to my skin and dress. With a jerk I loosened it up, ripping off some of my hide, too. Normally it felt blood-warm. It only went cold when black magick was at hand, so I knew that we had bigger troubles than the angry troops.

Lances, guns, and dark spells. Ain't this a swell time to be stuck in stays and a skirt?

Before I could chant up a defense shield from my soul-store an iron snake coiled around my waist and lifted me up. Gloriana spun me hard and put her well-dressed self between me and the musketry. With a shove she got me off of the wide leafy trail and out of the path of the cavalry charge.

"Go!" she ordered, emptying a saddle with an expert shot of her pistol. "Up that hill and lie down!"

Much as I didn't like cutting and running in the middle of a scrap, she made sense. We had no idea who else we might be up against or why. But it was a safe bet that little Verity was the prize. She always was. It looked like my disguise hadn't been good enough. So I pulled up my impractical hem and scampered up the rise to my left, zigzagging from tree to tree. Luckily the distance and angle made for poor shooting with those Charleville muskets. Just as fortunate, the woods were too thick for the horsemen to come after us without dismounting. And they seemed disinclined to do that.

I stopped before reaching the top of the high ground. Offering them a silhouette up there against the reddening sky was a dumb idea. So I hunched down to make a harder target until I found a handy old log lying on the ground. After setting a spell-shield around my back in case I got snuck up on, I poked my head around the end to see what was up.

Only one Redeemer had been ridden down by the rush of the lancers. He lay at the edge of the trail, a slight movement of his hand revealing that he still lived. The rest of Tyrell's men clung to the bases of trees, scattered on the same side of the path as me. Most of them had pistols, though a couple relied on the clubs and ropes they'd used against me. Gloriana knelt in the middle of their line, giving orders while she reloaded. Tyrell wasn't in sight, which was odd considering he wore a scarlet pelisse.

To my right the lancers turned and reformed to come down the trail again. I didn't see the sense in that. We'd all taken to the thick forest and there was nobody left in the open. The musketmen, maybe two dozen of them, kept us all pinned down. Even from my distant hiding place I could make out the shiny brass helmets with the big curvy crests and black horsetail plumes hanging down. Dragoons. That explained their inaccuracy. They used carbines, shortened muskets which were easier to carry on horses. Handy, but less barrel meant less effective range. But they also had nasty sabers, long straight monsters which would be bad news for the Redeemers if they got it in their minds to charge us.

After straightening their formation the lancers stayed put, points of their weapons up, the attached pennants dancing in the breeze. The dragoons' firing slackened. They were reloading. All of Bonaparte's men – or more likely the Proprietor's – seemed to freeze in place. For a long moment nobody on that side moved at all.

Somethin's up. What're they waitin' for?

My answer came in a way that I could've done without. From behind me and to my left a great stomping made me whip my head about. An instant later half a dozen huge lumpy heads came over the crest of the hill. I noticed, too, that the sun had set, though its ruddy glow still cast the long shadows of the hideous creatures which lumbered at us.

Around eight feet tall, with shoulders so broad they could barely squeeze between the trees, the things had faces like bulldogs, except that they only had one huge bloodshot eye. And no dog ever had such a horrifying mouth full of crooked teeth, all pointed and serrated like a shark's chompers. Their arms had an extra joint, making them so long that their swollen knuckles dragged on the ground. Only four knuckles, too, as their wagon wheel-sized hands had just three fingers and a thumb. The legs looked too short and stiff to be of much use for anything except the staggering gait. If the hill had been any more steep the monsters might've tumbled down it. All of them were covered in thick clumps of black hair and were naked except for grimy loincloths. For that I was grateful, because imagining what might be there just about made me sick to my stomach.

The smell of the creatures almost did that anyhow. A combination of rotting meat and a summertime privy, the stench amounted to a punch in the belly. Believe me, a witched nose sure wasn't a blessing right then.

"They aroma, it is foul, no?" asked a voice in a high-falutin' Gaullic tone.

I looked up to see the Duke lying in the crook of a tree maybe ten feet behind me and just as high above the ground. That's not where you expect to see a basset hound, normally. Every bit of him sagged, from his impressive brown ears to the jowls, eyebrows, and rear end. Even the skin on his stumpy legs drooped like oversized socks.

Yer no prize in the stinky department yerself, Mr. High and Mighty.

Much as I was tempted to say that out loud, I didn't. Instead

I asked him what the monsters were and what they were doing.

"Le ogres," he told me. "Brainless things, really. They will eat anything that moves, though they prefer human children." He peered down that patrician nose at me. "Inconvenient for you, no? Though I daresay your delicacy and flavor leave much to be desired. But who knows? Some shallots, a bit of truffle, a good white wine..."

"Hey, poochie!" I hissed. "No time fer your weird wit. What're they doin' here?"

"Is it not obvious? They are the hammer. And the soldiers are the anvil."

Now that he mentioned it, that made plenty of sense. The Redeemers couldn't very well stay put with man-eating fiends lurching down the hill at them. They'd have to run for it. When they did, the carbines and lances would dispose of them. Gloriana and friends were too lightly-armed for what faced them.

"We need to help the Redeemers," I told the dog.

He snorted as only a hound from Gaulle can. "You must be joking. I would not lift a leg to put them out if they were on fire."

"Do I have to remind you who was stuck in a cage in Iberion, turning a meat spit in a medieval kitchen, until a certain red-headed somebody came along and freed him from all of that shame?"

The Duke sighed, his lips fluttering. Drool flew in all directions. "Always she plays that trump card. Poor Evremonde should request a new deck."

"Hurry up and come down here. I got an idea." He gave me a horrified look. "It can't be that hard. You got up there, didn't you?"

"Oui, on the back of that silly winged equine. Did you think I sprang up here on my own?"

"I never know with you. Now hurry up. Make your way down that branch until it droops some. Then I'll catch you like I did in Carrasco's castle."

Thirty seconds later I lay beneath seventy pounds of smug hound, most of the wind knocked out of me. He didn't appear to be in any hurry to move off of me, either. Just lay there on his Verity mattress, slurping my face with his palm-sized pink tongue. *Yep. Just exactly like Carrasco's castle. More's the pity.*

I wiped the goo off with a sleeve of my dress, which was taking damage from abuse it'd never been intended for. With my Stone-strength I shoved the Duke off and told him to dash down to Gloriana to tell her that she had trouble in her rear. Armed with the dog's knowledge about the ogres, I hurried to get behind them.

"Hey, uglies!" I hollered when I got close to the shambling group. They were faster and nimbler than zombies, but not by much. "Lookin' fer a tasty dinner? Here I am."

Just as I'd hoped, they couldn't resist such a yummy morsel. Whatever command had sent them down the hill got interrupted by the sight of my potential deliciousness. Like trained troops they all turned together to start after me, disturbing arms reaching out to tear my arms off for drumsticks.

They panted and snuffed like doggies on the scent. Some of them made a kind of grunting moan, as if they hadn't been fed in months. For all I knew that was the case. After all, somebody was controlling them. Maybe he used hunger to get them to do his bidding.

At the top of the hill I nearly ran smack into that somebody. Two somebodies, to be accurate.

A pair of Bullies, hands joined, in a purplish bubble of magick.

They looked like all of the others I'd seen. Little blonde boys about seven years old, pale as the dead, with long fingers swollen at the tips like a tree frog's. Their eyes were black and lifeless, with no more pity in them than a corpse. Wearing the clothes of 1804 Gaulle, a careless observer might've walked up to give them a cuddle. Which would be the last thing that person ever did. For once you locked eyes with one, your will was captured and you did as they commanded. Slaves of the Merchantry's Proprietor, Bullies were adult mages who'd been caught breaking the rules and had been transformed into this form to work off their crimes until their penance had been done. Then they'd be restored to their true selves.

Cursing in a way that would've really riled-up Ma, I looked at their feet so that they couldn't spell me with their glance. They hadn't noticed me yet, since they were linked to combine their power to control the ogres. Not fully trusted with great individual power, Bullies needed to join forces to work big spells. Right then they were focused on getting the monsters to turn around. Once they managed that, I'd be in their sights for sure. I only had a few seconds to fish in my reticule for the best weapon to use against a Bully.

My trusty hand mirror.

The Merchantry needed an easy way to handle these little devils in case they got uppity. So built into them was a glaring weakness, if you'll pardon the expression. If a Bully saw his reflection he'd cease to exist. Something about not being able to handle the sight of his warped soul. I didn't care about the details. All I knew was that it worked. But only if you surprised them.

Which I did. Halfway, anyhow. The nearest one got caught before he even knew I was there. One second after I held the mirror up to his face he gasped. Then he sunk in upon himself like a leaky balloon before exploding in a mess of orange and violet sparks. An afterimage of a tiny skeleton hung in the night air before blowing away in the wind.

While I was congratulating myself on my warrior-girl cleverness the other one snatched at me. Only my Stone-boosted reflexes saved me. If a Bully got hold of you he'd capture your mind the same as with a gaze. Taking care to look lower than his face to avoid those obsidian eyes, I waved the mirror at him. But he held one hand in front of them so he wouldn't catch sight of himself. So we ridiculously danced around, him trying to grab me seeing and me working to avoid him the same way.

I had the advantage, though, since all I had to do was retreat. He had to make contact and get a good grip. Bullies weren't very physical. You could run away from one easy enough, if all he wanted was to clutch at you. So I ran backward, making sure not to smack into any trees in the dark. Just when I was congratulating myself on my wonderful battlefield skills I did the very thing I'd been expecting since leaving the *Kiss* that morning.

That stinking dress.

I stepped on the hem with my heel and went down on my butt. Hard. On an exposed tree root, too. Wincing, and cussing some more, I got ready to throw up a quick magick shield, not knowing if it would even work against a Bully's proprietor-made power. My spell-skills weren't the world's greatest, since I was just learning. Mostly just defense barriers and force balls. The other experiments were still hit-and-miss. But I didn't have to worry about any of that, because the little creep gave up the chase and went back to his ogres.

"You know," Jasper said, "we could just team up and obliterate his ugly corpus. I'd be more than happy to help."

"I know, but there's no tellin' who's watchin' and I want 'em to think that I gave them the real cup."

"Have it your way. But a Morphageus boomerang would solve all of your problems right now."

"While maybe announcin' to a bunch of his Merchantry friends that their Holy Grail is flingin' magick about. He might not be alone. Thanks, but I'll save my magick corset for an emergency."

The Bully had already scooted a good ways off. He must've

had more juice than I thought, because he controlled the one-eyed monsters just fine by himself. Maybe my doing away with his friend while they'd been linked had just transferred that guy's power to this one. Whatever the reason, the surviving Bully regrouped the ogres and sent them back down into the Redeemers.

Not all of them, though. As I tried to sneak up on the controlling mage and whack him with a big stick, a growl from my left told me that the Bully had some insurance this time. A long double-jointed arm as thick as a telegraph pole swatted me a good one. If Jasper hadn't been dogpaddling in my noggin that might've concluded poor Verity's save-the-world business. A split-second before the ogre's blow landed one of the steel corset bones flowed along my arm like quicksilver. The enormous paw collided with a brass bell that seemed to grow out of my flinching hand. Its clang deafened me, but at least my skull didn't crack like an eggshell. That was small consolation as my puny frame absorbed that tremendous punch and started to roll down the hill. In two seconds I was traveling at the speed of a galloping horse.

"Whee!" cried Jasper. "Finally, some fun and excitement!"

I disagreed. Giving up my noble plan not to use him, I wished the bell into a bullwhip with a grappling hook at the end. A flick of my wrist lassoed a sapling and stopped my dangerous descent before I could collide with a real tree. As fast as I was going that would've been the end of me. With a strained grunt I pulled myself up and leaned against the slender trunk, panting. The

Jasper-whip went back to his corsety purgatory, complaining all the way.

The ogres' speed had built up with the hill's slope being so steep here. In no time they'd crash into Gloriana's men and then very bad and gruesome things would happen. Smelling fresh meat, the creatures sent up a loud eager moan of hunger. Drool leaked out of their misshapen mouths, staining their furry chests. Those dreadful hands opened and closed as if getting ready to wring Redeemer necks. I winced in sympathy for those poor men about to be devoured.

The hound, though, had done his job well. His warning had come in time and Gloriana had used her resources cleverly. With a hoarse roar the lead monster came on, single eye widening as he reached for his meal. That terrifying sound turned into a confused whimper as something caught his legs at the shins. He disappeared face-first into the brush. All four ogres behind him met the same fate, pitching forward and planting their stubby noses into the ground.

A simple rope tied to a tree and yanked at the proper moment had felled the malodorous creatures.

Gloriana shouted an order and the Redeemers fell upon the ugly things, beating them with club, stabbing them with knives, even discharging pistols into their hairy bodies. Howls of unnatural rage and pain echoed through the dark forest. But in the next moment men screamed just as loud. Bodies flew as if launched by catapults. They made sick wet thuds when they struck trees. A couple gurgled as hideous teeth chomped into their innards.

It seemed that the ogres' skin couldn't be pierced.

"Well, that's a disappointment," said Jasper.

Though the clumsy monsters had trouble getting to their feet once downed, they were still plenty dangerous. Those extra-jointed arms had quite a reach even lying down. They felt pain when struck, to judge by the noise they made, but nothing could do real damage. Bullets stuck fast as if half-absorbed. Sword blades snapped. The Redeemers needed help, and quick.

"Mommy, can Morphageus come out and play?" Jasper pleaded. "Pretty please with sugar on top?"

"I'll allow that it looks like I may have to pitch in," I admitted. Nothing living could withstand Jasper's rune-covered blade. I'd once cut a tree down with a single swing.

Before I could decide whether to help the Redeemers and ruin my careful lie about the cup, Gloriana showed that she deserved her job as leader. She rolled beneath a giant's hammer fist, leaped over the grasp of another ogre, and plunged her smallsword into a huge lidless eye. Gray-green blood gushed out, soaking her blade. The ogre stiffened, its whole great bulk spasming like it had been struck by lightning. It gnashed its teeth so hard that they broke off. Then with a sigh it relaxed. And kept on relaxing to an impossible degree. Greenish sparks tumbled out of its mouth and nostrils. Soon it was nothing but an empty skin.

"Okay, that was worth all of the aggravation," announced Jasper.

"Sure was. Maybe they're related to them Furies. They have the same weakness."

"Or the Merchantry sorcerers just lack imagination in monster-makin'."

The Redeemers agreed. In less than a minute the remaining ogres had been served the same way and turned into the world's ugliest gunny sacks. We all cheered our victory, the men slapping one another on the back and crowing to the stars. I added my voice as I worked my way down to them. Even Gloriana managed a smug smile. She treated herself to a sip on her flask and tipped her top hat to me when I got near her.

I started to tell her about the Bully up the hill, the one who still had at least one ogre and plenty of black magick available. My Stone still lay cold as an icicle on my skin, so the nasty runt hadn't gone away. But no sooner had I opened my mouth to let her know about that threat then I saw that I'd overlooked another one.

While we'd been fighting the ogres the dragoons had moved through the trees like skirmishers. Now they knelt at the trail's edge, not thirty feet away, aiming their carbines.

Before I could even blink they fired a full volley at us.

"Your confusion is understandable." He waved the LeMat at
them. "This is called a revolver. It can fire nine shots without
reloading. A somewhat...advanced...design."
"Yeah, " I muttered. "So advanced it won't be
invented fer another fifty years yet."

11 / Night Fight

Even with my Stone Warden's reflexes I couldn't manage a
Morphageus defense or a magick shield in time. All I could do
was flinch and hope that no lead found me. Stinky white smoke
roiled all about us. The sound of two dozen muskets nearly
broke my witched eardrums. With my eyes closed, I listened for
the thud of bullets into bodies and the cries of the wounded. But
what I actually heard was something a lot less likely.

Whoops and cheers. Cackles of glee. Tiny ones.

Peering through the fog of the gun smoke, I saw disbelief and
confusion on the hard faces of the dragoons. And it wasn't just
because none of their targets had fallen, amazing as that was.
No, what really upset them was the swarm of orange embers
swirling in front of their muzzles, laughing and pointing.

Scorch had returned. And this time he'd brought all of his
friends from the *Kiss's* gun deck. They'd snuck into the carbine
barrels and ridden the .69 caliber balls just like they did the
ship's ordnance. Steering them as if riding horses, they'd made

certain that the bullets had traveled as far as possible for maximum thrills while missing the Redeemers and me.

"Guess you'll have to show your appreciation to that little troublemaker, huh?" said Jasper. "That'll hurt."

"No, sayin' thank you to my magick sword is what hurts," I shot back. "This'll only sting a bit."

I had no time for so much as a howdy right then, though. For the dragoons' shock had turned to outrage and battle lust. Their officer, a young lieutenant, barked an order. They all stood, leaned forward, and rushed us with a great shout of 'Long live the Emperor!"

Some kept their muskets, bayonets fixed. Some dropped their firearms and drew their straight heavy swords. This didn't look good. They outnumbered us by almost two-to-one, plus their weapons were better. Swords and bayonets were pretty darned accurate compared to the guns of this time. And our fire-sprite allies probably couldn't swing the odds in our favor again.

The dress clung to my knees and feet. There was no way that I could fight determined soldiers in it. Besides, it was already halfway ruined from my tumble down the hill. Turning Morphageus into a dagger, I sliced the skirt and chemise all the way up on both sides, freeing my legs. My bonnet was long gone, trampled under clumsy ogre feet. I scooted behind a tree, hoping that the dragoons wouldn't notice me and would focus on the Redeemers. Gloriana's band were no friends to us and I only cared for their welfare because I wanted answers from them.

It turned out that Tyrell's sister could take of herself. And her troops were no slouches, either, despite mostly carrying only knives, clubs, and ropes. Their pistols hadn't been reloaded after the scrap with the ogres. But somebody had trained them well in the art of using an opponent's own momentum against him. Time after time I saw a dragoon lunge with sword or bayonet, only to hit air as a Redeemer pivoted away at the last instant, grasped the weapon arm, and spun the poor soldier into a tree or the ground. Others used their ropes like whips to tangle wrists or necks and take down an enemy. Gloriana's smallsword stung like a fearsome wasp. How she managed to parry heavy saber strikes with it was beyond me.

Bonaparte's young officer knew his business, though. In all of the flurry of blows and cries he managed to maneuver eight of his men around the Redeemers and uphill. Despite Gloriana's men having evened the odds in the first minute of the fight, they now found themselves flanked and pushed onto the trail.

Which was just what the lancers had been waiting for.

Triumphant shouts rattled the darkness. I could see fine with my enchanted eyes, but it must've been unnerving to the Redeemers to hear the rumble of hooves in that murk. The trail was wide enough to gallop three abreast. Long lances across their snorting horses' necks, Napoleon's cavalry bore down on Gloriana's band. She urged her men to rush across the trail into the woods away from the flanking dragoons, and some managed it, but most were caught in the open. A couple panicked and stayed on the trail, trying to outrun the charge.

Column isn't a good formation for horse soldiers. They really ought to be in a line for best effect. But with trees on both sides the lancers dominated the narrow battlefield. Their spikes skewered two of the luckless Redeemers clear through. A third took a gaping wound in his face which looked like a second mouth. Freeing their points, the front line searched for new victims as they thundered down the trail. Behind them, the other three rows leaned down, ready to pick off anybody missed by the lead group.

Only they never got the chance. Right then I found out why Romulus had given me that smug wink.

The most awful profane language you ever heard swarmed our ears. All from hoarse women's throats, too, or so it seemed. I knew right away what caused it and laughed. *This is gonna be good.* From gaps in the leafy canopy overhead small winged objects dropped, pouncing on the lancers. Nasty hooked beaks normally used on fish slashed at their hands and faces. Gaullic eyes took gouges. Lances fell from bleeding, numbed fingers. Reins got yanked out of hands. Webbed feet kicked at horses' muzzles.

Matilda's seagull squadron had arrived from the *Kiss*.

Since even a well-trained troop of cavalry generally didn't practice against aerial attack, especially one that arrived in inky darkness, the whole formation went to pieces at once. The lancers took to batting at the nimble birds like they were swatting at mosquitoes. With shouts every bit as profane as the salty language of the birds – though to them it just sounded like ordinary gull screeches — they cursed their attackers. What had been an unstoppable charge turned into a whirling melee as horses stopped or bucked or reared. Mounts spun, trying to snap at birds and often throwing their riders. They tripped on falling lances. Many backed up into the line behind. It all became a tangled mess.

Which didn't stop the dragoons from continuing with their business. Before the Redeemers could take any advantage of their good fortune that clever officer ordered his force across the road to continue the battle. In another moment the fight with swords and bayonets had been rejoined, partly on the road and also in the trees.

Again our side had cards up its sleeve. As the soldiers raced into the woodline one of the trees reached out and clobbered that obstinate lieutenant. He dropped like a dead man when the thick limb whomped him on the back of the head. I had to remind myself that nobody else could see as well as me and that such a thing had to be even more scary and unsettling if you were on the receiving end. For a second I thought that we'd actually found allies in the trees again, but a closer look showed me what was really going on.

Romulus had swiped himself a Redeemer camouflage suit.

It didn't fit his great bulk very well, but at night it didn't have to be perfect. As it was it served to scare the pants off of the dragoons. Another one went flying into his fellows with a terrified wail. To their credit, though, they just gave the animated tree a wide berth and kept after the Redeemers. I got the feeling that there was some sort of bad blood between them.

Considering that Gloriana's group had started as disaffected soldiers in Napoleon's army, that might very well have been the case.

Several surrounded Gloriana, who used her smallsword in one hand and a truncheon from a fallen comrade in the other. It reminded me of how Pitcairn liked to fight with a belaying pin in his left hand. They might have studied under the same master. Her hair flew about like a storm cloud, the hat having been knocked off. She kept four men at bay with well-judged thrusts, swipes, even kicks. *Boy, did she go to Shade school or somethin'? I bet even Sha'ira would have her hands full with this one.* Two of the four went down, clutching gushing wounds. But more arrived to take their places, clearly hoping to avenge their fallen leader.

Romulus had plastered two or three more dragoons, but he'd also been hemmed in by several bayonets. Backed up against a tree, his movement restricted, he needed help, too. Matilda's gulls were still busy harassing the lancers, keeping them occupied so that they couldn't recover and continue their attack. I was stuck on the other side of the road, sawing off the skirt of my dress so that I could react if need be. Though jumping into the fight might be of use, it also might be just what the soldiers wanted. If they were working under Merchantry orders then getting me out in the open would be just peachy for them.

But they didn't need me. From the north end of the trail came a thumping of hooves. A single horse, dashing in to lend a hand. I grinned and squinted, expecting to see the mighty Alcibiades, fearsome Valkyrie warrior, appear out of the murk. He'd been biding his time, waiting to pounce.

It wasn't, though. What arrived was the horse of the lancer whom Gloriana had shot out of his saddle. And a raging hussar rode him, curved saber ready to do some damage.

Tyrell smacked the tar out of a pair of lancers with the flat of his blade. They slumped out of their saddles as if suddenly asleep. Another tried to draw his own sword, but was too late and caught the hussar's hilt alongside his temple. A fourth managed to get off a pistol shot, but Tyrell ducked and the bullet plowed into the fur busby. As payment he backhanded the poor guy with his fist. *That's funny. He's tryin' not to kill 'em.*

"Must be professional courtesy," said Jasper.

"Or maybe he's rememberin' our conversation."

Between the merciless seagulls and the savage hussar the lancers could take no more. Either mounted or on foot, they fled south along the trail, leaving the fight to the dragoons. Those mounted infantrymen seemed more than happy to do just that. They'd drawn some blood on Romulus already, paying for it with a few broken bones. Gloriana's fine coat had suffered some slashes. One of her foes lay in the grass, double over and clutching his belly. Several one-on-one duels continued all around them, too. But things looked less than rosy for our side.

Tyrell turned his horse away from the disappearing lancers and rode to the edge of the trail. He had a pistol in his fist, now, to complement the saber. With no warning he dropped a man with a bullet to the thigh who was about to lunge at Gloriana from behind with his bayonet. Everyone stopped to look at where the shot had come from.

"I'll thank you gentlemen to cease your annoyances to my sister," he said.

"Or what?" laughed one of the soldiers. "You'll shoot us with an empty gun?" He made a move to dash at the hussar.

The mounted man coolly thumbed the hammer and shot the man's helmet crest through. As the dragoon clutched his aching head and sank to the ground, another bullet shattered a carbine threatening Romulus. "Your confusion is understandable." He waved the Lemat at them. "This is called a revolver. It can fire nine shots without reloading. A somewhat...advanced...design."

"Yeah," I muttered. "So advanced it won't be invented fer fifty years yet."

While I was being all smug at Tyrell's demonstration I got another rude awakening. A pair of great hairy hands snatched me up into the air.

The ogre had managed to creep right up behind me, witched ears or no. That bully must've spelled him somehow to make no noise or smell. However he'd done it, I found myself ten feet in the air, staring down at so many sharp teeth that it was like gazing into a sword shop.

Jasper made tut-tut sounds. "My, my...isn't this a humiliatin' end to your glorious quest to save the world?"

I squirmed, but even Stone-strength couldn't pry those huge hands loose. "Yeah? How about a little help here, O Battle Edge of Doom?"

"Well, since you asked so nicely."

Dozens of steel porcupine quills sprang out of my magick corset, pricking the supposedly-indestructible monster flesh. With a surprised yowl the ogre let me go. I fell a long time and hit the ground hard (*probably shoulda thought about that part, Verity*), rolling downhill toward the edge of the road. Those quills slowed me down enough that I could avoid crashing into any trees. Absorbing them back into the corset, I looked around for help. But my friends across the way were busy negotiating the dragoons' surrender and the mishmash of angry Gaullic voices drowned out my predicament.

The giant's feet pounded after me. By the time I'd scrambled onto my own toes he'd cut me off from any aid. Now he towered between me and the others, stinking something fierce, a thick tree at his back. In the dim light nobody could've seen what was happening. I considered whomping him with some magick, but he was awful big and it might've only annoyed him more than he already was. Plus I figured it might attract that Bully. Two uglies at a time was more than I thought safe to handle. Hollering did no good. Everybody across the way was still kicking up a fuss about their own entanglement.

A sick rumble like a distant avalanche came out of the thing's cave of a mouth. Foul ooze dripped from those five-inch stalactite teeth. Right then I really wished that I couldn't see in the dark. It might've helped my morale some. And a second later that desire got magnified when the ogre picked up something from the trail, hefting it in one paw while pointing at me with the other.

He'd found a fallen lance.

Jasper was no help. "You know, there's a joke about Guinevere and Sir Lancelot runnin' through my head right now and..."

"Aw, stow it. That ain't gonna get me outta this."

"No appreciation for my bon-mots. All righty, then. You could turn me into a slingshot and we could poke out that pesky eye."

That sounded good, but it might attract that Bully. Then again, I wasn't in much of a position to pick and choose my survival tactics. And I figured the little squirt was likely to pop up any minute and get some revenge for his fellow mage. He knew where I was. Shoot, it was kind of obvious that he'd tracked me by my natural magick signature. I hadn't been slinging bucketloads of spells all day. Just as I'd made up my mind to take Jasper's advice, I saw that the ogre wasn't pointing at me with his free hand at all.

He was protecting his seeping eye.

Swell. Either he's got enough smarts to learn from his friends' mistakes or the Bully is doin' it fer him. Either way, gettin' a shot past that guard is gonna be tough.

Not for the first time that night I let my thinking get in the way of self-preservation. While I was ruminating on my next move, the ogre thrust the steel-tipped spear straight at me. He was a darned sight faster than I expected. I whipped up my arm to block it, Morphageus changed into a round Viking shield. That is, I did my best to raise the arm. It only traveled about six inches, then stopped.

What the heck?

Some invisible force pinned my arm to my side. With an *eep!* I flung my whole body to the left, landing in tall grass. The ogre roared, pulling the lance back for another jab. My arm was still stuck fast. I wished the shield into the other hand while scooting backwards on my rump until I could get safely away and stand again. That freed the first hand but froze the new one. A quick glance showed me the faintest of purplish shimmers around it. At the same time my Stone grew cold again. *The Bully's nearby. He's doin' this.*

My shield boss turned into a pair of clapping hands. "Well-reasoned! Let's hear it for the little lady!"

I scissored my legs apart as the ogre poked at me again, too low for a kill but scary nonetheless. He yanked it out of the ground, spraying me with dirt. *Gotta think of somethin' before the Bully gets it in his head to pin both my arms. Here's hopin' he only has enough power for one at a time.*

Rolling uphill to make the third strike miss, I felt around with my one good hand for a fallen branch, a rock, anything that might help me ward off that deadly point. At the same time I kept an eye out for the stumpy sorcerer. It wouldn't do to bump into him and get tranced. As the ogre pursued me to where he practically straddled me and couldn't miss, fatal lance aimed right at my belly, I set my fingers on an old hunk of hide. Out of reflex I pulled it over me, knowing that it'd never stop that spike from running me through.

"Woo!" sang Jasper, "is this ever gonna hurt!"

Before I even had a chance to wonder at his good spirits in the moment of my grisly demise, the lance hit me like a mule's kick. All my breath left me with a *woof!* Ten kinds of agony thrummed through me. I waited for the gush of gore. Soon my vision would fade and that would be it. Off to Valhalla I'd go, riding on the back of Alcibiades. *That'll be nice. No more monsters, no more fightin'. I could do with a spell of that.*

"Not so fast, missy," Jasper laughed. "You ain't getting' away from me that easy."

He wasn't joshing. The ogre gave me a confused frown. He pulled the lance back and examined the tip. Even with only one eye he could tell that not only was there no blood on it, for which I was real grateful, but the point had been blunted. *From a dry hunk o' leather? That ain't possible.* While the monster was deciding whether to stick me again or just lean in to chomp my head off, I squinted at the hide.

It was one of the dead and withered ogres.

Flinging the indestructible skin at my foe, I struggled to my feet and ran up the hill. When I returned Morphageus to corset form the Bully spell freed my arm. I tucked in behind a tree, hunting for him, ears cocked for the ogre, who stomped after me again, sniffing and grunting. My toe hit a rock, a smooth one the size of my fist. I picked it up as the creature lumbered up to me. *Wish I had Tommy's knack fer throwin' stuff. He never misses. Not ever.* Knack or no, I squared off and flung the rock.

And the ogre exploded into a thousand bloody hunks of meat.

For a second I patted myself on the back for my cleverness,
until the spell showed me what she saw.
Me, destroying everything good in the world.

12 / Directeur

I managed a choked "Yurp!" as I cringed. It seemed like half of the ogre's disgusting innards rained all over me. Wiping my eyes clean, I spun around to see who'd helped me out. Sure as shooting I hadn't blown the thing up with my rock. Heck, I'd missed him by two feet.

"Thanks fer nothin'," I muttered to Jasper.

He gasped in pretended shock. "Yet again you scorn your magick sword? What did I do now?"

"You could've helped me aim that rock some, O Grand Scimitar of Destiny." I still couldn't see anybody close by. Across the trail, though, Redeemers, dragoons, and my friends all stared like they were at a carnival freak show. Boy, was I familiar with that.

"Well, excuse me for livin', Miss High-and-Mighty. I figured you didn't need any assistance with such a puny adversary. Is old goat-smell dead and gone or not?"

"Sure is. I'm wearin' most of him. Yuck!"

"So clearly you had things under your usual faultless control."

"Except fer the missin' him by a mile part. Somebody came to our rescue. But I don't see nobody." I touched the Legacy Stone. Warm again. "Maybe the Bully did it and skedaddled."

I kept hunting for my savior, but nobody appeared. Romulus and Tyrell were headed across the trail to me. The dragoons had started to mount their horses and hightail it out of the vicinity. They looked pale as sheets. Something had spooked them. Of course, most of the things that happened to me tended to scare the willies out of normal folks. But it hadn't been the ogre business. No, they were pointing up at the sky as they spurred their steeds.

Pointing right above my head, actually. Where a winged monster hovered in a gap in the trees.

With a little yelp I jumped back, ready to defend myself again despite how exhausted I felt. And how sore. My tummy hurt so much from the lance that I might upchuck any second. Good thing for me the flying thing made no aggressive move. It just hung there in the night sky as if lassoed to a star. How it did that when its wings didn't even move befuddled me.

Just then the thing started to spin like a top. It picked up speed until it became a blur. At the same time it also rose away from me. I grew woozy watching the beast. What little food was in my stomach started to launch itself out.

And the ground whacked me a good hard one in the nose.

Ah...just me keelin' over again. That'll sure impress the Redeemers.

To make my humiliation complete, I heaved up a whole mess

of goo out of my mouth. There was blood in it, too. That lance strike must've busted me up some inside even though the ogre skin had kept it from actually penetrating into my vitals. I shivered and moaned. Ten kinds of red pain radiated from my middle. Though I was no doctor, I knew that this was awful bad, especially with the state of medicine in 1804.

"Ahoy there!" cried a spunky feminine voice from the treetops. "The little lady heeds some assistance. She has quite fainted, I fear."

Romulus was already kneeling beside me. Ernie sat on one shoulder and Matilda perched on the other. Big fingers poked and prodded my belly.

"Ow!" screeched Jasper in my head. "Holy mother of — what's that?"

"That's me in some big trouble," I thought back.

"Where's dat cup?" asked the giant Marshal. "She needs to heal."

Tyrell plopped himself down on my other side. He wrapped my trembling hands around the cup I'd given him. "Here. Use it to heal the worst of the injury."

The upstairs lady called out again. "She needs a free-will volunteer to take the damage. That's how it works."

Before the words were out of her mouth Romulus laid his hand atop both of mine. "That'll be me. I done it before."

"No!" commanded the woman, who sounded old but spry. "I do not propose to present the Equity with a dead Marshal if this goes wrong. Our relations are strained enough as it is."

"Me, then," proposed Tyrell. He leaned in close to me and whispered, "It's my fault, after all."

The boss in the sky didn't contradict him. But I tried to, with what little strength I could muster. "Leave me be. Don't want nobody sufferin' on my account."

He touched my cheek like a father at his child's sickbed. "But that's how this works, little Verity. We sacrifice for you because you must do the same for everyone."

Jasper moaned, "Somebody commence with the healin' before I end up as a Gaullic headstone! This hurts!"

The Hussar's hand clutched mine so hard I feared the bones would break. Gritting my teeth, I saw through my fog that he did the same. Sweat ran down his cheek. My guts started itching like a whole ant colony crawled there. As with all of Jasper's spells, the weird odor of brimstone and lily stung my nose. Nobody else seemed to notice. Just like in Virginia some weeks before, blue-white lights like a swarm of tiny fairies swirled up out of my injured area. They hung in the air for a moment, then sank into Tyrell's body. Just like that he coughed up blood. It dribbled down one corner of his mouth.

"Not there!" warned Romulus. "Wish it someplace else, fool. Where it be less likely to kill you."

My Redeemer friend (he was a friend right then, at least) nodded and closed his eyes. The cluster of lights popped out of his torso and drifted onto his left forearm. Like before, they got absorbed, making him grunt with new pain. A dark bloody patch spread across his blue sleeve, some of the gore dripping onto the ground. New hands wrapped a linen bandage tight around the spot. When I hugged him in gratitude they also snatched the cup away from me again.

"Idiot," murmured Gloriana, shaking her head at her brother.

"Is it done?" asked the lady up above us.

Romulus raised an eyebrow at me as Ernie ran along his arm and hopped onto my belly. The mouse jumped up and down on it a few times. When I didn't scream bloody murder he saluted and scampered away. I sighed and relaxed. Nothing hurt. All of the agony was gone.

"It is," reported Romulus.

"Any graves to be dug?"

Tyrell let out a grim laugh at that. "Only if I get gangrene." His voice dropped low again. "As if she'd care."

"Right, then. Coming down. Make way, all. This thing steers like a cow."

As if I weighed nothing Romulus scooped me up in his mighty arms and carried me to the edge of the trail. My vision cleared with the healing, and with Stone-sight I could see that the dreaded flying monster was a hot-air balloon with a bag painted black for night concealment. Its wings were actually some kind of fabric-covered steering vanes, connected to the tiny wicker gondola with levers and wires. The contraption was a lot smaller than any balloon I'd ever seen. Clearly only one person could get aloft in it, and even then it'd be a near disaster every minute it was aloft.

The pilot, that woman who'd been giving orders to everybody, looked to be nearly seventy years old. Round-cheeked, round-bottomed, and round-bellied, she might have passed for Mrs. Santa Claus with her fluffy white hair and twinkling eyes. Only the thick green goggles perched on her battered top hat, along with her long gray canvas coat and leather gauntlets, spoiled the illusion.

Plus the whopping strange gun she carried in the crook of her arm.

Basically it was a blunderbuss with a bell-shaped muzzle and short wooden stock. We had them on the *Kiss* for discouraging boarders. Loaded with small bullets, bits of rusty hardware, and broken glass, they ruined the prospects of anybody who found themselves in front of them. This one, though, had an iron cylinder on top, a metal hose running from it to the firing chamber, and a pressure gauge in the rear. Beneath it hung a lumpy box which might have held ammunition of some sort.

"Before you ask," said Jasper, "no, I can't turn myself into one of those. Too bad. It'd be a good look for me."

Several Redeemers grabbed ropes thrown from the gondola and hauled it toward the ground while its pilot pulled a cord to dump air from the bag. Once it had settled on the uneven surface of the hillside she opened a door and stepped out. Tyrell and Gloriana supported the old lady's arms and escorted her to the flat trail. The Hussar's newly-ruined arm was in a makeshift sling. Behind them the airship sagged as the hot air leaked out. It got tied to a tree, one lightly-wounded man left to guard it.

When the new arrival stopped dead-smack in the middle of

the dirt road, still holding that odd gun, all of the Redeemers knelt in a semi-circle, facing her. Even proud Gloriana did so, removing her hat. They performed a strange salute, touching their fists to their foreheads, then kissing the clenched hands and sort of shaking them at the woman. She nodded with a warm smile, like a grandma adoring her little ones.

"My, aren't you sweet?" she said, fingers idly tapping the barrel of her weapon. She passed it off to the first Redeemer to her right and clapped her hands. "All right, that's quite enough of that. Everybody up. There's work to be done. Gloriana, are we secure?"

Tyrell's sister avoided her somewhat disappointed look. They'd all been surprised by the lancer-dragoon assault and no mistake. "Yes, ma'am."

"Are we certain?"

"The Bully has fled through the ostium. All ogres are neutralized. No one else is at hand. The gulls say so."

The granny's adorable expression darkened. "My old ears may be defective. Gulls, you say? As in...birds?"

Matilda soared lazily past her head. From her black-ringed yellow beak came, "Yes, birds, you old biddy. Unplug your wrinkled ears and pay attention." Then she let loose with truly awful curse words and insults.

"Ah, I should have known. Pitcairn's prize chickens. I wonder how they taste with a good white wine?"

If she thought that'd intimidate the *Kiss'* scouts she was sadly mistaken. Those web-footed girls had fought demons and

Furies. Matilda pooped at her, just missing a buckled boot, and flew off to join the others on the ground across the trail. Romulus and Tyrell both choked back laughs. That earned them a savage glare which looked really odd on such a mild granny face. They bit their lips and turned away, shoulders still shaking.

"Now, then," continued the boss lady as she tugged off her white leather gloves, "if we are quite finished with all of the frivolity, perhaps we might move on. There are pressing concerns to address, you know."

Still leaning against Romulus so I wouldn't fall over again, I waggled my fingers at her. With the other hand I reached into my rucksack, hanging on his back. "And the first o' them pressin' concerns is: who might you be? We ain't been properly introduced, have we?"

She looked at me eye-to-eye, being just my height, and smiled like you would at somebody who'd just wet their pants in church. "I know who you are. The annoying impulsive waif who's causing us all of the bother. Or am I mistaken?"

I was up in her smug face before I had time to think twice about it. *Impulsive? Me?* "Causin' **you** bother? Well, ain't that a fine how-d'ya-do! Listen, lady, I never volunteered fer this business. If anybody's gettin' bothered it's yours truly." Romulus and Tyrell started snickering again. In my head Jasper was whooping it up and egging me on. But I didn't need his juvenile encouragement. Too much had come my way in the past three weeks to let this old bat look down her nose at me.

"And another thing," I snarled, quivering from anger. Never

rile a redhead. "I ain't no waif. Learned that word in school from Miz Finch, I did. 'A homeless, abandoned, or orphaned child.' None of that applies to me. Got a house, got friends, got a Ma and a Pa. My name ain't Pip and it ain't Oliver Twist. So I'll thank you to shut yer gob and tell me who the heck you are and why I should care." With that big finish I stuffed my mouth with the big chaw of tobacco I'd snuck from my pack.

You could've heard a gnat's footsteps on that trail, it had gone so quiet. The Redeemers' mouths all hung open like trap doors on a gallows. Nobody laughed now, not even Romulus or Tyrell. No wind, no shifting of feet, nothing. About the only noise I could make out was Jasper, debating with me about whether I'd just paid him enough for the favor I wanted. I figured my credit was good. Too bad the stuff tasted like rancid manure. How anybody could think it was a delight was beyond me.

That old lady's motherly expression never changed. But in the back of her eyes I could see something blaze up. A cold deadly fire like you'd imagine would surround Hades on his underworld throne. In fact, her whole attitude struck me as so heartless and cruel that I thought she might very well be that Hellenic god in disguise.

I sure hope that ain't so. This likely won't work then.

"O, ye of little faith," Jasper sighed.

She chuckled so low that hardly anybody would've noticed except me. "Such an ill-mannered brat. Your witch mother should have taken more time to instill some respect in you. But I have a few moments to improve your education in the social graces." As she spoke she brought her hand back to give me a good hard smack across the face, something not even my own mother had ever done.

The blow never landed. I'd been expecting her to resort to something low and had prepared for it. Before her hand could even start its swing I gave her both barrels.

A passion glamour.

It worked just as well as it had with General Lee in Richmond. Her vicious face went blank for an instant, then twisted in horror as the spell stole the most awful fear out of her mind and showed it to her on my face. She sucked in a hissing breath. Her mouth twitched. Those crone's hands shook like leaves in a gale. My Stone-boosted hearing could even pick up her heart pounding. For a second I patted myself on the back for my cleverness, until the spell showed me what she saw.

Me, destroying everything good in the world.

I stood atop a heap of bloody corpses, wearing black armor and waving Morphageus, runes alight along its dripping recurved blade. Widows wailed, fatherless children blubbered. Winged demons from the Obverse gnawed on hunks of flesh as they whipped slaves along a rocky rutted road. Lightning from a clear sky blasted fleeing armies. Furies plucked victims from homes to tear them to gory shreds. Behind me a battalion of Bullies held hands and led a vast horde of the undead into Paris, into Rome, into Washington City.

All fell before them. The very Redeemers who stood around us on the trail were also in the vision, their weapons useless against the banestaffs of Shades. Every one of them perished in the most disgusting way, consumed from within by purple fire. Among them stood the old lady, crying like a mother watching her children die in a plague. And a dark figure who I understood to be the Proprietor, white-blonde hair dancing in the foul wind, held out a hand to his new lieutenant, the general who would use the power taken from me to murder and maim until no resistance was left to oppose the Merchantry, neither in our world or in the one that held my father prisoner.

Napoleon Bonaparte.

We both gasped and stumbled apart. Two Redeemers caught her before she fell. I bumped into Romulus or I might've gone down myself. I'd had nasty dreams before, either sent by Sha'ira as warnings or by Merchantry sorcerers to terrify me. But this was so darned real it hit me like a friend's funeral.

I wished the glamour away. It had served its purpose and then some, rebounding into me like a badly-thrown boomerang. Spitting out the chewing tobacco, I gulped air and tried to ignore Jasper's complaints.

"No fair! I was just gettin' to the good part."

"Tough luck, boyo. I'm about to heave again, and this time all of my innards just might come up with it."

Held up by her men, who all clustered around her, the feeble but tough woman looked at me like I was a zoo exhibit. "What are you? What did you do to me?" She raised her voice, intending it for the Redeemers. "And who told me that she'd been disarmed?"

Gloriana showed her the cup. "She is. I have the tin cup right here. She did no magick, ma'am. She just stood there. No chants, no gestures."

"No magick?" The old eyes rolled. "She just forced a vision on me that an ancient demon mage would have been lucky to manage. You think a child can pull that from her soul-store?"

I shrugged, my head aching from that same vision. So exhausted from holding spells for disguise and translation, plus fighting Redeemers and ogres, not to mention marching all day, I let my red hair and freckles return. Mouths gaped again. It struck me that I was pretty close to naked now, dress, bonnet, and shoes long gone. Standing in my skivvies and stays, covered in dirt, scratches, bruises, and confusion, I just wanted dinner and a nap. Plus, I really needed to heed the call of nature before I embarrassed myself right in front of everybody.

"Not from my soul-store, no," I said, voice tired and hoarse. I gathered my will and let Morphageus liquefy out of its corset shape and flow down my arm. It pooled in my palm like quicksilver, then became a rusty tin cup identical to the one in Gloriana's hand. After that sank in on the Redeemers, it snaked out of my fist in its natural sword form.

"Heeeere's Jasper!" cried the boy's voice in my mind.

"I'm the Stone Warden, like it or not. And I reckon you're the one they call the Director?"

Recovering from her shock, the top-hatted granny nodded to me. "Madame Directeur Prisme Seychelles, to be precise. And it is time that you know exactly what the stakes are."

"The sword? Oh, heavens no, child. It's just a fancy butter knife. Powerful, yes. None can match it. But the Proprietor would hardly go to such trouble for another silly cleaver. "Hey!" Jasper called out, indignant. "I got feelin's, you know."

13 / Plots, Plots, Plots

With a disgusted snort Gloriana glared at the false cup, then twapped her brother upside his handsome head. "Idiot!"

He gave her that charming grin that had probably bewitched everything in a skirt since he was ten years old. "Oh, I don't know about that." Before she could react he snatched her fancy flask from her coat. Golden fluid, probably old, swanky, and expensive, filled the battered mug. "Now we don't have to share spit."

In my head Jasper let out a pathetic whine as the brandy's scent stung my nose. My belly lurched at the very thought of alcohol, but sword-boy sounded like a puppy on the wrong side of the fence from his food bowl. "Ain't happenin'," I told him, reforming Morphageus into its true cup shape again. "It took a magick miracle to heal my belly just now, remember?"

"And you might need a bunch more of those before we're through, missy, as accident-prone as you are. Demon-inflicted wounds are nasty things, they say. And you never know when a zombie horde might jump you again."

"I'll take my chances. My poor gut-muscles are achin' from all of the upchuckin' as it is."

I left Tyrell and Gloriana, still fussing with each other about who was most to blame for me fooling them, and scooted after the Directeur lady. Several Redeemers were buzzing around her like flies at a manure pile. You'd see the same thing at Mr. Ford's theatre back home, no-name actors and writers following the owner in a cloud, hoping to get noticed. This looked to be a similar sort of kissing-up.

Well, she'd better not be expectin' me to kowtow to her. I didn't do it fer Dionysus or Venoma and I ain't about to start now.

Madame Seychelles shooed her troops away as I approached. They scattered but stayed just out of earshot, like they feared I'd put another whammy on her. She yanked her head to say that I should follow her, then hobbled off of the trail and up into the trees a bit. Figuring that I was none too likely to find out was up without doing as she asked, I trudged along after her. As I went I worked up a fine head of steam, all ready to breathe some fire at her if she got huffy toward me again.

That lasted about eight whole seconds. Just as I caught up to her she climbed out of that formidable overcoat and held it out to me. "Here, child. You'll catch your death. That would do neither of us any good, would it?"

Shucks. And here I was all pumped up fer a tussle.

I mumbled something that might've sounded like an agreement and climbed into the coat. It turned out to be a darned sight thicker and heavier than it looked. Felt like wearing a horse blanket soaked in molasses. How a granny so old and frail managed to move in it was a mystery.

"Smells like fresh bread," Jasper observed, making 'that's yummy' noises, "and old cheese, and somethin' else —"

"Lily, partly," I said, sniffing. "She's got magick. Gee, what a surprise that is."

"Well, you do run with a witchy crowd. A regular spellin' bee, your life is."

I shook my head at the pun. "A fact I lay at your door."

"Who dropped in on who, hmm? I don't recall chasin' you down and draggin' you into my chamber."

"Oh, yeah? Well, let me tell you —"

I hauled my in-head jabbering up short, realizing that Madame Seychelles was peering at me through her silly smoked goggles. That didn't make sense to me, seeing how it was dark as a demon's prayer in the woods.

Like she could read my mind, which wouldn't have surprised me any, she said, "Special design. Liberated from the Merchantry. I expect they stole them from the Obverse. They are most mechanically advanced over there, in addition to their marvelous magick. Very helpful in these conditions. Though I doubt that they are as effective as your eyes, eh?"

"Couldn't say, ma'am." *No sense in bein' rude. You catch more flies with honey than vinegar.* I swiveled my head around, squinting. My arm pointed up the hill. "Can you make out that yellow-and-black striped caterpillar? About sixty yards off, three branches up?"

Jasper gasped. "There's nothin' there. Not polite to lie to old ladies."

"Aw, shush," I told him, my face not letting on to her. "She has it comin'. Besides, I need to get her on my side."

She gazed in that direction for a while, then shook her white head. "It would appear not. Morphageus does indeed increase your natural powers, which are formidable in their own right, if my spies are accurate."

"Spies, huh? Like Tyrell?"

"Such vitriol in that tongue. He has wounded you?"

"That'd be the nice way of sayin' it. I can think of others, but I was raised to avoid that sort o' language around my elders."

Madame Seychelles cackled and clapped her hands. "Priceless! Yet you have no trouble assailing them with terrifying glamours."

That fire I'd lost was burning again. "Not when they deserve it."

Instead of getting all huffy like before, she gave me a warm smile and sat on a big fallen log. She patted the spot next to her. "Fairly spoken. Sit down before you fall down. You look all done in."

I sure couldn't argue with that. We'd done nothing but march and fight all day, not to mention the magick. That takes it out of a body, even a witched one. And when did I last eat or drink anything?

Jasper wasted no time helping me out with that one. "Eons,"

he whimpered. "And that was just licorice. Unless you count that wonderful chaw of tobacco. Yum-yum!"

The thought of that made my empty belly heave. Plopping my tired backside down on the log, I sighed as the weight came off of my bare feet. Too bad the weight on my mind stayed put. "Things're gettin' powerful complicated. I expect you have somethin' to do with that. But I figure you can untangle some of it, too."

The grandmotherly head nodded. "Perhaps I can. But that may not make you feel any better."

"Oh, I sure enough expect that to be true. Every other time somebody's explained this mess to me it hasn't exactly made me sing and dance. The more I learn the more I want to crawl in a hole and hide."

"Welcome to the post-Affluxion world. It's rather like opening a trunk to find another one inside. And another one after that...forever."

I let out a sour laugh. "And each one has a fun surprise inside, like razors or rattlesnakes."

"Or magick talkin' swords," said my magick talking sword.

The leader of the Redeemers shrugged. "If you live, you'll have days where you fervently wish for a mere rattlesnake."

If I live? Thanks fer the honesty, but a little encouragement would be nice right now.

"Right now I'm wishin' fer an explanation. I've wasted three weeks gettin' chased by monsters, demons, sorcerers, zombies...you name it. Precious little rhyme or reason. No matter what I do, the Merchantry or you or some other nasty gang is waitin fer me."

Jasper sang in my brain. "And everywhere that Verity went, fiends were sure to go."

With a nod Prisme sighed. "That's because you are such a prize that all who play this game go to extraordinary lengths to secure you."

"Everybody wants Morphageus."

She yanked her goggles back on top of her hat. "The sword? Oh, heavens no, child. It's just a fancy butter knife. Powerful, yes. None can match it. But the Proprietor would hardly go to such trouble for another silly cleaver."

"Hey!" Jasper called out, indignant. "I got feelings, you know!"

I frowned and considered. "The Stone, then." Reaching into my chemise, I tugged on the maillon chain and hauled out the blunt jasper arrowhead.

"Of greater value, yes. The Obverse authorities dearly want it back. It is a sacred relic there. And it bestows great gifts on the bearer. But by itself the Sagestone is a mere rock, considering the stakes. Two worlds, both in crisis, with millions of lives in the balance? That reddish bauble isn't worth all of the men and materiel being expended."

"What, then? I ain't got nothin' else."

Seychelles threw up her liver-spotted hands. "Mon Dieu! Such an obtuse girl!"

My cup turned into a rag doll and applauded her. "Finally!

Recognition of my perspicacity. I've been sayin' that very thing for weeks now."

"Oh, shush," I told him. "I'm tryin' to figure this out." To Prisme I said, "Can we cut out the guessin'-games and just say what we mean. I could really stand some shut-eye."

"So could we all, though I fear that you are destined to always fall short in that regard." The elderly lady shook her head like I was the densest thing since granite. "You are the prize, Mademoiselle Sauveur. Just you, alone. Stripped of sword and stone, you would still be pursued by all the minions of the Merchantry, as well as by those of us who would deny them their catch."

"But why? Don't make no sense. I'm a kid who just wants to go to school and play-act with Tommy. Sure, there's that dumb prophecy, written by some feller who really needs Miz Finch to learn him better versifyin'. But I don't take no stock in that. And I ain't seen no cause to think I'm such a world-beater."

"Yet here we are, sitting in a dark Gaullic wood while every hellish fiend on Earth seeks to snatch you up. Could a normal girl have survived so long? And not merely survived, but thwarted their designs, even defeated gods? You badly underestimate your qualities."

"What qualities? From where I sit I have a knack fer stumblin' into ambushes and blunderin' into other folks' business."

"True enough, but you always escape. And on the way out you manage to make fools of your enemies and foil their plots."

"Fer instance?"

"Well, in Iberion you destroyed a large cache of weapons and ammunition."

"Yeah. So? I needed a diversion."

"They were destined for Merchantry infiltrators who planned to annihilate a column of Redeemers near Toulouse. Medieval Iberion was a perfect place to hide them until needed."

"I didn't know that, though."

"Perhaps not. But it is often better to be lucky than clever, they say. And you tend to have more luck than the average person, don't you? The very next night in Cumae three more depots of Merchantry arms perished in the flames of the dying city."

"And again, I'm tellin' you that I had nothin' to do with that. Shoot, I never even knew they was there."

"Yet it did happen, and you helped bring it about."

"Them zombies would've attacked the city anyhow. I just happened to be stuck in it when —"

When your crazy aunt came after you with her magick so she could collect the bounty on your coppery head. She controlled the zombies and sent them there.

Madame Seychelles gave me a knowing smile as I paused. "Ah! You begin to see?"

"And them other times when weird stuff happened? Like the attack of the Hellfiend Legion, fer instance?"

"They would have massacred a troop of Marshals disguised as Yankee cavalry if they hadn't changed their minds to apprehend you for the reward."

"The Furies who jumped the *Kiss*?"

"Were slated to assassinate a head of state en route to a peace conference. Diverted at the last moment."

"What great plot got ruined when that iron monster tried to ram us and I got half-drowned by the mer-men?"

She laughed out loud, not caring who heard. "Mine, I'm afraid. I was on that submarine. We had hoped to take you on board and make today's little contretemps unnecessary." A finger tapped me on my freckled pug nose. "Captain Nemo was quite perturbed when you jammed his propeller."

"You seem to like mechanical toys. And they ain't necessarily from 1804, neither."

"No. Like Tyrell, I was abroad when the Affluxion struck. In Boston, surrounded by all of that vaunted Yankee ingenuity. Engines, gears, pistons. So much more predictable than magick. Less to go wrong, barring the occasional boiler explosion."

"So if you wasn't in Gaulle in my time of 1850 then you must be —"

"I am the original Prisme Seychelles, not a copy."

"Where is your copy, then?"

"We had to, um, sequester her until this wretched mess is cleaned up."

"A polite word for prison."

"True enough. I can wallow in the social niceties when required, but do not mistake me. I am as savage as an aggrieved kraken when required."

What the heck's a kraken? "I ain't seen a lot o' them social niceties so far, except fer the loan o' this coat. Where I come from betrayin' and ambuscadin' are frowned on."

"Is that so? When last I checked you Americans were gleefully butchering one another right and left."

"I could say the same about Gaulle. Bonaparte's no angel, is he?"

"Decidedly not. Which is why you were so regrettably detained. But that can wait."

I thought about her duplicate self. "What about Tyrell's double? You got him in a dungeon, too?"

"He has, like his original, proven to be resourceful."

"Meanin' he got away."

"Quite. And it isn't a dungeon, you know. A lovely old castle, actually. Good food, kind servants. Warm, cozy."

"Somehow I doubt she sees it that way."

"You misunderstand. She does not know that she is being held. Rather, she believes that she has been made a baroness. That other Seychelles has no desire to leave."

Which made me think of the only other person I knew who was stuck in a jail. "I'm bettin' that Tommy don't feel the same way."

"Your unfortunate friend taken by Venoma? Difficult to say. The Proprietor's guests are often spelled into believing that they are in a happy familiar place. He may not wish to escape, either."

"More likely he's bein' tortured fer fun. They do that, I hear."

"Sometimes, yes. The Merchantry attracts the dregs of this world and the Obverse both. But he is of high value and they will likely not wish him damaged or uncooperative...yet."

That made me growl like a mama tiger. "If they so much as bruise an eyebrow on him I swear I'll —"

Prisme waggled a finger at me. "Ah, ah, ah! Careful! That is precisely why they took him. To make you charge in there, steaming at the ears, no thought to your own defense, and be captured the instant you crossed the threshold."

That was sensible advice, of course. As I thought about it, it occurred to me that something wasn't right. The whole thing seemed, well, dumb. Venoma had spit poison in Tommy's face from several yards away, then snatched him up, jumped into the Washington Monument's ostium, and been magically transported to...where? I had no proof that Tommy was in London, only her telling me to get myself there before the next moon. And why trance Tommy when I'd been so much closer? It would've given her the sword, the Stone, and me, just like that. Come to think of it, we'd fought twice that night and she'd never tried the venom trick, even when we were nose-to-nose. Well, nose-to-snout anyway.

She let me get away from her. Why?

What if the whole thing was some elaborate scheme to make me do just what I'd done: go gallivanting off half-cocked so that I'd be easier to grab? There sure wasn't any shortage of grabbers. Hellfiend Legion, Reb zombies, Assassins Guild, Furies, fraudulent Union troops, Redeemers, undead Dionysian Bacchantes, my own aunt, you name it. I was beginning to feel like the brass ring on a carousel.

"All them fingers are startin' to pinch," I sighed.

"What's that?" asked Madame Seychelles as she cleaned her goggles with a hanky.

I told her what I'd been thinking. It took a goodly while. When I came up for air she beamed at me like I was her blue-ribbon piglet at the county fair. "So perceptive! Always thinking ahead and behind at the same time. Seeing what isn't there as well as what is. That's why you're still alive, still free, and still dangerous."

"Dangerous? Look at me. I'm shiverin' in my skivvies, starved, nearly ogred to death. Dangerous to who?"

"Everyone, of course. Didn't you pay attention to your own passion glamour?"

"Yeah, but how likely is that to happen? I'm not a big believer in prophecies and predictions."

"You should be. That is what Obverse Sages do. They accumulate knowledge, then use it to see patterns and likelihoods."

"Who's an Obverse sage? Me? Don't think so. I'm a half-breed mutt with no trainin'."

"Oh, there you are wrong. Your mixed bloodline does not dilute your abilities. It enhances them. A child of two sorcerers and two worlds — believed impossible, by the way — who can wield the Morphageus with no training, defeat three Shades, outwit a Hellenic god, and preserve her sanity and wit when by rights she should have gone mad? What a gift to whoever can ally with her! What a valuable resource in the war to save mankind." Her eyes took on a possessive glint. "And that is why you'll help us before you go on to London."

Ah...here it comes. "Help you do what, exactly?"

"Why, kill Napoleon Bonaparte, of course."

"My apologies," I told her with a shrug.
"My Avengin' Scimitar o' Doom,
burstin' with the awesome power o' the
cosmos, has the maturity of a five-year-old."

14 / Big Plans for the Little Corporal

I jumped up and stepped away from her, hands up. "Whoa, whoa, whoa, whoa! Now wait a cotton-pickin' minute. I ain't killin' anybody."

Madame Prisme rolled her eyes and snorted. "That's an odd attitude for someone with your record. How many deaths have you caused in only three weeks as Stone Warden? Shall we start with the ten thousand acolytes of Dionysus in Cumae?"

"They was already dead."

"Fair enough. What about all of the Obverse sailors on the *Croatan*? The poor men of the Hellfiend Legion? Or the shock troops of the Proprietor in Virginia? Were they undead as well?"

"No, but they was sure tryin' to make me dead. Self-defense is a crime now?"

"Assuredly not. And that is what the assassination of the vile Corsican would be."

"How? He ain't come after me that I know of."

Her lips pursed. "Not strictly true."

"Yeah? More plottin' that nobody's bothered to let me in on

yet? Why ain't I surprised?"

"The information you seek is all up here." She tapped her top hat. "And the key to unlocking it is...one little life."

"Gee, that's all? I only have to murder one person? No big deal, huh? To you, maybe. But it leaves a sour taste in this girl's mouth."

"I imagine so. But there are worse tastes, believe me. Shame, humiliation, and grief, to start."

"All of which would come with stickin' a knife in an innocent man. No thanks." I started to stomp off, muttering that at least the demons were honest about what they were up to.

"Innocent?" she cried, sounding nothing like the calm and controlled Redeemer boss now. I heard a wife's pain and a mother's lament. "As innocent as Savonarola or Attila. You are a child of 1862. Did they not teach you in school of his monstrosities?"

"Uh, they kind o' skipped that part. Tended to talk mostly about his military genius, as I recall."

"A genius for torture and murder, more like. He cared nothing for his enemies and little more for his own men. Why do you think the Coterie Redempteur exists? Because of a policy dispute?" The Redeemer Directeur quivered like an unbalanced steam engine, showing signs of blowing apart. I looked around for some of her men in case I needed help with her.

"A hundred thousand dead slaves in Haiti, butchered in the most creatively awful ways. All for daring to seek freedom. And half that many again of his own troops, so he could claim dominion over a rock in the ocean." Despite the night's murk, I could see a shadow pass over her sagging features. "I lost my whole world there...husband and son. Yellow fever. Martyrs to his sick ambition and desire for control." Those bleak eyes seemed to flare like lanterns. "So do not dare to speak to me of his precious innocence. He took my Henri's when he forced him to kill and maim those Haitians. He stole my Georges' when he made him give the orders for it." Wiping an eye, she choked back a sob. "And he cost me mine when I discovered what sort of beast I'd been cheering for all of those years."

That threw a different light on things, of course. But I still couldn't stomach what she was asking of me, no matter how vile the man might be. Besides, there was a catch.

"But he ain't your Napoleon, is he?" I pointed out, as gentle as I could. "You said yourself that you rode out the Affluxion in the States United, like Tyrell. So neither of you is hatin' the actual feller. This Bonaparte in Paris right now is an imitation made by the Merchantry's spell. Doin' him in won't be justice."

That made her gag. "Oh, please! You know how things stand. The magick exactly recreates actual history unless extraordinary effort intervenes. This Corsican upstart is every bit as bad the real one. The same attitude, the same ruthlessness, the same blood on his hands. Perhaps not Haitian blood in this instance, since his troops never actually sailed there but only believe that they did. The mechanics of the Proprietor's curse matter little. More will die if he is not dealt with." She took my hands in hers. "You are of the modern world. You know how it all ends. This is

1804. Eleven more years of war, disease, starvation. Secret police kidnapping 'troublesome' citizens. Whether he is the bona-fide Napoleon or not, the same number of people will perish because of him. Nearly five million. Five million! Those who campaign outside Gaulle's borders, though they may not truly march to Austerlitz or Jena or Moscow, will die just the same. Squads of Merchantry agents will do away with them in an appropriately gruesome manner, then report their heroic deaths in battle."

"Then you should overthrow him, arrest him, try him. Not sneak in and just murder him. How does that make you, us, any better than he is?"

"Oh, I am under no illusions about that. Tainted we shall be if we do this. In a manner of speaking, though, we are putting down a rabid dog. Distasteful work, yet it ensures the safety of the community. And as for arresting him, nothing would bring me more joy than to pluck him from his warm bed and hand him over to a judge and jury. But the laws are his, as are its operators. Anything we do to him will be illegal, in the eyes of the people. Plus, he has the Grand Armee at his back. His success has made them too loyal to oppose openly."

I tried another angle. "You don't need me. You ambushed us good and proper, despite my Stone-senses and my experienced friends. We had a couple of Marshals and a Shade and I'm still yer prisoner. And another thing. I attract attention. The wrong kind. Ma says my magick gives off a beacon like a lighthouse. Bad guys...and bad things...flock to it. Might as well be a dead skunk in buzzard territory. I'll just bring down ogres and Bullies and all manner of trouble on you."

"What you say is true. In fact, I am counting on that very thing."

"Huh? That don't make no sense. Why would you want a horde of demons or Shades or some giant green Merchantry hamsters to crash yer fancy dress ball?"

Jasper said, "You think you're bein' funny. But those hamsters are no joke."

"What? There really is such a thing?"

"If you can imagine it, so can they. Remember that eight foot tall purple tick in Virginia?"

Seychelles nodded to Gloriana, who was approaching us. Tyrell's tough sister held up a gloved hand and stopped where she was. The Directeur turned back to me. "Because while the minions of the great enemy are occupied with your spry self, they shall not be keeping a watchful eye on my team."

"So I'm the sacrificial lamb then? Thanks a bunch."

She giggled. It sounded weird coming out of her old face. "Sacrificial dragon, I would say. You have a positive knack for getting yourself out of trouble, dear. I harbor few fears about the outcome if your lighthouse beacon, as you call it, draws some annoying moths. In fact, I am more concerned about your adversaries. All of those poor dearth-demons, heading for their bleak afterlife. I suppose even Obverse fiends have mothers, eh?"

I shook my head at that. "Ma'am, you sure got a powerful high opinion of my monster-whackin' skills. I hope they turn out to be justified."

"I'm certain they will be. After all, you are not alone on your quest, are you? You bear a fancy butter knife, after all." Prisme raised an eyebrow at my tin cup.

Morphageus reformed into an actual butter knife, though this one was four feet long and covered in fiery runes. "Well," said Jasper in a silly deep manly voice, sounding like one of the conceited actors at our theatre, I don't like to brag, but..."

"My apologies," I told her with a shrug. "My Avengin' Scimitar o' Doom, burstin' with the awesome power of the cosmos, has the maturity of a five year-old."

"Says the kid standin' in her underwear holdin' absurd kitchen cutlery," Jasper shot back. He turned into a jumbo egg beater and stuck a metal tongue out at me.

Madame Seychelles took all of this in with a straight face, like she saw that sort of thing every day. *Maybe she does, in her line of work.* "No apology required. This Jasper, as you call him, is precisely the sort of character needed on this mission. Indispensable."

"Who's indispensable?" he cackled. The eggbeater melted and reshaped itself into a gumball machine. It spat out a pair of little round red candies which became bloodshot doll's eyes. They looked back and forth between the old lady and me. "There! Properly dispensed, if I do say so myself."

The Directeur of the Coterie Redempteur showed that she had her limits as far as appreciating Jasper's value went. "I may have spoken too soon. What in the devil's name is he doing now?" She had a smile on her face when she said it, though.

Before I could get an answer out I found myself holding a tin cup again, only it was the size of a milking bucket and bore the words 'Property of Lucifer' across it. The smell of brimstone just about gagged me. This time no lily scent mingled with it. *Smart-aleck.* "Showin' off. He does that. If you ignore him he sometimes stops. More than likely, though, he'll just keep it up until you pretend to admire his undeniable wit."

With a soft chuckle she snapped her fingers – a neat trick while wearing gloves – and a shot glass full of whiskey appeared from thin air. *See? I knew I smelled magick on her.* It floated up, supported by nothing more than her thought, and poured itself into the cup. By the time I stuck my nose in to look, the liquid was gone.

"Whooee!" Jasper crowed. "That's the good stuff, there! You Gaulles sure know how to make a fellow feel welcome." His speech started to loosen. "Let's put on our dancin' shoooes...!"

I didn't share his gratitude. We tended to feel what the other felt, more or less. Thankfully, I didn't sense anything when he defended me from baddies. No chance I'd enjoy the impact of bullets, claws, teeth, and spells. But this wasn't one of those times. Already my face felt warm. Dizziness crept into my noggin to match the clumsiness of my limbs. Words came out as thick as syrup in winter.

"This is happenin' awful fast, boyo. I get the distinct impression that a certain magick sword of my acquaintance is goosin' up the effects fer my benefit."

He got coy. "Um...maybeee..."

"Well, knock it off. I'm in the middle of very delicate negoshee...negothee..."

"...athuns," he finished.

"Yeah, them. So I don't need you gummin' up the works."

"Sheesh! Try to show a girl a good time and all you get is a wagonload of grief." The fuzziness inside me faded. "There. Happy now?"

"I salute your gentlemanly restraint, O Blade of Bombast."

"A paragon of virtue, that's me." The cup turned into a bottle of headache powder. "Besides, when you get a hangover, I feel it, too. One of the drawbacks of this arrangement."

Stuffing his ramblings into the back of my mind, I focused on Madame Seychelles again. "You got magick. That's plain. So why do you need mine? Surely you know I ain't got a good grip on it yet. Who knows what I'm liable to do if I lose control? Might transmogrify your men into hairy turtles or somethin'." I recalled my horrifying trip along the edge of the Obverse with my loony Aunt Regan. "And I sure as heck can't latch onto a Chauntline. Ma says that might blow my head off."

The Directeur took my arm and guided me back toward the trail to where Gloriana still waited. "If you'll permit me an observation, your mother is a powerful practitioner but a bit overprotective. Who can blame her? You are her sole child, after all, and the Stone Warden to boot. Not to mention the fact that you are the unique progeny of Obverse and Earth. That makes you more precious than all the gems of the Indies."

"Yeah? Why's that? "

"Does no one tell you anything? How can you be so ignorant of the blessings bestowed upon you by your father?"

That made me think about the hollow, forlorn look on Ma's face every time I'd ever mentioned Pa. "Probably 'cause Ma don't much see it as a blessin'. Curse, more like."

"Indeed, the boundary can be a fine one."

"So what is this great inheritance I supposedly have?"

"Only that you are able to drink from a greater well of magick than anyone who has ever lived."

Really? Why do folk have to talk all mysterious and showy, like they're in a novel?

"That sounds peachy, but what exactly does it —"

"I mean that when you embrace a Chauntline, you are pulling energy from the Obverse, not just Mother Earth."

"And that's somethin' special?"

"I should say so. It would be like having an inexhaustible supply of musket balls, instead of having to reload each time. Actually, to be more precise, it would be like having a rapid-fire cannon that constantly feeds shells into the breech."

"Big stuff, then?"

"Very big stuff. It makes you able to defend and attack at the same time. Boosts the energy of Morphageus immeasurably. And you can pop over to the Obverse as easily as skipping through an open garden gate, whereas everyone else must prepare a complex and tiring spell."

I shook my head at all of that. "Hold on now. If I'm the only half-breed that's ever been, how can you know that any of this is true?"

"Our cleverest minds say so. As do our opposite numbers in the Honourable Merchantry. More to the point, the Obverse sages believe it. They naturally have researched and experimented on this very thing, ever since you were prophesied."

"I don't want to burst anybody's bubble, but this girl ain't ever done any o' that. I wouldn't even know where to start."

"Of course not. No one knows any skill at birth. One must be taught. And we can introduce you to just the right tutors as we make our way to Paris."

"Ah. So you just naturally believe that I'm gonna help you exterminate Napoleon?"

"I do. Because I have the means of transporting you to London in time to rescue your friend. Your cooperation in this venture is my price. It shall not be easy, however. Only last month poor Cadoudal was guillotined for attempting this very thing."

I gulped. How come nothing I ever blundered into was ever safe? "Gee, ain't that just swell."

That earned me a grandmotherly pat on my head. "Nothing ventured, nothing gained, dear."

As we set our feet onto the trail Gloriana leaned in to whisper into Prisme's ear. Normally I don't eavesdrop on that sort of thing, but I figured this was a special situation, what with me bein' a prisoner and all. Couldn't hurt to learn everything I could. So I reached out with my witched hearing to pick up the words. *Oh, really? Wonder what Romulus and Ernie'll say to that*. Then I tucked them into my memory for safekeeping. They'd probably come in handy.

We headed back down the trail a piece, Tyrell's sister tucked in behind us. That snotty attitude of hers was nowhere to be seen around Madame Seychelles. *Probably a good policy when yer boss is a mage with an ogre-slayin' gun*. Ahead waited Tyrell and Romulus. The Redeemer sat on a fully-packed Alcibiades, while my giant Marshal bodyguard sharpened his Bowie knife on a whetstone. More of Tyrell's comrades made their way toward them. Something was up. It looked like we wouldn't be sleeping quite yet.

"More Bonapartist cavalry headed our way, ma'am," Tyrell reported, wounded arm still hanging in its sling. "Word of that fracas got back to the garrison in Bayonne. It certainly was noisy enough to alarm the neighborhood."

"How far out?" Prisme asked. She tugged on her coat collar to let me know that she needed it back. I shrugged out of it and started shivering. Even in summer a Gaullic night could chill you when you were just in your undies. Jasper came back into my noodle and complained about his working conditions.

Tyrell answered, "Less than hour. We'd best get moving. I have some men laying a false trail to the southeast which should draw them away unless their captain is particularly clever."

"Excellent. I shall jump ahead in my balloon to the

rendezvous. Convincing our reluctant partners to cooperate will require a gentle hand and sophisticated tongue, I think."

"Agreed. Will you be taking Miss Verity along?"

Madame Prisme struggled into her gondola with the aid of a pair of Redeemers. "No. Too many spies in the air, of late. I shot several tenacious ravens on the way here. Had to hide in a cloud, as well, when a pair of winged dearth-demons came too near. Our enemy knows that his prize is at hand. Keep to the woods and watch her close. That troublesome Bully escaped. Doubtless his handler is nearby, waiting to release more mischief."

"Our vigilance will be all that you could wish," Gloriana assured her.

Prisme chuckled at that and lowered her goggles onto her eyes. "Careful with such declarations. My wishing capacity is extensive." She tested the controls of her guidance vanes, then peered at her stove. The fire had been restored, its flame causing the balloon to float a foot above the ground. Only two ropes lashed to trees prevented it from taking off.

"If we avoid contact with the enemy we should meet you two hours past dawn," said Tyrell, twirling his moustache. "In case of a delay Marshal Romulus will send word via gull or pelican."

"Let us hope it does not come to that. But trouble flies toward Miss Verity like iron filings to a lodestone. Expect the worst. Give it your best if it shows its head. Farewell, all!"

The massed Redeemers all gave her that funny fist-to-forehead salute, which she returned, adding a matronly finger wiggle. With a roar the flame belched up into the gasbag. When the restraining ropes were untied the balloon shot into the starry sky with more speed than I expected. Once it cleared the trees it caught a light breeze and moved northeast, aided by the flapping of the vanes.

"Right!" called Gloriana, striding up the trail, "let's move! Flankers out left and right. Gibert in the van. Valois, you take the rear. Look sharp, all! No surprises this time or I'll have your bollocks."

Everybody hustled off to take their positions. Tyrell launched Al into the air to reconnoiter. I left them all to their tasks, since I was so beat that my yawns sounded like foghorn blasts. Romulus scooped me up so I could climb up into the magicked backpack for a nap. There I found Ernie, snoring beneath the hound's ear. Two seconds later I was sawing logs, too.

*The big basset hound opened one eye and looked
up at Ernie in that sneering way that only
overthrown Gaullic royalty could manage.
"Monsieur Mouse, in the past those who have
disturbed my sacred rest have found themselves
scraping ordure from my cesspits."*

15 / Verity's Eventful Knap
Sunday, July 15, 1804

I think I slept pretty good, not waking until our trip was over.
Even then I might have kept on snoozing if it hadn't been for the
nasty dream I had. It was mostly the same as the one sent to me
in Iberion and a couple of times since: Tommy in a dark pit,
getting pecked by ravens who wore ruffs like Shakespeare while
a line of Bullies in poofy skirts danced the can-can with
Napoleon. You know, the usual stuff. The Gaullic Emperor wore
his typical military uniform but on his head was a crown of
thorns. That was new. Accompanied by horrifying yet absurd
dearth-demons who looked like pot-bellied cathedral gargoyles
and had flames shooting out of their rear ends, Venoma cackled
and pointed to an almost run-out hourglass.

Ever since becoming Stone Warden I'd been sent dreams by
friend or foe. By now I'd learned to tell your everyday ones from
those telegraphed into my head. They *tasted* different,
somehow. I'd even figured out how to separate those sent by

friends from those used as nasty weapons by the Merchantry or whatever other shadowy troublemakers were keen on harassing me. And this ugly piece of work sure was one of that last kind. Somebody not only wanted me to hurry up and get to London, but they wanted me disturbed and fidgety, too.

But Sha'ira, who'd been the first to Dreamwrite me and who'd done it to warn me of the dangers I'd face, had taught me a way to control some of the emotional upset that the icky dreams, the attack dreams, brought. Just as she'd helped me control seasickness and battle stress with a special chanting, she did the same for the nightmares. The trouble was, though, I had to do it from inside the dream, while still asleep. That meant I had to know that I was in a dream and try to control things. Not an easy thing, let me tell you. At first I'd just made the bad feelings worse. I kept at it, though, not wanting the baddies to win. Lately I'd managed to get pretty good at it. Maybe Jasper's Stone-boosted magick helped. Whatever the reason, this time I fought back.

And it felt good. While repeating the chant until my dream self buzzed and floated, I reached out to the other characters with magickal force. Invisible lines tangled the demons and smacked them into one another until they lay in a dazed and steaming heap. I raised a sparkly blue shield around poor whimpering Tommy with one hand and yanked dozens of stones out of the ground with the other. Those smooth pebbles hung in the air like a squadron of balloons. Snapping that second wrist, I sent the rocks into the ravens like a musket volley. Black oily feathers exploded into the air, accompanied by anguished squawks. That left just Venoma. She spat her gooey poison out of that sharkish mouth to paralyze me. It splatted against the iron knight's helmet I wore on my head, sizzling but doing no damage except for Jasper's indignant complaining. He flowed off of my face and reformed into a crossbow. The huge demon discovered discretion in her valor and leaped backward, causing the bolt to barely miss, though it opened up a black gash along her ugly right cheek. My arrow bounced off a rude stone wall to twirl back to me as a boomerang. When I seized the hourglass to flip it over and restart its time, though, the wretched thing grew fangs and snapped at my hand.

That woke me up, panting and sweating. The Duc du Evremonde grunted and rolled away from me, still in his own deep doggy dreams. His hound funk, a thick smell like dirty wool socks, came close to suffocating me. It filled the whole knapsack, which was the size of a biggish garden shed on the inside due to Ma's magick. Whatever spell she'd put on it to make it that way also kept out any sense of motion or upset. Lying on my pallet beneath an army blanket, I might have been in a real building with a solid foundation. There was no sensation of movement or jostling, even though I know that I still rode on Romulus' broad back.

After splashing water on my face and meditating some to make my heart stop pounding, I felt around for Ernie's plump mousey self. I hoped I hadn't smooshed him flat in my sleep. No sign of him. Looking in the various boxes, bags, and barrels of food did me no good, either. The tiny Marshal of the Equity was nowhere to be seen. But his silly Cockney voice, always too loud for his size, came from above me.

"Wake up, Miss Snores-a-Lot!" he called from the sunny opening of the knapsack. He wore a tiny bicorn hat sideways on his head as if he were a four-inch-tall Napoleon.

"Look who's talkin'," I laughed, rubbing at my sleepy eyes. "You sound like a locomotive strainin' uphill when you sleep."

"Well, neither of us can hold a candle to the Duke there. We should sell tickets."

The big basset hound opened one eye and looked up at Ernie in that sneering way that only overthrown Gaullic royalty could manage. "Monsieur Mouse, in the past those who have disturbed my sacred rest have found themselves scraping ordure from my cesspits."

That earned him a hooting laugh from Ernie. "You don't say? Well, there's a new world ordure now, Yer Grace. So I suggest you gets yer bum outta that comfy spot and come get breakfast before I feed yer portion to Matilda's gulls."

Like a shell from a Parrot rifle the dense-bodied doggy shot up and out of the knapsack, colliding with the mouse on his way. Before I could blink I was alone on my pallet.

"Say," said Jasper with fake disinterest, "did I hear somebody mention food or was I just havin' a delightful dream?"

"If you were, you'd be the only one." I grabbed a washcloth and some soap and commenced to scrub off yesterday's mud and ogre blood. A sealed water keg and a basin made it easy.

"What I wouldn't give fer a happy dream."

My tin cup wriggled itself into the shape of a crossbow. "Oh, I don't know. I thought that adventurous little vision of yours turned out pretty darned well, considerin'."

"You think so? I figured you were lendin' a helpin' arrowhead there. How'd ole Venoma taste? I'm guessin' she won't be winnin' any gastronomy prizes."

He transformed into a rag doll sticking a finger down its throat. "And you'd be right. Like lickin' a moldy mortician's table, only not as sweet. Blech!"

"Just be glad her blood's not as poisonous as her spit."

"Oh, it is, just not to me. One of the benefits of bein' the Jaunty Edge o' Justice. That and my homespun charm." The doll puckered up for a smooch, lips expanding to five times normal size.

The conversation went on like that while I finished my bath. When the basin had turned black as the Proprietor's heart I put on fresh drawers and my favorite outfit of cotton shirt, denim overalls, and straw hat. I added the belt so I could hang the tin cup on it. Since my disguise looked to be a total bust, I figured I'd be better off feeling comfy and ready for action. Judging by Madame Seychelles' warning, a tussle was more likely than not.

When I poked my head out of the knapsack, blinking from the bright summer sunshine, I found that I'd prepared too late for that. Romulus told me that I'd slept through a nasty fight with some more of Bonaparte's horsemen. It seemed that their captain had been as clever as Tyrell had feared. He'd taken the bait and followed the false trail laid by the Redeemers, but he'd also hedged his bets and sent a troop north, just in case.

"Luck fo' us they spit they force," Romulus said as he oiled a horse pistol taken from one of the unlucky men who'd engaged us.

Tyrell nodded agreement. Blood, not his, spattered his white arm sling. "Too bad we had to kill them all. Couldn't risk any survivors spreading the word of our whereabouts."

My jaw dropped. "What? You massacred prisoners? Why, that's about as lowdown a —"

His moustache twitched. He winked at Romulus, who grinned at my outrage. "They's okay, miss," he assured me. "Tied to trees a hundred yards off the trail. Gagged, too. By the time they gets loose and reports it'll be too late."

I felt like spelling them into ladies' dresses, but instead I wriggled out of the ruck, which lay on the ground between them, stomped off and muttering how it wasn't nice to mess with little girls. To make me feel better I headed for the fire, tended by Gloriana and three of the Redeemers. We were camped behind a barn at the edge of the woods. They'd bought eggs and bacon from the farmer and were frying them all up in a pan from Tyrell's saddlebags. A pot of coffee and some hardtack completed the meal. Alcibiades, still in his dark disguise color, munched grass nearby, needing no tether to keep him close. Everybody looked worn out, with dark bags under their eyes and stiff joints.

"Not much sleep for y'all last night, huh?" I asked, accepting bacon from one of the men. In my noggin Jasper nearly wet himself with joy.

"Sadly, no," he said. " We were about to bed down when the cuirassiers charged us from flank and rear. Our outposts gave us a little warning, but not enough to form a proper defense."

"That led to a running fight," Gloriana continued, hat cocked back on her head. "Hit and run. Naturally we took to the trees for cover and to inconvenience the horses. But we got scattered in the dark. The Bonapartists fought well even dismounted. Things looked bad for a while."

"But here you all are," I pointed out, chewing. "So you must've come together in the end."

"I wish we could take credit for that. But, alas, we had to be rescued." The sour look on her face told me that those words really hurt to say.

"Aw, it weren't much of an accomplishment to maroon that bunch o' scallywags," bellowed a familiar and beloved voice behind me.

I dropped my bacon and whirled to hug the Dread Pirate Roberta. Due to a Merchantry curse, whenever she left the *Kiss* she turned into a parrot. The scarlet macaw with the wire spectacles on her beak dropped from a tree limb right into my arms. She nipped my ear as she crawled up to perch on my shoulder. "Sure am glad to see you!" I told the *Penelope's Kiss'* first mate. "The seagulls need some o' yer special brand o' discipline."

That earned me a chorus of utterly-foul abuse from every

direction, though it ended in laughter. Matilda's girls strolled all over the surrounding pasture, looking to beg or steal from the humans' breakfast. They took spectacular yet good-natured verbal offense at my joshing. Jasper seemed to be taking notes in my brain as he absorbed their creative language.

"Never ceases to amaze me how they can invent completely new combinations," he said with glee. "You'd never think that the words 'head' and 'beak' would work with those particular verbs."

Roberta cackled, "Them swabs is beyond discipline. I just point 'em at the enemy and get out o' the way."

"So you and the gulls rescued the Redeemers? That's twice now that Matilda's crew has —"

Matilda strutted up to filch a bit of egg from one of the men. "We weren't involved, dearie. Tyrell asked us to keep an eye on the troop to the south, in case they doubled back. Only just arrived, we did. No, you'll have thank somebody else for this one."

"Who, then?" I asked, seeing the answer approach just as the words left my mouth.

A stone's throw away, an elegant green and gold figure oozed through the trees like a deadly phantom. Sha'ira wore her bow slung across her back, one hand on the hilt of her scimitar. Her hood covered her long black hair to keep away the morning chill. Beside her a burning ember rode the air currents like a drunken bee.

"Make way!" cried Scorch, heading straight at us like a

burning arrow. Gloriana snatched up the coffeepot with a gloved hand to save it as he dove headlong into the campfire. The sprite stretched out in the coals, bit of flaming debris kicked up as he wriggled in blazing bliss.

"Aahh, that's the ticket!" he purred, happy as a hog in mud. "Who knew that Gaulle would be so bloody frigid in July? A body could turn to ice in this nasty weather."

"It must be all of sixty degrees," chuckled Roberta. "Remind me never to take him on our next polar expedition. We'd have to stick him in a bubblin' stewpot for the whole trip." She leaned down and offered her white beak to me. "Verity, be a dear and clean these specs fer me, will you?"

I obliged her by plucking them off and wiping them with my shirt tail. Jasper was still trying on profane seagull expressions for size, which was annoying but a distraction I was used to after three weeks with him. By the time I returned Roberta's glasses Sha'ira had arrived at the fire. The red morning sun glinted off of her moonstone pendant, making it glow all rosy. Her facial tattoos and hawk's nose gave her a harsh beauty, but that striking appearance earned her no lusty stares from the men. *If she took down enough enemy troops last night to save their hides, especially if she had to use her Chauntline magick, these fellers are probably terrified of offendin' her. Can't blame 'em.*

"Well met, Verity," said the tall Arabe, bowing her head a fraction of an inch. The breeze made her brocade robe billow behind her. "You are well-rested?"

That was a gentle tease, as close as she generally ever got to being funny. Shades, even retired ones, had little sense of humor. She knew that I'd happily snoozed the night away while she and the rest had defended me with their lives. But she also knew that if needed, I'd have busted out of that pack with Morphageus in its full glory, eager to help thrash the baddies.

I gave her an innocent smile, playing along. "Why, yes, thank you. Peaceful as could be. But I hear that you were tossin' and turnin' all night long."

"Indeed...tossing Gaulles and turning defeat into victory." She sent a sly sidelong glance Gloriana's way as she said that. Tyrell's tart sister bristled a bit at that, but not enough to start an argument. Her men sort of hunkered down and got real interested in their food. I got the impression that I'd missed more than one intense engagement while I'd been asleep.

Scorch called out from the fire, "Don't pretend you did it all yourself! Yours truly was givin' it to 'em. Oh, yeah. Those Boney ponies sure hate it when you send a fireball up their —"

"But perhaps we should share the glories of the fight equally," offered Sha'ira. "After all, the Coterie Redempteur did not succumb to superior force. They battled nobly, giving better than they received, in order to give us the time to arrive and lend our weight to the cause. Otherwise there might have been nothing left to aid."

Gloriana made a wry face. It might've been because the Duke was giving her that miserable 'I'm starving' look that basset hounds use to charm folks out of their meals. I swear, after a few seconds of that you want to carry them on your back to a swanky restaurant and order them two of everything. But more likely it was an admission that she'd be dead or captured without Sha'ira. "You speak diplomatically, m'lady, but let us be frank. You fairly pulled us out of the fire last night." She raised her flask in grudging salute.

"Pulled you out of the fire?" complained Scorch. "What sort of talk is that?" He backstroked his way through the ashes, whole body glowing like iron in a forge. "You soft-skinned normals have no idea what's good in life."

Tyrell appeared with tongs and plucked Scorch out by the collar of his coat. The sprite's wings buzzed but couldn't pull him free. Like he did that sort of thing every day, the wounded Redeemer held his tiny body up to a cigar and puffed it into life. Scorch yelled and threatened but it did him no good. Only when the cigar was a going concern did the tongs part and release him.

Romulus had come over with Tyrell and between them, Sha'ira, and Gloriana I got the gist of what I'd slept through. The cavalry attack had come just before dawn, as the Redeemers were getting ready to bed down. Warning shots and cries from the picket posts alerted them to the danger and allowed them to flee the trail in two bunches. Gloriana led one and Tyrell the other, though he was slowed by the wound he'd taken for me. Doing what he was trained for, Alcibiades took to the air as scout and fighter both. He'd alerted those on the ground to enemy flanking movements while also diving down to unseat cuirassiers on the trail or in clearings. With me slumbering on his back Romulus hadn't been able to pitch in like he might have otherwise, but he accounted for a few unlucky assailants. Quite a few of them fell to Redeemer bullets, blades, and even fists.

But the success didn't last. Somehow the Gaulle soldiers were guided to each of our detachments, arriving at the perfect moment and position to apply the most pressure. Gloriana said it was like they could see in the dark. Her brother thought they had spies near us who had some mysterious way of instantly reporting to the enemy's officers. They doubted that it was somebody in the air or else Al would've noticed and dealt with him. I suggested that they check for insect spies, like the tick on Al's rump in Virginia. Everybody thought that was a grand idea and started in on it before the story was even finished. A Dreamworm was also possible. The thought of that made me feel sick.

As dawn approached things had gotten real sticky. Several Redeemers were down with wounds, though none too dangerous. The cuirassiers had linked up their lines into one and had nearly encircled us. With their pistols and carbines they made it plenty hot despite Tyrell's LeMat equalizer. One big rush and we would've been done for. I'd have been captured and sent off to the Proprietor before even knowing anything was up.

That obviously didn't happen. Instead, our foes began falling with arrows in their limbs. Some of the shafts carried fire on their tips, fire that laughed and taunted them. The dry grass burst into a wall of flame between them and the Redeemers. When any of the soldiers tried to retreat he met a well-armed ghost. Heads cracked. Joints bent in painful ways. One or two terrified men who made it to the trail got snatched up by a flying demon's teeth and flung back into the trees. Seeing this turn of events, Gloriana led a counter-attack that carried the day. Twenty minutes later the Bonapartist cavalrymen sat glum and bruised, wounds dressed and their hands and feet bound. After putting out the grass fire before it could set the trees alight, our band melted away, being sure to take a long winding route to get to the barn where we all sat breakfasting now.

"They say everything tastes better outdoors," I snickered, "especially when you've just whupped up on a bunch o' fellers."

The floppy-eared hound swiped another bit of bacon from some poor Redeemer's hand. "It is true. One's cuisine is much enhanced by *le victoire*."

"Though it was a near-run thing," observed Tyrell. "Another minute or two and we might have been overrun." He raised an eyebrow at Sha'ira.

She nodded in agreement. "Forgive my tardiness in coming to your aid. I have been shadowing your movements, waiting until I was truly needed. We had enough of our number captured without my adding to the tally. By the time I realized that our pursuers were gaining, I was hard-pressed to get up to you." She snagged Scorch out of the air. "It seems that someone lay intoxicated in a blacksmith's forge and needed fetching, hmm?"

Our fire-sprite threw up his hands and shrugged. "Yeah, well...what can I say? I'm a sucker for a pretty set of cinders. You know what I mean?"

Right then a tree cleared its throat as we passed.

16 / Marshaling Our Forces

Breakfast and story-telling done, we packed up and got ready for the last leg of our trip. Apparently we had another ten miles to go before meeting Madame Seychelles again. That meant sending men ahead to make sure our way was clear and no more excitement waited for us. We had precious few healthy folks left. Nearly every one of the Redeemers had a battle wound or at least some aching body parts from running and fighting. I felt none too spry myself after tussling with the ogres. Even Romulus had taken a few bumps and bruises. That was saying something, since he didn't take damage like a normal human. He'd caught a club to the head back home on the day I'd found Jasper without showing so much as a scrape.

The good news was that Roberta was with us now. She and Matilda's saucy girls could keep their sharp eyes out for trouble in all directions. So close to the sea as we were, nobody would think twice about seeing so many seagulls. Roberta, though, had to fly in short bursts over less-inhabited areas, because seeing a bright red-and-blue parrot sure as heck would be cause for comment. Our brilliant pirate queen was the feathered equivalent of a hussar. She even matched Tyrell's uniform.

With as many busted-up boys as we had now, some transport was needed. Gloriana bought the use of the farmer's horse and wagon for the day, promising to return them by nightfall. I got the impression he didn't much care, since she paid him enough to buy a royal coach. Those who couldn't walk went into the back, pistols taken from the luckless cuirassiers loaded and kept just out of sight. Tyrell rode ahead of it in all of his splendid martial glory, gold braid just about blinding us. His plan to satisfy the curious was to explain that he was escorting wounded veterans of the Grand Armee home to their families.

I walked behind the wagon with Romulus, since I wanted to talk about what was going on. The Duke had wasted no time mooching a ride, which didn't surprise me any. Already he was napping. Ernie sat on my shoulder, knitting needle spear in one paw. That dopey little bicorn hat was still perched between his little ears. He didn't say where he'd gotten it and I didn't ask. It looked like Scorch had forgiven Tyrell for taking advantage of him earlier. Now the sprite fluttered around the cigar, feasting off its heat. Sha'ira, as usual, couldn't stay still. One minute she'd be off in the trees to the flank, checking for trouble. The next she'd glide on ahead or behind. Sometimes she'd hold up an arm and Roberta would swoop down onto it from out of nowhere to fill her in on what she'd reconnoitered.

"So, where we headed anyway?" I asked. "And am I likely to enjoy it?"

"A sort of a bolt-hole," Romulus answered, drinking from his wooden canteen. "A big one."

Ernie laughed at that. "A really big one."

"We has to cut east a bit," explained the big Marshal. "Take us out the trees. More open country fo' a ways. Exposed. But ain't no help fo' it."

The mouse near my ear licked his lips. "But it's through the vineyards. So that's a nice benefit."

Jasper perked up when he said that. "Grapes? Wine? Where?"

"Settle down, boyo," I warned him. "You ain't about to get hold of any more joy-juice. Yesterday's little escapade was plenty fer a while."

"Speak for yourself, spoilsport. I plan to enjoy my summer holiday in Gaulle. Folks pay good money to experience this. The sunshine, the peerless cuisine, the —"

"—The abductions, the monsters, the screamin'..."

"See? An adventure getaway. You don't get that sort of thing sittin' at home, you know."

"Actually, I seem to recall exactly that sort of thing back in Washington. Demons, Bullies, poop monsters. That's why we ran off with our tails between our legs."

"Like this?" My cup melted and reformed into a cute little toy metal pup. It yapped and scampered along my arm to lick me on my freckled pug nose. The tongue felt warm. I caught a whiff of brimstone and lily before the doggy bounded back the way it had come.

I snorted and shook my head. "Not hardly. Wasn't there a lot less happy-happy and a lot more dear-Lord-won't-you-save-me-now?"

Jasper hung himself back on my belt as a cup again. "If you refer to the unfortunate beaver incident, I was barely involved."

"I do, among others. Gettin' transmogrified into a giant hairy rodent weren't my idea of a fine ole time."

"Hey!" objected Ernie.

I winced a little. "Did I say that out loud?"

"You did," he informed me. "And we're dyin' to find out why."

"Just reminiscin' with you-know-who." I tapped my noggin with one finger.

"Ah! Relivin' the good old days, eh? Must be a simple task since you've had that bloody blade for all of what? Three whole weeks?"

"Yeah, but it seems so much longer."

Things went on like that for about two more miles. Jasper blabbered on, filling my head with silliness. Romulus wouldn't give me any details about where we were going or why. We left the forest just as he'd predicted, putting the sea to our backs and climbing a steepish hill. As we did so I turned back in that direction, thinking maybe I could see the *Kiss* out on the ocean. But we weren't high enough. She probably was far away from us anyhow. And Ma, too.

What I did spot, though, on a much larger height a good half mile away, was a funny wooden contraption atop a skinny limestone tower. It looked a little like a lighthouse, except that in place of the lamp it had a big ladder with a double-hinged horizontal crossbar on top of it. Each end resembled a long thin house shutter. One pointed straight up and the other hung down at an angle.

"What in tarnation is that thing?" I wanted to know.

"Optical telegraph," said Tyrell, trotting up on Alcibiades. "Splendid invention of the brothers Chappe."

"Looks like a broken-down windmill."

"It does, but by design." He gazed at it through his binoculars while I snuck an apple out of my knapsack and tossed it to the Valkyrie horse. "The varying arrangements of the vanes represent words, phrases, and such. Much like naval signal flags."

"Signaling to who?" I wondered aloud, recalling how we always seemed to be getting caught by somebody on this trip.

"The next tower in the chain, generally. There are dozens of them, all over Gaulle, put in place by the government to coordinate forces." His gloved hand shot out to the north, where another hill also had a tower. "See there? Far enough away that you need a telescope to read the message."

Having no telescope, I used my witched eyes instead. Just as he'd said, a signal station just like the one I'd wondered about clung to the peak of a hill miles away. Its vanes were being moved into a new position as we watched.

"Do you know the code?" I asked Tyrell.

He shook his busby. "No, the books are changed often for security. But they certainly are busy, aren't they?"

"Too busy fer my comfort. You think maybe that's how the

soldiers keep findin' us?"

"Perhaps. But they are useless at night. And slow for complex communications. So the coordination of our last battle was managed by some other means. Still..." Tyrell gave the towers another long examination, then turned to Romulus. "We should increase our pace. This country betrays our every move."

Romulus nodded and jogged up to the wagon to tell it to get a move on. Alcibiades finished his apple, winked at me, and carried his peacock of a rider far ahead to check in with the advance scouts. That gave me a chance to grill Ernie for information.

"Okay, spill the beans. Where are we goin' and what'll happen we get there? I'm tired o' ugly surprises."

"Parlay, that's what."

"A meetin'? With who?

"My boss." He looked around as if he might be eavesdropped on in the middle of the Gaullic countryside. "Tough old bird, she is. Don't get on her bad side, duckie. She'll have yer guts fer garters, she will."

"The head of the Equity's here? And she's a...she?" It seemed like the freedom fighters lined up against the Merchantry all had lady leaders. That made me kind of happy. Then again, the Assassins Guild was all women and that was no group you'd want to spend the holidays with.

"Old as the pyramids she is, and just as stony." He leaned down to whisper in my ear. "They say she posed for the Sphinx...the lion part."

I snorted at that, but who could say he was wrong? After all, Romulus had been a guard dog for the Roman Emperor Hadrian.

We all took a right turn at a crossroads and headed straight east. Church bells rang out the call to Sunday mass. Now the land flattened out some, though it still rolled enough to get your attention when walking. On every side of the dirt road unending rows of grape vines stretched, the greenery hanging on old wooden fence post affairs. From a distance the fields looked like a lush green pasture with big cat scratches in them. Red-tiled stone farmhouses were scattered around. This area looked to have more plants and less people than the coast. Only a few folks passed us on the road. Nobody gave a hoot about the wagonload of injured men, but plenty stopped to stare at Romulus. *Not a lotta colored folks hereabouts. Especially fellers the size of a shed. Shoulda thought about that, I suppose.*

Tyrell explained to the curious that Romulus was a mighty Eastern warrior who had left his army to join that of the Emperor. The little Gaulle's might had so impressed the giant that he'd begged to see the land which bred such men. Since nobody could have ever visited the land of the pharaohs to contradict this, people nodded and moved on. But when they did they tended to laugh as they went.

"What's so funny, I wonder?" I said, not paying a lot of attention. My mind kept thinking about the meeting to come.

Jasper was giggling like an idiot. "You didn't catch that?" His voice rose in glee. "Oh, boy! That made my day!"

"Yeah? Well, make mine, too. I could use some mirth."

"I doubt you'll see the entertainment value. Tyrell told 'em that you were the simple-minded jester boy sent by the Turkish sultan to keep up the homesick giant's spirits."

"Ha, ha, ha...ain't we a card?" I wanted to throw something at Tyrell, maybe Morphageus transformed into a whacking big anvil. Knock that silly bear rug off of his handsome head. Then I recalled how he'd taken that injury so I could be less a little less dead than otherwise. *I guess he can make a little joke if he has a mind to. But I'm keepin' score, mister.*

The fun and games petered out as we approached our destination. Coming over a rise, surrounded by plump purple grapes which resembled precious gems hanging in clumps, I caught sight of an honest-to-goodness castle. Not the scary fortress kind like Carrasco had in Iberion, but one like you'd expect in a fairy tale. Tall slender spires with pointed roofs. Whitewashed stone walls so clean and pure it blinded you to look at them in the summer sunshine. Tons of ornate scrollwork all around the windows and eaves that made it look like a whopping great wedding cake. A clear green moat covered in pale swans and baby ducks. I expected to see Lancelot and Guinevere come across the drawbridge on snowy horses covered in pastel fabric.

"Now that's what I call a proper castle," said Jasper. "You think they'll have any pigs roastin' in their hearth? Or maybe a whole ox? I'm famished."

"When ain't you famished?" I wanted to know. "The day that

happens is the day I put on a hoop skirt and fill out a dance card for a cotillion."

"I'd like to remind you that I spent eons underground, waitin' for your clumsy fingers to find me. I'm seventy-seven hundred thousand meals behind. And travelin' with you sure ain't helpin' me to catch up any."

I took the hint and reached into my rucksack for something yummy to fill the void. All three of our voids, actually, since you couldn't have any food in your hand without Ernie pouncing on it like a terrier on a rat. Since I was rummaging around while it was still on Romulus' back, that meant some for him, too. We all shared some biscuits and cider while admiring the lovely castle some more. The closer it got the prettier it became.

As we passed through the last vineyard before setting foot on the well-tended lawn of the place, I caught sight of several pairs of booted feet to either side, just visible below the vines. Not ordinary 1804 peasant boots, neither, but well-made 'my-life-depends-upon-them' fighting footwear. Some had spurs. I counted at least four bodies to my left and right, crouching out of sight. Naturally that made me nervous and suspicious, so I mentioned it to Ernie.

"They be Marshals of the Equity, missy," he said, words garbled by a hunk of biscuit. "You don't think we're gonna bring in our Grandmaster without security, do yer?"

"Sort o' obvious, though. If I can spot 'em right off then so can the Merchantry or anybody else with a pair o' eyes."

"These blokes are just the coarse filter. They scare off the amateurs. We've got plenty of hidden muscle about. Most of 'em ain't quite...human, if you catch me meanin'.'"

Right then a tree cleared its throat as we passed.

I really gotta remember that things ain't like I thought they was three weeks ago. Otherwise I may get ambushed by a hostile gooseberry bush one o' these days.

Romulus gave the tree a nod and made a complicated sign with the fingers of one hand. To anybody casually watching it would've just looked like he'd scratched his cheek. But it was some kind of signal to the tree, Marshal to Marshal. In seconds the root telegraph system would pass on the message that the famed Romulus was about to arrive. From tree to shrub via grass and weed, the alert would travel to whoever was in charge of the castle defenses. Nobody would interfere with us now.

As I marveled at the wonder of a building ahead an idea struck me. "Say, this is post-Revolutionary Gaulle. Ain't castles and palaces a thing o' the past? Didn't they tear 'em down and burn 'em and loot 'em?"

"Sometimes," Tyrell replied, reappearing on his golden horse. "Though the farther from Paris they were then the more likely to stay up. Pillaged, yes. This one was stripped to the walls by the locals." He jerked his head toward the wagon and smiled. "Its owner was no friend of the common man. But Bonaparte turned out to be a lover of all things royal, as you know. Emperors rarely live in shacks. Many chateaux were renovated and distributed to his family and favorites."

"So much fer bein' a man o' the people."

"Precisely why we founded the Coterie Redempteur, to save the Revolution from itself." He gazed into the distance as if he were back in his real time, before the Affluxion created this pretend version. "If only we could have managed it."

Obviously there was a story in that, but right then we passed through the castle gate. Tyrell shook his head of sour memories and urged Alcibiades, now back in his glorious golden coat, forward. I had my own bad recollections to face. The last time I'd been in a castle the lord had turned my friends into pigs and whaled away at them with an immense axe. It'd taken some sharp work and a whole bunch of magick to get out of that one alive. Getting cooped up in one again didn't exactly make me sing for joy.

The wagon stopped to wait for clearance to enter. When I got up to it I saw that the Duc du Evremonde looked as glum at the prospect of going in as I felt. It was easy to guess why. When I'd met him he'd been a prisoner, a slave, turning a spit in the kitchen of that other castle. I'd rescued him on a whim against the advice of Jasper and made a friend for life. He'd repaid me by tackling that nasty Falcon just as he'd been about to shoot me with a poison arrow.

"Hey, poochie," I said, rubbing one great dangling ear and feeding him a biscuit. "Lookin' mighty morose. Don't much like castles, huh?"

"Au contraire, little pup," he said, long nose sniffing the air. "I love castles. Particularly this one."

"Appreciator of swanky architecture, eh? Sure is purty."

"Non, that is not why, though you have an eye for beauty and proportion seldom seen in an untutored yokel."

"Um, thanks. I think."

"You are welcome, funny-looking biped. But as fine a structure as it is, I adore it for quite a different reason." The dog sighed as his chocolate-brown eyes swept over the whole place. "I cherish it because it is mine."

My eyebrows shot up into the brim of my straw hat. "Yer fibbin'!"

The Duke turned his noble houndy head to look at me like I was the poorest tenant on his estate. "Please...though I have stooped to falsehoods in the past – the prospect of a dance with Madame Guillotine made liars of us all – in this instance I have no need or inclination to indulge in storytelling. This edifice has been in my family since Henri IV." That head sagged. "And I lost it."

This must be the day fer Gaullic regrets. Tyrell and Evremonde may hate each other's guts over the Revolution, but they got that much in common.

The horse whinnied and with a lurch the wagon got into motion again. Alcibiades stood on the drawbridge waiting for it, his scarlet-and-gold popinjay rider posing atop him like somebody was about to paint his portrait. Seeing as how this was Equity territory, I figured Tyrell was making a show for his team. Al did his part, his coat shining like polished brass in the July sun. Roberta, a real popinjay in the old-timey sense of parrot, floated past him and through the main gate with an amused snort at his pretentiousness.

He led the wagon into the castle courtyard. Romulus, Ernie, and I strolled in right behind. My Marshal friends showed no signs of worry, but their leader was our host and they knew what to expect. Hard experience had taught me to keep a sharp eye out for trouble in new situations, especially trouble of the strange and witchy kind. But I sure got surprised this time.

Madame Seychelles greeted us with, "May I present Revered Equity Grandmaster Vigor?"

My eyes popped out. The Grandmaster was an adorable ten year-old girl.

"New Marshals shall join our ranks,
and the Coterie will expand."
"Ooh!" shouted Jasper. "You know what that means?"
I sighed, knowing what was coming. "Do tell."
He turned into a party hat with feet and did a little dance.
"Celebratin', that's what! Shakin' a leg, swingin' yer partner!
Probably with al-kee-hol!"

17 / A Vigor-ous Discussion

"You know," Jasper said, "I never cease to be amazed by your ability to run into the weirdest stuff possible, even when surrounded by talkin' pirate parrots and charmin' magick swords."

I couldn't disagree with him. "Yeah, it's a special gift I got. But look on the bright side. No poop monsters yet."

My cup turned into a hand and rapped its knuckles on my noggin. "Knock on wood."

Vigor grinned at everybody like she was at her birthday party. The ancient Grandmaster wore a pastel pink dress suitable for a respectable girl of 1804. Six inches shorter than me, she had curly hair, dark brown with a few blondish highlights, and one of her front teeth was missing. Her features were even and pale. Rosy-cheeked and bright-eyed, she was the cutest thing ever.

"Well met!" she said to us all, arms wide in greeting. She led us into the main hall. Her voice had an odd accent, seeming to be a blend of Gaullic, Britannic, and something exotic. Ernie had told me she was from the land of the pharaohs. Maybe that part stayed with her even if she'd witched her appearance to blend in with the locals.

"Hey," I whispered to Ernie, who still sat on my shoulder, "she looks pretty well-preserved fer bein' as old as you said she was. So, is it clean livin' and healthy food or what?"

"The last one. Or what. See that big silver ring on her finger, with the sparkly black jewel? She's a Sword-Bearer, like you."

"Really? Ain't likely to cut much with that thing."

"Says the girl with Morphageus on her hip as a tin cup. All magic swords can disguise their shape. Generally they're some kind of jewelry until called on. But they only have one false form. Yours is the only sword able to shape at will, and the only one with a life-force inside."

Jasper purred and turned himself into an engraved silver trophy. "That's because I'm special."

"I grunted at that. "You sure are. How'd I get so lucky?"

He pretended to be hurt. "So bitter at such a tender age. My self-worth is decaying from your sarcasm." The cup turned into a little moldering skeleton.

I left off talking to them because little Vigor was addressing us again. "Equity and Coterie Redempteur assembled under one roof in common cause against the great scourge. My old heart swells." She stepped closer to me, beaming like I was her long-lost sister. "And the new Stone Warden, as foretold!" Those clear brown eyes squinted as she looked me over. All conversation in the great hall ceased. I felt like a prize sow at auction. "Madame Seychelles, you were not guilty of exaggeration in your description of her."

While everybody laughed at the odd girl in the dirty bare feet, overalls, and battered straw hat, I showed a polite smile while considering the situation. Considering how pleased she seemed to be that the Redeemers had agreed to meet with her people I gathered that they had some bad blood between them. From the way Romulus and Ernie talked, and from hints dropped by Tyrell, the struggle against the Honourable Merchantry involved some considerable disagreement as to strategy, tactics, and even the whole point of the fight. Vigor and the Equity wanted the Proprietor's operation dead and gone, swept away and flushed down a sewer. The Grand Mage needed to be released from bondage and his magickal might restored. But the Redeemers hoped to capture the locomotive and use the power of the train for good. Breaking it up and selling the cars wasn't part of their plan.

Things might get dicey, Verity. Watch yer step. Don't be surprised if each side has its own twisted ideas about what to do with you.

Vigor announced, "Welcome to Ponteau, one of the great chateaux of Gaulle. Unoccupied since the Revolution, though thankfully spared demolition. We have the use of it for a few days, as it is due to be occupied soon by a favorite of the new Emperor."

A mournful howl drowned out anything she might've wanted

to say after that. All heads turned to stare at the saddest stumpy-legged old basset hound in existence. He slumped in a corner near the curving staircase, the absolute picture of wretched desolation. His floppy skin pooled around his backside as he sat there, snout to the sky, letting out all of his doggy misery.

"Sounds like somebody lost his best friend," Tyrell taunted, busby under one arm. He'd left Alcibiades outside with a feed bag on.

"Pretty near," I said, giving him a nasty look. Sliding up next to him, I jabbed him in the ribs with a sharp elbow. "Quit bein' mean. We got enough grief comin' at us as it is without addin' to it our own selves."

The doll-sized zombie in my hand lifted its head and stuck its decaying tongue at him before reforming into a cup again. Tyrell let out a sour laugh at my defense of Evremonde. "Grief? Someday you must let me tell you all about grief, and how that cur was responsible for much of it."

"Maybe that's true. And maybe that cuts both ways. Reality tends to sit in the middle of things, I've noticed."

He shook his head and eased away, making a point of not looking at the dog. I scratched the Duke under his floppy jowls. With all of our other troubles, this was the sort of thing I didn't need. *These two're gonna blow up one o' these days. Hope the shrapnel don't wreck our whole operation.*

The entry hall filled up with more people than just those of us from the *Penelope's Kiss* and our Redeemer captors/allies. Now the escort of Marshals joined us, along with more of Madame

Seychelles' crew. Apparently Gloriana's platoon had just been a small strike force. Prisme had brought plenty of others with her. And Vigor had obviously made sure she wasn't outnumbered.

Those numbers included the usual strangeness, of course. In fact, more than the usual, on both sides. Sure, we had a hound who used to be a Gaullic aristocrat, a two thousand year-old fellow who'd once been a dog himself, a parrot in spectacles, and a talking mouse wearing a Napoleonic hat, but that didn't put us in the running for Best Bunch of Oddities. Just a quick survey of the new arrivals showed me a stag with a monocle, two middle-aged women with elephant trunks, Siamese twins sharpening one knife between them, and a dark-skinned lady whose hair moved as if it was alive. Compared to that and much more in view, we represented the Dull-as-Ditchwater Freedom Fighters League.

"I'm guessin' most o' these folks use magick to look normal when they're on missions?" I asked Romulus in a whisper. I didn't want to offend anybody.

"Some," he answered. "Not so many as you'd suppose. They makes use o' dere diff'rences. Remember, they's some strange places now, since the Affluxion."

Looking at the trio of unicorn men, I guessed so. There seemed to be more unusual Marshals than Redeemers, which made sense. Vigor's group had been old when Hector was a pup and that was no figure of speech. They roamed all over the world trying to keep it from barbarity. And that meant operating in really bizarre new places because of the botched Merchantry spell that had warped reality. The Redeemers, though, had been created only a few decades before my time, responding to Napoleon's betrayal of the Revolution and the Merchantry's involvement in making that happen. So they probably tended to stay in Gaulle, especially since there was no real Empire now, not like in actual history.

Madame Seychelles herded us into the Great Hall like a bunch of wayward chicks. That gave me time to take in the architecture, which was something to see, let me tell you. Though the furnishings, tapestries, and such had been looted years before, somebody had cleaned the place up, probably to prepare for Napoleon's flunky to move in. Even bare-bones as it was, it sure got your attention. We passed by the biggest set of stairs I'd ever seen, wide enough to fit a pair of loaded army wagons side-by-side. It wound upwards as a complicated double-circular affair with white marble banisters thicker than my whole body. Hourglass-shaped pillars decorated its entire length.

Our group shuffled through a passageway into the hall where we'd be holding the meeting. Longer and wider than the hull of the *Kiss*, its curved ceiling was carved into deep square recesses full of relief sculptures of scenes from mythology. Since this was Gaulle, more than a few of them made me blush. *What is it with naked wrasslin' that thrills the grown-ups so much?* On the solid wall to my right were two ornate fireplaces tall enough for Romulus to stand up in and big enough across that you would've had to pack a lunch to walk from end to end. Neither was in use, since it was July. Each had a mantle you could play baseball on top of. The wall facing them was mostly glass, floor to ceiling. Eight of the most gigantic windows I'd ever seen filled it, broken up into dozens of leaded fragments like clear stained glass. In between were intricate stone decorations like you'd see in a cathedral, if you ignored the nude fauns and such. Covering every bit of empty space, mostly on the hearth wall and the ends, several hundred sets of antlers hung, like a crazed hunter's idea of coat hooks.

"I'm guessin' that stag with the monocle's a little less thrilled than everybody else about the venue change," said Jasper.

"It don't make me too happy none, either," I told him, screwing up my face at all of the ostentatious murder trophies.

The only furniture was a matched set of high-backed red-leather wing chairs at the far end. Vigor and Prisme plopped themselves there, the Equity Grandmaster's feet unable to touch the floor. Madame Seychelles just managed to get her boot heels there. Behind each of them stood several of their senior followers. Gloriana and Tyrell represented the Redeemers, along with some others I didn't know. Clustered next to tiny Vigor was a hard-edged set of folks, unshaven men and steely-eyed women. Most everybody on both sides wore some version of the clothes of the local era, though the social class varied quite a bit. Some looked like lords and some looked like impoverished peasants. Most were somewhere in between. None seemed like anybody you'd want to see on the other side of your sword.

"Tough bunch, hmm?" noted Jasper, turning into a rag doll

again and shaking in pretended terror. "This must be what all the Merchantry demons are doin' at the prospect of squarin' off with 'em."

"Laughin' till they piddle all over themselves would be my guess. Ain't never seen a demon or anybody else who worked fer the Proprietor do any tremblin'. Except maybe when talkin' to their boss. I imagine plenty o' that goes on."

"Then they must need a team of custodians for their board meetings." The rag doll melted into a little mop. "Tile floors would probably be a smart design choice."

"With good drains. 'Cause other fluids would cover his floor, too. Redder ones."

Seychelles raised a hand to quiet the murmur of conversation in the hall. Not everybody was talking to a telepathic magick sword. "If you please. We cannot afford to forestall our business. The enemy will doubtless soon notice both your absence from your accustomed spheres of influence and the unusual concentration of us in this vicinity. Therefore we ought to decamp before dark. Much must be decided. A great deal depends upon what paths we choose. And there are ceremonies to be held, as well. New Marshals shall join our ranks, and the Coterie will expand, as well."

"Ooh!" shouted Jasper, the mop's strands separating into tiny hands which clapped for joy. "You know what that means?"

I sighed, knowing what was coming. "Do tell."

He turned into a party hat with feet and did a little dance. "Celebratin', that's what! Shakin' a leg, swingin' your partner!

Probably with al-kee-hol!"

"Yeah, with the world hangin' in the balance and Tommy's life at stake, that's just what you would be thinkin' about."

Now Vigor was talking. I shut down Jasper's tomfoolery so I could listen. It was a dead certain thing that my life was about to get affected by the decisions of strangers. Again.

"We must take care not to let petty parochial interests trump our larger purpose," said the little girl who wasn't. That made a bunch of the Redeemers starts to grumble. "I do not mean 'petty' in a pejorative way, to belittle your cause, but in its sense of 'small,' al la petit. Pardon the Gaullic joke. Of course to the Coterie your goal of bringing down Bonaparte is all-important. In your position I would take the same attitude. It would be my life, and the life of my family and friends, at stake. All who live care for those closest to them first and foremost." Heads nodded all around the hall, both Redeemers and Equity.

She continued. "But, if you will excuse me, I am not in your position. Those who reared me and those whom I reared have been dead for nearly five millennia. Now my family are all who draw breath, be they in Britain, Egypt, America, India, Italy...or this dear France where we now are met." Some folks frowned at that. I was one of them. *What's she talkin' about?* She smiled and shrugged. "I do tend to fall back on the old names, what nations called themselves before the Affluxion. An old woman's prerogative, surely?"

A gruff voice from someplace in the hall called out, "It matters not what you call them. But it does matter that you and your

Marshals propose to abandon us to this puffed-up Corsican's sick ambitions. Did you not live through it the first time? You know what will happen if he isn't stopped now."

"Austerlitz!" shouted a bitter new voice. "Trafalgar!"

"Bloody Spain!" a third added. "The Russian debacle!"

More Gaulles added their opinions to the mix. Battle after battle, outrage after outrage filled the air. "Jena! Eylau! Friedland! Waterloo!" Soon the cries mingled into an echoing hubbub that gave me a headache. Just as I was about to turn Jasper into earmuffs Seychelles stood and stopped it all with a single gesture.

"Manners," she said in a voice that was both calm and piercing at the same time. "My children, you do yourselves no credit to behave thus. Nor do you reflect well on me."

With that a few dozen fists touched foreheads. When they had been kissed and shaken toward the sky, she nodded. "My thanks. You must be aware that the Lady Vigor is not ignorant of history. But neither is she uncaring of your plight. Let her speak, please."

That earned her respectful silence. Vigor smiled and spoke once more. "As I said, the world in its wonderful entirety is my family now. The Equity must safeguard and renew all of it. Permit me an analogy. If a mother protected her children from a hungry bear, would she hurl one to the beast in order to save the rest? Not knowing if that would assuage it or merely whet its appetite? Or would she slay the bear and preserve them all?"

Many heads nodded in understanding and agreement. The

Marshal with a bruin's head didn't join in. Once more the strangeness of my situation hit home. *Gee, you really gotta watch yer mouth around this crowd, huh?*

"This is the position in which I find myself. The Coterie Redempteur wishes the Stone Warden's aid, and that of the Equity, in overthrowing this new Emperor who is so very much like the old one. A copy of disturbing accuracy. Certainly the world, even as twisted as it now is, would be better off without him. Millions of lives would be saved. Untold wretchedness avoided." The Redeemers applauded in agreement. "But how do we know that this would come to pass? This awful Affluxion spell works with terrible effectiveness. You all have seen it. History is not easy to alter, is it? The inertia of settled events does not give up its power without a struggle. Rarely does any significant event unbend. And even then only because the Merchantry wishes it to, with few exceptions. Our efforts bear much less fruit.

"But say that this time you are successful. Bonaparte perishes. There is much rejoicing throughout the land. All well and good. But who is to say that this will bring improvement? Remember, the spell was never intended to remake history. That was an unintended consequence of the Merchantry mages' hubris, of not comprehending the new forces with which they toyed. No, the spell generates melancholy, misfortune, suffering, privation, destitution, violence...all that powers its black magick. The more war, the more sickness, the more crime, the greater the Merchantry's foul energies. So removing this

Napoleon may bring short-term benefits to you and yours; however, eventually the spell will reassert itself and bring another evil just as fiendish, if not more so."

That wasn't what the multitudes wanted to hear. The griping started up again. And once more the Directeur intervened. "Now, now, let her finish," admonished Prisme. "So impatient! Don't complain until you have true cause."

When the grumping had subsided Vigor said, "But though the outcome is uncertain, that need not prevent us from treating the illness even though it may reoccur. Despite my misgivings, gently battered by your good Directeur's verbal assaults, I have consented to lend the weight of my Equity Marshals to your cause."

That brought joyous shouting from the Redeemers, so long and so loud that I feared the saucy carvings in the enormous ceiling would loosen and fall onto my head. *There's a great way for yer grand quest to end. Clobbered on the noggin by a naked plaster satyr. Yippee! Won't that make fer a swell epitaph?*

Naturally, Jasper had some suggestions. "Let's see. 'Right here doth lie a luckless kid/Upon her brain a stone did skid.' Or maybe 'This poor dead kid needs a new hat/A naughty sculpture squashed her flat.' Good, huh? Byron couldn't do better."

"Naw, the second one don't scan. Keep yer day job. Which is protectin' me from imminent harm. So get to it."

He turned himself into a cast-iron chamber pot. I sighed, took off my hat, and jammed it onto my head, knowing that it was the only way to shut him up. The cheering throng around me kept up the noise, except for the nearest ones who elbowed their neighbors and pointed at the funny little girl in the unusual outfit. No big deal. I was used to it.

Vigor, frail though she seemed, stood on her chair and shouted them all into submission. "There is a caveat, however." Silence reigned again. "Two of them, actually. The first is that this offer shall not be repeated. We shall aid you against Bonaparte once only. If the Coterie fails, you face the consequences on your own."

Madame Seychelles nodded agreement. "That is all that we ask. Lend us your honest strength and we do not fear failure. And the second caveat?"

The little Grandmaster pointed her ringed finger at me. "The young Stone Warden must agree to the entire scheme."

*"That's right!" hollered Jasper, though nobody could
hear him but me. "Big Daddy's back in town!
Gonna thump me some dearth-demon butt
and then relax with a stogie and a beer."*

18 / A Challenge

Jasper hopped off my head into my hands and turned into a skull. The jaw dropped like a gallows trapdoor. "Whoa! When has **that** ever happened?"

My mouth felt like it was in the same position. "Uh...can't recall. I'm guessin' never."

Every head in the place turned to look at me. Some of those heads had the wrong number of eyes, but I was in no position to judge, only being half-human myself. Since I didn't know how common that knowledge was, I kept it to myself. My life had enough complications in it without adding inter-dimensional hybrid bigotry to the mix.

I gave the crowd a silly girlish finger-waggle of a wave. "Hey there, y'all! Name's Verity. Verity Sauveur. Pleased to meetcha."

That didn't reassure those who hadn't already known who I was. A lot of eyes rolled. Even more lips twisted with barely-contained laughter. Maybe they'd expected a nine foot-tall bearded giant with a halo, speaking words of thunder with blood dripping from his jaws.

"You know, I can make that happen," Jasper offered, "if it's a look you think you'd like. Only cost you a dozen licorice whips and two shots of that splendid Gaullic brandy."

"Yeah, I bet you'd love that. Me looking like somethin' out o' some mythology book, heavin' my guts out in this swanky castle."

"Well, I'm so bored! We haven't fled in terror or been attacked by unspeakable horrors for ages." *By ages I guess he means a whole day.*

I stuffed him into the back of my mind to concentrate on addressing the multitudes. It was easy to see why they had a low opinion of me. Most of them had spent years, or even centuries, learning their fighting arts while seeing their friends and loved ones done in by the Merchantry. Now I showed up, barefoot, not even a teenager yet, with three weeks of experience, expecting to give orders and lead the way against Napoleon and then the Proprietor. Shoot, I would've doubted me, too.

"Sorry I ain't in gleamin' armor. Not all that tall, neither. Heck, don't even have proper shoes on." I nodded at the two ladies at the head of the cavernous room, one old enough to be my great-granny and the other seemingly even younger than me. "But I'm of a mind to remind all y'all that Prisme and Vigor there don't exactly fit the mold, and I dare any of you to cross 'em." I headed in their direction, figuring that a little proximity and reflected glory couldn't hurt my cause. The mass of Redeemers and Marshals parted like I was Moses. *Well, that's a start, anyway. Hope this quest don't take forty years.*

When I got to the dais their chairs rested on I mounted it and turned, standing between them. After waiting a second or two to see if lightning might strike me for presumption, I spoke some more. "Whether y'all like it or not, I am the Stone Warden. I can tell you plain that I sure don't like it much myself, but I didn't get a vote. Three weeks ago I was playin' alongside the Potomac River in the capital of the States United, no idea in the world about magick or Redeemers or Marshals or Merchantry. Ignorance sure was bliss, that's fer darned sure."

That earned me a laugh that finally seemed to be more with me than at me. *There's progress, kiddo. Baby steps.*

"Unless they're just laughin' at yer Gaullic pronunciations," snickered Jasper.

"But here I am. People who know the lay o' the land say that I've been chosen, that the prophecy came true, though much too soon, and there's no getting' outta it. All I know is that I fell down a hole and ended up with this contrary old thing."

I raised my arm up as high as it'd go and willed Morphageus into its natural shape, the recurved black blade's fiery runes outshining the summer sunlight that poured through the hall's immense windows. Beneath my shirt the Legacy Stone turned as warm as a steam engine boiler. Those same disbelieving eyes and sneering mouths now betrayed their astonishment as the rumors were proven to be true. The Stone Warden did walk amongst them. And in her freckled fist she held the most powerful sword in two realities.

"That's right!" hollered Jasper, though nobody could hear

him but me, thankfully. "Big Daddy's back in town! Gonna thump me some dearth-demon butt and then relax with a stogie and a beer."

"Thanks fer ruinin' my big moment," I thought at him.

He made a raspberry sound. "Hey, girlie. It's my big moment, too, remember."

A broad shouldered fellow with a pointed blonde beard and matching long hair stepped out of the crowd. Unlike the others, clad in 1804 clothes, he wore a gray tunic, tall boots, and tight leggings. This Marshal looked like my perfect idea of Robin Hood. For all I knew that was precisely who he was. You couldn't laugh off any wild idea with this assembly.

"All very well, yes," he said in a voice like a conceited actor playing God. Britannic accent, too. *Geez, the guy's a walkin', talkin' cliché. Sure easy to look at, though.* "A splendid display. Let us grant that the girl is who she claims to be." He waved a hand at Prisme and Vigor. "Who you claim her to be. So what?" The burly vision looked around at his peers. "Strength without skill. Might without control. Power without perspective." When nobody responded he aimed a battle-scarred hand at me. "She's a mere infant! We trust the soul of the planet to...that?"

Any other time I might've been offended. Every five minutes some adult was second-guessing me, belittling me, scorning me. It got real old. But I'd expected it this time, given those who were attending this shindig, and had made up my mind to make an example of the first loud-mouth who popped off. That it was this oaf who was so full of himself just made me that much happier.

I'd been muttering a chant under my breath ever since he'd opened his handsome mouth. Ma had taught it to me the very day I'd left the *Kiss* to go on this trip. Magickal energies from my soul-store surged out of my feet, lifting me a few inches off of the dais. From experience I knew that my eyes were blazing with an unsettling white light that Morphageus and the Stone amplified. That explained why the cleverer folks moved away from the fair-haired fool. They knew what was coming. He'd been too busy talking to pay attention.

No sooner had the word 'that' left his lips than blue lightning corkscrewed down my arm and out of the end of the blade. It felt like working a marionette with hot vibrating piano strings. More complex than the heavy-handed force blasts I'd first learned to fling, this one wrapped around him like a great hand, picked him up by the scruff of his neck as a mama cat might do to her wayward kitten, and hung him on a big set of antlers above a fireplace. He dangled there like a terrified and huffy Christmas ornament.

Actually, I found myself in a similar predicament. The spell discharged, I lay sprawled across Madame Seychelles' lap, legs swinging over the dais, utterly worn out. Sweat ran down my face and every other part of me. I was as soaked as if I'd run a footrace in a fur coat. Bugs crawled all over my skin. Really, it was leftover vibration from calling up the spell, but that's what it felt like. With a wish I shrunk Morphageus back into a tin cup and just lay there, panting.

"Woo-eee!" yelled Jasper. "Now that's some quality witchery!

My little Verity is all grown up." He kept on in that vein but I faded him out. Other voices were trying to be heard. They all mingled together, but I could still pick them out if I tried.

"Did you see that? She **is** the one. That's certain."

"Irresponsible, discharging such force in a crowded hall."

"That'll teach Herkimer to spout off to strangers."

"She's twelve going on fifty if you ask me."

"Glad I didn't speak up like he did. Came near to it."

"But look at her. Drained. Exhausted from one spell. How could she fight an experienced demon or mage?"

Good point there. I won't be much use if I can't keep this up like Ma does.

Jasper butted into my thoughts again. "But you can, O Whipped One."

"Nonsense. I'm a wrung-out wash cloth, boyo."

"Wrung-out, my Aunt Fanny. That's just how your system's interpretin' the new effect. The novelty reads as depletion. Ignore it. Feed it back into your soul-store. And let the room recharge you. There's lots of support here. They want to believe in you, to cheer you, to follow you. Draw that in like a sponge sucks up water. Go on. You know how."

Another voice gave me a different motivation for moving. "Might I have my lap back, dearie?" asked Prisme. "I can't feel my feet."

"Oh! Um, sorry." I relaxed and let the warmth of the room's supportive feelings in. Jasper was right, I didn't have to be taught how, it just happened of its own accord. Hard to explain, though. It sort of felt like every pore in my skin became a mouth and breathed it all into my core. Two seconds later new energy puffed me up as if I'd had the most perfect night's sleep ever. The buzzing evaporated and I hopped onto my feet again, all perky and feisty.

Oh, boy. A body could get used to this.

Jasper laughed. "Think that's somethin'? Wait'll you straddle a Chauntline. That'll feel like steppin' on a nail compared to this."

With that charming image in my head I looked out at the hundred faces before me. Nobody so much as cleared a throat. Just rapt expectation. Clearly they were waiting for me to say something noble and inspiring. Since I'd just drank up their love to re-spark myself, that was the least I could do.

"Whee doggies, weren't that a thing, huh?" I cried, beaming. "Sorry about showin' off and all, but that there feller got my dander up, he did."

"That's your idea of noble and inspiring?" Jasper complained.

"Aw, hush yerself. A few of 'em are so full of bile I could feel it when I did the sponge thing. Need to play the hayseed until I can smoke 'em out. Maybe they'll underestimate me. Be easier to handle 'em that way."

Applause came my way. But not from the crowd. They were still absorbing the magick attack and my recovery. No, the clapping came from one set of hands only, and from high up the wall to my left. Still swinging from the antlers, Herkimer kept it up and boomed, "Bravo! That's more like it!"

When my audience predictably turned to see what he was up to, the strapping fellow yanked a dagger from his boot and slashed behind his head in one blurred motion. The antler tip holding his collar broke. Free to fall, he nimbly landed on the acre-sized fireplace mantle, then leaped forward, rolling in mid-air and ending up on the floor in a graceful pose I wouldn't have expected from so big a man. What didn't surprise me was the smug smirk and the wink he gave me before sticking the knife back in the boot.

"Pardon my boldness, Stone Warden, but hard experience has taught me to be wary of brash claims, particularly where magick and children are concerned." He strolled toward the dais with two-mile steps. "In the Scepter'd Isle many think they are called, but so few are chosen. Hard it is to watch little ones immolate themselves with energies they do not respect and are not qualified to wield." He paused. "Even worse is having to do it for them, when they can control the power but feel that they need heed no advice."

It didn't require any great mind-reading abilities to see that the last part applied to his own child. The pain, written in the sorrowful lines creasing his face, told me that as sure as if he'd bellowed it out loud. Herkimer had killed him or her to save others from undisciplined sorcery. I couldn't imagine how awful that must've felt.

"I don't fit either o' them descriptions," I announced, hopping off of the dais. "Morphageus ain't killed me yet. And my Ma is a Chauntline mage. She taught me the right and wrong o' magick.

How to rule it and not let it be the boss o' me."

"How admirable." We were nose-to-nose now, or at least nose to torso. "But there is more to being Stone Warden than blasting stumps with spells and scoring points on mortals. You were given the Morphageus. It comes in the form of a sword for a reason." He moved past me to another Marshal dressed as he was, one who wore a rapier from Shakespeare's time on his hip. With a nod to his fellow he plucked the long narrow blade from its scabbard. That made everybody near us skedaddle like there was a burning fuse at hand. In an eye blink we had twenty feet of empty space around us.

"You know," sighed Jasper, "I sort o' figured we'd be fightin' an enemy or two before long, but gettin' run through by our allies seems a bit much."

I twirled my tin cup while considering our situation. "Not sure how much of an ally this Herkimer is. He's an honest-to-goodness Marshal, so I gotta think he can't be a spy or a traitor. Ole Vigor seems real hard to fool that way."

"Unless this whole thing's been set up by the Proprietor. I wouldn't put it past the Merchantry to think long-term and put this guy in place decades ago, just in case he might get this chance."

"Gee, thanks fer reassurin' me, boyo."

"Hey, I calls 'em as I sees 'em."

"Yeah? Well, help me call this one a draw, at least."

Little Vigor stood, frowning. "Herkimer, have you lost your mind?"

He shook his long blonde locks and hefted his friend's sword. "Quite the contrary, m'lady. My thoughts are clear as a spring morn. Do you not see?" His voice raised to include the rest of the hall. "Am I the only one here who understands our predicament?" The wicked point of the rapier jabbed at me from ten feet away. "Our savior here has strong magick. That much must be conceded. But it is not enough. She must also do battle without such aid. What if her soul-store be depleted and no Chauntline be near? Will she then submit to a foe, or strive on with steel and flesh? Our future depends upon the answer, does it not?"

"Can you not see that she is a babe?" Vigor asked, stepping down and moving between us. "Selected by fate too soon. And not a moon has passed since. How can she fence against you, of all people? Have you no sense of fair play?"

Herkimer scoffed at that, despite her being his Grandmaster. "You say that to me, who lost my family to Merchantry treachery?" Shaking his head hard, he exposed the left side of his head. That ear was missing, sawn off with little delicacy. "I'm reminded of it every time I pass a looking glass. The enemy cares only for victory. None of its minions will balk at cutting her throat while she sleeps. You say she is not grown? Not ready?" The rapier swished the air in a figure-eight. "Then let me make her ready."

Madame Seychelles was on her feet now. "I shall not stand by and watch you butcher this girl just to make a point."

"If you coddle her now then my point is already made. Let us see what she is made of. Perhaps I will prove as wrong about her swordplay as I was about her magick." Vigor and Prisme exchanged looks as if they were talking to one another as Jasper and I did. A conversation sure seemed to be happening, one way or the other. "Come, come, I shan't carve her up. We shall play to first blood. A little pinking won't kill her."

I was really getting irked at everybody talking about me like I wasn't standing right there. Tugging at my maillon neck chain, I brought out the Legacy Stone. "Hey, y'all! Don't I get a vote? The way I see it, it's my decision. I'm the one who has this." I waved the tin cup, letting it grow into Morphageus again. "And this."

"You see!" cried Herkimer, grinning. "She matures already. You would have sold her short."

"And she'd already short enough," Jasper snickered.

"Har-dee-har-har-har," I shot back in my thoughts, already thinking ahead to the 'friendly' duel I'd walked into.

Vigor looked at me hard. "You need not agree to this. I can order it halted."

I pulled off my straw hat and tossed it to Romulus. For the first time I noticed that Sha'ira stood beside him. *Where'd she come from? I swear, she has more magick than she lets on.* "Naw, he's right. If I can't even handle a simple tussle like this, what business do I have goin' after Bonaparte or the Proprietor?"

"In that case, may you acquit yourself well," Seychelles said, appearing beside her. She held out both hands as if grasping a large invisible ball. "But let us not take unnecessary risks, eh?" Her hands outlined my head and body, all the way to my unwashed bare feet. A tightness settled over my skin, like after a bath with too much lye soap. Finished with me, she did the same to Herkimer. "This little spell will protect all of your vital areas. No mortal strike can pierce. Deep scratches on limbs are possible. Neither shall die through intent or mischance."

"But it'll still hurt like hell," Jasper cackled.

My mind stifled him and raced to ponder all of the variables. Herkimer was big, but that didn't mean he'd lack grace or speed. Assuming that could earn me a scar. I called up all of the fencing lessons I'd had in the past three weeks. One of the benefits of being half-Obverse, according to Ma, was being able to learn something after one exposure, perfectly. The Sage blood had evolved for that, so they could take in knowledge and wisdom hard and fast. To that end I'd been taught years' worth of stuff, all stored in my muscles for recall. Whether I'd make use of the right technique at the proper time, though, was something I'd have to figure out on my own.

Before worrying about that, I figured I'd work on his mind a little. Every little bit would help. I tucked the Stone back into my shirt and saluted him with my sword. "You're from the Scepter'd Isle, you say? I'm headed that way."

He returned my salute, adding a flourish. "Well I know it. That's why I'm here. I'm to be your guide once you arrive on our shores."

"Good to know. You obviously know how to handle a sword.

Who taught you?"

"Maestro Saviolo, primarily. Though I have studied with di Grassi and Fabris, as well."

I'd read about those fellows in my stage combat researches at the theatre. Now here I was about to fight somebody who'd been taught by them. Personally. It was like learning musical composition at Mozart's house. Careful, Verity. *Your chances just diminished quite a bit.*

"Impressive," I told him, meaning every word of it. "My tutelage has been more...informal."

Herkimer donned gloves and stretched out his lunging muscles. "How so?"

"I was taught by a buccaneer and a woman."

That made him smirk again. "Yes? Do I know these masters?"

"Perhaps. The one is Aloysius Pitcairn."

His eyes widened, though he hid it well. "Say you so? A worthy name indeed. And the lady?"

Time to spring the trap. "Just her," I told him casually, jerking my head at Sha'ira, scourge of the Assassins Guild, bane of demons, walking nightmare to all Merchantry soldiers. She bowed.

This time he couldn't hide his nerves. One eye twitched and he licked his lips. "Ah..."

And right then I lunged at him.

I punched his boy-bits with all my might. Air whooshed out of the man's lungs. The same happened with every other fellow in the room. Sympathetic ohh sounds followed.

19 / A Touch, a Touch...

I hoped to get inside his guard before he could react, but he had the reflexes of a rattlesnake. The same fangs, too. His blade deflected my thrust before my front foot even landed in its lunge. Wide open to his riposte, I flung my rear leg across and twisted my body while spanking at his blade. But he deceived the parry with a neat disengage and went for my leading thigh. Only a slap with my free hand saved me. Before he could turn that into a backhanded cut I lurched past him, spun, and came back on guard.

Well, there's that question answered. He sure can move quick considerin' he's the size of a warehouse. Take yer time and fight with yer brain, kiddo.

"This brain?" asked Jasper. "This very brain that I'm stuck in? That's your secret weapon? The gooey one with the tiny logic center?"

"Aw, stifle yerself. I'm busy and you ain't allowed to help. No magick fer this fight, remember?"

"Boring! Boring! Boring!" He let out an evil laugh. "Fine. If you need me, I'll be rummagin' through your girlish fantasies."

He was welcome to try. My fantasies were less girlish than a circus strongman's. At least it'd keep him from distracting me. I had plenty to keep me occupied without worrying about his antics. Herkimer was flirting with my blade, his point first on one side of it, then the other. Teasing. Probing for a weakness. While he did so I silently chanted a calming mantra and took stock of my advantages.

Though I wasn't to use spells, I still had the Stone and my own natural gifts from Ma and Pa. Nobody could expect me to set those aside, even if there was a way to manage it. So I had more speed and strength than a normal person. On top of that, my mind worked so fast that it almost slowed down time. And every skill I'd ever learned, every fight I'd ever been in, every experience I'd ever had, was right there ready to be made use of.

Including all those choreographed stage scenes with Tommy where Verity the Valiant overcame impossible odds. One in particular.

Oh, boy, that'd be swell if I can make it happen. It'll take some maneuverin', though. And luck.

At that instant I needed ability more than luck. Herkimer tried to use his bulk to bowl me over. He should've stuck with his speed and clever bladework. Somebody was always trying to overwhelm me with their size. I had a lot of practice countering that sort of predictable attack. Sha'ira had made a special point of showing me ways to redirect strength. So when Big, Blonde, and Smug cocked his arm back to deliver a horizontal cut-her-in-half stroke, I didn't flee. Instead, I slid straight into it, inside his arm.

His blade bit only air, far behind me. With Stone-strength I belted him a good one with the fat acorn-shaped pommel of Morphageus, since I was too close to use point or edge. I'd aimed for his head but he was so much taller than me that all I got was the meat of his shoulder. Still, it was a sturdy whack and he went flying. He'd have gone down if he hadn't collided with a clump of his fellow Marshals who were busy placing bets on our fight. From the sound of things the odds were about even.

I wish I had your confidence in me, fellers.

Pursuing, I flicked my point at his forearm to score first blood and end the fight. Herkimer had other ideas, of course. That impressive limb was long gone by the time my cut arrived. He glided to his left front, nearly dead even with my right side, twisted his palm to the sky, cocked his wrist as far as it could go, and tried to angle a thrust into my back. A nice idea, if I hadn't seen Commander Pitcairn punto reverso the demon captain of the Croatan. I turned my hip and parried him in tierce, grinning at the amazement on his face. It must have been his most dependable kill. With a croise' I stripped his sword from his hand and back-cut the shoulder to win. And I never had to use my sneaky Verity the Valiant move.

That had been the plan, anyways. I hadn't counted on him being nimble enough to dive beneath Morphageus in a forward roll. It took him out of danger but also away from his fallen sword. With a shrug I turned, keeping myself between him and his rapier, and saluted.

"I don't suppose you will be magnanimous and kick my sword over here, eh?" he asked with a sheepish grin.

I let him think for a second that I was about to consider doing just that. Then I shook my head. "As I recall, it ain't actually yer sword, is it? Wouldn't wanna scratch up that nice hilt on these rough flagstones here."

To the crowd he called out, "See? She's advancing her knowledge already. Never give up an advantage to a foe. You all know that." He reached a brawny hand into his boot to take out that long dagger he'd displayed before. Then he repeated that on the other side. "But you should also press that advantage before your opponent finds a way to even the odds."

Two knives. Ain't that just swell? Now I'm the one who has to stay away and he's the one who'll want to get inside.

That changed things. My three-foot blade was a help, sure, but he could deflect and hold it with one knife while slashing me with the other. Though the Stone and my natural gifts made me fast, probably quicker than Herkimer, I wasn't likely to last long with twice as many possibilities to defend against. And from the smug look on his face, he believed it, too.

"Shall we dance?" he inquired, like some rich lord trolling for a girlfriend at a ball. That really made me want to smack that smirk off of his handsome mug.

Then it struck me. *Never give up an advantage to a foe, he said. Guess I'll take him at his word, then.*

Roaring and feinting a big rush at him, I forced him to slide back a couple of steps to prepare a defense. As soon as he did, I backpedaled until my rear foot bumped into his fallen sword. *Ah! Hello, pretty!* Everybody around me laughed out loud when I picked it up, hefting it in my left hand. It weighed about three pounds. I wasn't used to that. Morphageus always weighed a few ounces only, never more than a single pound, no matter what form it took. But still, insurance was welcome, no matter what. Now the odds had shifted again...to me.

"My, my! You were right, Herk!" hollered the weapon's actual owner. "She's quite the apt pupil." Guffaws surrounded me as the gamblers scrambled to increase their bets.

The big Briton grimaced at that. One thing I've learned about all men, be they boys or old codgers, they sure have a powerful hatred of teasing, taunting, and humiliation. And I'd already served him a healthy dose of that with my spell. Now I was force-feeding him some more and he really didn't care for the taste. I hoped that would work in my favor, but it also made him unpredictable.

"So it would seem," he spat, advancing. "Time for a more advanced lesson."

He came at me like a determined freight train, gaining momentum until I could feel his tremendous strides thrumming up into my feet through the stone of the floor. Unlike before, though, he kept his head even though anger boiled in him. The daggers stayed in proper position, his eyes were clear and observant. It wouldn't be as easy this time to take advantage of his impetus. All of my lessons raced through my brain like pages in a flip-book of drawings. Several options offered themselves as he rushed at me. All of them, though, had the drawback of being predictable to somebody with his training and experience. So I did the one thing he'd never expect.

Nothing.

It some gumption to stand there, points drooping to the ground, while the fair-haired ox came at me like a runaway barrel down a ramp. My mouth went dry as a sandbox. A twitch in my leg started of its own accord and didn't want to stop. I was sure the whole assembly could hear my little heart banging away. This was either going to be the most satisfying ending to a duel ever or I was likely to need Tyrell to accept a couple of broken bones to go with that arm wound.

When Herkimer got to within three paces I finally raised my swords. But I didn't aim them at him. Didn't offer any attack or defense at all. Instead, I crossed the blades, hilt to hilt, and made a nice horizontal package of steel.

And tossed them to my determined opponent.

Against his will he stutter-stepped and caught them in the cradle of his astonished arms. The daggers fell as pure reflex made him latch onto the bundle of blades. Blood thumping in my ears, I dropped into the same split I'd done with Tommy at Ford's Theatre that day I'd found Jasper. My coveralls just let me do it. *So far, so good.* Before Herkimer could recover from his stroke I took him out of the fight as only a ruthless girl can: I punched his boy-bits with all of my might.

Just so you know, it hurts a girl to be hit there, too, but it seems to *mean* more to a boy, somehow.

Air whooshed out of the man's lungs. The same happened with every other fellow in the room. Sympathetic *ooh* sounds followed. Though I wasn't looking, I knew that all of their knees had collapsed inward. They always did. I scooted between Herkimer's legs just before the swords fell from his nerveless hands to clatter where I'd just been. Scooping up one of his own daggers, I climbed the man-mountain's back until my face was right next to his.

Then I smooched his cheek.

He gasped and shrugged me off like a horse does a fly. I landed on my feet, panting, sweating, and shaking. Herkimer reached up to the spot my lips had touched. His fingers came away bloody. The kiss had concealed the sting of his dagger's treacherous point, stinging him with a tiny quarter-inch cut.

Hey, first-blood is first-blood, right?

With a rumbling growl like the fiercest bear ever seen, the great Briton snatched me off my feet before I could react. Marshals and Redeemers alike cried out in alarm. Some rushed to rescue me, others actually drew weapons, all hollered to Herkimer to calm down. Those immense arms nearly crushed the life out of me, despite my Stone-strength. I dropped the dagger in shock. Just as I was about to call on Jasper to transform into a wolf trap and break his ankle, it struck me what was happening.

I was getting a big old warm hug.

Herkimer shook with laughter. It felt like I was sitting on the limb of some living tree as it guffawed. I have some experience with that sort of thing, you know. My would-be rescuers stopped in their tracks and looked at one another, frowning. On the dais, Madame Seychelles held a brass pistol contraption as strange as the ogre-slaying blunderbuss she'd had in the forest. Her mouth curved in a relieved smile as she saw what was happening. Beside her, Grandmaster Vigor gripped a long slender single-edged sword with a beautiful basket hilt. In its pommel was the jewel from the gaudy ring she'd worn, which was nowhere to be seen. She, too, nodded and relaxed.

"Have you ever seen the like?" boomed Herkimer, rubbing my rusty head. For once I didn't mind. "I declare, that was worth a fist to the bollocks, eh? And what a fist!" He returned my kiss to the cheek with interest, drawing it out and ending with a big lip smack. My stomach lurched as I shot up into the air. Before I knew it my backside rested on his shoulder, as secure as on any bench. His ham of a hand wrapped around my waist. The other arm rose to gain the attention of the bemused crowd.

"Miss Verity Sauveur is the one and true Stone Warden!" he announced, sounding really happy for a fellow who'd just taken one in the drawers. "I so testify to all assembled. Furthermore, let it be known that my heart and blade are hers until the one falls silent or the other shatters."

Nobody made a sound. A hundred pairs of eyes stared at us, but not a tongue moved. Herkimer's eyebrows collided with one another. "Am I to be alone in this pledge?" he bellowed.

That was all the urging they needed. A sea of arms, most with some sort of deadly device in hand, rose in agreement. And like with the sea, a great roar swept over us as eager throats bawled out their agreement with his declaration. Even stoic Romulus had his Bowie knife out, joining in. Soon it all became a ritualized chant: *Ver-i-ty! Ver-i-ty! Ver-i-ty!* Love and devotion hit me like a warm oven. That was different. Usually when somebody hollered my name like that it was because I'd gotten into a fight with Artie Radley at school or tied tin cans to a cat's tail.

This felt a lot better.

Herkimer marched me around, still on his shoulder. Hands reached up to touch me like I was some sort of holy relic. That changed things some. *Okay, now this is gettin' weird. I can just imagine what Sha'ira or Jasper'll say. Uh, come to think of it, where is the annoying Scimitar of Sarcasm?*

"Over here where you callously left me," he griped. "Jeez, one little impossible vanquishing and you forget your friends. That's alright. I'm used to it. I was stuck in a hole for a few thousand years, after all. What's a couple of minutes on a grimy Gaullic floor in an abandoned castle, trod upon by booted feet?"

"Aw, shush yer belly-achin', you. I swear, complainin' must be yer magick power." I craned my neck, hunting for the recurved blade with the twisting vine pommel. "Don't see you. Where you hidin' yerself?"

"Right where I fell, missy. Next to that other sword, the poor plain one with no mind of its own. A lousy conversationalist, by the way."

"Gee, a sword that don't jibber-jabber night and day? I should be so lucky. Hold on, I'm a-comin'." I slid down off of Herkimer's shoulder, accepting thumps on the back and worshipful grasps of my hand. It took a while to worm my way through the press of bodies, but eventually I got back to where the swords had dropped.

But only the unmagicked rapier was there. No Morphageus.

Not good, not good, not good! Losin' yer sacred magick talisman the very minute they all but found a religion around you ain't the way to impress the masses.

My witched eyes scoured the floor to see if somebody'd kicked the thing. With so many people milling around that was more than likely. An even greater possibility was that a helpful hand had picked it up for me. I spun all around, hunting for that good Samaritan, though why he'd have left Herkimer's weapon on the floor made little sense. Nothing doing. The longer I went without seeing Morphageus, the more suspicious I got that some Redeemer had gotten it into his fool head to try a little Stone Wardening for his cause. *Hope not. They say that the sword kills anybody who tries to use it except me.*

But would it? Really? Jasper said so, but I was never a hundred percent sure when he was joshing. Sometimes I got the impression that he'd go off with the first floozie who promised him candy and liquor. He was a boy, after all.

I saw no sign of my fancy-dancy Blade of Destiny. On the chance that somebody in the crowd was sneaking off with it, I got ready to turn it into something inconvenient, like a cranky porcupine. Jasper saw that thought in my mind and yelled,

"What're you doin'? I'm right here!"

"Like heck you are. I only see the one sword and you ain't it." I picked up Herkimer's borrowed rapier, figuring his friend would want it back. Those things were really expensive in their day. I doubted that he owned more than the one. *Hard to believe he ain't come to claim it.* With my hand on its hilt and my nose a foot from the floor, I saw a small gold coin wedged between two of the flagstones. On its face was an image of Napoleon with a wreath on his head, looking like some ancient Roman. Along the edge it read *Premiere Consul.*

As I squinted at it, the head of the newly-minted Emperor winked at me.

"Hey, toots! How ya doin'?" it said in Jasper's voice.

"Pretty good. I got me a pricey sword and a forty-franc gold piece. Things're lookin' up."

Just to remind me not to say stuff like that, when I tried to grab the coin somebody's toe banged into it and sent it rolling. With a grunt of disgust I hustled after it, sword reversed so I wouldn't poke somebody with it. Again I had to thread my way through the packed bunch of people, only this time I was bent over looking for the coin. New kicks kept it moving. Several times I bumped my head into indignant posteriors. In between my *excuse me's* and *beg yer pardon's* I tracked the darned thing's progress by listening to Jasper's thrilled "Whee!" noises.

Eventually I found him, lying at the foot of the dais after running into it. As I arrived he turned into a leaden toy Bonaparte and reeled about like he was drunk, babbling in a bad

Gaullic accent. "Mon Dieu! My royal progress, she was not in ze straight line. Ze Imperial head does ze wobblety-wobblety."

"Serves you right," I told him. "You could've stayed put as Morphageus."

He dropped the funny voice and turned into a tin cup again. "No, I couldn't. There were some people who looked at me with acquisitive eyes, like I was a barely-smoked cigar in a gutter."

"You sure? These are the true-blue cream of the crop, I hear."

"That's one theory. It might hold if we didn't know about Merchantry shape-shifters."

"Imposters? Spies?"

"If there aren't any then I'd think that the Proprietor's reputation is less than deserved."

He had a point. We hadn't managed to escape the eyes of the enemy at any time for the past three weeks. Our various pursuers had proven their ability to infiltrate nearly anyplace. There was no reason to think this chateau was any more secure than rural Virginia or the *Penelope's Kiss* or even my own dreams.

Madame Seychelles interrupted her whispered conversation with Grandmaster Vigor to give me a warm but puzzled smile. "You spend so much time frowning at your cup, dear. I'm reminded of sad dipsomaniacs who peer mournfully into their glasses."

Jasper asked, "Dipso-what? Hey, is she insultin' your cup?"

"Naw," I explained, "she's funnin' with me." To the Directeur I said, "If you could hear what he thinks is sparklin' wit you'd be mournful, too.

Vigor laughed like a schoolgirl, which was just what she looked like. She held up her hand to display the huge black jewel in her ring. The sword had vanished. "I expect so. Which is why I am glad that Stormbolt has no spirit of her own."

"Really? I thought all magick swords talked. But then, I've only met one until now."

"No, yours is...unique. In so many ways." She stood as the doors of the Great Hall creaked open. Her followers and Prisme's brought in tables, benches, and trays. "Ah! Luncheon. Splendid. Time to initiate new Marshals. I hope you are ready for your ceremony, Miss Verity."

"And what about the poop monsters? Every time I turn around sewage is walkin' upright and lumberin' after me. I swear, if it happens again I may never get the stink off me. That'll put a cramp in my marriage prospects."

20 / Verity Submits to Marshal Law

I must've looked like a goldfish to the girl, my eyes got so big. My open gaping mouth probably added to the effect. "Huh? What? Who?"

"Oh, that's really gonna convince 'em they made the right choice," Jasper snickered.

Vigor's lip twitched, but she politely avoided laughing at my ignorance. "Another surprise? Vexing, is it not?" She turned to eye Romulus and Ernie, who suddenly seemed very interested in the ceiling. "Gentlemen, is this how you train your charge? She claims not to know about her impending installation into our happy band. Have you an explanation for this lapse?"

Romulus hemmed and hawed for a minute, then gave up and pulled Ernie off of his great rock ledge of a shoulder. "Ernie here's the talker. I mostly just punch bad people."

The plump little mouse found himself dumped onto the back of Vigor's chair. He took off his silly bicorn hat and bowed. "Well, Grandmaster, we've 'ad a bloody awful time of it. First Venoma jumped us in the alley as soon as we came out o' that theatre, then there were Bullies, banestaffs, ravens, zombies. She weren't adjustin' none too well to her new status as it was. Every time it seemed like we'd have a minute or two to sit her down and show her the lay o' the land, so to speak, some new awful thing'd 'appen and off we'd run again."

Vigor understood him perfectly, since she was a Marshal herself. "So you couldn't spare any time at all to inform her that every Stone Warden is brought into the Equity as a matter of sensible policy and ancient tradition? Nor explain to her what that entails? Her duties, obligations, and privileges?"

Ernie looked like he wanted to climb into the nearest cesspool and hide, as that would be less miserable a fate than disappointing his Grandmaster. "The, um, short and pithy answer would be no, m'lady."

Vigor poked him in his round furry belly. "Short and pithy, indeed. Like a certain mini-Marshal I know. Your punishment shall be dire." She pursed her lips and considered, drawing it out to prolong his agony. "For the duration of this luncheon, you shall peel my grapes."

Sighing with relief, realizing she'd been playing with him the whole time, Ernie bowed again and bounded off on his new mission. I figured that Vigor might get one grape out of three, but she probably knew that already. Before she turned back to me I caught her winking at Romulus, who grinned, returned my straw hat, and headed off with Sha'ira, saying they would relieve some guards so those Marshals could eat.

"If I didn't know better." I said, "I'd almost think you set that whole thing up with Romulus beforehand just to mess with poor ole Ernie."

She feigned innocence. "Me? Sweet maiden that I am?" We both laughed at the same time. "I'm as old as the pyramids, honey. I bore easily. After the first thousand years you take your entertainment where you can find it."

"Then tell your ignorant new Stone Warden what's up with this initiation business. That should be a boatload o' laughs."

Her face grew serious at that. "Not so many as you might hope for. The bearers of Morphageus always wear the spurs of the Equity. Just as you are the hope for the world in this instance, we have always sustained that hope until it would be needed again."

"Wait a cotton-pickin' minute. Again? I ain't the first and only Stone Warden?"

"Heavens no. You are the twelfth. Why would you think that you are the first?"

I tapped my tin cup. "Because a certain somebody's been kind o' hintin' that I was." I recalled his mention of having served Joan of Arc. "Though he ain't too good at keepin' his story straight."

"Is that so? From what I've heard in past incarnations, that would be very much in character."

"You say there's been eleven others? Then what about that dumb prophecy? The one written by the world's worst poet. That sure sounds like I'm the particular chosen one."

"Oh, you are, believe me. For this crisis. And if you fail, there will not be a thirteenth bearer of Morphageus." From her grim expression I could tell that she wasn't joking this time.

"Ah...no pressure on yours truly, then." I frowned, thinking back to other stuff Jasper had said. "He claimed he'd been in the chamber where I found him for eons. Let on that I was the first to find him. Was he out-and-out lyin' about that?"

"Not necessarily. From what we have learned from the others, as well as the Grand Mage himself before his capture by the Proprietor, the sword's spirit remembers little of each previous incarnation. Shadow memories at best. It was intended that he would always have fealty to his current bearer. Less messy that way. The spell that put him in the sword makes that happen, though there are some... imperfections... in that magick."

"Imperfections? You mean errors, like with the Affluxion spell?"

"In a way, though not nearly so severe as that. But springing from the same source."

It hit me like a bright flash in a dim room. "The Obverse. He's partly from the Obverse. That's why everybody wants it, wants me, wants the Stone. All of us are half-breeds, split between the worlds. Somehow that makes us extra-powerful. And extra-dangerous."

"Well-reasoned. It all springs from your father, who dared to cross over and marry a mage from this side. It should have been a barren union, but the Sagestone changed the rules. You were the result. Blood of both, magick of both, able to twist the barrier that separates Obverse from Earth. Which means you can unmake the Affluxion spell and return the lost balance."

Ah...well, that give the Merchantry a great reason for wanting to get rid of me. And fer its enemies to want to use me fer their own ends. "Unmake? How?"

She shrugged. "Good question. That's for you to discover. Otherwise we'd have done it ourselves." Ernie scampered over, climbed onto her chair, bowed, and presented her a peeled grape.

"Swell. Seems like every time I figure out one thing, it leads to two new posers."

"Oh, that's just life. You don't have to be a baby Stone Warden to experience it. We all feel the same way. Even creaky old ladies like me." Coming from somebody who looked like she still slept with a dolly, that was pretty funny.

"Tell me, then, creaky old lady: who's this Proprietor anyway? What's he look like? How will I recognize him if he shows himself to me? I'm really gettin' tired of all the mystery."

"I wish I could help you there. But he uses magick to constantly change his appearance. Some say he has to, that his excessive employment of dark sorcery has warped his looks beyond even what a dearth-demon must endure. Others say that he just likes to play dress-up. Either way, it would naturally behoove a man so reviled, with so many bounties on his head, to remain disguised."

"Then I might've met him already and not even have known it?"

"Possibly. Though one would think that if that had happened, he'd have taken the opportunity to capture or slay you."

"I suppose so. But he strikes me as one o' them too-clever fellers who likes the sound of his own voice and gets a thrill from playin' games with people."

"As I said, after the first thousand years you take your entertainment where you can find it."

"He's been around a while, too, huh?" I thought of Romulus having guarded a Roman emperor and of Tyrell being in his nineties. And supposedly I wouldn't age, either, so long as I had Morphageus and the Stone. "A lot o' that goin' around."

"So I hear. It's not as much fun as people think it might be."

"What about Jasper? Morphageus, I mean. How old is he, really? Does anybody know?"

"Uncertain. And with the blending of the worlds, it may have little meaning. Time doesn't exist in the Obverse in quite the same way as here. It passes more quickly and more slowly, all at once. I don't pretend to understand the science of it. Gives me a headache."

"Jasper got serious once, in Virginia when I got the hypos and tried to throw the sword in the ocean. He stopped me, of course. But then he told me how he ended up inside Morphageus."

Vigor's eyes sparkled. Her interest was like a living thing. "He did? Truly? Tell me. Leave nothing out." She patted Prisme's chair, which was empty because the Directeur was lunching with her Redeemers. Tyrell and Gloriana were bending her ear, casting sneaky glances my way as they talked. I plopped my butt down and got comfy. It felt wonderful. *When was the last time you sat in a padded armchair? Before this whole quest started, at least. Boy, the things you miss when you're runnin' fer yer life.*

I told her the story just as Jasper had given it to me. It took some concentration, because watching everybody else stuff their faces with the local Gaullic cuisine made my tummy rumble something fierce. At times I worried that Vigor couldn't hear me talk over the noise. But I managed. She heard about Jasper being a new apprentice to a great sorcerer so long ago that he couldn't even tell me the year or the place. He hadn't even learned anything yet. Sweeping and mopping was all he'd been allowed to do. It'd been the other boy, the cruel blonde one with mismatched eyes – one blue, one green – who'd been the bright shining star. A dark star, though. Always savagely but secretly punching and abusing Jasper. A nasty, arrogant kid who thought he knew more than their master.

Then they came under some sort of awful magickal assault. That mean boy had vanished. The master tapped Jasper on the forehead with his ring finger, a ring with my Stone set into it. In an instant the poor boy's life-force had been forged into the sword, or the sword into him. That part was kind of vague. And he'd been waiting for me ever since, with a few detours, until the night I'd fallen through the floor of the Ford's Theatre basement and found him.

The Grandmaster of the Equity stared at me as if I were some holy scroll with the key to the universe. With all that had happened to me, I couldn't discount that. "Incredible! Two moons, you say? Recently eclipsed? And this master lived in the open desert? With this very Sagestone on his finger?" She shook her head in utter disbelief, like I'd told her Mr. Lincoln kept slaves. "Incredible!" she repeated.

"Why so?" That food was really calling to me now. If it got any worse I'd have to tie myself to a mast to resist it. I tried to catch Ernie's eye to tell him to bring me something.

"Because it proves that the Morphageus came from the Obverse to this world. Two moons which could eclipse at the same time. That's the Obverse for certain. An event that happens once in ten thousand years. Said to be a portent of world-changing events. Two worlds, in this instance. And the Grand Mage used to spend time in the Mondrahn Sahni, the Trackless Waste, to clear his mind and develop new magicks. This all makes sense. He put much of his new-wrought power into the boy-sword and hid it on this side. His ancient wisdom went into his ringstone, which he hid in plain sight in the library of your father, as an ordinary sagestone. That remained in the Obverse. Then he became a peripatetic wise man, traveling all over the Earth, but always remaining far away from both Morphageus and his old ring. It was only in the past few hundred years, around the time in which the Scepter'd Isle is now stuck, that he emerged from the shadows as the Grand Mage once more."

"And now he's a prisoner of the Merchantry? That's where they got the power to make the Affluxion?"

"So it would seem. It took them more than three centuries to arrange it. Even with most of his energies dispersed into the two talismans, he was more than a match for any cabal of mages on either world. That is why the worst elements of the Obverse made a pact with the Proprietor and his Merchantry ruffians. Only such an unnatural wedding of magicks could bring him down. But at such cost! The deals that were struck will bring only slavery, suffering, and death. And predictably, there has been a falling out. Such a partnership was bound to be unstable. Now we have strife between the various players."

"I know. Them various players are the ones who keep ambushin' us everyplace we go. It'd help if I knew who they all were and what they wanted."

She smiled and nodded toward the Directeur. "You mean apart from our esteemed allies-of-convenience in the Coterie Redempteur?"

"Yeah, I already knew about these guys. Well, I didn't know that they'd jump us and blackmail me into sendin' Napoleon off to would-be-Emperor-heaven."

"I feel the same way about that. But annoying as it is, it's preferable to doing without their aid. The Redeemer network in Gaulle is even more extensive than the Equity's. Madame Seychelles has many secret groups of partisans operating throughout the country. Even in Bonaparte's inner circle. Since the Coterie began with disaffected officers of the Corsican, it has always been able to call on old loyalties."

"I ain't too sure them old loyalties is likely to help 'em much if they insist on thinkin' they can turn the Merchantry to sweetness and light. Redeem it, as they say. That's just looney."

"Again I agree. But one can hardly expect them to take any other course. Remember, they had no difficulty following Bonaparte when he was First Consul, the Gaullic Emperor in all but name. Guillotining aristocratic opponents and peasants alike was all well and good when they were the beneficiaries and the executions were all of the 'right' sort of people. So long as they could plausibly convince themselves that they were on the side of the angels. But once he declared himself in his position for life and was found to have conspired with the Merchantry to make that secure, they began to see the handwriting on the proverbial wall. Thus the Redeemers were born, to overthrow him and the Proprietor both, then employ the magick of the Merchantry for the world's betterment."

"Don't they know that can never work? Them demons and such from the Obverse ain't gonna let 'em just jump into the driver's seat and take the reins. I hear tell that the whole point of the arrangement was to get shed of the controls and restraints they have on the other side. Ain't likely they'll just roll over and let the Redeemers undo that."

"We have told them so many times. Pleaded. Begged, even. Prisme will not listen. She is bound and determined to make Gaulle great but good, famed throughout the world for throwing down the Proprietor and returning everything to the way it was before."

"Except she still wants Gaulle on top of the heap."

"I fear so."

"Say...if the Redeemers get their way and undo the Affluxion spell, does that mean the world goes back to March 20, 1850? Will I be a newborn baby again? Will Pa come back? Or will all of this just stay the way it is, with the Merchantry powerless, and not get any worse?"

"No one knows. Whatever action is taken involves tremendous risk. There are groups who do not want us to succeed for that very reason. They fear that the whole world could be destroyed, that the extreme magical forces arrayed to hold the Affluxion spell in place could very well shatter the planet if interrupted. One of them, the Graue Adler, is more than willing to see you dead rather than take the chance that you will make things worse."

"Graue Adler sounds Teutonic." And my unfilled stomach sounded much the same.

"It us. They are from the Imperium Sacra, on Gaulle's eastern border, where it is 1642. Constant religious civil war there. The Thirty Years War. Life is somewhat less than precious. Beware the Gray Eagles. Your youth will not protect you, nor will the fact that you are a girl."

"I get the feelin' that they've already tried or you wouldn't bring 'em up."

"That they have. They engaged the Assassins Guild to take your head only days after you found the Morphageus. And they had no qualms about acquiring banestaffs to do it."

"Them three nasty ladies weren't just after Sha'ira then? I was what they was after?"

"Exactly. Though they didn't mind mixing business with pleasure, since the two of you were together. Not that they are interested in the Merchantry one way or the other. The Guild is politically neutral. It's bad economics for mercenaries to care about a cause."

"I been sleepin' with one eye open ever since that ruckus on the beach. From what I'm told, they don't quit just because they had one setback."

"No, they do not. Again, bad economics for hired swords to fail."

I lifted a hand and kept count on my fingers. "So, let's see, fer one we got the Honourable Merchantry of Esteemed Gentlemen. They want me in London so they can have me, the Stone, and Morphageus all in one tidy bundle."

"Apparently. But they are not monolithic. Some factions there do not want the Proprietor to get all of that in his hands. They fear his power will grow beyond their control."

"What? He has a Board of Directors to answer to?"

"He does. The Nine Factors. Though they give him a free hand in nearly everything, particularly after arranging the brilliant coup which brought them the Grand Mage, a majority of five can overrule him. At present there are three cliques of three, a most unstable arrangement. If two of them band together the Proprietor can be tamed."

"Unless he arranges an unfortunate accident or two."

"Well, the makeup of the Nine Factors has been known to change abruptly."

"I'm guessin' that these three little bands have their own troops, their own magick, and their own schemes. 'Cause nothin' gets nastier than office feuds."

"Of course. One is solidly with the Proprietor, another backs him but is lukewarm about it, and the other smiles and smiles while sharpening a knife for him. It is that last set, the Bitter Apples – named for their leader's family crest — that you must watch for. They sent the Furies to your ship. And they bought the services of the Hellfiend Legion to stop you."

"I knew somebody had. Heck, their vicious commander flat-out admitted it."

"The plan was to sequester you in the States United as a bargaining chip, far away from the Proprietor's grasp. If you were in his dungeon then they would be lost."

I raised up another finger. "So there's two. And the Redeemers makes three. They hope to use me as a weapon against Napoleon first, then the Merchantry, to somehow turn it into daisies and sunlight and cute little puppies. Who else?"

"The Obverse, of course. At least, those who were party to the inter-world arrangement with the Merchantry. Specifically, the most hated of the dearth-demons, House Shedim. Even in the Obverse they are loathed. You must understand, the Obverse is not some black monstrosity with boiling pits of blood and vampire bats carrying off children. By and large it is a pleasant place, not unlike your time, except that they use magick instead of machines. Like here, spells come from life or death, nature or suffering. The difference is that in the Obverse there is a penalty for dark magick. It twists the soul and body, so that all may see your guilt and shame. This was put in place by the Grand Mage, long ago. House Shedim, where Venoma comes from, would like to break that curse and rule over their world. To that end they spent centuries tracking the Grand Mage, learning where he hid his talismans, and negotiating with the Proprietor. At last their plan bore fruit, on the very night of your birth."

"So they sent the *Croatan* after me, and nearly cooked Ma in a stewpot. Real nice bunch."

"Well, they are demons. Human flesh temporarily dulls the pain."

"And what about the poop monsters? Every time I turn around sewage is walkin' upright and lumberin' after me. The Bullies spelled 'em up in Washington, twice, and my creepy aunt did it in Lusitania. I swear, if it happens again I may never get the smell off me. That'll put a cramp in my marriage prospects."
Uh-huh. Like you'll ever have any suitors, once word gets out about your not bein' entirely human and all. Plus, your dowry's a tin cup and loads o' disaster.

"It's an easy spell, believe it or not. And it disturbs humans in a particularly visceral way."

"And all the zombies? Is that easy, too? 'Cause my viscera really don't like them guys."

"A bit more complicated, but the same general rules apply. Animating dead tissue is similar to the magick you used on Herkimer. We call it a puppeteer charm. The variants are fascinating. You can learn to do it to vegetation, paintings, tattoos..."

"Swell. Next time I'm jumped by a gaggle o' sailors I'll give 'em what-fer." I spread my fingers. "Merchantry, Bitter Apples, House Shedim, Coterie Redempteur, Assassins Guild. There's one hand. Anybody else got it in fer poor little Verity? I wouldn't wanna insult anybody by omittin' em from my list."

"Just the Papal Fief. They have a particular issue with you."

"Aw, yer pullin' my leg! What's the Pope got to do with any o' this?"

"Remember, on the Great Boot it is 1508. Any and all witches must be stopped."

"Ain't that just peachy? And of course they got a happy band o' witch-hunters on my trail."

She shrugged and smiled. This was all getting to be a little ridiculous. "Satanem Laqueum. Satan's Snare. Apart from wanting to rid the world of witchcraft, the Papal Fief would rather the Affluxion Spell not be re-set. They rather enjoy their dominant position on the peninsula as it is."

"Have I run into these Satan's Lackeys fellers yet?"

"We believe not. They seem to prefer to operate in Europa, close to home. Despite the historical time differences, they have cells in nearly every nation: in traditional homes of the Church like Gaulle and Iberion, but even in Protestant Zeelant, the Scepter'd Isle, and the Cantons. Airlann and Scandia are uncertain, as their statuses are not historical. But we assume that Pope Julius has a presence there, as well. Otherwise suspected witches would flee there to hide."

"How will I know 'em if I see 'em?"

"Their initiation ritual includes a forearm brand: a cross with a sword blade for the bottom arm. Plus, they favor small pistol-gripped crossbows. Those fire some very clever types of ammunition. And they often disguise themselves as sailors, in order to watch the ports."

Well, crud. Now I'm gonna be suspicious o' every man on the **Kiss**. *Wait! What'd she say about a brand?*

As if she'd read my alarmed thoughts, Vigor laughed. "Don't worry. Your Equity rite involves no pain, scarring, or even embarrassment. Unless you count being in the same club as Master Ernest here."

The stout mouse had just handed her another peeled grape. He made a sour face with his whiskered snout. "Quite right. The embarrassment only 'appens after you get confirmed."

Watching him go, it occurred to me that my aunt had made a serious accusation against him when we'd cornered her in that statue in Cumae. I asked the Grandmaster about that, and also about who Regan might be working for.

"That I do not yet know. If I had to guess I'd say the Bitter Apples. She is the sort of agent they would employ. A rogue with no ties to anyone else and personal animosity to drive her. But she might just as easily be in the Proprietor's employ, as a safeguard in case your will to rescue your friend Tommy should falter. After all, if you harden your heart and decide not to go to London, the Merchantry loses this hand."

"Ain't much chance o' that. Unless he ain't even there. I don't have no certain knowledge that he is, except that Venoma said so. Don't recall her nose runnin', so she told the truth at the Washington Monument, but that don't mean she weren't overruled later."

"The Equity will endeavor to confirm that he is, indeed, in the Proprietor's hands before you cross the water. His personal control. Since a scion of House Shedim took him, it is always possible that a double game is being played." She looked at Ernie, standing on the lunch table and tugging at another purple grape on the bunch. My hound lay just below, hoping something would fall into his drooly jaws. "As for your diminutive friend there, Regan told the truth. Partly, as is her wont. He did, in fact, betray the Equity once."

"Yeah? I can't hardly believe that of him. He's saved my bacon more times than I can count."

"This was long ago, though the guilt still tears at his soul. As you know, he was human. A Yeoman Warder at the Tower of London. Ravenmaster, in fact. When a Merchantry spy tried to suborn him into helping steal the Crown Jewels by substituting their ravens for the King's, he alerted the authorities and foiled the plot. He has hated ravens ever since. In revenge, a curse-bomb was mailed to him. When he opened it, he was permanently transformed into a mouse. Only the Proprietor himself or the Grand Mage can reverse the spell."

"Sounds to me like he's a hero, not a villain."

"At that point, yes. But the Merchantry is expert at vengeance. They did not stop there. His beloved wife Millie was poisoned. Typhoid in her sewing basket. She pricked her finger on a needle and the fever began. A Merchantry minion made it very clear that if Ernie did not aid them in another foul plot she would certainly die. But if he gave good service then her health would be restored. Certain incriminating Equity documents had to be purloined. In a torment of indecision he hesitated until the last moment, then snuck in by a drain pipe through which no human could have passed and stole the papers."

"That's awful. No way out then?"

"None. Who could have been so callous as to make any other choice? Alas, it was for naught. After he delivered the packet and demanded the salvation of Millie, the Proprietor's man laughed and declared that traitors were in no position to make demands. She passed away that very night. In his new cursed form, Ernie couldn't even hold her in his arms as she died."

Poor little feller. Havin' to live with that on his conscience. If it'd been me I'd have lost my mind. "I hope he at least tracked that scum down and got even with him."

"Alas, no. Though the spy did not survive the night either, Ernie did not have the satisfaction of dispatching him. That happened in the Proprietor's office, when our security spell activated and consumed the man in fiery boils. Took thirty seconds. We've never had a file stolen since."

"Any other time I'd feel sick to my stomach, but I'm so starved my belly ain't payin' attention to anything except that heap o' vittles there."

Vigor stood, apologetic. "What have I been doing? Rambling

on so and my new inductee wasting away. By all means, go. Feed until you burst. One never knows when another meal as fine may come our way. The times are uncertain, are they not?"

I headed for the table, my tummy empty but my mind full. I'd asked to be told what the score was and I'd gotten it in spades. Now I had to find a way to use it all and stay alive. Tommy waited.

With a pat I woke up the Duke. Several pats, actually.
Basset hounds have a lot of inertia to overcome.

21 / Tyrell Redeemed

I attacked that table of goodies like it was all of the nasty enemies Vigor had just told me about. Cheese fell to my wrath, bread surrendered, meat and fish begged for mercy. Even when my hollow belly had become a solid and swollen keg of happiness I still stuffed more yummies into my overalls and under my hat. Ernie even lost his unpeeled grapes to my gluttony. When I got my knapsack back from Romulus I'd stash it all away. During my culinary massacre Jasper, who hadn't said boo the whole time the Grandmaster had been explaining life to me, kept up nonstop squeals of delight that bordered on the obscene.

"Oh, oh! Is that brie? Howdy, God! I've died and gone to heaven!" was a typical expression. I sort of felt the same way myself.

"If this is the way the Equity usually eats I'm more'n happy to join their ranks," I told him, jamming black bread with honey into my face.

"Same here. Your magick sword will defend their larder till the last trumpet." With that the tin cup turned into a bugle and scared the beejeezus out of half of the seasoned fighters by blaring out a cavalry call that made dust fall from the ceiling. The Duc du Evremonde tried to run off in three directions at once. Scorch lit out like a Congreve rocket, landing on a mantle and glaring at us.

"Sorry, folks! Jasper's just expressing his appreciation for this banquet. Our compliments to the chef."

"I'm here to tell you," he said in my thoughts, "you're pickin' up enough witchery points right now to lasso the moon, girlie. Though I actually oughta dock you for not tellin' me what Gaullic cuisine was like. Holy Hannah!"

"Hey, it ain't like I ever been here before to find out."

"Well, now that we made it here, we ain't ever leavin'. This is too good to give up."

"Aw, you know we hafta go to London to get Tommy outta lockup. "

"I suppose so. But let's be optimists. Maybe Britannic food is just as good as this."

I didn't have the heart to tell him, folks.

In a big chapel just off of the Great Hall they'd laid out some pallets in a corner. Those of us who needed naps and didn't have to pull guard duty or to prepare the initiation ceremony got to snooze some. After finding Romulus out front, retrieving my pack, and dumping my filched food inside I flopped my weary bones down for two blessed hours of sleep. For a pillow I had my fragrant hound, who'd never met a nap he hadn't liked. Beside me lay the Elizabethan rapier, still unclaimed. Though I'd looked all over I hadn't spotted Herkimer's friend to return it to him.

That horrid dream didn't come back to assault me again. Apparently smacking Venoma and her friends around the night before had left an impression on House Shedim. The trouble was that I expected them to try that much harder the next time. And I wouldn't have the advantage of surprise anymore. So I expected plenty of tossing and turning come nightfall.

Nothin' like the likelihood o' getting' butchered by yer own nightmares to keep you up at night. Might have to get Sha'ira's help again. There's probably special tactics and rules fer dream-battles. Maybe we can link up while we're both asleep and she could help me. That'd scare the pants off o' ole Venoma...if she ever wore any.

Waking up around two o'clock, to judge by the sun's angle, the first thing I saw was Tyrell's boots with the fancy-dancy spurs. The rowels were gold suns and looked brand-new. I doubted he'd ever been dumb enough to jab them into Alcibiades with any regularity. Getting bucked off in flight would have more than the usual consequences. He sat on the floor beside me, brushing his just-polished toes until you could almost see yourself in them.

"You snore adorably," he told me. "I wanted to hug you and make goo-goo noises."

I yawned and stretched. "It's a special magick power only granted to Stone Wardens."

"Hopefully not the only one. Bonaparte is well-protected, and by much more than muskets and sabers." He pocketed the brush and stood, busby under one arm.

"Yeah, Vigor told me he made a pact with the Merchantry to secure his flanks. That's why you want to do him in? Fer conspirin' with the real enemy?"

"Do we need a reason besides him being just another ruthless despot? Come along, you need to get ready for your initiation."

With a pat I woke up the Duke. Several pats, actually. Basset hounds have a lot of inertia to overcome. "I'll be plain. The little Grandmaster don't think too highly o' yer motives. Says you Redeemers didn't mind him squashin' the Revolution so long as you officers benefitted from the new arrangement. But when he threw in with the Proprietor you saw he didn't necessarily need y'all."

To reinforce my point the hound's great pink bath mat of a tongue slobbered all over Tyrell's perfect boots, ruining the shine. I swear the dog let out a snide chuckle while he did it. I suppose you take your aristocratic vengeance however you can. The hussar must've been worked up by my accusation, because he saw that and just shrugged.

"You think it's that simple? That we're just a bunch of spiteful louts looking to get even with our boss?" He held up his left arm as high as he could in its sling. "This hurts like the devil, I'll have you know."

I'd figured he'd try to guilt me into dropping the subject. "I do know. And thank you kindly fer preservin' my life. It weren't the first time you done it. But that's sort o' yer job, ain't it? Yer group needs me. It don't necessarily mean that Captain Tyrell's a particularly nice feller."

His face darkened with a painful memory. "No, he isn't. He threw in his lot with a man who offered salvation but delivered hell. Played the boy and his friends for fools. They watched the Revolution collapse under its own weight. Factions with their own agendas slew one another in the name of political purity. The Paris mob would cheer a man to the rafters one day and cheer his executioner the next. We kept the guillotine so busy that the basket-makers died of overwork. Civil war racked the nation. Half the armies of Europa marched for our borders to restore the detested monarchy. Mother Gaulle soaked up so much blood that our shoes squished when we walked across her. We were exhausted. Is it any wonder that we embraced the first stout fellow on horseback who promised to make it stop?"

Tyrell shook his head. "The list of my crimes would raise the price of printer's ink. All committed in the name of duty – so I told myself. Men can rationalize anything, I've learned. Theft, murder, extortion, kidnapping, enslavement. I participated in those, and worse. My specialty was trumping up duels against Bonaparte's enemies. Though the term acquired a disturbing looseness as time went on. Pistol or blade, it made no difference. I laid them in their graves. Genteel assassination is all it was. Took to drink, I did. Of course that made me even less of a gentleman.

"Oh, I tried to better myself. But I didn't leave the Army or Bonaparte. One can know oneself to be a blackguard, hate oneself for it, and still continue the offenses. My grand attempt to atone for it all was to take a wife. The widow of an innocent man I'd killed in one of those sham duels. He'd published some minor complaint about the Corsican. Got himself on the wrong column of a sheet of paper in some Ministry. Poor fellow hardly knew which end of the gun to hold. Upset me so much my aim suffered. Took him a week to die of gangrene."

Why's he blurtin' this out? This was a lot more than I'd bargained for. But I needed to hear it. It looked like getting grabbed by the Redeemers was the best thing that had happened to me in a while. I was finding out all sorts of handy stuff. "So you married your victim's wife? How on earth did you manage that?"

"With more mendacity. Nd false repentance, pretended remorse. That and a hussar's uniform accomplished this marvel. And thus I entered holy matrimony, lying through my teeth. What a fine way to achieve wedded bliss, eh?"

I thought I could see where this was headed. "But..."

He threw up his hands. "It worked. Against all logic we were happy. I foreswore my former avocation and returned to strictly military duty. Genevieve undertook my redemption. One day at a time, our past notwithstanding, life conquered death. Never had I known such peace. For ten months. Then..." He trailed off into the darkest of silences.

"You lost her, huh?"

"In childbirth. So common. So ordinary. A daily occurrence, yes? But I took it as a sign that my deeds had cursed me. Only the baby prevented me from committing more atrocities."

Baby? He has a kid? "The child survived. That's nice."

"It was. For six weeks. She'd been born weak. A heart defect, I think. I knew that she couldn't last, but every day that I was permitted to hold that tiny wriggling red-haired bauble was a black patch scrubbed from my soul."

Hold on. Red-haired, did he say? "So that's why you keep bailin' me outta trouble. I remind you o' her." *So he'd had a good heart-felt reason to take my ogre wound in the forest.*

A tear trickled down his cheek until his dark moustache absorbed it. "She snored adorably. I would hug her and make goo-goo noises."

That was my cue. I put my arms around him and squeezed. He wasn't my real Pa, but he was here. "I'm supposed to be takin' you to task, not comfortin' you."

"You've comforted me every day since I met you. I shamelessly pretend she's grown up and is helping me save the world."

Jasper chimed in. I'd been expecting him to. "Should I turn myself into a hanky so you two can dab your eyes? Or maybe a sad violin, for mood music?"

"Aw, stifle yerself. This beats poop monsters any day."

"Yeah, if he ain't playin' you for a sucker."

I slung my pack over one shoulder. The hound had vanished. I imagined he was off someplace, gloating over his enemy's misfortune. "Did you found the Redeemers after that?"

"I did. I vowed, we vowed, to do whatever we could,

consistent with our honor, to atone for our support of the First Consul. Gloriana stood with me that day, and Prisme, who is my age, actually. She thinks her orders carry more weight with that gray hair. You know, she rarely uses magick, despite being good at it. A Merchantry mage spelled her family into oblivion. That's why she loves her gadgetry so much."

"But she gave you your permanent youth, right? And your sister, too?"

"As a practical matter. We need health and energy to perform our missions. Most of the others chose not to do that, out of hatred for the Proprietor and the Obverse."

We left the chapel and returned to the Great Hall. I still wasn't happy about him setting me up to be captured, but his confession threw a whole new light on that. And on his treatment of me. Since Gloriana had been bound and determined to go after me, he'd participated to make sure I hadn't gotten hurt in the process. It was a little creepy, having a guardian angel who was old as the States United, with a daddy fixation and wagonloads of guilt. *A girl could do worse, though. And with so many homicidal groups after me, I oughta be thankful for whoever I can get on my side.*

I vowed to find a way to work on him and Madame Seychelles, all subtle-like, to get them to see that the Redeemers' belief that they could assume the Proprietor's power and make a happy, joyous, peaceful world with it would never work. For one, that energy came from death and disease and madness. Nothing good could come of it. Whatever spell you cast would pervert whatever it touched, no matter how nice it seemed at first. For another, the demons would never let it happen. Unless we found a way to destroy them along with the Merchantry, they could always hide in their true world and plot more mischief. Even if we freed the Grand Mage and he helped us go after House Shedim and its allies, the Coterie Redempteur's cherished goal would die.

"And just how is Verity the Valiant plannin' to accomplish all of this subtle schemin'?" Jasper wanted to know. "My experience so far has been of you blowin' up powder sheds, openin' up the gates of Hades, rampagin' around an Obverse ship whackin' body parts off o' monsters..."

"Okay, okay, okay, I get yer point. I'll have to cogitate on that. Take some lessons from Ma and Sha'ira, maybe. Or Pitcairn. Learn how to nudge and not shove."

"Let me know when you plan to start. I wanna sell tickets."

"You know, maybe my cosmically-charged magick penknife could try to be more supportive. That'd help loads."

Our gripe session got interrupted by the dark-skinned lady Marshal with the living hair. Her four-foot-long black locks fascinated me, seeing as how I kept my hair almost boy-short. Like I'd imagine Medusa's snakes would behave, thick plaits moved on their own. It sort of looked as if she were underwater and currents disturbed them. Sometimes they'd rearrange themselves and playfully bat at one another. At other times, the whole thing would settle down as if it was just normal glossy hair and hang loose down her back.

"I'm starin', ain't I?" I said. "Sorry. That ain't polite."

"Think nothing of it," she told me with a warm smile. "I well know it is a strange and fascinating sight."

"Yeah," snickered Jasper. "She looks like she's wearin' an octopus on her head."

"Shush, you," I thought at him. "Can't you be nice at least once?" To the lovely lady I said, "I think I'm just jealous 'cause I ain't got much hair." I took off my straw hat to show her.

Her big brown eyes widened. "You have little cause for envy, little one. Though it be short, it glistens like bronze at sunset. What a treasure!"

That made me feel better. "I'm Verity, by the way. I'm responsible fer this mess, I suppose."

She dipped her head a fraction of an inch. "I am called Dymastis. I am most happy to meet you."

"Are you Hellene? Your name and accent sound like some I heard in Lusitania."

"Your ear is good. I am, indeed, from Hellas, though not from Lusitania, but the homeland. Phocis, near Delphi."

"Does everybody there have hair like yours?"

She smiled at that and let it float free again. "Oh, no. I am decidedly in the minority. I am a wood nymph."

Now I was really jealous. *A goddess. Yeah, that would explain why she's so pretty it hurts to look at her. No snub nose or freckles on that amazin' face. And they must've used her body to design them statues. That Empire dress don't hide her charms much.*

On cue Jasper said, "Hurts to look at her? Speak for yourself. Whoo-ee!"

"Do I have to get a dog muzzle fer you? Down, boy!"

"I am your mentor for the ceremony," the goddess informed me. Dymastis waved me toward the dais. Nobody was there now. In fact, other than three nervous young lads who were also about to be made Marshals, the enormous room was empty. Those fellows crept over to stand behind me and hear what was expected of us. *It better not involve gettin' wet, gettin' naked, or gettin' drunk or I'll make the biggest stink you ever heard.*

"Hey, missy, don't I get a vote?" Jasper protested.

"Absolutely not. I already know yer opinion o' all three o' them indignities."

"Indignities?! You mean glorious opportunities. You are just about the dullest girl ever, you know that? I'm ashamed to call you my bearer."

"Yeah, well shame is exactly what I'm worried about, so you can just get all o' that outta yer perverted little spirit-mind."

He faded out, grumpy and pouty. Tyrell also left as soon as the nymph took over Verity-watching duty. She explained what was expected of us at our initiation, only two hours away. It was easy to listen to her. On top of her inhuman beauty her voice sounded like the low notes on a wind chime, with lyre accompaniment by a muse. The hair only danced a little bit, like it was in a soft breeze, so as not to distract us. As a girl I had some immunity to her charms. What agonies the three boys were going through I could only guess. I did notice that she had to repeat a lot of her instructions to them.

To my great relief our tasks were simple, understandable, and free of obvious humiliation, except for the chance of forgetting our assigned bits of the ceremony. Some marching around, some call-and-response, that sort of thing. It was like what I'd heard a lodge induction was like. Lots of pompous ritual designed to bring us into the fold and believe that we were part of something important. Since I had the advantage of being part Obverse Sage, quite apart from my Stone-aided brain, I memorized it all in nothing flat. The love-addled men-folk took a bit longer. But eventually they, too, declared that they had it down and headed out, sighing for Dymastis as they left.

"I expect you get a lotta that, huh?" I asked her, dropping my backside into one of the chairs so I could reach into the rucksack. Jasper was already claiming hunger pangs and I needed to eat something on his behalf.

"It is fairly incessant, yes. But it comes with being a goddess." She knelt beside me and had her amazing hair hold open my pack to make it easier to search for goodies. "We survive on love and attention from mortals. So complaining about it would not only be uncharitable but suicidal."

I found a bread roll and a jar of honey. "How does a wood nymph from Hellas end up bein' a Marshal o' the Equity? Ain't you tied to yer grove or whatever?"

"Until the Affluxion, yes. Then the bonds of men and gods were burst apart. That is why you have encountered so many of us in your adventures so far."

I recalled the attack on the *Kiss* by a flock of angry Furies with muskets. Deep in my pack I still had the pectoral gem from one of them. It might come in handy one of these days. "Yeah, nothin' like bein' personally challenged by Dionysus to make you wish you'd stayed home."

That made her laugh, a beautiful melody that sent chills up my back. It had a different effect on Jasper, but I shut him up. "I can well imagine. Though when all was said and done it was he who wished he'd stayed home."

"Probably so. But I can't take much credit fer that. It was Athena, Artemis, and Apollo who whupped up on him." And Hades, who sent his Furies to open up Cumae's passage to the underworld and robbed Dionysus of his undead maenads.

"Your modesty borders on fibbing. They would never have come to your aid if you had not called upon them. And your courage and cleverness preserved the citizens if not their city."

"Shoot, I just react with my gut and hope fer the best." I bit into the honey-slathered bread, which finally made Jasper stop his mortifyingly-inappropriate comments about her various fine attributes.

Dymastis stood, her hair curling around her like a black shawl. It sure got your attention, contrasting with the peach-colored dress that made her look barely-clothed at all. "Then let us hope that your gut, as you call it, remains as wise as you are courageous. For your road is long and treacherous. Many lives and futures depend upon your decisions and deeds."

"That's just what I'm afraid of."

"Do not be. A Marshal's fear should be only of the foe, never of her own worth."

Easy to say when yer a goddess, I suppose.

She bowed and left me with my honey-dipped roll and a feeling of emptiness. It hadn't taken very long in her company to grow attached. It wasn't just her physical beauty and melodious voice. Being near her felt like a warm hug from your grandma, reassuring. I half-wanted to build an altar to the stunning creature. Jasper 'desired' a lot more than that.

"You just get them there icky thoughts outta my head right now, mister," I warned him, "or else I'm gonna turn this here cup into a wire brush and jam it in my ear."

"Go ahead. I have an itch that needs attention. Right on top o' your cerebellum."

In that vein we volleyed back and forth while I took the Duke outside for some fresh air. He was really perfuming the Great Hall. Soon the ceremony would start. I needed Ernie or Romulus to give me the straight dope on what being a Marshal really meant.

"Oh, I don't know about that," Jasper said, in his usual contradictory mood. "While they're turnin' red in the face guffawin' at yer epic wit you could whack their heads off with the Broodin' Blade of Reprisal."

22 / A Hard-to-Swallow Ritual

My two Equity buddies scared the pants off of me with their talk of dedicating your soul to the cause, freely surrendering your life to the Order if the Grandmaster deemed it necessary, and generally giving up every shred of individuality and control. They strung that business out for a good fifteen minutes, letting me practically dissolve into a puddle of outraged terror, until finally breaking down and confessing that I was just going to be an honorary member. It was a courtesy title, since I was Stone Warden and savior of mankind and all.

After nearly choking the jokesters – and where did Romulus suddenly get a sense of humor, anyway? – I asked, "It must have some rights and responsibilities, the way Vigor and her crew keep goin' on about it. Do I get a membership badge? Is there a secret handshake? Discounts at dry goods stores?"

"I wish dat were true," Romulus said, his eyes scanning the horizon for any sign of soldiers or other trouble. We were in a small grove of apple trees behind the chateau. He sat on his haunches like the great mastiff he'd once been. "Then Mr. Clemens back home might've kept his thumb off da scale."

Standing on top of the hound's back, Ernie burped. Apparently he'd been eating non-stop while I'd napped. His big belly looked like he'd swallowed a whole apple. "No badge. Anything that identifies yer can get yer killed if captured. Just the coin. They told yer about that, right?"

I shrugged. A big, winged thing was racing in at us, lower than the trees. "Sort o'. An ancient Egyptian gold piece, no bigger than a fingernail but chock full o' magick."

"That it is. It translates for yer, so you won't have to rent a spell from yer sword."

"Spoilsport!" pouted Jasper.

Romulus waved at the incoming flyer while talking to me. "And it lets you cross borders without the Affluxion spell takin' hold."

"Shoot, I can already do that, thanks to the Stone and Morphageus. Probably without 'em, too, since I'm half-Obverse."

"True," said Roberta, landing on Romulus' tree limb of a forearm. "But it never hurts to have extra powder in yer hold, matey. Besides, some borders are a darned sight stronger than others."

"Like the Scepter'd Isle?"

"Abso-darned-lutely. It's all we can do to push the *Kiss* through it sometimes, and that witched ship was built by the Proprietor himself. We'd never get onto that swampy patch without it. The Affluxion curse would cloud our minds and make us think we were there when really we'd just be rottin' in a

Merchantry prison hulk with raven peckin' at our gizzards."

"Well, okay then. It might come in handy, especially if I was to lose the Stone or the sword."

"Can't lose me," claimed Jasper. "I'm like a bad penny. I always turn up."

"What else does the equity coin do? Flight without wings? Make me bulletproof?"

Ernie scratched the Duke's ear for him with the butt end of his sharpened knitting needle. "Have yer seen either of us catchin' musket balls with our teeth or soarin' alongside o' Alcibiades? No, nothin' that spectacular. But it does let us recognize each other without usin' words or gestures. A warm buzz in our heads tells us when we're close to one o' our own."

Romulus nodded agreement. "And it lets us past Equity traps without gettin' blown up or witched to death. That's a handy thing."

I shuddered as I thought about how Tyrell had described the horrible death of the Merchantry spy at the hands of a document's security spell. "Y'all got a lotta them things?"

"You bet yer bilge pump they do," Roberta assured me. "Once I saw a Merchantry soldier try to sneak into an Equity bolt-hole to lay an ambush. His blood turned to acid and he sizzled from the inside-out. Gratifyin', in a disgustin' sort o' way." Her feathers fluffed up at the thought.

That made me cringe. "Almost like a banestaff strike. Boy, the Equity plays fer keeps, huh?"

"We have to," Ernie explained. "That's what's kept us around fer so long. The baddies like the Merchantry and their ilk don't respond to gentle persuasion. You has to get their attention with their own methods sometimes. Remind me to tell yer what they did to a poor gent who tried to murder the Grandmaster. She may look like an innocent little girl but when she's riled —"

"No, thanks, I'd like to keep that nice lunch down. Is that all the coins do?"

"It is," said Romulus, "except fo' da personal magick. Every Marshal gits a little somethin' extra dat's partic'lar to him. Nothin' fancy, no fireballs from da hands or suchlike."

"I'm guessin' yours is that you can take a lotta damage, huh? I seen you get clubbed over the head and not even blink. Gave me a powerful headache just to watch it."

"You's right. Takes a gun, knife, or spell to make much o' an impression."

I gave Ernie a wry smile. "What's yours? Lemme guess. You can eat ten times yer weight and still keep fightin'?"

The plump rodent wrinkled his snout at me. "Very funny. It just so 'appens that one's a natural inborn talent, duckie." To demonstrate he patted his tummy. "No, I can go days without sleep if I've a mind to. Handy fer guard duty when everybody else is bushed."

It occurred to me then that I hadn't actually ever seen him sleep much. "Nifty. What do I get, then? Can I choose my own, or is it a surprise?"

"Surprise. The Grandmaster knows best. I wanted to be eight feet tall with iron teeth, but no."

I tried to imagine Ernie as a goliath rodent, feared by all. It made me blow snot out of my nose. "Then Romulus would've been ridin' on **yer** shoulder." The thought of carrying a coin around all of the time made me think. "Say, it don't sound very practical, keepin' a spelled coin on ya all o' the time. How d'ya manage it?"

"Easy," said Romulus. "You don't carry it. You swallows it."

My eyes bugged out at that. "That's even worse! Why, every day you'd have to visit the outhouse with a tin cup and —" I felt that lunch starting to climb back out of me after all.

Roberta rolled her parroty eyes behind her spectacles. "She don't grasp the 'magick' part, do she?" The big red and blue bird gave me a schoolmarm look. "It don't come out the other end. No scamperin' off to the ship's head to catch the little bugger."

"Yer absorbs it," announced Ernie with a wink.

They gotta be joshin' with me again. "Uh-huh. Right."

"Ain't a joke," Romulus assured me. "Part o' da spell. It becomes part o' yo' body, next to da heart. Stays dere fo'ever."

"Can you feel it?"

"Not really. You kin sense da energy, but not da metal."

This is gettin' weirder and weirder. "The Equity sure must like their magick."

Ernie shook his head. "Actually, the Grandmaster don't much care fer it. She uses as little of it as she can, even though she's so good with it she's terrifyin'. Causes dependency, she says. Like opium. Wants us to rely on our wits and not on sorcery. That's the enemy's weakness. So we have it for basic stuff, like the coin.

And special security precautions. But little else."

That was all I found out, because Sha'ira strolled up to tell us that I needed to get myself into the Great Hall. The ceremony was about to start and I was the guest of honor. I hustled off with the foundling rapier, leaving the hound with the Marshals and the Dreamwriter. But before I got out of earshot I heard the tall Arabe tell Romulus and Ernie to be watchful. On her patrol she'd spotted some suspicious shapes in the woods a few miles off.

Ain't that just peachy? Probably one o' them nasty groups Vigor filled me in on. Or several of 'em, with my luck. One o' these days I'm gonna go without a monster attack and expire o' the surprise. There's an epitaph: 'Here lies the last Stone Warden, done to death by good news.'

"Hey," said Jasper, "it sure beats that whole 'your blood turns to acid' business."

"You got that right. Maybe my special coin power will be to smell out booby-traps. That'd be nifty, huh?"

"Naw. Yours should be not pukin' your guts out all of the time. Do you have any idea how repulsive that is when you're a suave magick sword who feels everything his human does?"

I stuck my finger down my throat just to make him cringe. "As a matter of fact, I do."

Right then I bumped into Dymastis.

"Did you not eat your fill at luncheon?" she asked with a twinkle in her beautiful eye.

Wiping my gooey finger off on my overalls, I shrugged. "Just makin' sure the Equity coin'll fit. I bet yer rethinkin' this whole 'honor the Stone Warden' business now, huh?"

That made her laugh. "Well, you certainly are different from the Maid of Orleans."

"I hope so," Jasper said. "Because we all remember how that little episode played out."

Which bothered me some. That Stone Wardens hadn't always succeeded in their quests, or at least hadn't survived winning. I should bear that in mind from now on, that all of the magick might not see me through this in one piece. Especially since none of the others had been as young and clueless as me.

The initiation ceremony wasn't very eventful for the most part. Well, not for me. An ordinary person with an ordinary life would've had an ordinary mental collapse. We put on white robes like we were a nervous choir of four, each of us with a serving Marshal as a sponsor. Romulus went with me, though I knew that Ernie stowed away in his shirt pocket. He said he wasn't about to miss out on me gulping down that gold piece.

One at a time we marched up to the dais through a gauntlet of Marshals to where Vigor stood. Her robe was purple with gold piping, shot through with magickal rainbows of fire when she moved. On her head was a wrought circlet of maillon that must've cost an unholy amount of money. That mermaid-worked meteor metal was the rarest substance on earth, and the toughest. A big black faceted jewel, the twin of the one on her ring, hung from it. She looked like she had a third eye, which was probably the point. Each inductee knelt on one knee, said his name, and accepted the tiny coin from her. When she asked if he took on the mantle of the Equity of his own volition and swore to dedicate his life to justice for all the world's peoples, he said that he did and popped the coin into his mouth. As it went down his gullet Vigor snapped her wrist. A tornado of stars swirled out of her ring, surrounding the hand. When they faded the magic sword Stormbolt remained.

You know, not too long ago seein' somethin' like that would've sent me screamin' fer the hills. Now I just yawn. Guess you can get used to anything.

Vigor set the scary-sharp tip of the sword against the new Marshal's chest. That spectral shimmer flowed out of her gown, down her arm, and into the steel. For a couple of seconds it looked like a Damascus blade sunlit from within. Then the energy dove into the fellow's body. He jerked as if wasp-stung. His Grandmaster set her small hand atop his head and the same twitch struck her. Eyes back in her head, hair standing up as if she stood on a Chauntline, she spoke in the low dry voice of the truly ancient woman she was.

"Poison," she rasped. "It shall not bite. Nor tongue of serpent nor hand of man may envenom you. Go now, and deliver justice to the low, to the meek, to the poor. When the Equity has need, you shall answer."

Two more times that happened, just the same except for the trance-gift. The second of those was to be unseen by all but the strongest minds. To the third she gave a cunning tongue, to be instantly believed and obeyed. Only a mage could resist. I hoped my talent would be as useful as those. Getting the magick ability to make people laugh at my jokes might make me feel good but wouldn't help the grand quest very much.

"Oh, I don't know about that," Jasper said, in his usual contradictory mood. "While they're turnin' red in the face guffawin' at yer epic wit you could whack their heads off with the Broodin' Blade of Reprisal." He turned into a six-inch long headsman's axe as he spoke, peeking out of my initiation robe.

I tucked him back inside, wishing him into a rabbit's foot and making him drop into a pocket of my overalls. "Go brood in the dark fer a while, will ya? I need to pay attention to this. Don't wanna accidentally contract myself again, like I did with a certain annoyin' somebody."

He muffled his voice just to be sarcastic. I ignored it and concentrated on Vigor. Now I knelt barefoot before her, running through the procedures so I wouldn't mess up in front of Romulus and Ernie. When she nodded a greeting I nodded back. *Well, so far, so good.* The rest of it went just like with the three young men. She asked me if I was joining the Marshals of the Equity of my own free will and handed me the coin. Licking my suddenly-dry lips, I said yes, which was maybe three-quarters true. That seemed good enough for her. When she raised one eyebrow and the corner of her mouth, that was my cue to gulp the gold piece. It was no bigger than a nail head and had a worn image of Cleopatra on its face. Swallowing it was simple.

Hmm. Tastes like peppermint. Wouldn't have guessed that. I also wouldn't have guessed what happened when Stormbolt touched me.

*"Congratulations! You've just managed to desecrate the
cosmic beauty of two universes by spewing up
your lunch all over the astral plane. I salute you!"*

23 / Spiritual Vomit

It had looked so minor when the others had their seizures. They'd stiffened up for a few seconds and then relaxed into mellow acceptance of their new status. My experience was different. At least, it lasted longer from my point of view. Those stars that cycloned out of the sword blade burst behind my eyes like some astronomer's nightmare. All that remained in my sight was an immense spiral galaxy with Vigor's forehead gem at the center. I felt like I was a comet, white-hot and streaking through the void. Planets and suns whizzed past as I accelerated. The only sound was a melodic cry. Once I'd seen a musician play water glasses by rubbing his fingers along the rims. That's sort of what it resembled, only it penetrated clear through me, rattling my bones. But a scary as the experience was, it felt familiar. Manageable.

Because it was the same soul-stretching ride I'd taken in Lusitania when I'd grabbed Aunt Regan's wrist on the Chauntline.

Sure enough, that sound focused itself until it was obviously the same communal scream of despair as on the first trip. What I'd thought were planets out of the corner of my eye turned out to be faces in agony. Meteors headed for me and just missing were really the clutching hands of dearth-demons. This time, though, I knew what to do. Repeating the chant *Nhana pana yolnyu*, I made everything slow down. Like going from an out-of-control locomotive to a handcar, it all eased off. Now I was floating in space, bobbing a little as a cork in a bathtub might. Instead of terror, I felt calm. Control. So much so that I could look around and see where I was and what was going on. And that was when I noticed something about the pained faces and the demons.

They were one and the same.

I was in the barrier between my world and the Obverse. The souls of those who used black magick, the kind dependent on suffering for its fuel, drifted away from their owners' bodies like boats with no mooring lines. Only in this case the boats got sucked down a whirlpool and then smashed against rocks until they no longer looked like they used to. This limbo, this no-place, was where that happened.

It was also where you crossed over to the other plane. There were gates. I'd thought they were just balls of gas or will-o'-the-wisps hanging in the blackness. But when I maneuvered myself up to one I could see that it was a ring of light. Peering inside, I saw a magnificent city with impossibly tall and narrow buildings in a geometry that made my eyes cross. It had been built on a mountainside. Waterfalls amongst the structures created amazing rainbows between the elevated streets and green-glassed towers. The sun threw a pale reddish light, not like our bright yellow-white star. I saw no trains, no carriages, no wagons. What I did see, though, made me gasp.

Flying carpets.

Now I knew that I was seeing the Obverse for the first time. If I stepped through that gate I might find Pa waiting for me on the other side. What might he think, seeing his newborn baby all grown up and carrying the burden of his Legacy Stone? All I had to do was drift up to it and —

Just as I got within spitting distance of the scarlet-and-violet ring the cityscape view got blocked out by a huge black shadow. A moment later an eye the size of an armoire, yellow-green with two vertical pupils, appeared. It blinked, sideways, and a sickly-wet animal rumble poured out. I changed my mind about going in. They'd told me the passages were guarded and now I saw that they weren't lying.

Curious, I glided around to the other side of the gate to see what was there. As I did so I saw that the thing wasn't even two inches thick. And once I got to the reverse face my eyes widened. There was the very Gaullic chateau I stood in, warm sun bathing its pale stones. My witched eyes spotted figures of guardian Marshals amongst the vines and trees. No giant monster secured this side. *Maybe that's our problem. No wonder the Merchantry floods the world with evil beasties. We make it easy for 'em. Well, let's just see what happens if you pass through here.*

The instant my body touched the gate everything winked out. Dizziness grabbed hold and spun me like a top. I got really sick to my stomach and upchucked. Everything came up so hard that I feared that the oversized Obverse creature must be squeezing me. My knees smacked into the ground, followed a second later by my hands and nose. Panting, the world spinning around me, I felt blood oozing out of my nose and ears.

Except that it wasn't. I hadn't gotten sick or bled or even left the dais. From the look of things that whole out-of-body episode has taken maybe three breaths. Nobody stared at me with any more wonder or disgust than usual. Vigor hadn't even opened her eyes yet. She was still tranced, about to pronounce what special Equity talent I would display from now on. In fact, not a soul in the Great Hall reacted to me in any way different from how they'd received the three fellows who'd gone first. Only Jasper made any comment.

"Congratulations! You've just managed to desecrate the cosmic beauty of two universes by spewing up your lunch all over the astral plane. I salute you!"

"Aw, put a sock in it. It was only spiritual vomit."

Vigor gasped and croaked out her declaration. As she did so her eyes flew open and she stared at me like my hair was on fire. "Channel-walker! This one may pass without hindrance between the realms."

A collective gasp from the hundred spectators. It seemed to be a big deal.

"She needs no ostium nor sacred portal," the Grandmaster

continued. There was amazement in her voice. Vigor stared at her sword, at her hands. I frowned, confused. Something wasn't right. From the mumbling of others around me, I wasn't the only one who thought that.

The little girl stumbled back and with a clumsy trip fell into her chair. Stormbolt collapsed like wet sand and became a mere ring on her finger. She stripped the maillon wreath from her hair. "I can give her nothing. This gem has no power that she does not already possess. The child is beyond me, whether she knows it or not."

Huh? That whole business with the gate was just...me? Without a Chauntline? How the heck did I manage to do that?

Now Vigor looked like a ten year-old girl again. No trace of the five millennia she'd lived showed on her sweet face. All of the spooky attitudes she'd displayed during the ceremony had evaporated. It reminded me of the fake mediums who conducted séances in Washington for the rich and gullible. They always pretended that some spirit from the 'Great Beyond' had taken charge of their minds and bodies. Only Vigor hadn't pretended a darned thing.

"Wasn't that a nice initiation?" she sang to the crowd, apparently not seeing the shock on their faces. Standing, she held her arms out to let Dymastis pull off the purple robe. The maillon headpiece disappeared into her reticule. Now back in her 'civilian' attire, that same frock she'd been in at lunch, the Equity Grandmaster grinned like she was at a country ball.

"Uh, yes'm," Romulus agreed. Ernie crawled out of his

pocket, looked at me, and held up his hands. I shrugged, letting him know that I was as dumbfounded as everybody else.

"It's always a treat to give these nice young people a gift to help them as they start off on this difficult life." She patted the three young fellows who'd been inducted with me on their backs. "And Miss Verity here shall need every bit of aid we can bestow."

Now there's a completely true prediction that no medium could compete with.

With that she ambled off of the raised platform to chit-chat with the Marshals. Madame Seychelles appeared next to me, all dressed up for ballooning, from her top hat and goggles to her long cinder-proof coat and gauntlets. "You look like you just went a few rounds with a den of Darwins, dearie."

Having done that very thing when the Croatan had attacked us on the *Kiss*, I knew just what she meant. "Feel like it, too. Saw more'n few of 'em on my trip."

"You don't say? Then it's true, what she said? You can stroll over to the Obverse whenever you like, without a portal or guide?"

I bit my lower lip. "Maybe. I done it twice. Made it into the barrier, anyways. No idea how I managed it, though. Couldn't do it right now if you held a knife to Ma's throat." The memory of that fearsome gargantuan whatever-it-was hit me. "And as far as actually settin' foot on the other side, there's a, um, complication."

She laughed and nodded. "Yes. I understand the toll-keeper is a grumpy old Gus."

Jasper piped up at last. I'd been waiting. "Oh, maybe he just needs somebody to pull a thorn out of his paw and make him a friend for life."

"Right," I said, walking toward the exit with the Directeur. "I'll make sure to turn you into a big pair o' tweezers fer that little job."

Herkimer stopped us halfway to the door. "There you are! You are a difficult girl to catch, despite your fame." He rubbed at the dinky scratch I'd put on his cheek. "Though perhaps I should have not tried so hard this morning."

I figured another part of his anatomy would've been more tender than his face, but what did I know about men's nether regions? "Sorry 'bout that."

"Oh, don't be. I most decidedly got what I asked for." The big blonde fellow pulled at his chin beard. "I say, you haven't seen my partner, perchance? The one whose sword I used? He seems to have scarpered."

"The tall narrow guy? Face all angles?" Come to think of it, I hadn't set eyes on him since the duel. I'd given Dymastis his rapier, hoping she'd be able to return it. *Can't imagine somebody'd just up and go without such a pricey and necessary item.*

"Aye, that would be him. Young Babington. Grim demeanor, yes. Always looks like he hasn't had a good outhouse result for a month. Probably due to his religious difficulties." Herkimer glanced about and lowered his voice, which meant that it could only be heard for five miles instead of the usual ten. "Papist, you know. Inconvenient to be one of them in the Scepter'd Isle right now. Since he's always served the Equity well and upsets no apple carts, I've looked the other way. But Her Majesty's treatment of them after so many assassination plots has made him a dour one, indeed. Can't be pleasant to see Walshingham's boys haul off your friends to Little Ease in the dead of night, never to be seen again until they appear on the scaffold."

Alarm bells clanged in my head. They were distant, but still worrisome. Jasper chose right then to bring them nearer by turning himself into a foot-tall church with belfry. The bulky Briton snorted and asked what the devil my cup was up to now.

"Devil's the right word. He's feelin' bored and unappreciated. That makes him do all manner o' silliness to entertain hisself. Really he's only happy when somethin' bad fer my health is goin' on." After what Herkimer had just told me, that might be any time now. I gave suspicious glances all around the room, half-expecting armed men to burst out of the fireplaces or crash through the spectacular windows of the Hall.

"What do you fear?" he asked, seeing me scanning the room like a mouse for a hawk.

"Not sure. But since yer Grandmaster gave me a master class on who's who and what's what I'm startin' to see baddies in every shadow." With a thought I shrank Jasper back into a cup, but now I kept the handle locked in my fist, ready for another transformation. I noticed that as the afternoon sun lengthened those shadows that the sky was clouding up some. *Hope that don't ground Prisme's balloon. I can see by her face that she's thinkin' the same thing.*

"Not Babington, surely? Do you know how many times that lad has saved my life? Hurled himself in front of a troll's spear in Scandia. Spit him like a pig. A miracle he survived."

"Yeah, but that's just what a good traitor would do, right?"

Now Herkimer was getting a trifle offended. Accusing Babington reflected badly on the blonde bear's judgement. "Careful now. I like it not that you leap to aspersions on such slight —"

I gave him a hard look. "Then where is he? Ain't seen hide nor hair of him since our altercation. Left his pricey cutlery on the floor and vanished. He ever do that before?"

Already he was having doubts. He furrowed his brow and pondered. "Hmm. Now that you make mention of it, he has seemed distracted of late. And he begged to come on this journey with me, even though it made us more conspicuous. It's not in his nature to absent himself without leave. As for the rapier..." It was clear that its abandonment bothered him.

A thought struck me. I grabbed his arm and steered him back toward the crowd and the dais. "Find that sword. Take it apart. Use a hammer if you have to. Eyeball it good and tell me what you find. Go!" Off he went without any more argument, a man of action happy to have something to do, even if it might indict a man he trusted.

Madame Seychelles had none of his indecision about Babington. Already she was charging for the door, intent on getting to her gasbag. "Your instincts have already become

Redeemer lore. I, for one, do not intend to ignore them. If it should turn out that the young man is loyal to the Equity then no harm has been done, except to his feelings. Those will mend. But our cause cannot risk hurt to you. Particularly after what I saw at that ceremony."

Just to be on the safe side, I started chanting under my breath to whip up some magick from my soul-store and keep it handy for making a shield or flinging a blast of force. As we passed through the enormous double doors I raised a hand to do just that. But nothing bad came our way. The Directeur, moving with more agility than somebody her age ought to have managed, steered me up the marvelous double-spiral stairs.

"I'm on the roof," she explained, her bizarre pistol in hand now. "Balloons attracts less attention there, amongst the spires and chimneys. Plus, we get to a safe height, out of musket range, that much quicker." Her hand yanked back a ratchet on the side of her weapon.

"Nice hogleg yer packin', ma'am," I said with a nod to her odd firearm.

She picked her skirt with the free hand to make climbing easier. "You like it? That clever Captain Nemo made it for me. Such a handy boy." Her gun was hefty, about the size of Tyrell's LeMat revolver. There the resemblance ended. Its brass barrel was long, fluted, and looked like somebody had hollowed out a fancy candlestick. The breech fit into a polished mahogany handle with beautiful carvings. Prisme's piece didn't seem to use gunpowder at all, but a strong spring.

"Shoots nice and quiet," she told me, leading the way around the next turn. "No loud bang."

I squinted at the thing while keeping an eye on the steps. "Don't shoot bullets?"

"Lead is for barbarians. And it's one-size-fits-all." She tapped a round bin beneath the barrel. "This fires glass globes full of special sauce. Acid, poison, whatever one needs. Salt, sometimes. Nothing drops a dearth-demon faster than salt in the wound."

"Really? That's handy to know." *Seems an awful simple remedy fer such a nasty enemy.*

"Stick with me, honey, I'll further your education. You don't always need a crutch of magick to get by in this world."

Pale blue fire coated my hand, just in case. My alarm bells were really bonging now. "Though it never hurts to have some ready to go."

"Actually, you'd be surprised how often a spell can cock things up worse than they already are." Madame Seychelles giggled like a schoolgirl as she said that.

That turned to shrieks of agony as a crossbow bolt pinned her gun hand to her chest.

"If this pot gets any thicker,
it'll set like concrete," Jasper said.

24 / Vicious Eagles

Two more bolts shattered on my energy shield a split-second later. With Jasper's help I'd raised it without a conscious thought. While I dragged Prisme back around the turn of the stair I caught sight of three gray-hooded figures at the top, blocking access to the roof. Each held a small bow with a pistol grip. They reloaded with cool efficiency and one began descending toward me. Coming up the stairs from our left were two more, already aiming their bolts.

How the heck did they get in here with all of the Marshals and Redeemers on guard? That was a dumb question with only one smart answer. These guys were Marshals and Redeemers. Either traitors or shape-shifter imposters. *Gee, I really gotta have a talk with Vigor and Prisme about their interview procedures.* As if to confirm that guess, I got a glimpse of one of the three above. Sure enough...Babington the true believer.

The two new arrivals were the biggest threat, since the others weren't loaded or in sight again yet. I swung my left arm around to get the shield up before the pair of arrows could be loosed. Seeing the blue shimmer, they paused and held off firing, not wanting to waste their ammunition. But they kept climbing at us, waiting for the others to come down. Then I'd have a problem.

"Hey, lemme out, lemme out!" whined Jasper. "I wanna play!"

That sounded like a good idea to me. Maybe the mere sight of Morphageus would intimidate my new friends into retreating. The recurved blade flared into existence in my hand, runes glowing like new-forged steel. I could fade them at will, but this time I wanted them out in all of their glory. At first it seemed to work. The hooded fellows stopped in their tracks and put their heads together for a discussion. Just as I started to relax, though, they drew long curved daggers with their free hands, cried "Die, witch!" and charged.

I set Madame Seychelles down as gently as I could, with her back against the heavy stone balustrade. She whimpered with the pain of the wicked wound but was still lucid. Standing one step down from her, I braced my bare feet and waited for the attackers to commit themselves. Since the staircase was a good twelve feet across, the one on my right tried to flank me while his partner made a frontal assault to take all of my attention.

That might've worked if I'd been your typical schoolgirl in denim britches. Unlucky for them, that wasn't the case. With the Stone calming me and speeding up my thinking, I knew in a flash the best way to handle them. I tossed Morphageus at the flanker's head. It swoop-swooped at him, nice and slow. He ducked it and laughed. At the same time I pushed my defensive platter of energy at the other one, like you'd throw the cover of a dustbin. He took it full-on and rolled back down the steps.

The man to my right took advantage of my exposure to loose his bolt at me. But just as he pulled the trigger Jasper came back at him as a boomerang, clobbering him in the back of his hooded skull. The arrow went high and harmless. When he landed on the stones I saw the cross/sword scar on his forearm. While the aboriginal throwing stick flew back toward my waiting hand, I learned an unpleasant fact.

That first enemy, the one rushing down the stairs, had turned the corner and had me dead to rights. I looked straight into the deadly barb of his arrow. And now I had no sword and no time to throw up a new shield.

I made to leap over the rail and take my chances on a hard landing. Before I could bunch my legs and spring, though, the assassin jerked and shrieked. That turned to gurgles as hideous blisters and running sores erupted on his face. Disgusting fluids dripped from the hem of his robe. The bow fell from useless fingers. He trembled, all of the visible flesh seeming to melt. When his eyeballs burst like stomped grapes I turned away and lost my lunch for real this time.

"What a waste!" Jasper lamented.

With a sick sigh the corpse flopped onto the stairs, rolling one and lying still, steam rising from it. Madame Seychelles grunted, despite her misery. "Humph! So that's what those purple ones do. I'd always wondered." She'd grabbed the Nemo pistol from her cruelly-pinned hand and shot him down for me, just as calm as could be.

All of a sudden I wished I hadn't been so mean when I'd glamoured her. That'd been a bigger risk than I'd known. "Yer one tough granny, you know that?"

I got a sweet smile back. "Of course I do, dearie. You think the Coterie follow my orders because I bake them cookies? Now help an old girl up. We need to decamp."

With an eye toward the remaining two killers, I got a shoulder under her good arm and lifted her onto her feet. The other pair were both out cold but could revive at any time. And there might be more on the way. Somebody down in the vestibule sure was keeping friendly traffic away from the staircase. We couldn't stay where we were. But while I considered what might be our best course, I thought to poke around for some information.

"Hey, Babington!" I hollered up at the conscious pair. They seemed a bit stunned that their little plot hadn't worked. Neither showed his face around the final corner upstairs. "Your friend Herkimer's gonna be awful upset that you been with the Graue Adler all this time and played him fer a fool."

"The merest justice, that," he retorted. "The great ape was a fool before I ever met him. Protestant stooge!"

"Yer kiddin'. That's what this is about? Whose church is on top?"

"Why not? Makes as much sense as whose king is on top. Look around, sorceress. Living gargoyles walk the Earth. Demons have come from hell to establish dominion. Witches cast spells even as children. Men have cast their lot with the forces of darkness and despair. Can you honestly say that we are in the wrong to fight this?"

"You know, he kind of has a point," offered Jasper.

"Yeah? Didn't I find you in a black pit, just waitin' to corrupt my innocence?" To Babington I said, "I fight it, too, you know. The Merchantry is the villain here, not me. Why don't you take out a few o' them?"

"Says the baby witch with the magick of ten. Your smooth corrupting words shall not shake my faith!"

"Witch...yeah, maybe. But I'm no Satan-worshipper. This power don't come from him." *Assumin' he's even real. But with the way things are now, I'd be crazy to discount it. Besides, there's that troublesome smell of brimstone from Jasper's spells.*

"An easy thing to say. But from where else would it spawn? His Holiness assures us that all magick is black, born of suffering and evil. We must cleanse the world of every one of you."

I considered asking him about the power to turn water into wine and where that stood in his appraisal of magick's wickedness. A theological argument would just play into his hands. Babington was clearly killing time, stalling until reinforcements could arrive. We had to get off the stairs and find safety. Plus, Prisme's wound was bleeding freely now.

"Bold move, strikin' at this meetin'. You gotta know that this is a suicide mission, right? They'll never let you escape."

"What of it? My polluted body is but a vessel for my soul,

which shall sail on to heavenly glory. After all, it was good enough for my Lord, who cast out devils and died for it."

Measuring the angle of the corner he hid behind, I thought I might be able to heave the boomerang up there and get him, with Jasper's gleeful guidance. But that'd still leave his accomplice in murder untouched. And if I guessed wrong Morphageus might bounce off of a couple of walls and fall at their feet, an easy prize. *Naw. We need to sneak back down into the lobby and take our chances there. And I got an idea how to do it, too.*

A puppeteer charm. That's what Vigor had called it. If it had worked on the strong Herkimer, who'd been struggling the whole time, it ought to work on an unconscious religious fanatic. Heading downstairs, all clumsy with Prisme's weight to support, I asked the Directeur if she could bank one of her hideous glass bullets up at Babington to keep his head down. Weak now from shock and bleeding, her voice tired, she shook her head.

"No, they break on first contact and discharge their toxins. You can't ricochet them."

"Too bad. Guess I'll have to try it my way then." Hoping I didn't bounce the magick right back into our faces, I whispered a chant and flung an invisible baseball of force at the landing overhead, trying to carom it like a billiard ball. A second later I heard a curse, not in Babington's voice, as somebody got knocked over like a bowling pin.

"Well-done," praised the Directeur. "Your control is impressive after only what, three weeks? A shot like that takes most practitioners years to master."

I gave her a shrug and a sheepish smile. "I hear it runs in the family."

"Clearly."

Now we'd made it to the unconscious Adler I'd shoved with my defensive shield. Half-conscious, actually, because he'd started to come to with a groan. Before he could gather all of his wits, not to mention his knife, I called up the same spell that had hung up Herkimer to dry. With Morphageus to channel it like I was using a paintbrush, I wrapped him up in energy and made a detailed picture in my mind of what I wanted. It took a whole lot of strength and concentration but I yanked him onto his feet. But when I tried to walk him toward the lobby I found that I didn't have enough oomph left to manage it. My arm shook and sweat matted my hair. *Nope. I ain't got the mustard after the ceremony. That took a lot outta me.*

Just as my living marionette wobbled and started to collapse, a hand grabbed my wrist. With unexpected force Madame Seychelles, eyes sparkling with violet lights that ran down her arm, said, "Let me help you, sweetie. It's the least I can do. You'll have to be quick, though. I fear my reserves are quite low, what with this pinprick and all."

Like getting a second wind during a long run, I felt myself renewed. The aching and tiredness went away. *Now I know why them Bullies all hold hands when they attack us.* My arm stopped wavering. Now I had all of the finesse I could want. More magick poured out of me and into the unlucky Papal Fief assassin. He marched down the last two steps and into the entry hall of the chateau like it was his own idea...and promptly caught several arrows to the body.

I'd expected that, though, since the Graue Adler were so zealous. They'd fired at the first person to come down the steps, figuring it'd be yours truly. Not being as cold-hearted as them, I'd wrapped my puppet in a thin protective barrier. It wasn't bulletproof but it was defense enough for the low-powered hand bows. Hoping that all of the slayers were busy reloading, I leaned Prisme against the banister and bounded down amongst them. Luck was on my side. All but one of the Gray Eagles was busy yanking back on his bowstring. That one rushed his shot, still surprised that his comrades had pin-cushioned their own man. A quick twist of my body was all I needed to make him miss. Seeing that their prey had turned on them, the murder squad plucked their daggers from their robes and set to it.

Despite everything they'd been told, plus what they'd seen with their own eyes when I'd dueled Herkimer, my enemies still seemed to think I was your normal kid. Shoot, I could hardly believe otherwise myself. They came at me in an almost casual way, careless and uncoordinated. That sure helped me out, because even so I knew that four-on-one wasn't great odds in a fight. I just hoped I could hold them off without too much bleeding on my part until some loyal Marshals heard the ruckus and came to my aid. *Where is everybody? All these guards and none of 'em has noticed this tussle?*

Not trusting to magick until I could recharge it, I stuck with all of my hard training from Shade and pirate. The first fellow to come at me got my big straw hat in his face, followed by a Stone-aided kick to the belly that sent him careening into the man behind him. Both ended up sprawled on the floor ten feet away, weapons dropped. Another darted around them to slash at my face. Morphageus not only parried that but snapped his blade off at the hilt. No earthly metal could stand up to mine. *Thanks, Jasper!* My big pommel caught him between his eyes and he slumped into a corner. So far I hadn't had to actually kill anybody. I hoped not to.

My last foe had no such scruples. He was bound and determined to slice me up like a stew carrot. And he was a darned sight better at his job than the others. *Probably the team leader. Watch yerself, kiddo.* A swarthy fellow with a neat black beard, hooked nose, and blazing eyes, he snatched up a fallen blade and came at me with double daggers. One would thrust and the other would cut. That made blocking them risky and confusing. If it hadn't been for the Stone boosting my reflexes I might not have lasted long. But like the others he didn't take me as seriously as he should've. Plus, he was an assassin, not a duelist. A quick stab in the back was probably what he was used to dishing out.

Still, I had a tough time of it, even with the extra reach my sword gave me. Backpedaling, making sure I didn't trip over his fallen friends, I blocked half a dozen blurred strikes. With a slick maneuver he got inside of Morphageus, wrapping the arm so I couldn't use the blade. That cost him the use of his own knife on that side, though. He launched a vicious stab at my heart with the other while I was tied up. I just managed to grab the wrist before the point pierced me. Now we were both immobilized, glaring wordlessly at one another. My strength clearly took him aback. His left arm began to loosen its snaking hold on mine. He was going to free his own knife by releasing mine, hoping he could get in a killing blow before I realized it. An instant before that happened, I evened the odds, though it sickened me to do it.

I snapped my knee up into his elbow while jerking down on his wrist. The joint snapped like a sun-dried twig. A steam-whistle scream came out of his mouth that was far higher than the sound Prisme made when she'd been shot. *Well, that oughta finally alert somebody. You could hear it in Boston.* His foot-long dagger dropped onto the flagstones, making yet more noise. My enemy flung himself away from me, right arm hanging useless and bent in entirely the wrong way. That didn't end the fight, though. Against all common sense, gasping in what had to be eleven kinds of hellish pain, he raised his other fist and prepared to come at me again.

"Mighty tenacious of you," I told him. "Let me guess. Yer bosses in Rome or wherever told ya this was a one-way trip, so goin' back home means you'll be just as dead there. Am I right?"

In a Teutonic accent he hissed, "You shall not turn my wits, sorceress! I will cut out your deceiving tongue first."

"Ah! A true believer, like Babington. Some bishop told you I was trouble, so here you are, all ready to sacrifice yerself fer the wrong cause."

He growled and made to rush me. When he swiped at Morphageus to get inside it again I dropped my point beneath his hand and set it against his chest. Twice more he tried it, with the same result. "That's what ya get fer havin' one sneaky move. When ya overuse it, it gets kind o' predictable." When he looked past me to the stairs I added, "Don't bother. No help that way. One's very, very dead and two have lost their appetite fer tanglin' with me. Babington and his friend up top ain't likely to chance Madame Seychelles' scary pistol. I know I wouldn't."

Behind him I saw the first two I'd taken down start to stir again. I couldn't waste time debating somebody who was beyond persuading. And I didn't want to coldly massacre them all, either, assuming that I could. Some help would be nice right about now. A few angry Redeemers and Marshals coming to rescue the 'last best hope of an ever-dwindling tomorrow', as Jasper would say. Still nobody responded to the fighting and screaming. Did they all go deaf at the same time?

A quick glance at the doors to the Great Hall showed me what had happened. It had been spelled. The tiniest flares of pinkish light twinkled on it. I didn't know what sort of magick had coated them, but that was why the cavalry didn't come. Somebody had done the same favor for the main doors to the front, too. We were sealed in.

"Kind o' hypocritical of y'all. I thought the Graue Adler hated magick and witches and such?"

His confused frown told me a lot more than his mouth

would've. He and his men hadn't spelled the lobby. The very thought truly offended him. "Hmm. My mistake," I shrugged, wary of his two buddies. They were cocking crossbows. "Somebody else did it. Yer gettin' help from folks with less scruples. Folks on the other side of these doors maybe?"

"If this plot gets any thicker it'll set like concrete," Jasper said.

"There you are! Where were you while I was engaged in furious battle with these guys?"

"Right with you, annoying brat. Helped you all the way I did. I nudge here, a nudge there..."

"Think you can nudge the doors to that Great Hall, then?"

"Maybe. Whoops! Hold on a second." My vision blurred and the room went all dark and stuffy. Loud metal bangs half-deafened my sensitive ears. He'd reshaped into a suit of armor, covering me head to toe just long enough to stop the bolts fired by the revived pair. *Don't they know when to stop?*

"Okay, you have yer uses," I admitted. "Now let's end this." I wished him into a new shape and smacked the double doors with a Morphageus sledgehammer. The shock went all the way up into my teeth. Those funny pink lights winked out. I hit the doors again, this time with a lot less vibration through my bones. With a creak the twenty-foot-tall barrier opened up, revealing a room full of folks all standing around having polite conversation.

"Jeepers!" I hollered. "A hundred dadburned freedom fighters loungin' in here and I had to whip the Graue Adler all by my lonesome!"

Eyes grew big and jaws flopped open as those in the Great Hall caught sight of the gray-hooded men behind me. When a couple dozen drew weapons and ran toward us, my recent enemies decided that self-destruction for their cause wasn't as nifty an idea as they'd thought. All three, dragging the still-unconscious one I'd pummeled with my pommel, made for the outside door. Now that the spell had been broken it could be opened, too. But at that moment Romulus appeared, coming in through those same doors. His giant mitts knocked two of them down and snagged the other's cowl, making the poor guy choke as he lifted him off of his booted feet.

"How'd da Eagles git in here?" he wanted to know. "And who locked dis door?"

"An excellent question," grumbled Grandmaster Vigor, Stormbolt in hand. Let us find out from these petty butchers. It shan't take long."

She turned out to be mistaken. In near-perfect unison the Graue Adler prisoners drew three-inch knives from their belts and slashed their own palms. Their leader gave the unconscious man a cut to the cheek. Moments later they all frothed at the mouth and died with victorious smiles.

"There's two more at the top o' the stairs," I announced. "One of 'em's Babington. Madame Prisme's about six steps up, shot through with an arrow. She's in a bad way."

A whole pack of Redeemers fell over themselves stomping up the stairs to help their fallen leader. Romulus went back outside with Sha'ira to secure the grounds, saying he'd send Roberta aloft to check the roof for more infiltrators. Vigor nudged the dead Adler's body with her sword tip.

"How did this happen?" she demanded. "What charm sealed the doors?"

A long-robed bald fellow in thick spectacles peered at a hinge, his nose practically touching it. After sniffing, he ran a bony finger along it and then licked the digit. "Dampener, with a soupcon of Impeder. No sound got through, and the spell took away the urge to enter or leave."

"Well, those witch-hunters certainly didn't cast it. They'd die first. As they just demonstrated." She pointed to the dead men. "Examine and identify, please. If young Babington was in on this, others of our Order may be involved, though I can hardly credit it."

As grim-faced Marshals with swords and flintlocks mounted the steps to flush out Babington and his accomplice, I snuck out the front door, where Tyrell stood next to Alcibiades, his LeMat in hand. He peered up at the eaves of the castle with binoculars, wary of sharpshooters. Gloriana crouched behind a column, eyeing the vineyards and orchards. Other Redeemers had fanned out into the lawns and gardens to flush any hidden Graue Adlers. The sun was getting pretty low in the west. We had maybe two hours of daylight left.

"You need to bustle out of here," Tyrell told me. "Strange as it may seem, you aren't safe amongst the cream of the Equity's chivalry."

I almost pointed out that it hadn't been the Marshals who'd kidnapped and blackmailed me, but I stopped myself. It appeared that I had enough so-called allies after my head as it was. "Looks like it. How's that kind o' thing happen, anyways?"

He shook his head. "Disaffected men, perhaps seduced by the Merchantry or Obverse. Promises of a new world order, promotions, honors. Unlikely with the Marshals, though. Vigor is very thorough with her selections and even better at turning them into righteous crusaders."

A memory came to me, of the tortured form of the spy who'd been shape-shifted into a tick and planted on Al's rump to track us in Virginia. "Maybe it's simple extortion. Grab a loved one, threaten doom unless you turn against yer own people. That scheme's older than Vigor."

"It is, indeed."

Gloriana spoke from her crouch beneath the horse. "There is a third possibility. They may all be imposters, their appearances altered to sow dissension in our ranks. Well within the enemy's power to achieve. Betrayal on top of murder is traditionally bad for morale."

I frowned and considered her theory. "Won't a spell like that decay when they're dead and give the game away?"

"Not if done by House Shedim. Their methods are more permanent, if more excruciating."

The thought of demons performing unnatural surgical operations on people, even if they might be willing, turned my stomach. A lot of things had that effect today, including trips to the Obverse, seeing Prisme kill a man with a vile poison bullet, and me destroying a man's elbow joint. *A lot more o' that sort o' thing to come, I reckon. Ain't gonna be much reasoned discourse where I'm headed. Just violence and treachery. I really hope to see Ma before we have to cross the Channel. That may be the last time if this all goes sour.*

"Is there a plan, if I just cut and run?" I asked them. "Or do I just take off on my own and hope fer the best?" Not that such a thing would be unusual, the way this great quest had been so far. The whole Iberion-Lusitania business proved that.

Jasper threw in his opinion. "Just you and me, kiddo, free as birds! Wanderin' the back roads of Napoleonic Gaulle. What could possibly go wrong?"

"Oh, let's count the ways. Dearth-demons, Gray Eagles, Assassins Guild, ravens, Bullies, zombies, renegade Marshals. And poop monsters. Can't ferget the dadburned poop monsters..."

"At that rate you'll have to count on your toes, too. Good thing you always go barefoot."

Tyrell raised his hand and pointed to a chimney on the roof. "Got him! Babington. His friend is right behind him, too. Tell the Grandmaster where they are. Perhaps she can apprehend them before they unhelpfully dispatch themselves." Gloriana rushed into the chateau to deliver the message. Her brother picked up one of Al's front hooves and inspected it, or pretended to. "Of course there are contingency plans. You need to get to Poitiers, straight north of here. Get your pack from Romulus, disguise yourself like a proper local girl again, and hide in plain sight. Glamour every one of Bonaparte's officials whom you meet. No one will be able to remember you when you've gone. That way pursuers will have the devil of a time tracking you."

"That's all fine and dandy, but how am I supposed to get to Paris and then London in less than a week. I'm still hundreds of miles away. Hoofin' it ain't gonna work."

A spry old voice called out to me from the front doors. "Oh, don't you worry your ruddy little head about that, missy! Your aerial conveyance awaits."

I whirled around just as Madame Prisme Seychelles strolled up to us, a map in her gloved hands. Drying blood covered her long traveling coat. Not only was she no longer gravely wounded, she was so perky and energetic that she seemed as if she'd grown younger. My face must've betrayed my amazement, because she tapped me on the snoot with her map and laughed.

"You aren't the only one with healing spells. Or healing potion, in this case. Alas, its effects reverse in a few days. But by then I'll have delivered you into friendly hands."

I worried about what'd happen when her potion expired. "And whose hands might they be?"

"Victoria Sponge. And immensely lovely and talented hands they are."

Jasper groaned. "That rodent is devourin' my licorice!"
The cup turned into a rag doll and stared at me,
hands on hips. "Well, take action! Flog him. Exile him."

25 / The Power of Fairy Flatulence

That made me snort. I looked at Tyrell, the picture of disinterested innocence. "Sponge! You mean Laurence's old girlfriend?" How many ladies named Sponge could there be, after all?

"She's not that old," he mumbled. I swear he was blushing.

"Former girlfriend, then. It is the same one, right? What the heck can she do fer us? Is she a Redeemer or a Marshal? A crack shot, maybe? Good with a blade?"

"Positively not. She's a musician, as I said."

"Oh, that's swell. At least we'll have classy tunes at our funerals."

Tyrell swung up onto Al's back as shots and cries came from the roof. Babington's last stand had begun. I doubted that Vigor would get her living prisoner to interrogate. He didn't seem the type to surrender. The hussar said, "I have to lend a hand there. Madame Directeur, I leave Verity to your capable direction. You have the address I gave you?"

Prisme patted a pocket. "I do, indeed. Rue de Poisson in Poitiers." *Fish Street?*

"She'll be giving a recital tomorrow night. Give her that note and she'll help you. Vicki is famous and respected. Her name will open doors for you. Adieu." He saluted and urged Alcibiades off down the lane toward the far end of the chateau.

Prisme took my arm. "Come, we must hasten to the roof, as well. Fortunately, my balloon is on this end. We won't be involved in that other unpleasantness."

Just inside the door we met Dymastis. She held my rucksack and hat out to me. "Marshal Romulus said you'd be needing these. He regrets that he cannot bid you farewell in person. His services were required in tracking a suspect."

Ernie poked his snout out of the top flap. He was, of course, chewing on something. "But I'm available, so all is not lost. Say, what's this stringy black stuff? Some sort o' beef jerky?"

Jasper groaned. "That rodent's devourin' my licorice!" The cup turned into a rag doll and stared at me, hands on hips. "Well, take action! Flog him. Exile him."

"Oh, calm yerself," I told him, slinging the pack onto my back. "There're plenty of yummies left fer the obnoxious talkin' sword. I can get the corncob pipe goin' once we're in the air. She has so many sparks flyin' around up there that a few more won't hurt."

The doll clapped its little hands. "Did I ever tell you that you're my favorite Stone Warden?"

"Yeah, but it's yer veracity that's open to question. I hear I'm yer twelfth bearer. Ferget to mention a few things, did ya?"

He reshaped into a cup and hopped onto my belt hook. "Um, maybe. The details are a little fuzzy. You know how it is. Eons of time, so much frenzied activity..."

I followed the Directeur up the stairs, pausing when we passed the pool of blood. Her blood. *Whoa, that's a lot. She must have a dandy health potion to make up fer losin' that much. And there ain't a mark on her hand where the arrow went through, either.* As we climbed I asked her about how the healing had worked.

A pained expression clouded her face, but it wasn't from any physical hurt. "The same as any other rejuvenative charm, except that the magic isn't in a soul-store or Chauntline. Some generous person has to volunteer to take the damage." She looked up at the landing, where four strapping young Redeemers lay, all wincing. Two had an injury to hand or chest, bleeding and bandaged. The other pair were pale and weak. "In this case, several generous persons." They all struggled to sit up and give her the Coterie salute, but she waved at them to relax. "So that no one would risk death, the injuries were spread out amongst them. One for the body wound, one for the hand, and two to make up for the blood lost."

After fussing over them for a bit, blowing kisses and touching cheeks, Prisme wiped away a tear and continued upstairs. No sounds came from the roof, so the two Gray Eagles were either dead or captured. Escape was pretty unlikely, with the grounds crawling with trained fighters and Tyrell in the air on his Valkyrie horse. Roberta and some gulls, too, probably. If they were still alive I didn't envy them their time with the young-looking Grandmaster. Somehow seeming to be ten years old only made her angry power more unsettling.

We turned to the left when we got to the roof. The chimneys were so thick that it was like walking through a strange forest of white stone trees. When we got up close I saw that most of them weren't chimneys at all, but turrets with windows and ridiculous heaps of ornamental work. Some of them were thirty feet high. A few were domed and had bells in them. All were covered in huge carvings of seashells, animals (lions and lizards were popular), Hellenic columns, and geometric shapes. Even the actual chimneys looked like tombstones for gods. Everything had so many extra cornices and moldings that it looked like the ideal afterlife for pigeons. Gray and steep, the peaks rising from the flat part of the roof were shingled in slate. They were the only plain spots I could see and that made me happy, like turning off an alarm.

Nobody threw fireballs or javelins at us. After the day I'd had that was a blessed relief. We zigzagged between two particularly silly turrets with statues of winged bunnies all over them and bumped into Prisme's balloon. It looked even more odd in daylight. The teardrop-shaped bag was made of midnight blue silk, covered in netting. Unusual writing in gold, swirly and beautiful like Arabe, ran along the bottom edge. Strong rope cables connected it to the wicker gondola which was so narrow that it would really be a tight squeeze for the two of us. At one end was a complicated wood and fabric steering rudder with two big flappable wings. Control toggles in the basket served to change direction and oar-like devices would propel the thing with the wings, if you had strong arms. In the center of the gondola was the stove used to heat the air inside the balloon and allow it to fly. I couldn't see any big fuel compartment and wondered how Madame Seychelles made long trips.

"My secret recipe, that's how," she told me. "Get in, dearie and I'll show you."

She opened the gate-like door and I wormed my way in after her. I had to pull off the rucksack to manage it. Prisme slid back until she was next to the steering machinery. That crazy blunderbuss of hers was in a scabbard affair next to her. Hopefully, the ether would be ogre-free during our trip. From a coat pocket she took a pale blue porcelain snuffbox.

"That's yer secret ingredient?" I asked. "We ain't likely to get far burnin' that stuff."

"A fat lot you know," she said with a wink. "This is the most dangerous stuff known to man."

I rolled my eyes as she opened the tiny box. "Why, we gonna sneeze our way to Poitiers?"

Madame Seychelles snorted at that. "Actually, you're at the wrong end of the body."

A tap on a floor pedal with her foot popped a small lid on the stove. She shook out something the size of a walnut. It landed next to the opening. Rather than being the fine powder I'd expected, it turned out to be a jumbled mass of something much more solid. And it moved. In fact, it stood up on two wobbly legs and...yawned.

"Whoa!" I squinted, not sure that I was seeing it right. "Tell me that ain't a real-life fairy?"

"I could, but I'd be fibbing." Prisme pocketed the snuffbox and waggled her fingers at the dinky winged creature. "Hello, Maybelle. Wakey-wakey, sleepyhead. Time to earn your keep."

While Maybelle rubbed her eyes and yawned again, I stuck my snoot real close to get a better look at her. The fairy was a little smaller than the four-inch-tall Scorch and, unlike our fire sprites on the *Kiss*, had only one pair of wings. She had white hair that hung down the middle of her back in a plait so it wouldn't tangle in those dainty flight-makers. If she'd been normal sized her eyes would've been the size of my palms. Huge, almond-shaped, and bright blue, they probably gave her night-vision as good as my own. Other than that she had a fairly normal pretty face. Her body and limbs were unnaturally long and slender. A butterfly would've outweighed her. As far as clothes went, she wore a green vest under a short sack coat, much as men of my time of 1862 would. Heck, she even had a tiny top hat perched on her head, cocked sideways. No trousers, though. Instead, her legs were covered in footless stockings with horizontal black stripes, beneath a gauzy skirt like our ballerinas would dance in.

"Is she drunk?" I asked. "Don't seem to be doin' too well on them spindly legs."

"Oh, no, she's sober," Madame Seychelles assured me. "For the moment. But that may change if she gets into the flower blossoms tonight. The girl's a holy terror when she's in her cups. No self-control. Flies in circles. Starts fights with innocent hummingbirds. Sad, really."

I thought of somebody else who matched that description. "Do all o' the wee winged folk act like fools? 'Cause our sprites seem awfully disposed to drink too much fire and get wild."

That got me a reaction from the fairy. She glared at me with one angry blue eye and took to her wings. Purple sparkles surrounded her in the air. The tiny girl hovered even with my nose, made a really rude gesture, and spit on it. To me it felt like a soft kiss, but I'm sure she thought it was a devastating retort. Then she flew over to Prisme and held up her palms to the sky.

"Don't act all innocent for her benefit," said the Directeur. She pointed to the open trapdoor in the oven. "You know perfectly well what needs to happen. Get busy, girlie."

Maybelle sighed and landed beside the hole. With a disgusted snort she yanked up her skirt, squatted low, and —

"Eew!" Jasper cried. "Did she just do what I think she did?"

A dense constellation of those purple lights billowed up around her, resembling embers from an angry volcano. They poured out of her bare backside and filled up the empty stove. For three full minutes that went on, even though that was totally impossible from a body the size of a thumb. I gawked at the sight like I was at a circus freak show. Jasper turned into a rag doll that covered its eyes with its hands in horror.

"Tell me when it's over," he asked with a whimper. "My tender eyeballs might rupture."

Eventually the violet cascade tapered off, ending with a sound like somebody blowing a raspberry. Still looking like she'd lost a bet, and maybe she had, Maybelle stood, let her wispy skirt fall, and stood with her arms crossed, staring daggers at us. I tapped Jasper on his noggin. His fingers spread to take a peek. Seeing that the offending activity had ended, he turned himself into a cup again.

"People have called it 'fairy dust' for ages," Prisme informed me, closing the little stove port, "but it's not that at all. It's really gas. A particularly concentrated and potent gas."

I risked a sniff. The smell nearly made me gag, but not because it was the usual...well, you know. It turned out that fairy flatulence had the odor of lavender and honeysuckle. But a few bushels of it really overpowered you, especially if you had a Stone-boosted nose. Made my eyes water, it did. My traveling companion showed no effect from it at all.

"Maybelle owes me a few favors," she said, giving the fairy a knowing glance. "Don't you? All those scrapes I got you out of, including a couple of prosecutions. You'd be stewing in a Fae jail if it weren't for me. Remember that." Maybelle stuck out her tongue, but she was trying hard not to laugh at the same time. *Hmm. Maybe we're more alike than I want to think.*

Prisme took out the snuffbox and opened it. "Fairies are nocturnal creatures. Troublemakers so often are. I had to wake her up out of a sound sleep. That's why she's so cranky. Usually she's a bit more polite than this." Maybelle rose up from the stove, shedding a few gassy flashes, and headed for her portable bedroom to resume her beauty rest.

My cup turned into a palm-sized store ticket. "Now servin'
Number Thirteen! Step right up, Assassins Guild. No pushin',
no shovin', you silly demons. House Shedim can wait until
it's called like everybody else. You, too, Merchantry goons."

26 / Stormbolt Earns Its Name

A white-hot bullet shot out of the just-closed filler hole. We all
ducked in surprise as the projectile ricocheted all about the
cramped gondola. I got Morphageus up as a shield to block any
magical attack, hoping I wouldn't get singed. Maybelle dove into
her snuffbox.

"Who in tarnation dumped a wagonload of blossoms all over
me?" demanded an indignant Scorch, stopping in mid-air to
brush purple debris from his coat. The flame surrounding him
subsided until only his hair was ablaze. His double pair of wings
hummed so hard and fast they sounded like a sawmill. He
looked at each of us in turn, accusingly. "It's getting so a fellow
can't even sneak a nap in a nice warm oven without some ill-
mannered buffoon —"

Catching sight of the fetching Maybelle changed his tune.
Scorch straightened his tie, brushed his fiery hair back. "Why,
hello there, you captivating creature. My apologies for including
you amongst the suspects. It's clear as morning dew that you
could never have done so dastardly a deed."

With a squeak the cute fairy ducked down low in the snuffbox, banging the lid down after her. Scorch stuck out his lower lip in a pout. The lid cracked open a bit to reveal one coy blue eye. Then it dropped back down. High-pitched giggles came from inside. Madame Seychelles and I both choked back snorts of laughter. This was the sort of romantic display you didn't often see unless you were at a particularly silly play at the theatre.

"She fancies me," Scorch insisted, buzzing down to sit on the edge of the gondola rail. "I can tell. It's so hard for a woman like that to say no to...this." He stretched his arms wide and lay back, ankles crossed.

Prisme raised one gray eyebrow at him. "And just what is...this, if I may be so bold as to ask?"

The sprite gasped at her ignorance of his renown. I jumped in to help out. "This here's Scorch, ladies' man and fire sprite extraordinaire on the *Penelope's Kiss*."

"I am most delighted to make your acquaintance, Madame Directeur," he said with a deep bow and a swirling arm flourish. "And might I say that the heat of your oven has a savory taste and aroma that I have seldom enjoyed. You should be mighty proud."

"Oh, I am," she assured him, opening the big door to check on the fairy gas' state. She closed it quickly to keep the violet cloud inside. "Though most of that is due to the exquisite Miss Maybelle whom you were chatting up just now. It's her you smell."

"You don't say? That's quite an agreeable surprise. In my

experience fairies tend to produce an off-putting aroma. I tend to favor a more charcoalish sort of experience. Too much sweetness disagrees with me. Cloying, don't you know." He ogled the snuffbox again. A goofy grin opened up on his face. "Maybelle, you say?"

"Maybelle Moonflower, maidenfair of the northern Aquitania." Prisme winked at me and continued in a teasing tone. "Unattached, I hear. Sworn to none...as yet."

"What a waste," he sighed. "She should be birthing litters by now. Sharing her bounty."

Boy oh boy, this is all gettin' a bit thick. I'm thinkin' we oughta take off before more bad guys arrive. They seem to be lined up fer miles to take a crack at poor little Verity. Probably have to take numbers and get served in turn.

My cup turned into a palm-sized store ticket. "Now servin' Number Thirteen! Step right up, Assassins Guild. No pushin', no shovin', you silly demons. House Shedim can wait until it's called like everybody else. You, too, Merchantry goons."

While the dinky but adorable mating ritual continued, I peeked over the edge of the basket to see what was up, since we weren't. All of the turrets, towers, chimneys, and roof peaks made it hard to spy out much. At the other end of the roof a gaggle of folks were fussing with something or somebody. From the way they acted they might've actually snared themselves a Graue Adler prisoner. That would be quite the success, considering their preference for dramatic death scenes worthy of the stage. Maybe we'd find out something useful. Lady Vigor probably knew some interrogation tricks that didn't bear thinking about.

Having her name in my head made me jump when she popped her curly head over the rail and said hi. My witched ears hadn't heard so much as the rustle of her dress. I needed to learn how to do that. It'd be a real handy trick to know. She laughed, seeming to know just what I was thinking. "I get that reaction a lot. Light on my feet, I am."

"I'll say. Usually I can hear a butterfly hiccup a block away."

"They are prone to that. Overindulging in hollyhocks is a prime cause." The Grandmaster opened the door. "I brought you something. He insisted. And that look he puts on is very manipulative, I fear. Approaches being black magick. If we could bottle it we could conquer the Proprietor himself."

Standing there was the saggy, baggy, floppy, sloppy, mopey, dopey, droopy basset hound, of course. His brown ears hung to the ground like big wet leaves. The skin surrendered to gravity everywhere. Even on his legs, where it pooled around his enormous feet like oversized socks. That impressive male undercarriage looked like it'd be a positive liability when running, but I'd never noticed him having a problem with it. I certainly hadn't been tactless enough to ask about it. Ma raised me better than that.

"Bonjour," groaned the Duke. "I am quite peckish. Have you any sustenance handy?"

"Yeah, and I missed you, too, you old fraud." I patted his head and buried my face in his jowls, sucking in the doggy funk.

"Plannin' on travelin' to Poitiers with us?"

"If you would be so kind. The sight of this glorious wreck of a house is too much for me to bear. So many bitter memories. I must seek solace elsewhere."

Madame Seychelles shook her head while she fiddled with the stove. "No room, I'm afraid. Tight quarters with this one already."

Right on cue those liquid brown eyes turned on their I-m-about-to-cry-because-you're-abandoning-me charm. If I hadn't known any better I might've suspected that he was using an actual charm. Anyway, he was wasting a perfectly good pouty face, because I wasn't about to leave him behind.

"Wait a minute," I said, "I got an idea." Dragging my rucksack from its corner, I lay it on its side and opened the top flap. "Come on, boy. In you go."

"He'll never fit in there in a million years, child," Vigor protested. "Why, he's longer than the whole blessed bag."

She stopped talking when the nearly yard-long hound disappeared inside like I'd cut a hole in the floor. "Neat trick, huh?" I giggled. "My Ma made it fer me. Real handy. Got a whole storeroom inside."

"Lady Ellen is a most capable mage. She must have learned that spell from your father. Those bags are common in the Obverse. Children use them for their school books and such."

"Really? She never said. Shoot, I didn't even know she do magick at all until a couple of weeks ago. Didn't bother to mention me bein' half-Obverse, either, until I pried it outta her just the other day."

"Well, it isn't the sort of thing one mentions in casual conversation. Particularly since that very fact is why so many loathsome individuals wish you harm."

I thought back to the day I found Morphageus. That afternoon, before that grand event had even happened, we'd been jumped by a pack of rich kids from St. Usher's. Though I hadn't known it then, it was actually a Merchantry headquarters. Those meanies had tried to kill us for no good reason. *Nothin' worse than a private school kid with a knife.* Now I knew why. It annoyed me that Horace and his plug-uglies had known what I was before Ma had worked up the gumption to tell me herself.

"Yeah, well, maybe if she had mentioned it I could've been on my guard. Besides, I deserved to know everything. Pa, Ma, me, all o' this craziness. Y'all need to quit treatin' me like a little kid."

"If you'll pardon me...you are a little kid. You'll forgive us all for believing what we saw until shown otherwise."

That's rich, comin' from her. "Says the ten year-old who watched the Pyramids get built."

That made her smile. "Strictly speaking, I helped move the stones. But your point is taken."

With a deafening roar the stove sent out a burst of violet flame that made the balloon's bag billow out. The gondola tilted a bit as we got more lift. Scorch flew through the fire with glee, then returned to whisper sweet nothings into the snuffbox. "What're y'all gonna do when I leave?" I hollered as the noise grew louder. "Rush ahead and meet us at Poitiers?"

"No, we will lay a false trail to keep your pursuers confused and busy. And the traitorous Mr. Babington was clumsy enough to fall into our hands mostly unbruised. Your resourceful Lady Roberta snatched his envenomed bodkin out of his hand before he could shuffle off this mortal coil with it. I have a few rather pointed questions to put to him."

Yeah, I'll bet. Probably with Stormbolt's point.

"What should I do at Poitiers? Bein' there don't help me none that I can see. I gotta get to London." I glanced over at the busy Directeur. "And Paris, too, I suppose. Time's awful short."

"That it is, presuming young Thomas's situation is as the House Shedim demon claimed. That will be confirmed in a day or two. If he truly is in Merchantry custody and in peril, as you say, then we shall take steps to get you there in haste. If not, we can adapt our plan to circumstances. Taking our time and being most cautious would be wise."

"Fine. But I'm gonna keep goin' hard until I have proof that Tommy's not gonna get his throat cut when the moon turns full again."

"I would expect nothing less. Meet with the redoubtable Victoria Sponge, as Captain Tyrell suggested. You will be in good hands with her. As soon as possible you must rendezvous in Orleans, at the Parc Floral de la Source, with the rest of the team – Tyrell, his sister, Romulus, Sha'ira, a few others I'm sending who may prove useful. Your mother, too, if Commander Pitcairn can free himself of his pursuers. Be ever watchful. If the Graue

Adler could infiltrate us so easily, that can only mean that others have the same information about your movements. They have a method of tracking you, that much is certain."

"Boy, is that true. Everywhere I go there's somebody waitin' fer me. It's like each day o' the week has its assigned monster or murderer."

Jasper chuckled. "If it's Sunday, it must be poop monsters."

The balloon was straining at its restraining ropes now. It wanted to be off. Madame Seychelles had her big goggles over her eyes and was testing the steering and propulsion controls. I noticed that she'd hooked up a chain-and-bar affair to the oar. That machinery led to a wheel next to the stove, where a boiler like on a locomotive, only smaller, sat. "Baby steam engine," she explained, shouting over all of the noise as it rattled into life. "To flap our wings. Unless you plan to do it all night."

"Only if I can do it while dead asleep, ma'am. I'm powerful tired."

"As I thought. You do just that, then. We're all depending on you to be sharp."

Jasper turned into a thumbtack. "Some of us are sharper than others."

I turned back to Vigor. "Looks like we're finally leavin'. You got anything else?"

"Only this." Stormbolt leaped into existence out of its whirlwind. Now I could see that its basket hilt was a riot of silvery shooting stars and sculptural whirlwinds. Not only that, the whole sword was made of maillon. *Holy smokes! Prob'ly worth more than Cornelius Vanderbilt's and John Jacob Astor's bank accounts put together*. She touched its tip against my chest. I felt a warm glow, sort of like when the Stone was in use.

"Now that I've recovered from your eventful induction, Marshal Verity, I need to gift you, after all. And I have a feeling that this will serve you well in the coming days."

"What is it? I don't feel much of —yow!" An itching burn flowed through all of my limbs. Just as I decided to jump in the moat to make it stop, it faded into a happy tingle.

"Inkchantment. A special type of puppeteer spell. With only your will you will be able to manipulate and even enliven any art, be it paint, ink, or pencil drawing."

"I'm not sure how helpful that'll be, but thanks."

The little girl patted my cheek like she was my granny. "Oh, just you wait, honey."

"Cast off!" cried Prisme. "Vigor, be a dear and do the honors, please."

Stormbolt neatly cut the four ropes holding us down. I hauled them back into the gondola as we lurched into the air, swaying to and fro. *Hope this stops, 'cause I ain't aimin' to upchuck again.* Before we cleared the nearest chimney the motion subsided. At least, ours did. Back on the roof there was a whole lot of movement, none of it good. One of the stone lizard carvings leaped from its wall, just missing the basket with a savage swipe of its claws. It landed with a booming thud, hissing and spitting, next to the little Grandmaster.

"You know," Jasper observed, "I seem to say 'you don't see that every day' an awful lot lately. Why do you suppose that is?"

"Probably 'cause yer great and glorious Stone Warden's on the menu o' every icky monster in two universes." *And what does it say about me that I ain't squealin' in terror at the sight of a statue hoppin' around? Shoot, I ain't even surprised by this sort o' thing anymore.*

While we kept ascending, slow and straight, since the balloon was still amongst the turrets and we hadn't caught a breeze yet, I watched Vigor deal with the sudden arrival of a marble reptile over twelve feet long. It turned out to be quite the education. She demonstrated what an experienced magick practitioner with a spellsword could do. I couldn't imagine ever being that good. *Heck, I can't even imagine livin' past the next week.*

That lizard looked like some small carnivorous ones I'd seen in a menagerie, except for the long-as-a-milk-wagon-and-made-of-stone part. Its snout was long and pointy, though not as much as a crocodile. Ditto for the teeth. There were plenty of them and each looked to be as long as my foot. At a good eight feet and active as a bullwhip, the tail was as dangerous as the nasty front end. In fact, the beast attacked with that part first, slashing at Vigor's legs to knock her down before devouring her. But the Equity leader leaped aside, ran along the chimney wall, and dropped back down behind her foe, sword held high.

"Spry little thing for bein' older than dirt, don't you think?" Jasper said.

"I'll say. And in a long dress, too. Glad I ain't up against her."

I looked over to Madame Seychelles, who was sliding the snuffbox back into her pocket. "Shouldn't we help out? Maybe give it what-fer with that ogre-gun?"

She leaned her wrinkled face over the side to take a look. "Oh, she's fine. If we interfered she'd regard it as an insult."

"Seems to me that gettin' yer head gnawed off would be a lot worse."

That got a big laugh. "Unlikely. Watch."

Before the lizard could turn around Stormbolt had chopped off three feet of its thrashing tail. Despite it being made of solid marble, the girl accomplished the surgery with an almost casual wrist flick. When her blade made contact an electrical charge shot out along its length, like a small and contained lightning strike. *Guess that's why it's called Stormbolt. The power of weather must live inside it.* To prove me right, Vigor whipped the sword in big circles over her head. A mighty whirlwind surrounded her. Every time the creature tried to bat at her with its claws it found its forefoot knocked back with great violence. Hunkering down, looking for an opening in the defense, it forgot about its own. That's when a great white-hot lightning bolt that Zeus would've envied blasted out of the tip of the magick sword. It hit the giant lizard in its open mouth. The thing exploded into a hundred chunks of smoking stone, breaking windows and carving channels in walls.

"See?" said Prisme. "Now wouldn't she have been cross if we had denied her the satisfaction of that?" She worked at starting the engine that would flap our wings and send us north.

"Maybe. But if I ever get jumped by a witched sculpture, feel free to wound my pride by killin' it fer me. I won't kick up a fuss, I promise you."

As if 'pride' had been its cue, the lion that had been carved next to the lizard shook its head and looked around. It was behind Vigor, who wasn't paying attention because she was poking through the reptile-rubble making sure the pieces weren't about to start more trouble. I hollered a warning, but we were pretty high up now and she didn't hear me.

"Scorch!" I yelled, whipping my head around to find him. "You need to fly down there and —" I didn't see him atop the stove or anyplace else. "Hey! Where'd that stinky spark go?"

Prisme tipped her head at the oven. "Inside. I'm afraid the happy couple are, um, otherwise engaged."

From inside the firebox came the happy raucous sounds of wee-folk having themselves the sort of good time that I'm not about to describe for you.

I rolled my eyes and grumbled. "Oh, oink! All men's the same even when they have wings."

The Directeur grinned. "So true." She sighed and thought about something, then laughed. "So, so true."

That was a conversation I didn't want to have, especially two hundred feet in the air. I considered turning Morphageus into a pair of wings and soaring down to help, but even if I survived landing between all those chimneys, not to mention the fight, getting back into the balloon would be a puzzler. Just as I was about to grab the ogre-gun and risk a shot, my tin cup jumped from my hip and transformed into a six-foot-long speaking trumpet. *Guess I owe Jasper some licorice whips later.*

"Ahoy, Lady Vigor!" I called through the giant cone. "You got the king o' beasts on yer tail!"

The Grandmaster turned her adorable head to look behind just as the marble beast pounced from its ledge twenty feet up. Again she bounded out of the way just as her attacker landed. How she managed that in a skirt was the greatest magick I'd seen all day. But her next trick was a close second. Squaring off against the stone cat, she invited it to leap at her with its deadly claws. When it did so she shouted something in no language I recognized – even my new Marshal's coin didn't translate it – and vanished into a sheet of rain gushing from a mattress-sized black cloud that popped into existence over her head. That lion shot straight through the falling water without touching her. She'd actually become the rain itself, so far as I could tell. *Whoa! That's a swell move. Maybe she can teach it to me.*

Bouncing off of a wall and growling its confused displeasure, the creature spun around in a circle hunting for his prey. The cloud faded and all that was left was a big puddle beneath the lion's paws. He finally gave up and decided on a victory drink. Lapping up the water with his huge kitty tongue, most of it went down his gullet in maybe ten seconds. When he stopped he frowned, as if he had a belly-ache. That turned out to be the case, because he yowled and roared, rolling on his back and tearing at himself with his teeth. In the middle of that he burst into white stony fragments just as the lizard had. Left standing in the middle of all of that destruction was Vigor, who brushed off a few dusty spots on her dress, then saluted me with Stormbolt.

Now we were out of range of even the speaking-trumpet, which I shrank back into a cup. No more sculptures jumped off the walls of the chateau's turrets and chimneys. In fact, everything around the castle seemed calm. In the west the sun was very low now, throwing long shadows of trees and buildings. The constant menace of the day seemed past. But I knew it wasn't. Because if there was one thing I'd learned in the three weeks that I'd been the reluctant Stone Warden, it was that inanimate objects tend to stay that way unless somebody with sorcery starts playing around with them.

"Hey, ya got a spyglass around here someplace?" I asked our pilot, my voice raised above the din of the flapper engine. My voice was likely to vanish if things didn't quiet down soon. Madame Seychelles blinked through her green-lensed goggles and pointed towards her ogre-gun. In a long quiver-like affair next to it was a brass telescope almost as big as the pintle-mounted one that Commander Pitcairn used on the *Kiss*. I dragged it out, extended it as far as it would go, and jammed my eye into the small end. Time was getting short. Before dusk set in and made a search that much more difficult, even for my witched peepers, I wanted to find the cause of Vigor's distress. Though looking was just for confirming my suspicion. There wasn't much doubt in my mind who it was.

Sure enough, straight south of the chateau about half a mile I spotted her, hidden in a thick patch of trees and floating a foot above the grass. My crazy Aunt Regan, Ma's sister and a twisted Chauntline mage, was chanting while waving her staff around. Just as I caught sight of her, she did the same to me. Since her pets were destroyed, she relaxed and stopped the spell. Regan threw back her gray hood. Like in Lusitania she wore a dark-blue leather mask. Just for me she peeled it off, smiled, waved, and vanished in a burst of green light.

Lilac light splashed up from the little hatch as Maybelle popped out of it, wings chattering. She'd lost her hat and one stocking. Both were in her hand. As she hovered she blew Scorch a kiss and giggled.

27 / Off to Poitiers

After that, the rest of the evening was downright dull. Or at least as dull as my life ever got. After all, we were flying in a hot air balloon fueled by fairy flatulence ignited by a pirate fire sprite. I had a basset hound snoozing in a knapsack that was as big as a carriage house inside. We had a blunderbuss that could explode ogres. And I had a sword that could take any shape and also talked to me in my head.

Not to mention the fact that I wasn't human. Well, not completely. Not much could compete with that.

We didn't bother looking for my nasty aunt. Regan had been in the opposite direction from where we were headed, so going back hadn't been practical. Anyway, I knew that we wouldn't have found anything. As I knew from having accidentally hitched a ride with her in Cumae, she knew how to telegraph herself short distances by skipping along that same Obverse barrier I'd visited during my Equity initiation. That was what she'd done as I'd watched. By the time we could've made it to those trees where I'd seen her she'd have been a dozen miles away. Strong magick. It seemed like it was in our blood. Ma, Pa, Regan, even me. *Travelin' Europa, yankin' on them awesome cosmic forces. Just another day in paradise for the Sauveurs.*

It was after dark now. We had plenty of light to fly by. There weren't any clouds and the moon was only a few days from full. I tried not to think about the moon. When it got all the way full that might be the end of Tommy, if Venoma hadn't been bluffing. Since demons couldn't tell a lie without their noses running and hers had been dry as Sahara sandpaper I figured that I couldn't hope for that. To occupy my mind I smoked my pipe, since I needed to recharge Jasper with a favor, while keeping an eye out for ravens or anything else with wings that could ambush us in the middle of the air.

But worrying about Tommy turned into fretting about all of the friends I'd left scattered behind me. Romulus, Sha'ira, Roberta, and Ernie back at the old Chateau Evremonde. Heck, even that treacherous Tyrell who'd so inconveniently saved me. Now I had a hard time hating him. By now they might all be in a Gaullic army hoosegow. There'd been so much commotion and strangeness at the castle that those signaling stations of Napoleon's had to have noticed. Maybe not, though. I hadn't heard tell of a plan to get all of the Marshals and Redeemers out, but I suspected Vigor had neatly arranged it.

Bonaparte's troops weren't the only potential problem. It sounded like all of the various groups I'd finally been warned about, from the Bitter Apples to Satan's Snare, knew where I was and were converging in a hurry. Though I'd snuck out in the balloon, that left my friends in the middle of my mess, fighting off magick, monsters, and murderers. I didn't like it that they were fending that off on my account, even if, as Vigor had said, drawing off pursuit was the intention.

And then there was Ma and the *Kiss*. You'd think that after nearly being turned into demon stew on board the *Croatan* that she'd never want to set foot on a ship again. But ever since then she'd stayed on Pitcairn's pride and joy, stitching up sailor's clothes and helping in the sick bay or galley when they were short-handed. It was me who kept leaving her, gallivanting off to Iberion, Lusitania, and now Gaulle. Despite her fearsome battle-magick I worried about her. I'd nearly lost her to the cannibals when I'd rushed off from Washington. Getting word that she'd gone down to some dastardly attack meant for me would make me a flaming wreck.

The wind had shifted to the north and was pretty brisk up high. Prisme turned off the flapper engine so we wouldn't attract attention. She said that if no trouble came our way and the breeze stayed constant, we'd be in Poitiers by dawn without having to fire up the noisy thing. That sounded fine to me. I planned to get some shut eye in my rucksack. Madame Seychelles insisted that she could stay awake a long time yet and I wasn't about to argue. I knocked out my pipe on the rail of the gondola and yawned.

Somebody else did the same, behind me. I turned to see Scorch climb out of the feeder hole of the stove like an exhausted man who'd fallen into a well. Though below him the violent violet fairy gas bubbled merrily away, he had no flame on him at all. Not so much as an ember stuck to his hair. He might've been a normal person, except for being four inches tall with wings. Those drooped down his back like damp newspapers. In fact, everything about him did. When he'd made it all of the way out of the hatch he collapsed on his face. I'd seen perkier drunks in Washington gutters.

"Miss Verity, Scorch the Mighty has met his match," he muttered, barely audible.

"You don't say?" I snickered, not sure this was a discussion I wanted to be a part of. *Still, you have to learn about the world if you're gonna save it, I suppose.*

"Oh, I accept the responsibility. After all, I pursued her. I sallied forth and tilted at that romantic windmill. How was I to know that it was enchanted?"

That all reminded me of the decrepit old fellow we'd run into in Iberion who had been doing that very thing. Those windmills had been enchanted, too, witched by my aunt into actual living beings with a mean streak. It had taken a Gypsy buck and an Arabe fighter to rescue him. "Bit off more than ya could chew, huh?"

"Decidedly. In fact, I was the one who got chewed. And then spit out again." With a groan he sat up. "As you may know, I am not without experience in the ways of love. Many a bewinged darling has found her way to me, departing the following morn without complaint, a smile upon her dainty lips. In point of fact, those lips always spread the word to their fellow maidens of the Fae. Often I have been hard-pressed to attend to them all." He shook his bedraggled head. "My, how the tables have turned."

I tried to keep a straight face, imagining my gallant little sprite getting wrung-out like a dishrag. Though I didn't know exactly what he and Maybelle had been up to in that stove, I had a pretty good idea. Before moving to Washington City we'd lived on a farm in Maryland. You didn't have to be a genius to figure out where new livestock came from. What made it all so darned fascinating for grown-ups was beyond me, though Ma insisted I'd soon change my tune on that.

Jasper finally woke up. Since he lived in my noggin, he had an uncomfortable way of timing his comments for maximum embarrassment. "And when you do, ol' Jasper'll be right there with you, takin' notes for your memoirs."

"Gee, thanks fer makin' this even more awkward than it already is, Creepy Sword o' Fate."

"You don't have to thank me. The pleasure's all mine."

Ya got that right.

Lilac light splashed up from the little hatch as Maybelle popped out of it, wings chattering. She'd lost her hat and one stocking. Both were in her hand. As she hovered she blew Scorch a kiss and giggled. When he whimpered and sagged she winked at me and glided over the pocket in Prisme's coat where her snuffbox lay. With another laugh she paused her wings and dropped out of sight.

"Scorch and Maybelle, sittin' in a tree," sang Jasper, "k-i-s-s-i-n-g..."

"At least," I snickered, watching the quenched fire sprite moan and drag himself toward the flapper-engine in search of hot coals to restore his strength.

"Perhaps she was sent by the Obverse as a fiendish trap," he said. "An agent of the demons intended to weaken the forces of good in order to make the Merchantry's task easier. That would explain so much."

The wounded warrior disappeared into the firebox. A moment later its sides glowed orange as he absorbed and magnified the heat of the coals. He let out a long satisfied sigh like a farmer dropping into a hot bath after a long day of toil. Madame Seychelles couldn't suppress her laughter anymore and let it all out. I joined her. Pretty soon we were almost as tuckered out from guffawing as Scorch was from romancing.

"I'll take a good belly laugh after a day like this," I said, spitting over the side. "You can only handle so many duels, assassins, and Equity initiations before ya go loopy in the head."

"Loogie on the head, yer mean," complained a Cockney voice from the darkness next to me.

Morphageus blazed in my hand before I knew I'd wished it. On the other side of the big basket Prisme had snatched up her ogre-gun and aimed it at the voice. By then I'd recognized it. I held up a hand to tell her it was okay. With the other arm I waved the newcomers aboard.

The Dread Pirate Roberta soared out of the murk to land on the railing of the wicker gondola. Riding on the parrot's back, just behind her head, Ernie was making a disgusted face and trying to get my spit off of his little bicorn hat. Roberta was chuckling at his plight. Soon all of us except the mouse were yucking it up at his expense.

"Go ahead, laugh," he said in a sour tone. "Ridicule the rodent, if that makes yer happy."

I fished out a bandana from my overalls. While I wiped his headgear Roberta managed to choke down her mirth enough to tell us what was going on and why they'd come to us. "I swear, Gaulle was havin' itself a reg'lar scalawag convention after you left. You sure timed it good, shrimp. Come sundown Venoma and Toxicus rode an ostium in lookin' fer you. Brought a boatload o' Darwins, too. I declare, them fellers is a darned sight harder to dispatch after dark. Faster, stronger, tougher hide."

I recalled fighting Venoma in Washington before I'd had any skill or experience. It wasn't something I was eager to try again even with my improved abilities. "They sure are. We were lucky they got anxious on the *Croatan* and jumped us in broad daylight."

"Well, we got lucky again. While the Marshals were givin' 'em their best broadside and the Redeemers were layin' into 'em with blade and ball, them three hateful girlies from the Assassins Guild showed up and pitched right in."

"Huh? Averna, Morrigan, and Nephthys? How's that lucky?"

"Because they went after the stinkin' demons, that's why. Never saw the like. Shades takin' down the Obverse."

Prisme frowned at that. "I wonder what has happened. The

Guild is staunchly apolitical. They never take sides, just payment." She adjusted her steering to turn the balloon more northeast-ish. "That's why they've remained in business for so long. No one will trust them with secrets if they think the Sisterhood has an agenda."

Roberta ruffled up her neck feathers and shrugged her wings. "Don't know 'about any o' that. All I can testify to is what I saw through these spectacles. Them ladies went through the Darwins like crap through a goose." She chuckled. "And we all know how **that** goes."

"Eight o' the animal demons went down in less than a minute," Ernie said, accepting his now-dried hat back from me with a grudging nod. "The Shades came right behind 'em, outta the same ostium like they'd been chasin' the fiends." He shuddered as if afraid they might pop up right then, even though we were a thousand feet up. "I thought that ginger one was scary when she came after us on the beach in Virginia. But tonight it was like she had a personal grudge against the demons."

"Don't make no sense," I said. "Shades're taught as kids to keep their emotions in a strongbox and never take 'em on a job. Interferes with the judgment."

"Well, her judgment didn't seem like it was impaired," insisted Roberta. She beaked her breast feathers to deal with an itch. "Two snakebirds jumped her and she sliced 'em up like holiday turkeys before they could get a lick in."

I asked, "Did they take on Venoma or Toxicus?"

"Nope, just the animal freaks. Can't blame 'em, though.

Tanglin' with House Shedim at night ain't a winnin' proposition fer a human, Assassins Guild or not." She looked me up and down. "Present comp'ny excepted, of course."

"Shoot, that was beginner's luck. Plus, Jasper was runnin' that fight, not me."

"You sure?"

"I'd only had Morphageus fer an hour or two. Ain't likely I was such a natural talent that I could block her every slash and bite without a heap o' magickal help, is it?"

Madame Seychelles steered us back to the original topic. "Lady Roberta, Master Ernie...what else happened at this violent encounter? Was it only House Shedim with Darwins?"

Ernie crawled along me to warm himself on the stove. "Don't I wish. Bonaparte's boys showed up, too. Fancy blokes on fancier horses, like Tyrell. Somehow our man Laurence bluffed 'em and they went away."

"That weren't the end o' our troubles, though," Roberta continued. "Some Bitter Apple mages snuck into the house and the Marshals had a devil of a time rootin' em out. Had to go room to room. So much magick bein' flung about that from outside it looked like an indoor fireworks show. Eleven marshals dead, they say."

Whoa! That's some serious casualties considerin' Vigor only brought forty or fifty with her. "Anybody we know?" I asked in a quiet voice, afraid of the answer.

"Naw. Though yer great lumberin' friend Herkimer caught himself a good slice across the ribs from Toxicus' tail-barb.

Romulus and Sha'ira gave a good account o' themselves, naturally. Led the counter-attack that drove the nasty brutes back into the ostium."

Ernie growled, "That ain't all. I was with that Gloriana, Tyrell's sister, so-called. If yer can call a magick-built copy your sister. Anyway, I was with her when she fought a Darwin in the vineyard. One o' them two-headed fox things. It got her down with a knife to her throat before I could jump in with me needle."

I frowned. *I thought we hadn't lost anybody?* "And it didn't kill her?"

"Nope. In fact, they had themselves a nice, pleasant conversation, all in whispers. I couldn't catch a word of it, more's the pity. But I'll tell yer one thing. They knew each other. That much was certain. Then he backed off and she pretended to belly-kick him into runnin' away. The whole bleedin' fight was cooked up fer me benefit."

We all stood there with our mouths open, digesting that. Was Tyrell aware of it? Was he in on it with her? Did Gloriana lead the enemy right to her own friends in trying to get to me? Why, if she needed me to help with her scheme to get Napoleon? Some sort of deal maybe, where the Merchantry would sacrifice him in exchange for the Stone Warden? Or was it even worse than that and she'd sold out for mere money or power?

"Can't say as I ever did like her much," I said finally, sneaking a look over at the Redeemer Directeur. Madame Seychelles kept command over her face, but even so I could tell that she was heart-broken. One of her own had sold her out. *That's gotta be tough.*

After a while she took a big gulp of the Gaullic night air and sighed it back out. "Alright, then. There it is. We should probably assume the worst and prepare for Poitiers to be crawling with Graue Adler, Bitter Apples, and Satanem Laqueum. To say nothing of the usual Bonapartist scum: spies, secret police, and the like."

Her mention of those Satan's Lackey's fellows made me think of something I'd seen back at the castle. "Hey, wait a minute. Vigor told me that them Satanem Whatever guys all have a cross branded on 'em."

"True. The vertical bar is a sword blade. Why?"

"'Cause some o' them Gray Eagle boys had the same thing."

She raised an eyebrow at that. "You don't say? My, my, this is getting...complex. They either want to muddy the waters by making us think that the Graue Adler are cooperating with them – not likely, the Teutons are Protestant militants – or the Papal Fief has somehow infiltrated their enemy's ranks. If I had to guess I would choose the latter. Though how they hide those marks I don't know."

I threw up my hands. "Shoot, beats me. I didn't even know any of these fool groups existed until this afternoon. Sounds to me like everybody's turnin' themselves inside-out stabbin' one another in the back while tryin' to get to me."

"It does sound needlessly complex. But that's the Merchantry for you. They love a good chess game more than a battle. And allying themselves with the Obverse only magnified that sort of thinking. On the other side everything has three meanings and five insinuations. Small wonder that when their mad spell went wrong it reshaped the world with that preference built in."

This was all giving me a worse headache than I'd had the first time Jasper blackmailed me into drinking rotgut Confederate whiskey. I needed to get a big book and write it all down, maybe color-coded to keep the various sides and their machinations straight. Compared to our Civil War in the States United the one that the Merchantry had on its hands was a game of tiddlywinks. *Criminey! Don't nobody on that side trust one another at all? As far as that goes, it don't look too much like the big cheeses on my side are any better. Ain't no way to run a railroad, that's fer sure.*

Jasper turned the tin cup into a toy locomotive. Smoke poured out of the chimney and the wheels turned. "Woo-woo! This is how you run a railroad. Woo-woo!"

"I'll sort it out later," I said to Roberta and Ernie. "My, um, trained companion and me both need naps. Anything else happen I oughta know about?"

Ernie yawned. "You mean besides that nutso Aunt Regan o' yers showin' up to abuse the masonry? But I figure yer already knew about that, didn't yer?"

I told them all about Vigor's fight with the vicious statuary, and how Regan had taunted me before winking out to wherever her next outrage was scheduled. How she fit into all of this was still a mystery. She'd claimed that she wanted to turn me over to somebody for a reward, but who? There was a list of suspects as long as your arm. And there was always the possibility that she was working for a group we didn't even know about yet. Or maybe she'd been lying about the whole thing and just wanted to make Ma suffer through me.

Roberta filled me in on the rest as I was opening my knapsack to crawl in and sleep. The upshot of all of the chaos was that a lot of Marshals were dead and only a couple of Redeemers. Either that meant something sinister or the Marshals just threw themselves into a fight with less regard for their own safety. Heaps of enemy bodies had been disposed of to keep Napoleon's troops and the local citizens from finding them. By the time inquisitive gendarmes had braved the night to see what had happened, the site had been cleaned up and vacated. Vigor was leading her picked squad on a wild goose chase to confuse any further pursuit. They'd meet us in Paris in two days. When she'd finished I thanked her and slithered into my pack. Duke lay on his back, snoring. With a weary smile I lay beside him and did the same.

Yanking myself away from the Chauntline with an agonizing wrench that felt exactly like ripping a bandage off a mortal wound, I collapsed into a girl-puddle, sweat and tears mingling on my face.

28 / One Step Over the Line
Tuesday, July 16, 1804

For the second night in a row I had no nasty demon dreams. I sawed logs until near dawn without having to fend off psychic attacks. To my delight, no abuse came my way while I slept.

Well, no otherworldly abuse assailed me. Strictly speaking, the basset hound's gassy discharge didn't count as a Merchantry ploy, though you'd have been hard-pressed to tell the difference in that closed canvas bag with your eyes watering. As I struggled to breathe in that toxic atmosphere, barely awake, I felt that I was suffocating and getting asphyxiated all at the same time. Blinking, I tried to focus but all I could see was a wall of fuzz. My snoot was jammed into a gooey cave of some kind. I pulled back a couple of inches and winced. My face was stuck up inside the dog's ear canal, the great velvety blanket hanging across my cheek. *Eeww!*

One of the hound's aristocratic eyebrows rose with sneering slowness. The Duke looked at me like I was a servant caught stealing spoons, a sort of disappointed sneer. "Do you mind?" the Gaullic tones asked. "That funny freckled nose of yours tickles."

I slid back a couple of feet, waving at the air to clear it without being too obvious. "Um, sorry."

He shook his head, causing those enormous ears to make a leathery flapping noise like one of Satan's bats come to claim me. "Ah, well, I suppose it could be worse. At least your proboscis is not as formidable as de Bergerac's."

"That cuts both ways," said Jasper. "We might've been at his other end."

Double -eeww!

"Do ya mind?" I asked in my head, hunting for my straw hat. "I ain't had breakfast yet and I'd appreciate it if ya wouldn't put me off it. When I don't eat, neither do you."

"Point taken."

We scrounged some food from the boxes and bags lashed to the sides of the magicked backpack, since I was eating for three. One bite for me, one for the Duke, one for Jasper. That's how it seemed, anyhow. An apple, some hardtack and beans, coffee I heated with a spell inside my Morphageus-pot. After changing into an itchy and confining blue frock so I'd blend in with the locals, Jasper around my wrist as a pretty bracelet, I crawled out of the rucksack to see what Poitiers looked like.

As soon as I poked my head out I bumped into Madame Seychelles' boot. The gondola sure was short on elbow room, being basically a one-person ship with just enough extra space for a few bags of supplies tied to the walls. The magick stove that heated the air for lifting took up most of the center area, with the little steam engine for the flapper and the steering controls crammed into one corner. Prisme peered into her spyglass in the direction we were drifting. I rubbed the sleep from my eyes and pulled myself up with a grunt to stand next to her and look out over the rail.

The balloon moved north, silent as a wish. To our right lay gently rolling country, some wooded, some in vines, some in pasture. I could hear some cows mooing below us, probably wondering what the heck that ugly cloud was above them. To our right the edge of the world burned with an orange-pink glow. We were so close to dawn you could almost smell the sun. Ahead lay the town, mostly low white stone buildings with several church spires sticking up like daggers. A curving river cut it in half. It was still a good two miles off. At a guess I figured it was probably about the same size as Washington, D.C. And just like home, it had troops all around it.

"Oh, ain't that just swell," I grumbled. "Bonaparte's already beat us here."

The Redeemer Directeur chuckled and rubbed my head. *All grown-ups everywhere must've told each other how much I hate that.* "It looks that way, doesn't it? But no, it's been a garrison town for a long time. And a university town. Crawling with soldiers and students."

"Oh, yeah!" crowed Jasper, making my head vibrate at such an early hour. "This sounds like my kind of place! Taverns, duelin' grounds, ladies of questionable virtue amblin' along the boulevards..."

I let my forehead rest on the rail and sighed. "Maybe I'll get lucky and we'll only have to deal with demon hordes and the Assassins Guild." The thought of my boy-sword running amok, or expecting me to, in that sort of free-wheeling atmosphere made my tummy rumble.

Prisme had let the stove go cold, as she planned to set down well short of Poitiers and hide her airship. Already we were sinking. In fact, the tops of the surrounding trees weren't but maybe thirty feet below us. She'd expertly gauged the whisper of a breeze and with her hand on the steering post the balloon was headed for a soft landing in tall grass. As if a gentle giant's hand was placing us on a shelf, we touched the ground with a bump so slight it amounted to a goodnight kiss. That was a relief, considering what I'd expected. The few times I'd taken to the air with Jasper wings or springs or some other homemade magickal contrivance I hadn't always come back to earth so painlessly.

With a pat on my bottom Madame Seychelles scooted me out the gondola door to lasso tree trunks with the tether ropes. In a minute or two our craft was tucked in a clump of elms, hidden from prying eyes well off of any road or track. With a tug on some lines the gray-haired captain released camouflage nets with false fabric leaves from the top of the bag. Now it'd take a careful inspection up close to notice us at all.

"Mighty clever," I told her, grabbing my rucksack and dumping the hound out of it. He pouted at having to walk, but I needed his wonder-snout to help keep out of trouble. Besides, I figured he probably knew the town.

The Directeur of the Coterie Redempteur removed her heavy long coat, top hat, and goggles. Underneath she wore a matronly gray dress a bit older, fashion-wise, than the time we were in. Inside her oversized handbag went Captain Nemo's terrifying pistol and some extra magazines. My reticule was a lot smaller and all it held was Gaullic coins, licorice whips to bribe Jasper, some cookies for the hound, and the bottle of magick potion pills Ma had put into the back of my knapsack. *Never know when you'll need a temporary itchin' spell or a charm against werewolves. And them's just the most likely ones on the label.*

"Bonnet, dear," Prisme instructed me, tying her wide-brimmed hat under her chin with a pink ribbon. "Going to be a hot one, I think. With your complexion it would burn you to a cinder." Making a sour face, I plopped my less-impressive chapeau on, too, grumbling about having to leave my beloved straw hat in the pack with my overalls. I knew that it wouldn't do to wander Poitiers in broad daylight dressed like a bum from sixty years in the future, but that didn't mean I had to like it.

While we got ready to head into town the Dread Pirate Roberta landed on a fence post beside us. Ernie clung to her back, as usual. He hopped onto the Duke's rump for the walk north. My parrot friend informed us that they'd spotted nothing unusual in their tour of the Poitiers airspace. No ravens, Furies, demons, or sharpshooters. Just loads of soldiers.

"They shan't bother us," Madame Seychelles claimed. "Unless a general call has gone out to all garrisons to be on the lookout for a sprightly red-haired lass and her granny." She wrinkled her nose. "But just to be safe, let us tuck that flaming mop of yours well under your hat."

Once that had been done we set off, leaving Roberta to guard the balloon and my precious pack. I ducked into the bushes to answer nature's morning call. *That's one advantage of a skirt over trousers, anyway.* Before rejoining Prisme I gulped down some licorice. Better to start Jasper off in a good mood than leave it until I needed an extra boost of something special. At least I didn't have to bribe him for translation spells anymore. As I stepped over a fallen log to go back, I nearly jumped to the moon, squealing.

I stood on an honest-to-goodness Chauntline. A big one.

It's hard to explain the feeling. Imagine that hot numb shock you get when you whack your funny bone, only it's traveling up your foot, through your belly and backbone, and filling up your head. A zillion ants danced on my skin. My already-fantastic senses doubled or tripled. Colors seemed so bright and rich that it was like living inside an oil painting. I swear I could hear quiet conversations in the town, two miles away. My nose caught the scent of the sea nearly a hundred miles off, though the whiff of cow dung at a farm fought for my attention.

Boy, o boy, this is a whole diff'rent kettle o' fish from the line on the Kiss. Even that one in Cumae ain't nothin' compared to it.

Of course Jasper noticed, too. "Yee-haw!" he hollered, like he was on a runaway stallion and having the time of his life. "This beats your trip to the Obverse hands-down! Oo-ee! Just feel that power. Mama Earth grabbin' you by the scruff o' the neck and shakin' you real good!"

"Glad somebody appreciates it." I sucked in great gulps of air and chanted to calm myself and keep from getting blown off of my feet. "Feels like a spankin' from God, if you ask me." *Holy Cow, I'm about to shiver into a thousand pieces and I ain't even embraced the line yet. Just standin' on it is like jumpin' rope on a locomotive goin' flat-out.*

"Go ahead," Jasper whispered. "You know you want to."

"Want to what?" I barked out a scoffing laugh. "Latch onto this thing? Are you loony?"

"Aw, come on. No guts, no glory." My bracelet turned into a chicken and clucked taunts at me.

"No!" I insisted, still concentrating on the same chant that had saved me when I'd ridden with Regan. "I ain't gonna."

"Ain't gonna what?"

"Embrace this Chauntline."

He let out an evil laugh. "As you wish!"

Before I knew what he was up to Jasper had reached down to join my mind and soul-store to the Chauntline. My spine bent back into a taut bow and my mouth gaped like a fish. I felt like I was trying to drink an ocean of fire. It took every ounce of willpower I could muster to channel the energy into the Morphageus sword. A greenish-white sphere shot out of the blade, brighter than the risen sun. It struck a granite boulder taller than me, turning it into steaming bits of powder. Amazingly, there was no sound when the rock disintegrated. It just sighed into nonexistence.

I understood how it felt. Yanking myself away from the Chauntline with an agonizing wrench that felt exactly like ripping a bandage off a mortal wound, I collapsed into a girl-puddle, sweat and tears mingling on my face. Every inch of me shivered as if I'd come down with the ague. Iron hammers pounded away at my skull.

Mages do this on purpose? Are they nuts?

Panting, I lay there for what seemed hours. Soon my panting was replaced by that of Duke, who washed my face with his hot doggy tongue. I groaned and rolled over onto my side, dreaming of all manner of indignities to visit upon Jasper as soon as I had the strength to do more than breathe. Using him to plug a sewer pipe would be a good start.

"Don't you dare," he warned me, the sword returning to cup form. "Remember, I can only do what you truly wish, even if you ain't aware of it."

My mouth was lined with wool and swallowing hurt. "You...are a lyin' cup. Ain't no part o' me wanted anything like what just happened."

"Ah, don't fib, now. I live inside your little gray cells." He turned himself into a perfectly-accurate brain.

"You got that right. Actually, I'm wishin' you didn't live anyplace at all."

The brain changed into a big cartoonish heart. "Your lips say no but your eyes say yes."

I hauled myself up by grabbing onto the big hound's loose

skin until I could sort of stand, though I had to lean against the dog to stay there. Everything vibrated and my senses were still scary-good. To ease all of that I nudge Duke into walking me away from the Chauntline.

Madame Seychelles brushed grass off of my dress. "What the devil happened, dearie? You look like a mule kicked you."

"That's pretty accurate, ma'am." I raised my cup, still wanting to throw it into a river and go home. "I stumbled across a powerful big Chauntline and my so-called partner here thought it'd be funny to give it a warm hug."

Jasper turned into his sword self at that. My eyes goggled when I saw that the black blade now had a golden glow around it, visible even in bright daylight. "So I see," said Prisme, taking my arm and steering me across the field toward a path. "It certainly charged up your soul-store."

She was right about that. A look at my hand showed the same sunny sheen. I could feel energy stuffing every crevice of my insides. Even off of the line my witched senses were still better than usual. Stone-strength, too. Though I didn't give it a try, I felt sure I could throw a rock through a barn wall. *Yeah, that'd be smart. Display my boosted powers by collapsing on my India rubber legs. All the citizens of Gaulle will unite in laughter.*

"So this is how experienced mages restock their powers? Seems like a dangerous way to go about it."

"For you it is, so young and freshly-taught. I'm a potion-speller myself. An old hand like your mother would bathe in a

Chauntline and purr." The Directeur pulled away from me. "But I expect you have reserves you aren't aware of."

Sure enough, I didn't fall. In fact, every step felt sturdier than the one before it. Most of the queasiness had already passed, along with the aches and dizziness. It almost felt like I'd taken on some of Romulus' near-invincibility. That got me to thinking. *Gee, maybe this is why I can't recall Ma ever bein' sick a day in her life, even when I'd had all manner o' sniffles, chicken pox, and what have you.*

"Sounds like somebody's gettin' herself ready to apologize to her much-maligned sword," said a smug Jasper.

At that I shrank him back into a cup and spit into it. Well, I tried to, anyhow. He made the bottom vanish and I hit my own foot. Ernie let out a laugh at my payback. So much for making my point.

Since I clearly wasn't about to expire from my reluctant ordeal, I made the best of it and kept on toward Poitiers with Prisme. My aura or whatever it was had faded out, absorbed back into me. I returned the cup to my wrist as a silver charm bracelet. Now I was about as girly as I'd ever been, except for the occasional wedding or funeral I'd been obliged to attend. The shoes pinched something awful and the hat ribbon tied beneath my chin choked me. How women managed to live this way was something I couldn't fathom.

"We should get to town in time to take a proper breakfast at a pleasant little spot I know," Madame Seychelles informed me. "Plausible identities would be helpful, don't you think?"

We cooked up a simple story to explain our presence in Poitiers. Prisme would be a lady from Paris who'd lost her grandson in one of Napoleon's battles and hoped to donate to the university in his name. He'd been a law student before running off with the Grand Armee. I'd be her great-grandniece, tagging along to get some edifying travel in before returning to school in the fall.

Getting all of the details right and practicing conversations so that we'd be less likely to get tripped up took a while. By the time we'd satisfied ourselves that we wouldn't get caught in a fib, the border of the town lay in sight. The sun was higher and warmer by now, though it was still only about eight in the morning. Our dirt path became a proper cobbled street as it entered Poitiers, clean and well-maintained. Apart from milk wagons and the like, there wasn't a lot of traffic about yet. Poitiers looked to be really old. Its architecture ranged from medieval Romanesque churches like Miz Finch had showed us pictures of in class to half-timbered Renaissance houses and some modern stone buildings at the University. Prisme led the way to the middle sort of place, a little tea shop with flowers in the window.

"Well, look at this," she said with a smile, pointing to the half-fishy sign above the door, "the *Mermaid* still a going concern. I'd feared Bonaparte's modernizing might have claimed it."

The Directeur pushed open the old oak door, which made a bell tinkle to alert the proprietor. I followed her into a cramped but neat room with a low ceiling and about eight round tables. Only three of them had customers, mostly sleepy fellows dressed for work at other shops. They nursed cups of tea or coffee while munching on biscuits or plates of eggs. My sensitive snoot picked up those scents, plus the aroma of cheese, bacon, honey, and loads of other goodies. Naturally, that made my mouth water, since my knapsack breakfast had been less than filling. Jasper started singing odes to the chefs of Gaulle in my noggin.

"And a fine good morning to you, ladies!" chimed a high woman's voice. The owner of the establishment wiped her hands on a long apron and scooted over to us. I saw that her voice was the only thing high about her.

She was a dwarf, a good foot shorter than me.

"Just because men must behave like apes in a menagerie
is no reason why we should follow their example."
In my head Jasper started making monkey sounds.
There's an example I'd really like to ignore.
If he starts flingin' poop I'll have a screamin' fit right here.

29 / Breakfast at the *Mermaid*

Don't stare, don't stare. don't stare…

My desperate reminder to be polite didn't work too well, since my eyes got big as wagon wheels. She pretended not to notice, though. I guess she'd grown so used to it that she just let folks gawk until they adjusted to the sight, then they could get on to real business. Sort of how I did when people would see me do some impossible thing like turn Jasper into a giant frying pan and whack flaming poop monsters with it.

"Welcome to the *Mermaid*, my dears," she said, all cheery and bouncy. "Looking for a fine breakfast, eh?" Our host looked to be middle-aged, with some gray in her chestnut hair but nothing like what Prisme had. Her cheeks looked so rosy that I thought at first she wore eight layers of rouge. But no, that was just her normal complexion. The twinkling brown eyes and button nose complemented those happy cheeks. On her head was a ruffled white cap that matched her apron. There was so much flour and other kitchen litter covering her that I figured she was the sole worker in the place.

"That we are, that we are," my partner confirmed, nodding and returning her smile. "We have traveled from Paris for business at the University and every tongue sings the praises of your establishment."

"I'm happy to hear it. And if I may say so myself, they told you no falsehoods." The little lady hobbled over to a corner table, facing the door. I noticed that her legs were too short for her body. Her arms, likewise, weren't in proportion. "Pray be seated and I will prove it with some tea to start."

As we set ourselves into the chairs she bustled off to prepare our breakfast. I used my new senses to investigate the place, but heard no diabolical plots against us amongst the other customers. Nobody snuck furtive glances at us or muttered to his fellow diner. My super-snoot couldn't detect any ominous stench of demons or black magick. The Stone stayed warm under my dress.

"That's nice," Jasper said. "At least this'll be one meal we can eat in peace, without divin' out the window to escape imminent doom."

"Yeah, well, the day's still young, bucko," I warned him.

Madame Seychelles looked like she'd been examining the *Mermaid* for trouble, too. Once she'd satisfied herself that the eatery was just what it seemed to be, she set her bag on the table and sighed. "So far, so good. As safe a place as any to start our search for the redoubtable Victoria Sponge. Captain Tyrell insisted that she would aid us, if only we can track her down.

Perhaps our host can direct us toward the precise Rue de Poisson address where she shall be giving her concert."

"Oh, that's easy." I shrugged like I'd had some great psychic power all of my life." There's a salon-thing happenin' at Number 42 at eight o'clock."

"You don't say? And you know this how?"

"From my careful eye fer detail, knowledge of Gaullic customs and geography, and from spyin' a poster fer the event on the wall by the door."

"Clever girl. Though I note that truly public salons are quite rare. Generally they are only for the special friends of the host."

"Maybe she needs the money. How much can ivory-ticklin' pay? A poor customer's gold spends as good as a rich one's."

"True enough. But I doubt that is why she did it. More likely she is advertising her presence to us."

"And to anybody on the other side who'd like to interfere."

"That is the problem with advertising. But we are likely to be safer in her company than out of it, if trouble arises."

I snorted at that. "This Sponge lady must be one tough piano player. What's she gonna do, whack 'em with her sheet music?"

Just then the *Mermaid*'s waitress, cook, and cleaning lady arrived with a tray. She set it down and unloaded teacups and a pot. We were eye-to-eye now that I was sitting down. I apologized for being a rude gawker earlier. With one hand she waved that off while pouring.

"Oh, stare away, young miss. If that sort of thing bothered me I'd not be in this line of work." One corner of her mouth turned up and she leaned in close to me. "But you know all about that, don't you? Being treated differently because of your unusual birth?"

Huh? Jeepers, ain't there one normal person in Gaulle who don't know about me, magick, and monsters?

I gave her my best confused expression, hoping to deflect the conversation elsewhere. We were supposed to be in disguise, after all. "Don't know what you mean, ma'am? I ain't unusual in any way."

A stubby finger poked at my hat. "Oh, no? That strand of hair I see there says otherwise. It's not at all common. Red as red could be. You don't get teased? Called funny names, like ginger-pate or carrot-top?"

Seeing that I'd jumped to the wrong conclusion, I laughed. "Some. Mostly boys my age. But I give 'em a good hidin' and they don't do it twice."

Prisme kicked me under the table. *Oops. Guess that ain't proper young lady behavior fer 1804. So much fer my great disguise.*

The Directeur sugared her tea while trying to salvage my goof. "You'll have to excuse my grand-niece. Chloe lost her mother at birth. She hasn't had the opportunity to absorb the social graces at her mama's knee. That's why I've taken her under my wing, so to speak. To polish off some of those rough edges." Prisme smiled at me, clearly enjoying every word. "Do well-brought-up girls fight boys, dear?"

Boxed in by our cover story, I played along, lowering my eyes and shrinking a bit. "No, ma'am."

"That's correct. Just because men must behave like apes in a menagerie is no reason why we should follow their example."

In my head Jasper started making monkey sounds. *There's an example I'd really like to ignore. If he starts flingin' poop I'll have a screamin' fit right here.*

"You seem to have done a wonderful job with her," said the waitress. "I can tell that she's a young lady of refinement and quality."

Jasper's ape noises turned into howls of laughter as he scoffed at that claim. I sighed and sipped my tea. It looked like I was in for a long, painful breakfast unless I could get some yummy jam into my tummy to pacify him. Prisme responded as if she'd read my mind, ordering us food in respectable proportions while managing to mention that we were in Poitiers to bestow funds on the University to remember our lost relation.

"Aye, the wars have taken many a young fellow from us," our server said as she moved off to get our goodies. "Bless you for preserving his memory this way."

I watched her disappear through a swinging door into the kitchen. "Well, that oughta get our make-believe identities spread around town in an hour. She likely couldn't keep a secret if you put a silence spell on her."

Prisme nodded. "I hope so. Strange. People are more likely to believe the village gossip than a pair of strangers. They'll take it as gospel coming from her."

"But just to make sure, we're gonna visit the University and play out the lie, right?"

"We are. Plus, that will give us an excuse to wander the streets and see how things are. We wouldn't want any surprises before talking to Miss Sponge."

"Why don't we just ask around, find out where she's stayin', and go visit her right now? Time's a-wastin'."

More folks entered the restaurant. Soldiers. Their blue uniforms had red trim and red epaulettes on the shoulders, with white crossbelts and tall black shakos for headgear. Madame Seychelles lowered her voice, cuing me to do the same. "Because it's almost certain that she is being watched. A visit now would attract the sort of interest we wish to avoid. But tonight, at the crowded salon performance, we shall be more assured of avoiding notice."

"Watched? Bonaparte's worried about a lady musician? That's takin' national security a little far, don't ya think? Even if she is Britannic."

The soldiers were officers, but they seemed to be only interested in breakfast. They paid us no mind. "Believe me, in her case he is right to be concerned. Victoria Sponge is nearly as great a threat to his Empire as you are."

Our host returned with a bigger tray than before, pausing to tell the soldiers that she'd be right back to serve them. She struggled over to us with her oversized load. I helped her get it onto the table before she dropped crockery and bacon everywhere. *Jasper would've cried like a new widow if that happened.* While she set out the bowls and plates Prisme asked her who the handsome young men in the splendid uniforms were.

"Ah, those are some of our fine gentlemen from the garrison here. Artillery lieutenants from the look of them. They are slaves to my cooking." She shook her head and chuckled. "Or slaves to the twins, at least."

"Twins?"

"Gabrielle and Giselle Seurat. Teenaged daughters of the University Chancellor. They dine here often. Or at least they pretend to while trancing the Emperor's finest. Golden curls, milky complexions, pouty lips. Wicked little charmers, they are. You'd think they were witches, they control the poor men so."

I wanted to tell her that in my experience with women and soldiers you could accomplish the same feat even if you were forty-eight and homely, but that would've derailed my goody-two-shoes disguise again. Instead I ignored Jasper's predictable and disgusting commentary in my noggin and asked, "Surely the wrong is really on the side of the ill-disciplined men-folk, taking after the maidens?"

The little woman's face contorted with mirth. She rolled her eyes and leaned in to us to wink and whisper, "Who said they were maidens? That would take a good deal of witchcraft...plus some time-travel."

With that, still snickering, she waddled off to seat the bewhiskered officers. Prisme stirred her tea with a knowing smile. "Yes, even an imitation Merchantry-made Gaulle still lives up to its reputation."

We finished breakfast without any trouble, taking our time and hoping the ballyhooed twins would show. When they didn't we paid the hostess, thanked her, and left the *Mermaid* for the University. Prisme thought playing out our cover story would help spread it around Poitiers while letting us visit and spy the important parts of the city. I'd rather have jumped in the balloon and high-tailed it for Paris and London, but apparently there were good reasons for not doing that. She sure seemed convinced that we needed this piano player as part of our grand design for tweaking Napoleon's nose.

So we hired a carriage and driver to take us around in style. That made my aching legs happy. Three weeks as Stone Warden had aged me a few decades, it seemed. Too much racing about, fighting monsters, fleeing for my life or somebody else's, getting pecked by giant ravens or charged by even bigger blood-sucking ticks. Not to mention getting turned into a beaver or being snatched into the air by a talking tree. After all of that a ride in an airship or coach was heaven. Our carriage was pretty swanky, with real glass windows and comfy springs that cushioned the rough cobblestoned streets. The driver was a plump, talkative fellow named Jean, invalided out of the navy with a bad foot wound, he told us. In fact, he told us so much that after a while I longed for a bit less telling and a little more quiet riding. It didn't help that Jasper kept imitating his voice while he was talking that blue streak.

But he turned out to be a blessing in disguise, since he gave us more information about Poitiers than we would likely have discovered for ourselves. Jean detoured us at Prisme's request and took us past the army camp, explaining what regiments were present and how they were organized. Nothing that Bonaparte would've considered to be too much intelligence but still handy for us to know. We learned the names of the garrison commander and the recent history of his men in Napoleon's campaigns. Some juicy bits, too, such as who was fathering children illicitly and who was married to more than one woman. Apparently the Seurat girls had broken many hearts and even more commandments in their brief career as the most-renowned coquettes of Poitiers.

After that we made our way to the University of Poitiers, with Jean keeping up his chatter. He told us that it was ancient and respected, having been founded in the 1400's. Descartes and Rabelais had been students there. It was the town's chief reason for existing, employing the most people and bringing in tons of money to the local economy. The Revolution had closed it briefly but it had been back in operation for eight years, though with a less religious curriculum. Jean said it graduated mostly lawyers and doctors. I could see from my window that the place was old. Lots of the buildings looked to have been built hundreds of years before. Students wore gowns and old-timey hats that weren't anything like current Gaullic fashion. In particular the chapel, probably the first structure to have been put up, resembled a small Gothic cathedral. From its belfry rang out a complicated tune, calling everybody to a meeting. Young men hustled toward it from every direction.

Our horse stopped in front of an ivy-covered brick house at the north end of the campus. Jean climbed down, favoring one leg, to unfold the iron steps and open our door. I got out after Madame Seychelles, nodding thanks to him. He touched his hat and said he'd wait for us. We strolled up the stone walkway and knocked on the arched door. A colored butler with a West Indian accent, possibly Haitian, answered it and let us in. A minute later we were sitting in the Chancellor's office.

Chancellor Erasmus Seurat was no classical Hellenic statue, so his wife must've provided the famed beauty of his daughters. Long and gangly, hair very thin, he looked like a daddy longlegs with a bespectacled turtle head sticking out of his high starched collar. His nose made a bigger and better beak than Roberta could claim. Though he started out our interview with an expression so sour he might've been a lemon-tester, that all changed when Prisme informed him that she was there to give his institution a gazillion francs in memory of her heroic late son, lost at the Battle of Marengo four years before.

"Is that so?" he asked in a nasal tone, narrow eyebrows creeping up behind his thick lenses. He sat up a little straighter and forced a smile. It made him look like a happy undertaker. "A tragedy, of course. Any young man's life cut short is cause for mourning. Though there is the consolation of his passing's having served the Emperor."

Lips tight, Prisme nodded. "Of course, there is that." *Boy there's some actin' fer ya. Pretendin' to like Napoleon while plottin' to do him in.*

"You say he was a student here? I confess that I cannot recall the name. Then again, so many boys pass through here."

"Jules was not here long. In fact, he had barely taken a class when the events of 18 Brumaire stirred passionate patriotic feelings in his breast. He left Poitiers to take up arms for our great General Bonaparte." Selling her story, the Directeur dabbed at a non-existent tear with her hanky. I did the same to help her out. "He perished during the Italian campaign. Marengo was his first and last engagement."

Seurat's face looked like he didn't know whether to sympathize with her loss or rejoice in the two million francs she proposed to donate. He settled on a dour middle-of-the-road expression. "It is hard, I know. So many of our lads did the same. Few returned. But at least the course you propose will enable others to be educated here, perhaps those who might otherwise be lost to farming or the trades."

Since Ma had done both of those he didn't score any points with me by saying that. But I had a part to play so I nodded in agreement. "You say rightly, sir. I dream that my aunt's contribution may help create a doctor who will save lives on the battlefield. A fitting tribute to Jules' memory, considering the circumstances of his death."

"That's right," Jasper said, "keep shoveling that manure. Maybe a fine garden of daisies will grow."

"Aw, hush, you. Don't throw me off my role here."

Madame Seychelles, calling herself Mistress Fouquet, spent some time discussing the practical details of her gift. Legal issues, banks, that sort of thing. Pretending to be a bored kid, which wasn't a stretch, I ambled around the office, poking into bookshelves and looking out of the window. Stormy weather was coming from the west. All the talk of a pretended dead boy just reminded me of Tommy, whose demise was likely to be very real in a few days if we didn't do something. I hadn't seen him in nearly a month and was already having trouble recalling his face. *Is that how nature softens the blow? By fading the loved one from your memory?*

"Ain't gonna happen," I promised myself. "I'll keep you in my mind clear as a Brady photograph till I spring you from whatever dungeon Venoma stuck you in. Then we'll go home and you can knock bees outta the air again with yer rock-throwin' skills."

My inner dialogue was interrupted by a side door banging open. A matched set of young beauties barged in, mouths going a mile-a-minute so that you couldn't understand a word they said. They precisely matched the description given us by the Mermaid's gossipy hostess. Both were blonde, both were fetching, both were as identical as a pair of tintypes made with a double-lensed camera. It was easy to see why the boys worshipped them. Only their different dresses helped tell them apart.

"Papa!" squealed the one in pastel green. "That awful Lieutenant Mayotte promised to take me to the recital tonight and now he claims he has duty with his regiment."

Her sister, wearing a white frock with little red birds

embroidered on it, waved off that complaint as unworthy of paternal notice. "Oh, who cares about your silly romantic mess. I have a real problem."

The first girl set her jaw. "Are you going to let Giselle talk to me that way?"

Giselle ignored her high-strung sister and pressed her case. "The dressmaker says that I have no more credit on my account with her. In fact, she tells me that she won't deliver my new gown for tonight's salon until she's paid in full. You simply must take action against the little harpy or my reputation will be ruined."

"What reputation?" muttered Gabrielle.

Seurat threw up his hands, waving them to gain their silence. "Girls! You are interrupting an important meeting. Mistress Fouquet has lost her son and wishes to generously endow us in his name."

The twins recalled their father's position and curtsied to Prisme with every ounce of breeding they possessed. She nodded in response and introduced me to them. After giving their own names and expressing their rapture at making our acquaintance, they pounced on Seurat again with their earth-shattering troubles.

Again he shushed them with furious arm motions. "One at a time! Gabrielle, you first. If the young man has duty, there is little I can do about it. Unless you suspect him of telling you a tale to escort some other lass to the party."

Her scowl proclaimed that this was exactly her fear, but she said nothing. While she stood there pouting, arms crossed, her father explained the hard realities of economics to Giselle. Eventually she stomped to the window to stare daggers across town at her faithless beau.

"Perhaps he's at the *Mermaid*," I suggested. "You might go over there and talk to him."

She frowned. "The *Mermaid*? I wouldn't be caught dead in such a place."

Right then her nose started running like a tapped keg. And my Stone froze to my skin.

Gabrielle was a demon.

This is the end of *Jasper's Magick Corset, Part One.*
Part Two, *Partying is Such Sweet Sorrow,*
will continue directly from this point
(an excerpt appears below).

If you enjoyed this book (or even if you didn't), please
leave a brief review on Amazon, Goodreads, etc.

Thank you for reading.

www.terrykroenungink.com

From *Jasper's Magick Corset, Part 2:*
Partying is Such Sweet Sorrow

Jean jumped down to hold an umbrella over us. That came in handy, because turning Morphageus into one in front of everybody might've started the evening on the wrong note. The big house's enormous covered porch or portico or veranda or whatever you called it was crammed with the upper-crust of Poitiers, chatting and flirting. Since ladies' dresses were so much simpler than in my 1862 – no silly hoops the size of hogsheads – a lot more folks managed to fit there than I was used to seeing. Dark and stormy as it was, they seemed to still prefer the outdoors to going inside. Most of the men were puffing on cigars or elaborate pipes, making Jasper drool in my head. If it was bad for you, or wrong, or forbidden, he loved it.

Since we were in a garrison town, the Grand Armee was well-represented. At least the officer corps was. All the poor privates were probably pulling guard duty in the rain. Since the lightning and thunder had grown fiercer in the last hour, I didn't envy them that. *At least we ain't up in that fragile balloon in this mess. That thing feels unstable even in the calm and sun.* The porch looked like a peacock convention with all the braid and garish colors. Just in the time it took to walk from our carriage I spotted hussars like Tyrell, artillery captains in green and yellow with front-to-back bicorn hats, and an infantry colonel in white with a raspberry-toned front piece and bearskin monstrosity on his head. All of them had cutlery on their hips that I wanted to steal. Smallswords with jeweled shell hilts, curved brass sabers in metal scabbards, long straight backswords with fancy tassels hanging from the pommels. I took note of them all just in case I needed to form Jasper into one as part of a disguise.

"Ah! Tobacco and edged weapons!" he gushed. "If there's alcohol and rich victuals your Uncle Jasper will be a happy fellow."

"Ain't no doubt o' that," I assured him. "This here's a high-class party and no mistake."

As we got up the steps and under the porch room, Jean bowed and made to return to his horse and coach. Prisme latched onto his arm and whispered in his ear for a good while first. After nodding understanding, he gave the whole area a thorough hard look and hurried into the rain. Before I could ask what that had been about she nudged me through the throng of grown-ups and into the entry hall. There I saw why the porch had been so crowded. You hardly had enough room to scratch an itch inside the house. How you'd get a hanging sword through there was a mystery. Booted feet stomped on my poor toes. Skirted backsides whumped into me. I even took an elbow to the head without so much as a beg-you-pardon.

"People's manners ain't what they oughta be," I complained to the Directeur, who didn't seem to mind as much as I did.

"You are right," she agreed, keeping hold of me so we wouldn't get separated. "I blame the Revolution for that. They took equality to mean that everything the aristocrats practiced, including common courtesy, was anathema." A lout belched and blundered into us. "Of course, copious amounts of wine and spirits also play a role."

Echoing the drunk's burb, Jasper hollered in exaggerated inebriation, "And this spirit's gonna whine until he gets some o' that!"

"Aw, hush," I told him, transforming Morphageus into a porcupine with a wrist strap. "I ain't lettin' my belly get within a mile o' the drinks table and that's that."

"Suit yourself." His voice had that dangerous I'll-get-even tone I hated. "But you never know when you're gonna need that extra little bit of magick to get out of a tight spot."

"Let me get outta this tight spot first." I jabbed the spiked bracelet into three different rumps in front of me. When their owners yowled and jumped I shoved them aside with my unnatural strength. Using that tactic we bulled forward, leaving a trail of indignant folks behind us, until we got into the ballroom where the recital was to be held. Once there the crowd thinned some, making it easier to breathe.

And a good thing, too. Because I gasped as soon as I saw the setup.

The house's architecture might've been more restrained than the bare-bones Evremonde chateau's, but the furnishings and art more than made up for it. Everything was lit with candles, there not being the gaslights of my time yet. But that just made it all look better, because the chandeliers, which resembled great ice sculptures ablaze with fire, cast a soft golden glow. Gas always looked harsh, plus it just about asphyxiated you with its fumes. This lovely light made everybody look good, no matter how homely. None of the expensive paintings, sculptures, or wall hangings needed much help, though. Nearly every inch of space that didn't have a person standing on it was covered by canvas, stone, or tapestry. I was no art expert but I knew enough to tell that a lot of Gaulle's most famous masters were represented, to say nothing of Hellas and the Papal Fief. Even the ceiling had decoration. Somebody had spent months on his back putting an elaborate mythological hunting scene there. Artemis and her hounds pursued a much-antlered stag across a stream.

"That ain't what she looks like," I muttered, recalling my time in Iberion when she, her brother Apollo, and Athena had helped save my bacon from Dionysus.

"Is that so, little miss?" said an amused lady next to me in a refined Britannic accent. "You've met her, I suppose?"

Without thinking, my neck still hauled back to stare upwards, I answered, "Only once. But she was my age and had shorter hair."

"Oh, good show," laughed Jasper. "Let's see how you get out of this one."

"You don't say? The virgin goddess of the hunt was, what? Eleven?"

"Twelve, actually." I put on a big, embarrassed wince and turned to the woman, hiding my wrist with my handbag long enough to turn Morphageus back into a bracelet. "My Ma says I have an over-active imagination." *Boy, ain't that a lie. I could never make up anything near as weird as what my real life has turned out to be.*

"Hey!" Jasper protested. "Why you callin' weird?"

"Gee, I wonder..."

ABOUT THE AUTHOR

Terry Kroenung taught literature for 30 years, mostly at Niwot High School in Colorado, where he inflicted his Shakespeare impersonations and love of Eeyore collectibles on tomorrow's leaders. An Advanced Actor/Combatant with the Society of American Fight Directors, he owns more swords than any sane human has any need of and spent countless hours choreographing fights with his students (thus, the gray hairs and nervous twitchings of his poor principal). As unplanned preparation for writing about Verity's adventures he served as an U.S. Army infantry officer on the East German border, a Confederate Civil War re-enactor in Virginia, and a pirate at street festivals. His youthful cigar smoking and whiskey drinking resulted in just as much misery as Verity feels when indulging.

The smart-aleck dialogue and puns come naturally, alas...more's the pity.

www.ingramcontent.com/pod-product-compliance
Lightning Source LLC
Chambersburg PA
CBHW030549260626
47157CB00006B/2247